## PRAISE FOR *NEW YORK TIMES*
## BESTSELLING AUTHOR
## CATHERINE COULTER

"Bawdy fare, Coulter-style . . . romance, humor, and spicy sex talk." —*Kirkus Reviews*

"A hot-blooded romp." —*People*

"Coulter is excellent at portraying the romantic tension between her heroes and heroines, and she manages to write explicitly but beautifully about sex as well as love." —*Milwaukee Journal Sentinel*

"Unexpected plot twists, witty dialogue and an engaging cast of characters." —*Publishers Weekly*

"Catherine Coulter delivers . . . straightforward, fast-paced romance." —*Minneapolis Star Tribune*

"Sexy." —*Booklist*

"Coulter's characters quickly come alive and draw the reader into the story. You root for the good guys and hiss for the bad guys. When you have to put the book down for a while, you can hardly wait to get back and see what's going on." —*The Sunday Oklahoman*

"Charm, wit, and intrigue . . . Sure to keep readers turning the pages." —*Naples Daily News*

# Jade Star

◇

## Catherine Coulter

A SIGNET BOOK

SIGNET
Published by New American Library, a division of
Penguin Putnam Inc., 375 Hudson Street,
New York, New York 10014, U.S.A.
Penguin Books Ltd, 80 Strand,
London WC2R 0RL, England
Penguin Books Australia Ltd, 250 Camberwell Road,
Camberwell, Victoria 3124, Australia
Penguin Books Canada Ltd, 10 Alcorn Avenue,
Toronto, Ontario, Canada M4V 3B2
Penguin Books (N.Z.) Ltd, 182–190 Wairau Road,
Auckland 10, New Zealand

Penguin Books Ltd, Registered Offices:
Harmondsworth, Middlesex, England

Published by Signet, an imprint of New American Library,
a division of Penguin Putnam Inc. Previously printed in Topaz
and Onyx editons.

First Signet Printing, April 1999
First Signet Printing, Revised Edition, June 2002
10  9  8  7  6  5  4

Ⓤ REGISTERED TRADEMARK—MARCA REGISTRADA

Printed in the United States of America

PUBLISHER'S NOTE
This is a work of fiction. Names, characters, places, and incidents either
are the product of the author's imagination or are used fictitiously,
and any resemblance to actual persons, living or dead, business
establishments, events or locales is entirely coincidental.

# Chapter 1

*Lahaina, Maui, 1854*

The warm, coarse beach sand was the odd pinkish color of the squirrelfish, the ocean as deep an aqua as the bluefin trevally.

"Come on, Jules, stop dreaming the morning away!"

Juliana DuPres laughed with the pleasure of a now-forbidden swim, tightened her kapa-cloth sarong more tightly over her breasts, and dashed into the swirling waves after Kanola. The tides were strong at Makila Point, but Jules, an expert swimmer, merely relaxed in the grip of the pulling crosscurrents until she was safely beyond them.

"Slow down, Kanola," she said. "There should be a school of parrotfish here and I want to see them." Without waiting for a reply from her friend, Jules drew a deep breath and dove down several feet to the coral reef below. She knew her eyes would be red and swollen from the salt water, but it didn't matter. Not only were there parrotfish, but yellowstrip goatfish as well, a treat. She thought to herself as her head cleared the surface: Father, if you truly believed in the glory of creation, you would open your eyes to the incredible beauty that surrounds you.

She grinned at her thought, and spit out a mouthful of salt water. She could just see Reverend Etienne DuPres stripped of his sweat-soaked black broadcloth, cavorting in the ocean and calling out the names of fish. Or lying on his back on the beach, his sallow face becoming healthy and tanned.

"Well, what did you see, Jules? An eel maybe?"

Juliana swam easily to where Kanola was resting on an irregular outcropping of coral that acted as something of a narrow breakwater. The coral was rough, pitted, and slimy. Jules dug her fingers into a crevice, holding tight to keep from being pulled back into the water. There was room enough for just the two of them.

Jules, her voice filled with enthusiasm as she pulled two soaked hunks of bread from a large pocket on the side of the sarong, told her friend, "Now, let's see just how hungry all my friends are. Maybe even that zebra moray who was slithering between my feet." She scattered the bread all about her. Within seconds more fish than she could count—even a whitetip reef shark—were swarming about her and Kanola. Jules smiled when their smooth bodies brushed hers. "More saddle wrasse than anything else," she said.

Kanola regarded Jules with the same affectionate smile she gave her own sister. Jules was only two years younger than she, but she clung tenaciously to her childhood pursuits, and, Kanola admitted, Jules knew more about fish than any haole she'd ever known. She listened to her friend go on about every sort of fish consuming the bread, then interrupted her with a raised hand. She said in English as idiomatic as her friend's, "Your papa has been after you again, I gather?"

Jules sighed, and fell silent for a moment. "Papa is Papa," she said. "Everything fun and natural is kapu—particularly," she added on a bitter note, "if one happens to be a female."

"I thought as much," Kanola said. "What has he done now? Forbidden you to swim?"

Jules nodded, a small smile playing about her mouth. "Three years ago," she said.

Kanola was startled. "However have you managed to keep it a secret from him all this time?"

"Thomas helps me, washes me down and all that. I assume that Papa thinks I'm just excessively susceptible to the heat and take a lot of baths, because my hair is usually wet. He doesn't seem to notice my red eyes."

"You are nineteen, Jules, a woman grown. There is more to life than searching out and cataloging fish, birds, flowers—" Her voice trailed off when Jules shot her an angry look.

"For instance," she said at her friend's obstinate silence, "there's John Bleecher." Kanola had been married for five years now and was the proud mother of two children.

Jules stared off into the distance, the endless expanse of ocean blurring before her eyes. "He used to be a friend," she said.

"I'm sure he still is," Kanola said. "And he's not a missionary. He'd give you no orders like your father does, or make you pray on your knees until you're stiff as a board."

"I wish he'd turn his attentions to Sarah. She wants to get married."

"Sarah is a stick," Kanola said.

"She's also beautiful, fragile, and soft, which is what I've always been told men want in a wife."

"And you, I suppose, are a hag."

Jules's hair had come loose on her dive, and masses of corky wild curls framed her face. "No, not anymore, I don't guess," she said. "But I'm about as fragile as one of my peacock groupers."

"Well, I think you're lucky you didn't gain your beauty sooner, else your father would have kept a closer watch on you."

"Spoken like a true friend." Jules grinned. "Incidentally, he still thinks I'm a scruffy twit, looks at me like I give him pain. It's the red hair, you know, that I got from my French grandmother, the immoral actress. Come on, let's swim out a bit more. We've the time and I've got a good fifteen more minutes before the sun does awful things to my skin."

That was certainly the case, Kanola thought as she watched her friend dive cleanly into the smooth water. Her skin beneath her sarong was as white as her hair was red, and too much sun, even on her lightly tanned face and shoulders, made her not only a blotched mess, but sick as well. Kanola slipped into the water after Jules, and swam after her.

"Would you have a look at that, Captain."

Jameson Wilkes followed Rodney Cumber's pointing finger. He studied the two very female figures swimming cleanly through the water. One was a native, clear enough, but the other— Even from this distance he could tell that she was different, a real find.

He was silent for a moment, then said to Cumber,

"Take three men and lower the boat. Bring the both of them to me."

"Aye, aye, sir."

"Beg your pardon, Captain, but the other one—she ain't no native gal, sir."

"No, Gallen, I don't imagine she is," Jameson Wilkes said to his first mate. "But then again, Bob, we won't be coming back to Maui, will we?"

Bob Gallen didn't like the direction he knew his captain's thoughts were taking. Plowing prostitutes in Lahaina was one thing, even bringing over those Chinese girls to be sold in San Francisco wasn't too bad, but capturing a white girl was quite another, and it made him feel funny. "What if she's a missionary's girl?"

"Then she's probably a virgin," Jameson Wilkes said. "Don't worry, Bob. If she's married, or is covered with the freckles that usually come along with that color hair, I'll set her quickly back into the ocean. Let's wait and see."

"I don't like it," Bob Gallen said.

Jameson Wilkes knew the moment the two women recognized their danger. He heard one of them scream, saw them flip over and race back toward shore. But his men would be faster, of course.

"Kanola, hurry." But Kanola wasn't as strong a swimmer. Jules slowed, and grabbed her friend's hand.

"Go on, Jules."

"No," Jules yelled, swallowing a mouthful of salt water. Wild, terrifying thoughts swirled through her head. She'd seen the whaler in the distance, watched it without a great deal of interest until she heard Kanola cry out. Then she'd seen the boat coming toward them.

She grasped Kanola's arm, pulling her with all her strength. But it was no use. The sun was shadowed by the men and the boat.

"Come on, little girlies," she heard a man's voice call.

"Dive, Kanola."

But Kanola was much heavier than Jules, her body no longer as lithe. Jules watched helplessly as one of the men grabbed Kanola by her long, loose black hair and dragged her over the side of the boat. Without another thought, Jules dove deep. She had to escape and get help. It was her only thought as she swam with strong strokes underwater. I must get help. When she could hold her breath no longer, she surfaced, only to see a swarthy grinning face directly in front of her, blocking her way to shore.

"That's enough now, girlie," Rodney said. He and another sailor grabbed for her.

Jules fought silently, but she was no match for the two men. Like Kanola, she was dragged over the side of the boat and dumped on the bottom.

"Would you just fill your eyes with this, Ned," Rodney said. "Not a freckle on that pretty little face. The captain'll be mighty pleased. Oh yes he will."

Jameson Wilkes was pleased. He watched his sailors bundle the two girls up the ladder. He quickly dismissed the native girl, his eyes on the flame-haired wench. He couldn't believe his luck. Even though her thick hair was straggling down about her face and down her back, he knew she was a beauty. She was tall, slender, straight-legged, and those marvelous breasts, heaving beneath the thin covering of her sarong. Like Rodney, he quickly saw that not one freckle marred her lovely white skin.

Jules was brought to a stumbling halt before a tall, very well-dressed man. He looked a bit like her father, but his face was seamed and dark from years spent on a ship. Her father usually carried an umbrella to protect his face from the harsh sun.

"My dear," Jameson Wilkes said, offering her a slight bow, "welcome aboard the *Sea Shroud*."

"Who are you?" Jules said. "Why have you brought us here?"

"My dear," Jameson Wilkes said in his deep voice, "I have but one question for you first. Are you yet a virgin?"

Jules stared at him as if he'd spoken Greek.

"Ah," Jameson said, his eyes glittering. "Come along now, and I'll tell you all you wish to know."

"Kanola," Jules said. "She's my friend, she must—"

Jameson stopped in his tracks. Slowly he turned. "Her status isn't in much doubt, but nonetheless, we will see." He walked to Kanola, who stood straight and proud, and with one fast motion he ripped off her sarong. Kanola lunged toward him, her nails aimed at his face, but three sailors grabbed her.

"My dear," Jameson called to Jules. "You see, it is as I expected. The marks on her belly. Childbirthing marks. She hasn't your worth. And like many native women, she's got too much flesh. No, unfortunately, she has no value. Come along, now."

Jules screamed, her voice high and thin, but she didn't have the strength of Jameson Wilkes and he dragged her to the hatch. The dim companionway loomed below. She heard Kanola call her name, then heard her cries of terror.

"I suggest you think about thanking me for protecting you from my men," Jameson˙Wilkes said. "Nor, my dear, do you want to look."

But she did. She saw Kanola on her back on the deck, men holding her arms and legs, and the sailor who had captured them pulling at his trousers. She wasn't stupid or ignorant. One couldn't be, in a whaling town like Lahaina, even if one's father was a minister. "No," she yelled, and her short fingernails tore down Jameson Wilkes's face. She escaped, dashed back toward the deck.

She rushed like a demon toward the screaming Kanola, cursing with the few foul words she'd heard from drunk sailors in Lahaina. The man turned, and she saw his hairy belly and a huge rod of flesh jutting out from his abdomen.

Jameson Wilkes caught her, pulling her back against him. "You want to watch, my dear? I'm sorry to deny you such an education, but I must." He forced her through the hatch down to the companionway.

He knew his men would rape the native girl. He also knew that such a sight would probably terrify this lovely creature, and that he didn't want.

"Kanola," Jules said. "You must make them stop. Don't let them hurt her."

"I swear to you they won't hurt her," Jameson Wilkes said.

"She's my friend. Make them stop."

"Captain, she got away from us." Jameson Wilkes didn't acknowledge his man's shout. He said to Juliana, "You see, your friend has escaped. Even now she's swimming to shore."

"She won't make it. We're too far from shore."

"Enough," Jameson Wilkes yelled. "I'll se͏ men after her to save her. Now stop fighting m͏

But she didn't. She managed to twist about and slam her fist against his jaw.

His head jerked back. He held her, and hit her jaw. Jules crumpled where she stood.

Jules was aware of the throbbing pain in her jaw before she opened her eyes. The pain held her for a moment, then memory flooded back. She gasped, jerking upright, only to realize that she was quite naked, only a thin sheet covering her. She clutched it to her chin.

"Well, at last. I didn't think I'd hit you that hard. Your jaw isn't broken. I'm not such a fool as that."

"Kanola, my friend," she said.

"Quite safe," Jameson said. "My men caught up with her before she drowned and escorted her to shore. You need worry no more about her."

"I don't believe you," she said.

He shrugged. "I have no reason to lie to you, my dear. Believe what you will." Of course the native bitch had drowned, but his men had tried to save her, although not to rescue her.

"Who are you?" she asked, staring at the man who was now sitting at his ease in a chair opposite her.

"Captain Jameson Wilkes, at your service, ma'am. And who are you?"

"Juliana DuPres. My father is Etienne DuPres, a minister in Lahaina. You will return me, now, sir." The sheet slipped, and she jerked it up.

"I wondered when you would realize how very— vulnerable you are, Juliana. That's a lovely name, incidentally. It suits you." He sat forward, his eyes intent. "You suit me, you know. Oh yes."

Jules stared at him. She knew all about the evil men of the whalers, for her father had ranted and raved about them and their wicked, immoral ways often enough. But to be faced with one of them, to be lying in the man's bed without a stitch of clothes on, was almost too much for her to grasp.

"She's dead," Jules said.

"No," he said. "As I told you, your friend is quite safe now. I suggest, my dear, that you think about yourself."

"I don't understand. Why have you done this? What do you want from me?"

"I am, I suppose, a wicked man in your innocent eyes, Juliana. But you needn't worry. I am first and foremost a businessman." She knows, he thought, studying her closely. Deep down, she knows exactly what I want.

"You're a pig," Jules said.

He laughed at that, but she saw that his eyes remained cold, as icy cold as the sleeting gray winter rains in Toronto, a place she could scarcely remember.

"My father will kill you."

"Your father? Now, that's amusing, to be sure it is. Your father, my dear Juliana, is a prig, a weak prig who can do naught but try to change all the natives into prigs. Don't you find it ridiculous that many of the natives that have succumbed to religion now dress like English and American gentlemen and ladies? It's all too absurd, you know. But back to your precious father. Perhaps he and your family will mourn you. For they will believe you drowned, and you will no longer exist for them."

Jules closed her eyes. He'd lied about Kanola, of course. She was dead, drowned. If she weren't, then everyone would know that Jules had been taken by a whaler.

"Wouldn't you like to know what I am going to do with you, Juliana? Where I'm taking you?"

Slowly she turned her face away from him. Obviously he didn't realize what he had admitted. "No," she said, "I don't want to know."

For the first time, Jameson was worried. The girl's face was deathly pale. He rose slowly, but was wise enough not to approach her now.

"You will rest a bit, Juliana, then we will talk. I would suggest that you remain in this cabin. My men, as you can well imagine, are not always polite gentlemen."

He strode to the cabin door, looking over his shoulder at her before he left. She hadn't moved. He frowned. Then he heard the soft, broken sound of her sobbing, and was relieved.

Excellent, he thought as he left the cabin. She's resilient. She would have to be. He had two weeks to bring her around before they arrived in San Francisco. He wondered how much money she would bring him. Then he felt the burning pain in his belly. It came more frequently now, particularly if he were angry or upset, or filled with anticipation, as he was now. He walked from the cabin, kneading his belly, forcing his mind away from the biting pain.

# Chapter 2

*San Francisco, California, 1854*

"Come on, now, Willie, I'm not cutting your arm off, for God's sake. Stop your bellowing."

"It hurts, Saint, bloody bad."

Saint stared down at the newly stitched gash on Limpin' Willie's arm. Good job. He picked up a bottle, saw Willie pale with fear, and began to talk. "Did I ever tell you about this stuff, Willie? No? Well, it's called iodine, and it's better than whiskey for what ails you. And cheaper. It was discovered way back in 1811 by a chap named Courtois, but there's controversy even about that, of course." Saint held Willie's arm over a basin and poured the iodine on the wound. Willie yelped and struggled, but Saint had three times his strength and wasn't about to let him go.

Saint continued holding Willie's arm while he patted off the excess. "Do you know what 'iodine' means, Willie? No? Well, part of it comes from the Greek word *ion* and it means 'violet.' Just look at your arm, as violet as can be. Now, you've come out of this not only patched up but educated as well."

Limpin' Willie had got his breath and bearings

back. He stared down at his purple arm. "Violet, huh, Saint?"

"The ladies will think you look like a bloomin' flower, Willie."

Limpin' Willie gave him a crooked grin, showing the inside of a mouth that contained only half its complement of teeth. "It still hurts like hell, Saint, but I'll live. Thanks, I owe you one."

"Actually, you owe me five. The rest, I'll take in a favor down the road."

"Anything, anytime, Saint." Willie paid his money and prepared to leave.

"Keep that bandage clean, Willie. And no picking pockets or bashing folk around for a while. And don't let the wound get dirty. Come back to see me in three days."

Willie took his leave and Saint stood silently for a moment in the doorway, shaking his head. Limpin' Willie was a Sydney Duck—one of that group of men from Australia who were criminals to their toes. But he was harmless as a puppy around Saint. At least Willie had had brains enough to come to him immediately. He shuddered to think what would have happened to that wound had Willie waited even a couple of days. He briefly imagined a one-armed pickpocket, but didn't laugh.

He left his house on Clay Street and made his way to Montgomery Street to the Saxton, Brewer and Company bank. Delaney Saxton was in conversation with one of his clerks, and broke off when he saw Saint.

"You've saved me, Saint," he said. "Old Jarvis here is trying to talk me into something mighty suspicious."

"Send Jarvis to see Limpin' Willie. The poor fellow's out of commission for a while, a gash in his arm probably gained while he was trying to rob somebody. It'll do him good to use his brain for a change."

"Patched him up, did you?" Del asked. "I think the Sydney Ducks would elect you mayor if you wanted it. Lord knows there's enough of them, and all of them in your debt, right?"

"Banking and doctoring, we both collect debts, don't we, Del? How's Chauncey?"

"No longer just a mother, thank God," Delaney said, a satisfied grin on his lips.

"You take it easy, Del, you hear? Little Alexandra is only three months old. You give Chauncey all the rest she needs."

Delaney Saxton raised an eyebrow. "I? You know very well that my wife's insatiable, Saint. I have nothing to say in the matter." He bumped his fist against his forehead and shook his head. "Good Lord, what a man will tell his doctor. You're worse than a damned priest."

Saint laughed, a rumbling sound deep in his chest. "Come on, boy, let's have some lunch. You're looking peaked."

"Boy? I'm the same age as you, old man." Del spoke briefly to his partner, Dan Brewer, then the two men strolled onto Montgomery Street. There was a light blanket of fog, typical for June in San Francisco, and it was chilly enough to appreciate vests under coats. They wove their way through the masses of humanity to Saint's favorite restaurant, Pierre's Culinary Establishment.

They both drank beers while waiting for Pierre's

bouillabaisse. "I wonder how Byrony and Brent are doing," Saint said after a moment.

"Knowing Brent, he won't write. He'll just show up in a couple of months, richer than he was when he left. Fact is, he should, of course, what with his father's plantation to deal with. In Natchez, isn't it?"

"That's what Byrony told me. Named Wakehurst. I wonder how the two of them will deal with all the slaves. I can't imagine Byrony liking the fact that people are actually owned. And Brent's been away from that kind of life for a long time."

"Well, I just hope he and Byrony mend their fences while they're gone. I'd sure like to see them united when they get back." Del paused a moment, shaking his head. "Ira and his dear half-sister, Irene, are still behaving with a bit of nastiness."

"You believe in divine justice, Del?" Saint asked.

"Not particularly. Why?"

Saint shrugged. "I think the Butlers are a bit overdue for it. It still upsets me to think of Byrony married to Ira and considered the mother of his half-sister's child."

"Incest," Del said with distaste, "is something I simply don't understand."

Saint didn't reply, his eyes on the huge serving of bouillabaisse Jacques had set in front of him.

Del said in an aggrieved voice, "I got about half as much as you, Saint."

"Well, you're about half my size, and besides—"

"I know. Pierre owes you favors."

"Yeah. Remember when he burned himself real bad a couple of months ago? I accepted payment in food. My housekeeper's cooking just can't compete with Pierre's."

Delaney laughed and spooned down a bite of the delicious fish stew.

"More and more families, thank heaven," Saint said. "In a couple of years maybe we'll be rid of our rough reputation. Never seen so many horny men as in this city."

"Nor so many happy prostitutes. This is also a town where women can make their fortunes."

Saint grunted something that Del didn't understand, but he didn't ask for enlightenment. Saint didn't approve of prostitution.

"You want to come over for dinner tomorrow night?" Del asked after a moment. "Chauncey would like to see you, and Alexandra, of course."

"Sorry, but I'm kind of committed."

"Ah, the widow Branigan."

"Jane's a good sort," Saint said. "Besides, one of her boys has a bit of a cold."

"Are you going to marry her, Saint?"

"You shackled men," Saint said. "None of you is happy unless all us carefree bachelors join you."

"Well, if you had a wife, you wouldn't have to take favors in food."

"Just because a woman has different parts, Del, doesn't mean she can cook."

Delaney laughed, and toasted Saint with the rest of his beer.

"Looks like you're a healthy young horse again, Joe," saint said, ruffling the little boy's hair. "Not to worry, Jane," he said to Joe's mother, who was hovering behind him. "The lad's just fine now."

"Thank you, Saint."

But Joe said, "I was hoping I'd get sicker. Mom

said you might tell me why you're called Saint if I was sick enough."

"Maybe. No luck this time, Joe. What's that delicious smell, Jane?"

"Bouillabaisse," she said. "I heard you liked it."

Saint, who was filled up to his craw with that dish, forced an agreeable smile.

It was close to ten o'clock before Joe and his older brother, Tyler, were finally tucked into their beds upstairs. Saint leaned back in his comfortable chair, his half-closed eyes resting for a moment on Jane Branigan. She was a fine-looking woman, with her coal-black hair and chocolate-brown eyes. A bit on the plump side, perhaps, but he was a big man, with big hands. The unbidden thought of his big hands covering her ample breasts and hips made him smile and his sex harden. A man with big appetites.

"I know what you're thinking, Saint Morris." Jane leaned down and kissed him. "You haven't a subtle bone in your big body."

"Probably not," Saint said. He pulled her down on his lap and laced his fingers together behind her back. Her breasts pressed against his chest, and he got harder. "You're a fine woman, Jane," he said, the words rumbling deep in his throat, and leaned her back against his arm to kiss her. She responded with enthusiasm, as she usually did, and before long his fingers were caressing her bare breasts. "Nice," he said. "Very nice indeed."

She pressed down against him, and he smiled even as he kissed her again, quite thoroughly.

They hadn't enjoyed each other in nearly a week, and Jane discovered that she wanted him as much as he did her. In their urgency, they didn't consider going to Jane's bedroom. He took her on the carpet in front of the fireplace.

"Ah, Jane," he said some minutes later as he watched her face contort with her pleasure. "It pleases me so much when you do that."

Jane pulled an afghan over them, then snuggled against Saint's chest. "It's been too long," she said. "That was very nice."

"An understatement, woman," he said and kissed her earlobe. He felt her hand glide down his chest, over his belly. "I'm only a man, Jane, be patient."

"Hmm," she said, caressing him in her hand. "Is that really all you are?"

It was close to midnight before they were dressed again and sitting at Jane's small kitchen table drinking tea.

He never spent the night with her because of her boys. Some nights, like tonight, when he was sated and sleepy, he thought of holding her, her arms wrapped around him.

"How's our little girl doing, Jane?" he asked, as he sipped the delicious tea.

"Much better. She wants me to call her Mary, which I do, of course. She worships you, naturally."

"Excellent, but is her sewing good enough for you?"

"Yes. She's a bright girl and she wants nothing more than to please. She still likes to stay in the back of the shop, away from the customers, but I expect she'll gain some confidence soon."

"It might take a while, since most of your customers are men," Saint said. "You've got three women working for you now, right?"

"Yes, and business is booming. Lord, I think our

little shop has made at least two thousand shirts since we opened last year, not to mention more flannel trousers than I care to count."

Saint pictured the fifteen-year-old Mary—her name in Chinese, he couldn't begin to pronounce—as she had been two months ago when he had saved her from being sold as a prostitute in a filthy crib down on Washington Street. She had been beaten for her unwillingness, and Saint had examined her carefully while she was unconscious. Luckily, she was still a virgin, but he could imagine that her maidenhead was only a technicality. Poor girl. He sighed, leaning back in the chair. So many poor girls, so many victims.

"I know what you're thinking, Saint," Jane said, closing her hand over his forearm. "You've done so much. It's just that the city is so very young and wild and there are so many men and—"

"And many of them bastards."

"True, but things are changing, you know. You're not a bastard, and neither are many of your friends."

"Things won't really change until San Francisco is no longer a city of single men and prostitutes."

"More families are coming all the time," Jane said, making Saint recall his own words to Del Saxton. She lowered her eyes to her lap for a moment. "If only Danny had survived—"

"I know, Jane, I know. Your husband was doubtless a fine man. He sure picked a fine wife and made fine boys."

"But *some* gold wasn't enough for him. If only you'd been in that camp when he came down with pneumonia, things might have been different."

"I'm not a miracle worker. Now, we've talked ourselves into a depression, and that's no good at all, particularly after what you did to my poor body." She laughed, as he had known she would. He rose and stretched. Jane eyed him. He was a fine specimen of a man. She was so lucky to have found him when she had. She watched him walk over to the sink. She loved the way his chestnut hair curled about his ears, the way his hazel eyes narrowed when he was concentrating. And she knew he didn't love her. They were good together, and, the good Lord knew, he'd helped her more than she could ever repay. Maybe someday.

"Let me fix this blasted pump, then I've got to get home," he said over his shoulder.

Saint was awakened at three o'clock in the morning by violent knocks on the front door. It was Caesar, from Maggie's brothel. One of the men, a stranger, had beaten one of her girls.

He cursed and ranted all the way to the Wild Star, Brent Hammond's saloon. The other half of the large building was a brothel, called Maggie's.

"Dammit, Maggie," he shouted as soon as he stepped into her sitting room. "How could you let something like this happen? Which girl got hurt?"

"Victoria," Maggie said. "The man is dead. Ceaser slit his throat. Come along."

Oh God, Saint thought as he stared down at Victoria, pert, vivacious always with a ready smile for him, except now. One eye was already blackening, her upper lip was split and swollen, and she looked as pale as the sheet covering her.

"Hold still, Victoria," he said as he sat on the bed beside her. "It's just me, Saint."

Victoria closed her eyes, biting her lower lip to keep from crying out. His touch was gentle, but she hurt, badly. "Your jaw's not broken," Saint said. He pulled down the sheet that covered her. There were teeth marks on her left breast and an ugly bruise over her lower ribs. He probed as gently as he could, feeling her tense. "Try to relax, Victoria. I'll be done in a minute. Your ribs are fine, but you're going to hurt for a couple of weeks."

He drew the sheet lower, and sucked in his breath. There was blood clotted between her thighs. "Maggie, fetch me some hot water and some clean cloths. Now, Victoria, tell me what the bastard did to you."

Victoria drew a shuddering breath and whispered, "He hurt me, Saint."

*Dear God, I can see that well enough.* "Why are you bleeding? How did he hurt you here?"

He listened with growing anger. The man had dug his fist into her, tearing her. "He wasn't normal, Saint, and when I started yelling, he got crazy and hit me more." She burst into tears.

Saint stroked her hair from her forehead, muttering soothing sounds to calm her as he waited for Maggie to return with the hot water. "It will be all right, Victoria. Just a few stitches, and you'll be fine, I promise." As he spoke, he remembered Maggie asking him once why he didn't want any of her girls. "I'd go to hell first," he'd told her, and he meant it. He knew, in all fairness, that Maggie was greatly upset now, for nothing like this had ever happened before. But dammit, something like this should never happen.

"All right, Victoria, I'm going to put you out for a while. It's just chloroform. You understand me? I just

want you to breathe in, deeply. Don't fight it, now."
She nodded, and closed her eyes as Saint gently
placed the dampened cloth with its sweetish liquid
over her nostrils.

He carefully stitched the torn flesh, then bathed
her and pressed soft cloths against her.

"Thank you, Saint," Maggie said when he rose. He
said nothing until he'd pulled a sheet and blankets
over Victoria.

"Would you like a brandy?"

He nodded, still looking down at Victoria. "She
won't be out for much longer. Yes, a brandy is just
what I need. Give her a bit of laudanum in water
when she wakes up. And have one of the girls stay
with her, Maggie."

He followed her from the room.

"This is damnable, Maggie," he said as he accepted
the brandy snifter from her.

"I know." He saw the pain in her eyes, and just a
bit of his anger melted. "I heard her scream, and ran
into the room. The man—well, I smashed him over
the head with a lamp, then called Caesar. The man
wasn't really unconscious and he began struggling.
He pulled a derringer, and Caesar killed him. Will
she be all right, Saint, truly?"

"Yes, in time. I think, though, that you've lost
yourself a whore."

Maggie winced at his term, but said nothing. It
was true, no matter how one dressed it up fancy in
one's mind. She shook her head and sank onto a
chair. "I'll see that she's well taken care of. But she's
alone, Saint. Like all my girls, Victoria chose to be
a—whore. Hell, she's getting rich off all the horny
men in this city."

"I wonder what her choice is now?"

"I'll take care of her. She's earned quite a bit of money during the past year. She'll be just fine."

*And she'll probably go through life now never wanting another man to touch her.* "She's going to need some close nursing for a couple of days. I'll see her tomorrow morning. Keep her quiet. I'll take the stitches out in a week or so."

"Thank you, Saint. Lord, I wish Brent were here."

"He and Byrony will be back soon enough. He couldn't have prevented what happened, in any case."

"No, I suppose not," Maggie said. She rose and shook Saint's hand. "Thanks, Saint, for coming so quickly."

"What did you do with the bastard who hurt her?"

"Caesar dumped him somewhere, I don't know."

"I hope it wasn't in the bay. Wouldn't want the fish to get polluted by such scum."

"I owe you, Saint."

Saint grunted, too weary to argue or preach anymore.

He went home and drank half a bottle of whiskey before falling into oblivion near dawn.

# Chapter 3

*Aboard the* Sea Shroud

Juliana felt bile rise in her throat as she looked down at the tray of food Jameson Wilkes had brought her. In normal circumstances she would have wolfed down the delicious-looking beef and boiled potatoes.

"You will eat, my dear."

She jerked around at his calm, hated voice. She'd seen him leave but hadn't heard him come back into the cabin.

"I can't," she said.

"I am prepared to make allowances for your shock, Juliana, but not when it comes to your health. I assure you that I will not allow you to become a skinny wraith. Now, eat."

"I'll vomit," she said. "All over your beautiful cabin."

"If you do," he said, coming to stand beside the narrow bed, "I will let you spend your days up on deck in full view of my men. And you'll be stark naked, my dear."

She took a bite of the potatoes.

"That's better. You will finish all the food on your

tray, every bit of it. I will be your dinner companion, so to speak."

"I have nothing to say to you, Mr. Wilkes—"

"You may call me Captain."

"Nothing at all, save to insist that you return me to my parents."

"You know, Juliana, you are really looking quite bedraggled. Your hair is encrusted with salt and tangled like a witch's mop. After you eat, I'll let you bathe. It will make you feel better, and undoubtedly make you appear more appetizing."

"I want to go home," she said, and he heard the break in her voice. "Please, please, take me home."

"You seem like a bright girl, too bright to waste your energies begging for what I cannot do."

"Cannot? You mean you will not. What do you want with me? My parents have no money.

"Your show of spirit does not displease me," Jameson Wilkes said. "Would you like me to thump your back?"

Her eyes widened in terror and she pulled back against the headboard of the bed.

"Finish your dinner," he said, sitting back in his chair, his arms folded over his chest.

Kanola, Jules thought, she's dead. He'll kill me too. She'd tried, during the long hours he'd left her alone, to reason out what was happening to her, but her grief and her fear had left her mind numb. She ate mechanically, chewing every bit of food ten times, as her mother had taught her to do.

When Jameson Wilkes removed the tray from her lap, Jules didn't move. She stared straight ahead at his shelves of books, saying nothing.

"Would you like to bathe first or shall I tell you where I'm taking you and why? You've gone mute on me, huh? Very well, listen well. We are bound for San Francisco, but I believe you already know that. As to your fate, I promise you it won't be so bad. You see, Juliana, I will sell you to the highest bidder at a very special auction. With your looks and your virginity, only a rich man will be able to pay the price. I venture to say that you'll be well treated. Indeed, I would say that the man who purchases you will keep you in some amount of luxury. In short, Juliana, you will be a rich man's mistress."

She looked at him blankly. "What do you mean, a man's mistress? You mean some man would hurt me?"

Jameson Wilkes could only stare at her for a long moment. Then he laughed. "A missionary's daughter," he said more to himself than to her. "How can you be so ignorant, having grown up in Lahaina? You do know what prostitutes are?"

"Yes. Terrible men pay money to debauch—"

"These so-called terrible men pay women money, my dear. And the native women are among the most unrestrained females most men have ever encountered. Now, a mistress is much more prized than a simple prostitute. A mistress is beholden to only one man. If she behaves well with that one man, she in turn is treated well—quite indulged, really. It is not a bad life."

"You would make me a prostitute, then?"

"Yes, plainly, you will be a prostitute."

"But you said that prostitutes are willing to do what they do, that they—"

"Unfortunately, you will not have that choice," he

said, cutting her off. "But it is not impossible, Juliana, when the man who purchases you, let us say, eventually has had enough of your charms, that you could marry and settle down with children, or even return to Maui, if you wish it."

She heard Kanola's cries, but could only imagine how the men had hurt her before she'd managed to escape them and jump overboard. "I will not do it," she said.

"Ah, more spirit. I repeat, Miss Juliana DuPres, you have no choice in the matter."

"I do. I would kill any man who tried to hurt me."

"And I, my dear," he said with deadly calm, "have two weeks to change that violent attitude of yours." He rose, staring down at her. "You know, you are almost lovely enough to tempt me. Ah, I see that such a notion repels you. Perhaps you believe me too old. But it is usually older men who are the rich ones. I will return shortly with your bath."

He left her alone. Jules looked toward the cabin door. It wasn't locked. But that fact gained her nothing. She had no clothes, and even if she did find something to cover herself with, there were all those sailors abovedeck. Even if she managed to escape them, what would she do? *Kanola jumped, knowing she wouldn't be able to make it to shore.* She came up to her knees and stared out the porthole at the endless stretch of ocean. Miles and miles from anywhere.

Jameson Wilkes returned shortly. "Cover yourself well," he said to her, then stood aside as a sailor entered with a stout wooden hipbath, followed by two other men who carried buckets of steaming water.

The men's eyes slid toward her when they thought the captain wasn't looking.

Jameson closed the door behind them, then turned and said, "Your bath, my dear."

She could only stare at him.

"Come, now."

"Get out," she said.

"No," he said. "This is your first lesson in obedience. Have you ignored the fact that it was I who stripped you? Come, I am well used to women's bodies, and will not lose my head over the sight of you."

"No."

She saw his expression change. She closed her eyes, humiliation and fear washed through her.

"Don't make me force you."

Slowly Jules rose from the bed, pulling the sheet with her. She walked to the tub, her eyes fastened to the soft Turkey carpet beneath her feet. He jerked the sheet off her.

Never in her life had another person seen her unclothed. Even her mother. Even Sarah, her sister.

"Get into the tub."

She did.

Although Jameson Wilkes had studied her closely and quite objectively when he'd first brought her unconscious to his cabin, seeing her move made his eyes shine with pleasure. She was lovely. Long white legs, nicely shaped. Her hips weren't full and rounded, but he didn't expect that. She was too young and hadn't borne children. She looked coltish, but certainly not sexless. He mentally added another five hundred dollars to the price he'd already decided upon.

He handed her some perfumed soap. "Wash your hair well," he said, and returned to his chair.

Jules tried to hide herself from him, but it wasn't

possible. Her breasts were plainly visible, no matter how she tried to curl down into the tub.

After some moments, there was a rap at the cabin door. Jameson Wilkes said, "Don't worry. You will have your privacy. It is just fresh water to rinse your hair."

Privacy, she thought, feeling what must be hysteria welling up in her, a condition she'd never thought would touch her.

When he told her to stand up, she obeyed. He rinsed her hair thoroughly, then fashioned a turban around her head. He handed her a large towel and helped her out of the tub. He said nothing as Juliana dried herself, then wrapped the towel around her. Her breasts, he thought, pleased, were nicely rounded and high, enough of a handful for any man.

He handed her a pearl-handled brush and comb.

Jules sat on the edge of the bed and began to untangle her hair. This is a dream, she thought, a nightmare, and I'll wake up soon, and shiver, then laugh at my own strange imagination. Then I'll go visit Kanola and play with her children—

"You know, your tanned face and shoulders will lighten up quite nicely, I think, after two weeks indoors. You'll be perfectly white all over. Nor," Jameson Wilkes continued, "will we have to darken your brows or eyelashes. All the redheads I've known have had to do so, you know."

Jules thought of the faded daguerreotype of her French grandmother that her own mother kept well hidden from her father. She'd had dark brows, and her eyelashes appeared thick and curling, making her eyes look sultry. Jules said nothing.

"Of course, such flame-colored hair as yours is unusual and not always natural. I much enjoyed assuring myself that it was natural."

She stared at him blankly.

"The very red curls between your thighs, Juliana."

This isn't happening, she thought. It can't be happening.

He saw the horror in her eyes, saw her quickly duck her head down, stiffen. Excellent, he thought. She was no delicate, swooning maiden. She had pride, and backbone.

"I fear the next two weeks might prove a bit boring and confining for you, my dear. But there is no choice, really. I noticed that you were looking at my books. I have a good selection. Not many young ladies like to read, but I have a feeling that you are different from your sisters. Now, if you will excuse me, I have other duties to attend to."

"I have no clothes. Please—"

"No, of course you do not. And you won't."

"But why?"

Jameson paused by the cabin door. "There are two reasons, Juliana. First of all, a gown would make you feel less vulnerable, less malleable, give you a confidence that would be illusory at best. Second, I want you to become used to being naked. You will be spending the majority of your time during the next months in your natural state, I would imagine."

"You are evil."

He was amused. "Didn't you hear your minister father rant enough about the evil of men?"

"I didn't really believe him."

"Oh, incidentally, Juliana, the trunk containing my

clothes is locked. I beg you not to try to pry it open. Such an act would displease me."

He left her then, sitting on the edge of the bed, wrapped in the bath towel, her wet hair streaming over her shoulders.

The pain in his belly sharpened a bit and he rubbed his stomach.

John Bleecher was walking beside her, and Jules knew he wanted to hold her hand. He was a nice boy—no, not a boy, not any longer. He wanted to marry her. Her father wanted her to marry John. But Sarah didn't, nor did Jules. She would have paired John with Sarah in an instant, but people never seemed to behave as they should. Sarah would worship him, attend to his every word with flattering and sincere attention. Suddenly John turned, grabbed her upper arms, and planted a very wet kiss on her mouth.

Jules began to struggle, but John didn't stop. His teeth ground against her lips, and she cried out. But it was no use, he was too strong.

"John, stop it, you idiot! How dare you—"

Jules came suddenly awake, jerking upright in bed. The cabin was dark. Her breathing was jerky. Of course John Bleecher wasn't there. She was alone. John had kissed her once, and when she'd frowned at him, he'd let her be. And her mind had turned him into a monster. Like Jameson Wilkes. Like those sailors who had hurt Kanola. No, she thought, I must face facts. They'd raped her, like animals. And that was what was in store for her. She wasn't certain what that entailed, exactly, and she didn't want to know.

She lay back down, pulling the sheet to her chin. What to do? Certainly there was no way to escape from this ship. But when they arrived in San Francisco— Surely she couldn't be kept a prisoner all the time. Surely when Jameson Wilkes tried to sell her, she could scream and fight and demand justice.

How many girls had he kidnapped? How many girls had he sold? What had happened to them? Were there more girls aboard his ship right now?

There were no answers, of course.

Jules fell asleep close to dawn. She woke slowly, feeling smooth fingers gliding up and down her bare arm. Her eyes flew open. Jameson Wilkes was sitting beside her, a bemused expression on his face.

"Don't touch me," she whispered, easing as far away from him as she could.

"That's something else," he said calmly. "I *will* touch you, often. You must get used to it. You must learn not to flinch or act terrified. Of course, the man who buys you will want a certain amount of innocence and timidity, but he won't want to have spent his money on a frightened, shrinking little virgin."

He reached for her again. Jules, without conscious decision, flew at him, her nails raking down his face before he could stop her. Her attack was effective because it was so unexpected. He finally grabbed her wrists and bent her arms behind her until she was biting her lower lip in silent pain.

"If you do that again," he said, "I will bring in three of my most vicious sailors and let them fondle you and kiss you." He shook her, until she cried out. "Do you understand?"

She nodded.

He released her. He rose and walked to the small shaving mirror above the commode. "You drew a bit of blood."

"I would kill you if I could."

He said nothing, merely washed the scratch on his cheek. "I believe I have your punishment," he said, his voice as calm as could be. "I had intended to give you another day or so—" He broke off and shrugged. He strode toward her, and Jules pressed her back against the headboard of the bed.

Soon she was lying on her back, her wrists tied above her head to the headboard. He slowly drew down the sheet.

"There," he said. "How lovely you are, Juliana." Jules closed her eyes, so shamed and humiliated that she wanted to choke from it.

She felt his dry, cool fingers touch her breasts, and yelled, but she couldn't get away from him.

Jameson straightened, smiling. "You will remain thus, my dear, until it pleases me to release you. When you are ready to be more cooperative, I will untie your wrists. Now, I have some work to do and I shall stay here in my cabin."

He walked to his desk, sat down, and opened a ledger. She felt him looking at her. She wanted to die.

The days and nights blurred in Juliana's mind. She wasn't certain, but she believed it had been four days now since Jameson Wilkes had kidnapped her. It was afternoon, and something within her simply snapped. She would no longer be an obedient, biddable possession. She waited, not moving, until she heard Wilkes's footsteps coming toward the cabin.

She knew his sound as well as she knew her own. When he entered, she very calmly struck him as hard as she could with an ivory bookend.

She stood a moment, staring down at him. "Now, you pig." She stripped him of all his clothes except his trousers. She couldn't bring herself to do that, though she'd planned to. She'd wanted him to feel as she did—humiliated, exposed, helpless. She donned his shirt, hating it because it smelled like him, then tied his hands behind him. In her fury, she kicked him hard in the ribs. Then she stood back, and the realization that what she'd done was for naught struck her hard. She heard the sound of footsteps coming toward the cabin. She raced to the door, but there was no lock. Slowly she backed up and waited.

Bob Gallen, first mate aboard the *Sea Shroud*, knocked on the door. There was no answer. He knocked again, calling to his captain.

Frowning, he opened the cabin door and stood stock-still for a moment, staring first at his unconscious captain and then at the motionless white-faced girl who was wearing his captain's shirt.

"Oh no," he said. He bent down to examine Jameson Wilkes. "He'll be all right, I think," he said, looking up at her. "Look, miss, I'm sorry about all this, but what you've done was utterly stupid. Jesus." Bob plowed his hand through his hair.

"Please," Juliana said, "please help me."

"I can't," Bob said. "Both of us would wish ourselves dead if I did." He quickly untied the captain's wrists and lifted him in his arms. He laid him on the bed.

"Get me into one of the boats, that's all I ask. Please."

He shook his head. From the corner of his eye he saw the girl race toward the door. He caught her and pulled her back. He shook her.

"Don't, for God's sake. You're not stupid. You know what the men did to your friend, don't you, before she jumped?"

"I don't care. I hope he dies."

"Look, Miss DuPres, I don't approve his taking a missionary's daughter, but I have no say in the matter. For god's sake, even if I managed to get you in a boat and away from the ship, you'd die soon enough."

"All of you are evil. God, I hope you die too."

Both of them froze at the groan from the bed. As if mesmerized, Jules watched Jameson Wilkes slowly sit up and gingerly rub his head.

# Chapter 4

"Well, Bob, may I inquire as to the reason for your presence?" Before Bob Gallen could reply—a difficult matter in any case, since he felt strangled with fear—Jameson Wilkes continued, "Ah, I see the problem. You look charming in my shirt, Juliana. Did you strike me?"

"Yes," she said, her voice shrill with fear. "I only wish I'd killed you."

Jameson Wilkes said nothing until the dizziness passed. "I underestimated you," he said more to himself than to her. "A mistake I shan't make again. Bob, you may leave now. I believe my faculties are sufficiently intact once more."

"Sir, really," Bob Gallen said, but stopped abruptly at the threat in his captain's eyes.

He turned on his heel, not looking at Juliana again, and left the cabin, closing the door behind him.

Jameson Wilkes rose slowly from the bed. "Your modesty prohibited you from removing my trousers?"

She would not cower before this evil man. She said, "After I got your shirt off, I saw how old and ugly you were. Do you think I would want to see more? You are repellent."

Jameson Wilkes was forty-one years old. He didn't

consider himself either old or ill-formed. In fact, he was proud that he was lean, with none of the paunch at his middle that most men his age sported. He wanted to beat her, but no. He saw her fear, realized her speech was all bravado, and reluctantly admired her for it. It had been years, he thought, since he'd thought of a woman as an individual, a being who was separate and distinct unto herself.

It was quite likely that the man who purchased her would be repellent. Probably fat, with sagging jowls. He allowed himself a few moments to feel regret, then quashed it.

He said in his calm voice, "Please remove my shirt."

Jules clutched the fine lawn material to her chest. "No."

He sighed. "If you do not remove the shirt this instant, I will call back my gallant first mate. He, I am certain, no matter what his chivalrous feelings toward you, will be pleased to see all of you."

"I won't," she said. She leaned down and picked up the ivory bookend. "You come near me and I will kill you."

She didn't stand a chance, of course. He was on her in an instant, bending her arm in an iron grasp until she dropped the bookend. He practically tore the shirt from her and threw her onto the floor.

"You deserve to be beaten," he said as he pulled on his ripped shirt. "But I can't mark you. There isn't the time for you to heal. And no man would want to buy damaged goods."

All bravado was gone, stripped away as surely as he had stripped away his shirt. She covered her face with her hands and sobbed.

Jameson Wilkes frowned down at her. Her hair
was in wild curls about her face and shoulders.
Never before had he dealt with a female like her. For
a moment he stood quietly, not knowing what to do.
He didn't want to break her, not completely, but he
couldn't allow her to be a wild thing, either. He
didn't doubt for a minute that she would never will-
ingly allow herself to be raped by the man who
would buy her. It would hurt his reputation badly
were she to kill the as-yet-unknown man.

Then he smiled, his decision made. Without another word he lifted her from the floor and set her
on the bed. He tied her wrists above her head and
left her.

That evening when he brought her dinner tray, he
said nothing to her of the afternoon's incident. He
even allowed her to cover herself with the sheet
while she ate.

"Do drink your wine, Juliana," he said. "It is from
my own private stock."

She shook her head.

"You've never tasted wine before?" He rose and
poured himself a glass. "Come, now, just a bit to see
if you like it."

Jules, numb, raised the glass and drank. The wine
was rich and sweet. Warmth crashed to her stomach.

Jameson Wilkes watched closely as she downed
the entire contents of the glass. He smiled. "Excellent," he said.

It would take a while, he knew. He had no idea
whether the amount of the drug he'd poured into
the glass was correct. The old Chinese gnome who'd
sold it to him had merely said that the dose "de-

pended." On what? Well, he thought, leaning back in his chair, he would soon see. The drug was a mixture of opium and other things, the old man had said, things that would make women utterly wild. Jameson wasn't certain that such things as aphrodisiacs existed. Certainly the myth about oysters was just that, a myth.

"We will be in San Francisco within a week," he said, cutting through the silence. "We're making excellent time, better than I'd expected. Did I tell you, my dear, that this was my last voyage to the islands?"

Jules was beginning to feel odd, somehow detached from herself. She heard his voice, understood his words. She said slowly, her tongue thick in her mouth, "I want to go home. I do not particularly like my father or my sister, but Lahaina is my home." She looked a bit startled at what she'd said, but continued in a soft singsong voice, "I collected flowers, and cataloged fish. I don't want to be a man's whore. I don't want to be like some of the women on Maui."

"You are a smart girl, Juliana. Perhaps the man who buys you will indulge you in your interests. Perhaps you should consider how best to endear yourself to your future protector."

"No," she said quite clearly. But Jameson Wilkes wasn't very clear anymore, and she blinked to keep him in focus. "My family would know." She realized she wasn't making any sense.

He was smiling at her, and she wondered at it. She also realized at that moment that she had to relieve herself. Always before, she'd been alone. "I must use the chamber pot," she said.

"Go right ahead, my dear."

Jules shook her head in confusion. "No," she said. "I can't, not while you're in here. Please leave."

This was interesting, Jameson Wilkes thought, studying her face closely. A loss of inhibition, an excellent start. "Of course you can," he said, his voice as soothing as honey.

But still she sat there looking confused, bewildered. He said very gently, "I won't pay you any heed. Go ahead."

Jules eased off the bed and walked to the chamber pot, which was stored beneath a small cabinet. She didn't realize that she was quite naked. Nor did she pay any more attention to Jameson Wilkes. When she was finished, she turned, straightened, and stared at him.

To his complete and utter surprise, Jameson Wilkes felt a powerful surge of lust. He'd believed himself immune to her body—to any woman's body, for that matter. It was a heady combination, her standing so confidently before him, but her eyes dazed and confused.

"What do you feel, Juliana?" he asked, forcing himself not to move.

"I don't know."

"Why don't you lie down? Surely what you're feeling will pass quickly enough."

She did, stretching languidly, her eyes closing. Her body felt tingly, strangely alive in places she'd never paid much attention to. But she wasn't frightened of the feelings.

Jameson Wilkes sat down beside her and carefully laid his hand on her breast. He felt her quiver.

He leaned down and took her nipple in his mouth.

Suddenly she lurched up, and struck him with her fists.

I didn't give her enough, he thought as he subdued her. But now I know. Probably it was the opium that had relaxed her so much, sent her into that other-worldly, detached kind of dream state. He'd seen it before.

"What did you do to me?" she yelled, struggling with all her might, even after he'd again tied her wrists.

"Why, nothing, my dear," he said. "Perhaps you're really a little whore at heart. Didn't you enjoy my touching you?"

She closed her eyes, not moving even when tears streamed down her cheeks.

Jameson Wilkes walked to the cabin door. He'd won. This time he ignored the stabbing pain in his belly.

*San Francisco*

It was near to midnight. There was a quarter-moon, but the fog was so thick that the night looked an eerie gray. Saint had returned to his house thirty minutes before. He had an appointment with Hoot Moon, an unlikely criminal with a personality as unlikely as his name. As he settled down in his favorite armchair to wait for his visitor, he wondered what the man had to tell him. Hoot Moon owed him, as did many other of his friends, for Saint had, through sheer luck, saved the man's life when he'd been shot in the head. He heard a furtive knock on the front door and rose to answer it.

Hoot Moon quickly slipped into the small entrance hall. He was a small man, vicious to his victims but possessed of a strange sort of honor that made him as loyal as a tick to his friends. He counted Saint among his friends.

Saint watched him slip off his thick cloak. "Why all the secrecy, Hoot?"

"You told me to let you know if any slavers came in," Hoot said in his low, hoarse voice, the result of a knife wound in his throat many years before.

Saint stiffened. "Who and when?"

"Jameson Wilkes, the old scoundrel, he just got in yesterday. Word's out that he's got something besides just the usual count of little Chink girls for that Chinese madame, Ah Choy. He's got him a missionary girl, Doc, stole her in Maui. I can't say I rightly can hold with that, no siree."

Maui!

"I know you spent a couple years there, Saint, in Lahaina. I wanted you to know right away."

Saint felt such a surge of rage, mingled with fear, that he couldn't speak for a moment. He got hold of himself. "Come on into the living room, Hoot, and let's have ourselves a drink. Whiskey."

Hoot scratched his ear and followed Saint. He downed the shot of whiskey in one quick gulp, then moved to stand by the fireplace to watch Saint expectantly.

"Now," Saint said, "tell me everything you know."

"He's having an auction tomorrow night, at the Crooked House on Sutter Street. He's really toutin' the missionary gal. He wants plenty of money for her, of course, her bein' a virgin and all."

"Is there a description of the girl?"

"Yep. Flame-colored hair and green eyes. About

eighteen, I think, maybe nineteen. Beautiful, according to what I heard, and real white skin."

Saint went utterly still. Oh yes, he knew who the missionary girl was, all right. Juliana DuPres. Jules. Lord, she'd been only fourteen or fifteen when he'd left Maui. His little ruby jewel, he'd called her, ruffling her thick red curls, always out swimming and searching out new species of fish, or hiking to find new plants. She'd quickly become "Jules" after that. And she'd tagged after him like a puppy, that pert little face of hers filled with worshipful infatuation. He could have told her to go to the moon and she'd probably have done her damnedest to do as he wished.

Rage filled him and he felt his stomach heave. He rarely felt the urge toward violence, but he did now. He wanted to kill Jameson Wilkes with his bare hands.

But that wouldn't help Jules.

"Whatcha say, Saint?" Hoot asked after many minutes had passed.

"We've got to save the girl, of course."

"Old Wilkes is gonna ask a fortune for her, I'll bet."

"He'd be a fool not to," Saint said. He suddenly remembered the day he'd left Lahaina. Jules had stood on the dock waving frantically to him. He'd seen tears in her eyes even from that distance. Then he'd seen her father, the damned prig, pull her away.

During the past two years, Saint had managed to buy four young Chinese girls from Ah Choy before they'd been debauched. But of course he didn't have enough money to buy Jules. God, what was he to do?

He said finally, "Hoot, find out exactly what hour the auction starts." He added quietly, "I think it's about time I called in some favors."

After Hoot Moon left as furtively as he'd come, Saint poured himself another whiskey and sat down again in his chair, his long legs stretched out in front of him, his fingers steepled. Until now he'd never involved his friends. There was always the chance of reprisals. Once before, two years ago, a friend had helped him, and had been recognized. He'd been found two days later with a bullet through his brain. But this time was different. He knew he could trust Delaney Saxton. After all, Del had saved his cook and housekeeper, Lin Chou, from one of those filthy cribs. Del, at least, cared. But Del was a new father. If he were recognized, there could be real trouble for him and Chauncey.

The criminal element in San Francisco knew no social boundaries. Some of the wealthiest men were utterly rotten, and it was impossible to tell who was involved in what. As for Hoot Moon and his sort, they were petty criminals in comparison. And, oddly enough, Saint trusted them.

He could borrow money from Del Saxton and buy Juliana DuPres outright. But the thought of paying, at the very least, a good five thousand dollars to that scum Wilkes made him want to howl. No, he didn't want Wilkes to get a cent. He wanted to smash the man's face into pulp.

Somewhere near three o'clock in the morning, Saint decided he wouldn't involve any of his respectable friends. He'd call in the favors from the Sydney Ducks.

*     *     *

Jules felt calm. When Jameson Wilkes tried to auction her off, she'd scream, fight, tear the place down. Somebody would help her. Not all men were like him.

She was still a prisoner in Wilkes's cabin. After she'd decided what she would do, she spent a good deal of time staring out the porthole at San Francisco. They were docked at the Clay Street wharf, Jameson Wilkes had told her.

He'd put a lock on the cabin door. "Just in case you get any outlandish ideas, my dear," he'd said in that calm voice of his.

She'd asked him two days before, "Isn't there anyone you care about?"

Oddly enough, he'd stiffened. But he'd said nothing, merely looked away from her as if seeing someone in the distant past.

It was dark now, and her nose was pressed against the porthole. There were so many lights, and she could even hear the shouts of men in the distance. She didn't look around when she heard the cabin door open.

"Juliana, it is time."

Jameson Wilkes drew back a moment at the hatred he saw in her eyes. But it was more than that, he realized. There was determination as well. It didn't require a powerful intellect to realize what she planned to do. He shook his head, and there was a flicker of regret in his eyes. He felt a sudden burning pain in his belly and automatically began to rub his stomach.

He handed her a gown, no underthings or petticoats, just a gown that was of a filmy material and a garish crimson color.

Jules only stared at the gown. He'd forced her to bathe that afternoon and wash her hair. She was now standing before him, a sheet wrapped around her. She drew herself up. "Surely, sir, that gown is in dreadful taste. Won't your gentlemen friends want to purchase a female who looks more a lady than a whore?"

He laughed. "Take the gown, my dear."

"No, I won't."

"If you refuse," he said, his voice as unruffled as always, "you will go before a roomful of men quite naked. It is your decision."

He calmly laid the gown on the bed, turned on his heel, and strode to the cabin door. "You have fifteen minutes, Juliana, no more."

She had no choice, none at all. She didn't disbelieve his threat. As she struggled to cover herself as best she could with the bright red dress, the memories of that night some five days before again filtered through her mind. Vague images, but they bothered her. She saw herself, as if through a haze, lying on her back, feeling strange sensations, feeling as though she were floating above her body, a body quite separate from her. Until he'd touched her breast—then she'd become herself again. She shook her head. It had made no sense. None at all. She raised her chin and waited for Jameson Wilkes to return for her.

She would best him. Oh, yes, she would.

# Chapter 5

The Crooked House on Sutter Street stood at the end of a cul-de-sac, and was, Saint knew, for all its rumored satanic rites and sexual perversions, nothing more than a whorehouse. A fancy whorehouse with only rich private members.

*Members*, he thought, shaking his head. That was almost funny.

He thought of Juliana DuPres and what she must be feeling. Terror, no doubt. He wondered if she'd changed much from that pert little straggly girl he'd known five years ago. So bright, she'd been, as bright as her flame-colored hair. He remembered her waiting for him several times outside the Seamen's Hospital on Front Street. If her damned father had known, he would have had a fit, of course, but somehow he'd never learned of those visits. No matter how depressed Saint had been, the sight of her had always make him smile.

Saint came out of the shadows at the sound of an owl. Hoot, he realized, was in place, as were, Saint hoped, the other dozen Sydney Ducks. A villainous lot, the bunch of them, but he'd take them over the bastards inside the Crooked House any day.

Saint felt a gentle tugging on his arm.

"Saint, they've already auctioned off three Chink gals. Wilkes ain't to be seen, of course. It's Danvers who's doing the dealing."

Saint adjusted his full beard and his black wig. Because of his height, he could, by standing on a crate, see through a side window. He nodded to Limpin' Willie, eased up onto the crate, which wobbled a bit under his weight, and peered again into the room.

There were at least twenty men, all of them masked, seated in chairs facing a small stage. He'd heard about the anonymity, the major rule, and thus the black masks. It prevented blackmail and a certain amount of embarrassment, he supposed. The curtains behind the stage were black velvet, as were the draperies in the room itself. He felt his blood boil when another quite young Chinese girl was forced out from behind the curtain, her long silken black hair covering her small breasts. He heard muted conversation, heard that sharp-voiced bastard Danvers calling out bids. How many more poor unfortunate girls before Jules? He didn't want the crate to break beneath him.

Juliana was wrapped in a thick cloak, her hands tied behind her, a gag in her mouth. Jameson Wilkes was seated beside her, his face utterly emotionless. She'd seen around the curtain briefly, seen the masked men seated in the darkened room.

It was some sort of club, she thought, with men here for the express purpose of buying women. But she wouldn't give up. Wilkes had to take off this gag sometime; then she would scream. I'll fight, I'll yell and—

Wilkes removed her gag. "Drink this now, Juliana."

She stared at the glass of wine for a long moment. "Why?"

"It will make everything easier for you."

"You had me drink wine before."

"Yes, and you will again, now."

She looked about her. Two of Jameson Wilkes's men stood behind her. "No," she said.

She felt the rim of the glass pressing against her teeth. She felt the wine seep into her mouth. She collected it, then jerked her head away and spat the wine full into Jameson Wilkes's face.

She saw his face go red with rage, and said, "Why don't you strike me, you bastard? But you won't, will you? You can't. You don't want to bruise your precious merchandise."

Jameson got a hold on himself. "You know, my dear, I'm tempted to feel a bit sorry for the man who buys you. But by then you will no longer be my problem." He looked at the two men. "Hold her head and keep her mouth open."

Jules struggled, but it was no use. She was forced to swallow the wine. She felt Jameson's handkerchief wipe off the drops that fell down her chin.

He stood back and stroked his chin. "Very nice. Keep breathing heavily."

"I hate you," she whispered. "You drugged the wine, didn't you? With more this time."

"Of course, but you knew that. You will be the most biddable creature imaginable by the time you're on that stage. Now, just sit quietly. I suspect that you'll be as pliant as I wish in another ten minutes." He chuckled a bit. "Do you know, I think I'll give your buyer a bit of the opium. Who knows, perhaps after you've been plowed, you won't need to be convinced anymore." He saw the horror in her eyes, and felt a moment of indecision. No, he thought, he had to sell her. He needed the money, he needed what the money would buy for him. He no longer denied to himself that he wanted her, wanted her more than any woman he'd ever known. But it wasn't to be.

Saint could feel the change in the group of men. There was a surge of anticipation, and the men were speaking to each other in excited whispers, sitting forward. His breath caught in his throat. Juliana Du-Pres was gently led onto the stage. Her beautiful thick hair was loose down her back, a riotous mass of curls. He sucked in his breath at the sight of her. God, she'd changed, she'd become a woman. She raised her head at the instruction from Danvers, and he saw the vague disinterested look in her eyes. He felt rage flow through him, realizing that she was drugged. He heard excited voices call out:

"Lord, would you look at those breasts—white as the snow in the Sierras."

"Turn her around and raise the hair off her back."

"No missionary girl ever looked like that. Wilkes wouldn't lie to us, would he? Lord, she's made to be on her back."

Saint forced himself to wait just a bit longer, until all the men were completely distracted by Juliana, their attention focused forward to the stage.

She looked like a puppet, her eyes glazed and vague.

He heard Danvers, the auctioneer, call out, "Well, gentlemen, we've a real prize here, a virgin prize. The bidding will start at three thousand dollars!"

The bidding had reached nearly five thousand

when one of the men called out, "How do we know that you haven't pushed up those breasts of hers? Let's see them."

"Yes, strip her down."

"Let's see those long legs."

That was it, Saint thought as he watched the auctioneer reach out to pull down the awful gown from her breasts.

He let out a banshee's shriek, the signal, and slipped off the crate. Within seconds the Crooked House was pandemonium. He himself threw himself against the side door, felt the wood give instantly at his surge of power. From the corner of his eye he saw all the Sydney Ducks pour into the room, yelling obscenities and brandishing pistols and knives. He'd given orders that no one was to be killed. He didn't care about bashed heads or robbery.

He rushed toward the stage. The man who was guarding Juliana was flailing at two Sydney Ducks. Then Saint saw another man, an older man, and he knew it was Jameson Wilkes. He was striding toward Juliana, his face grim.

Saint smiled. He reached Wilkes just as he grabbed for Juliana. He looked him straight in the eye, saw his surprise, and sent his fist into Wilkes's jaw. He watched with intense satisfaction as the man crumpled to the floor.

"Juliana," he said, lightly touching her arm.

She looked at him with no recognition at all. He grabbed her hand, and suddenly she began to struggle. He knew he had to get her out of here quickly. "Forgive me, Jules." He sent his fist into her jaw. He caught her against him and quickly lifted her into his arms. Just as he slipped out of the smashed side door, he let out three sharp hoots. Within moments the raiders had fled from the Crooked House, leaving its members staring at each other, some of them bleeding and robbed, bewildered and enraged.

Saint pulled off his cloak and wrapped it around Jules. He increased his pace, realizing that some heads had been knocked together. With his luck, he would soon have some patients to attend to. He had to hurry.

He made it to his house in just over ten minutes. He nearly laughed aloud with relief as he slammed the front door closed behind him. Moments later, he was carefully lowering Jules to his bed. Quickly he ran his fingers over her jaw. She would have a bruise, but that was all. She was still unconscious, but he imagined it was the drug—opium, likely—that was keeping her under. He had just covered her with blankets when he heard a knock on the door downstairs.

He closed his bedroom door, praying that she wouldn't wake up. He ripped off his ridiculous disguise as he walked downstairs.

He treated three gentlemen. When they left the reason for their cut lips, bruised jaws, and cracked ribs vague, Saint had a difficult time not laughing in their faces. His last patient was Bunker Stevenson, an upright, very wealthy citizen. "Damned misunderstanding over cards, Saint," Bunker said, and Saint forced himself to remain silent and make sympathetic noises. He listened to Bunker go on and on about the poker game, and wondered finally if he weren't, perhaps, telling the truth.

The other two men weren't from San Francisco. Saint smiled when one of them yelled as he was binding his cracked ribs.

It was nearly an hour before Saint returned to his bedroom. He lit a lamp and stood over the bed a moment, staring down at Juliana DuPres. Her hair was wild around her head. "You've changed, little one," he said, sitting beside her. He pulled off the blankets. He knew he had to make certain she was all right, and wanted to do it before she awakened. She'd be embarrassed enough as it was.

He drew a deep breath, and for one of the few times in his professional career was very aware that his patient was a woman. Damnation, he was a doctor, not a rutting bastard.

He stripped off the gown, not surprised that she was naked beneath it. The thought of what would have happened to her—no, he wouldn't think about it now. He gave her a quick examination, felt his hands trembling, cursed himself, and put her in one of his nightshirts—a nightshirt Jane had made for him that he'd never worn. It was like a huge white tent on her. After he'd covered her again, he slapped her cheeks. "It's time to wake up now, Jules. Come on, wake up, don't scare me."

Jules heard a voice, a man's voice, speaking sharply to her, but she didn't want to leave the blessed security of sleep. The voice continued and she felt light slaps on her face.

"No."

"Wake up, Jules."

Slowly she opened her eyes. She saw a man leaning over her, heard him call her name. He'd called her Jules. That was odd. Jameson Wilkes didn't know her nickname.

She blinked, trying to bring the man's face into focus.

But she felt heavy, so disconnected. He bought me, she thought suddenly, he's the man who paid for me. She reared up and struck at him.

Saint closed his hands around her shoulders and pressed her back down. "Don't be afraid, Jules. It's me—Michael. You're safe now. You're with me." She didn't respond for a moment, and he continued, "Do you understand, Jules? You're all right now, I promise you."

"Michael?" She tried to focus her mind on his words.

*Michael*, he thought. Only Jules had called him Michael, and not Saint, and he'd remembered. "Yes, it's Michael. You've been drugged, little one, but it will pass soon now."

"Michael," she said again. Suddenly she knew who he was, and she felt a bolt of incredible, unexpected happiness surge through her. She nearly gasped aloud with pleasure and relief. "Oh God, it must have been a dream, a nightmare. All of it—it was nothing. You're with me again. You've come back to me."

Saint had no chance to do anything. Jules threw her arms about him, buried her face against his shoulder. She said over and over, "You've come back to me. I always prayed you would. You don't know—so long since you left me, so long."

"No, no," he said, touching his fingertips to her lips. "We're not on Maui, Jules. We're in San Francisco."

But she was clutching at him, whispering, "I always loved you, always. You came back to me."

He grasped her arms and pulled her back. He looked into her face and told himself that she didn't realize what she was saying. "Listen to me, Jules. We're in San Francisco. I got you away from Jameson Wilkes and that godawful auction. You're safe with me now, in my house."

"You saved me, Michael?" She reached for him again, and he eased her against him, rocking her. He pressed his cheek against her wildly curling hair. "You really saved me?"

"Yes, and you're safe now."

Jules felt his large hands stroking down her back, pressing closer. She felt no fear. She felt secure and warm and happy. The past and the present merged and all she could grasp was her love for this man. "I love you, Michael," she said again. "You saved me."

"No, Jules, you don't love me. Hush, now. Would you like a glass of water?"

She didn't want water. She wanted Michael. She'd wanted him forever, it seemed now. He was holding her. His hands were making her feel strange things she didn't want to stop. She raised her hand to touch his face. "Michael." She raised herself and kissed him.

Saint was appalled at what was happening. It was that damned drug Wilkes had given her. He had to get away from her.

"Jules, no." She pressed herself against him, her breasts against his chest.

"I've always loved you, Michael, and now you've saved me. I belong to you. Please, Michael."

Please what, for God's sake? He struggled for reason. "Listen to me, Jules. You've been drugged, sweetheart. It's the opium that's making you act and feel like this. We've got to—"

She kissed him. He heard his own low moan. He

didn't know how it happened, but he was lying on the bed, Jules clutched against the length of him. "Dammit," he said aloud. He tried to hold her still, but she was wild against him, as if she wanted to become part of him. He had to do something. What had that bastard Wilkes given her? What had been added to the opium?

He knew she was beyond reason. He guessed that if it had been anyone else who had saved her, this wouldn't be happening. But he was her Michael from five years ago, and it was all tangled in her mind. But none of it was real, none of it.

"Jules," he said, desperate now.

"You'll never leave me, will you, Michael? Promise me that you'll never leave me again."

"I promise," he said.

She became more demanding, more urgent. He should leave her now, but he couldn't. He closed his mind to his own lust. He let her kiss him, let her move against him. Very slowly he eased his hand beneath the nightshirt. Her flesh was warm and smooth under his fingers. He closed his palm over her and gently pressed. She moaned, jerking against him.

"I'll help you, sweetheart," he said, his words warm in her mouth. His fingers found her, and he closed his eyes at the pleasure of it. She was warm, frantic. Within moments he felt her convulse, felt her legs stiffen, heard her wild cries. He saw the bewildered look in her dazed eyes, the confusion, then the release. Then she became still, slumping into him.

He forced himself to ease his hand away from her. "It's all right now," he said against her temple. "Everything is all right now."

And it was, at least for her. She fell asleep in his arms, her breathing soft and regular. Her last blurred words were "I love you."

Saint didn't move for a long time. Dear Lord, he thought, he'd never expected this. His sex was hard against her belly.

*I love you.*

No, she didn't, she couldn't. She was confusing the past with the present. A young girl's infatuation had melded with a woman's needs, and the drug had made her lose all sense of reality, of rightness. But the passion in her— He knew she'd never had a woman's release.

He breathed in the pungent, musky perfume Wilkes had made her use. He felt tired to his bones, despite his lust. Before he fell into a light sleep, he realized that he had a very real problem. Juliana DuPres was now his responsibility. What in God's name was he going to do?

On the heels of that thought, he heard again her pleasure, and his fingers tingled with the memory of touching her, giving her that pleasure. Would she remember in the morning? Remember what she'd said to him and what he'd done to her?

For his own peace of mind, he hoped she wouldn't.

# Chapter 6

Juliana cried out when Saint moved away from her. "Just a moment, Jules. I'll be right back, I promise you."

He pulled off his boots, then, unable to help himself, turned to look down at her. He wished he could see her as the young girl of five years before, but it wasn't possible, of course. He'd given her a woman's pleasure. It pleased him that he had been the first man to give her that gift. He could still see the dazed astonishment in her eyes. He closed his eyes against the image, but he'd been involved in her feelings— no way around that, even though he hadn't— Well, enough of that thinking.

If only, he thought, he'd met her for the first time this evening, rescued a stranger from Wilkes, not his Jules. But she was alive in his past, warm and loving and vivid, and his memories of Lahaina were rich because of her. He pulled her under the covers and into his arms, settling himself on his back.

He wouldn't feel guilty about it, he thought as he stared up toward the darkened ceiling of his bedroom. He'd simply done what he'd had to do. A strange cure for a doctor to employ, and that made him smile. Sex, he thought, made a man foolish; it overpowered his brain and complicated things. Well, there was going to be nothing complicated about this. But he pulled her closer, and his last thought before he fell into a light sleep was that she had to bathe away that awful pungent perfume.

He dreamed about an afternoon that he'd thought long forgotten, an afternoon some six years before. He was walking along beside his young friend, his step automatically shortened to match hers, not at first realizing that she wasn't behaving normally.

"The bird of paradise is so forceful," Juliana said, stopping a moment to sniff and lightly touch the vivid flower. "All sharp lines, beautiful colors, of course, but it's not delicate like the hibiscus."

This was her fifth stop to admire flowers. He'd had lectures from Jules on all the flora on Maui over the three months he'd known her. He was hot, tired, and wanted to go swimming, so he stopped her.

"Enough about the graceful hibiscus. Let's get into the water and you can show me some blackspot sergeants."

To his surprise, she ducked her head down, and a small "No" barely reached his ears.

"But you always want to go into the water," he said, patting her shoulder.

"Jules," Saint had said finally, giving her his full attention. "What's all this about? You've been acting strangely, I can't get you to go swimming with me, all you've wanted to do is prattle on about flowers. Now, what's going on?"

To his surprise, she turned red. He waited patiently, watching her pleat her cotton skirt with nervous fingers.

"If you're not going to talk to me, we might as well get me out of my misery and go swimming. What do you say? Want to change your mind? I'll make sure you don't get too much sun. Where is your sarong?"

Her head shot up. "I can't."

He stared down at her thin, intense face, surrounded with the riotous red curls. She looked as though she wanted to sink into the soft grass beneath her feet. He frowned, curbing his impatience. Then understanding hit him, and he wanted to laugh. But he said quite gently, taking her hand in his large one, "Come over here and let's sit down a minute. It's a great view, don't you think?"

He felt her trembling, felt her pulling back, but ignored it. So it was her monthly flow. Perhaps he should simply leave her on the beach while he swam. But she looked so strange; perhaps she wasn't feeling well. Once they were seated on a flat volcanic rock, he said matter-of-factly, "I'm your friend, and more than that, I'm a doctor. Your doctor. Now, talk to me."

She wouldn't look at him. "I'm dying," she said simply, her girl's voice high and thin and resigned.

"What the hell does that mean?" Even as he spoke, he realized suddenly that this must be her first time. She was thirteen, and he hadn't realized, hadn't considered that she— He felt a fool, a big bungling fool.

"Jules, you're not dying," he said. "You're bleeding, aren't you, for the first time?"

She looked at him, aghast. "Yes," she whispered.

He wished he could shake that pallid mother of hers until her teeth rattled for being such a damned prude. He proceeded in a calm, practical voice to explain to her the process of becoming a woman. "Do you understand now, Jules? There's nothing to be worried about, I promise. You're just fine. It's all very natural."

"You mean I'm going to do this *forever*?"

"Well, not forever, but for quite a few more years."

"But I want to go swimming."

He laughed and ruffled her hair. "You're just going to have to watch me for a couple more days. You don't hurt at all in your belly, do you?"

"Yes, but I don't care. I don't like this, not at all. It's not fair."

He hadn't thought about it in that way. "No," he said, "I guess it's not. But then again, Jules, I can't have babies. Do you think that's fair?"

He'd watched her playing with one of the native women's infants the previous afternoon. But she didn't take the bait, and repeated stubbornly, "It still isn't fair. You can still be a father, and that's almost the same thing. And you can swim all the time, all year round."

Thank God, she at least knew where babies came from, at least had a general notion. He supposed he should tell her that she could swim, but he could just imagine what she'd say to that.

Saint turned in his sleep, suddenly uncomfortable, then awakened with a start. There was a soft body pressed against him, a leg, knee bent, flung over his belly. Saint blinked away the dream. It was dawn, dull morning light filtering through the bedroom window. Slowly he raised a hand and smoothed her tangled hair away from his face. She wasn't a child anymore, hating what her body had done to her because it kept her from being a mermaid for five days. Why had that ridiculous dream come to him anyway? Because it was sexual in nature, he realized, even though at the time he'd merely been a good friend talking reassuringly to a young girl. Nothing more.

Saint suddenly realized that he was hard again. He had to get away from her, get things back into proper perspective. As he slowly eased out of her hold, he wondered if she still remembered that long-ago afternoon, and her girl's embarrassed confession, and her outrage at the unfairness of it.

She slept on, murmuring a bit, but not stirring.

As he bathed and shaved in the small bedroom down the hall, he wondered if that dream wasn't some sort of guide. Yes, that was it. If she remembered her wild behavior of the previous night, he would simply treat it as naturally as he'd treated her young girl's first monthly flow. He was still her friend, and her doctor. Nothing more.

She slept on even after his housekeeper, Lydia Mullens, arrived. He joined Lydia in the small kitchen, telling her about their guest over a cup of scalding black coffee. He told her what had happened the previous night, told her he'd known Jules when he'd lived in Lahaina.

"Wicked," Lydia said finally, shaking her gray head. "I've heard of the Crooked House, of course. You did a fine thing, Saint, yes, a fine thing." She looked toward the ceiling, frowning. "Poor little mite. What are you going to do, Saint?"

He downed the rest of his coffee, and rose from his chair. "An excellent question. Right now, I want her to wake up. Lord only knows how much opium that bastard gave her.

"I'll cook up a big breakfast for her," Lydia said. "Good food will clear out her system."

Saint nodded, and walked from the kitchen. Lydia stared after him, a thoughtful look in her eyes. She was fond of Saint, more than fond, she thought. He was like a son to her, a son to be proud of. She thought of her only son, dead now for three years. Rory had wanted gold so much, too much, and he'd died of dysentery in a wretched mining camp near Nevada City. And she'd come here alone with practically no money. She'd worked in the Stevenson home for two months, until the daughter of the house, Penelope, made her so furious she'd simply walked out. She blessed, every now and again, that awful cold she'd gotten, for it had given her Saint. And now there was a girl upstairs, a young girl who had dropped into his life out of his past.

She turned slowly away from the table and began to lay strips of bacon into a skillet. Saint needed a wife, but first she had to get to know this Juliana DuPres.

Jules felt a hand on her shoulder, gently shaking her, heard a soft man's voice speaking to her. She froze inwardly until her mind, less dull and heavy now, forced her to open her eyes. She saw Michael leaning over her, concerned, studying her. She felt so sluggish, it was an effort to keep her eyes open. Michael, she thought. He was here, with her. It didn't surprise her.

"How do you feel, Jules?" he asked, taking in the physical signs as he spoke. He knew how she felt without having to ask.

"I remember," Jules said.

He tensed, afraid to say anything.

"Is Jameson Wilkes dead? Did you kill him?"

He was relieved at her tone—angry, aggressive. "No, but I did slam my fist into his face. I don't imagine he'll feel very well for a while."

"Yes," she said again. "I remember. He drugged me, forced wine down my throat when I refused to drink it. I remember now that you hit me. My jaw hurts."

"I'm sorry, Jules, but I had to get you out of there fast. I think you believed I was one of those men, and you fought me."

"Well, I just hope that you broke his jaw." She yawned, and raised her hand to cover her mouth. She paused, staring at the long sleeve that fell over the tips of her fingers. She looked at him, puzzled.

Saint became all professional. "I'm a doctor, Jules. I had to make sure you were all right. That's one of my nightshirts, my only one, in fact. It's yours until I can buy you something else."

His very matter-of-fact voice would have worked if she hadn't spent two weeks faced with what men did to women. He'd stripped off that awful gown, seen her naked. She'd remembered Wilkes's looks when she'd been without any clothes in front of him. How had Michael looked at her? It was too much. She cried.

"Jules, come on, now, sweetheart. That's no way to greet an old friend after five long years."

He wanted to hold her, to comfort her, but he held himself still. He said, "Buck up, Jules, the world hasn't ended. Nothing happened. You're safe here. Don't turn into a watering pot on me now."

She sniffed, trying to swallow the tears, and dashed the back of her hand across her eyes. "You're right," she said. "You're not like Wilkes."

"No, I'm not."

"I don't understand how you saved me," she said, her attention wandering inward even as she spoke. Something was gnawing at the back of her mind, but she couldn't remember what it was.

"I was told by one of the Sydney Ducks that Wilkes had a missionary's daughter from Lahaina. When I heard the description, I knew it had to be you. The rest was planning, that's all."

He saw that she was frowning at a point beyond his shoulder. He waited patiently, knowing that if she remembered everything that had happened the previous evening, he would simply have to deal with it.

Jules said abruptly, her eyes suddenly intent upon his face, "You haven't changed at all, Michael. You're still large and hard and handsome, and your eyes still crinkle."

"I'm nearly an old man now, Jules."

"You're not even ten years older, that's all. I remember you used the same argument on me when I asked you to marry me when I was fourteen." A child's words from the past. Something nibbled insistently at the edge of her memory, but she couldn't seem to grab it, to understand. It was frustrating. Slowly she raised her hand to touch his face. "You still feel like you used to," she said. Then suddenly she said, her voice intense, "I dreamed you came back to me in Lahaina, and we were together again."

"A dream," he said. "And I did come back to you, in a sense."

"Yes, I suppose. Your eyes are so beautiful. The hazel is so much nicer than my slime green."

He laughed at that. "Oh no, not slime, Jules. Don't you remember how you got your nickname?"

She smiled, two dimples deepening in her cheeks. "Yes, but it's you who have forgotten, Michael. My nickname is from my awful hair, not my eyes."

He remembered the young girl telling him that she hated the name Juliana, and he'd said, looking at her glorious, wildly curling hair, "Why not 'Jules' then? That's close enough to 'jewels,' and that's like your hair. All right?"

"Not slime," he repeated, smiling gently at her. "Your eyes, like your hair, are jewels, green jade in this case."

"You make me sound like a gawdy piece of jewelry. Rubies and jade." She paused a moment. "I like the jade. That makes me sound exotic."

He heard Lydia call up and frowned. They'd spoken of nothing really. But at least she was responding to him normally. He said, "That's my housekeeper, Lydia. I told her about you, Jules, and she's made you breakfast. Are you hungry?"

"Yes," she said, surprised. "You know, I really am. For the first time in a long while."

He saw a flash of pain in her eyes, but for the

moment he ignored it. "Let me invite Lydia up to meet you. You'll like her."

Jules did like Lydia, but the housekeeper clucked over her until finally Saint sent her out of the room.

Some minutes later, Saint was thinking between bites of scrambled eggs that she was responding much better than he'd believed possible. And her eyes were brighter; she was more alert.

And she was so damned beautiful that it made him ache just to look at her. And she was in his bed, and not fourteen years old anymore.

When Lydia came back to remove the breakfast trays, she looked closely at Jules. "Good, you did justice to my food. You let Saint take care of you, young lady."

"You and that crazy name," Jules said.

"No one else calls me Michael," he said. He reached out his hand to touch her jaw. To his consternation, she jerked away from him, eyes wide with fear.

"I'm sorry, Jules," he said, dropping his hand. "I just want to feel your jaw. I did smack you pretty hard."

"I'm being stupid," she said, trying to make herself relax.

"No, you're being very brave. I'm proud of you."

She gave him a pitifully hopeful look. "I'm glad you haven't changed," she said. "You may feel my jaw. I won't be silly anymore."

She leaned forward and watched his face as his fingers, long, blunt, yet so gentle, touched her sore jaw. Without conscious thought, she leaned against his fingers, years of absolute trust inherent in the simple movement.

Saint felt a treacherous weight descend. She was

so vulnerable, so unsettled and confused, and he was her anchor. He looked at the gentle arch of her neck. Too delicate, he thought, too fragile. He drew his hand away, appalled. Again.

She smiled at him, a dazzling smile. He sucked in his breath. "You've turned into a beautiful woman, Jules."

"Me?" She laughed incredulously. "Well, maybe passable. John Bleecher did want to marry me, you know."

"Bleecher? The planter's son? That gangly boy who had pimples?"

"Yes, but now he doesn't. And besides, I didn't want to marry him, so I'm not certain if that counts or not."

"Just why didn't you want to marry him?"

Jules frowned. "Kanola asked me the same thing—" She broke off abruptly, memory flooding her. Kanola was dead. Tears welled up. She turned her face away.

"What's wrong, Jules?"

"Kanola's dead. Wilkes's men hurt her, I know it. I saw them holding her down and she was fighting them. She's dead."

Had Jules seen her friend raped and murdered? He wanted to ask her how Wilkes had captured her, but at that moment there was a knock on the front door. A patient. Damnation. "Jules—"

It was someone sick to see him, she thought. She swallowed and forced a smile. "I'll be all right."

"I'll be back up as soon as I've seen my patient." He rose. "I want you to rest, Jules. We've got to clear the opium out of your system."

"Can I have a bath, Michael?"

"I'll send Lydia up," he said, and left the bedroom, closing the door.

He felt a spurt of rage to see Bunker Stevenson waiting for him in his surgery. He still wasn't certain that Bunker hadn't been one of the men at the Crooked House. He said shortly, "I'll be with you in just a minute, Bunker." He pulled Lydia into the hall. "No one is to know she's here. Can you help her bathe, Lydia? I'll figure out what we're going to do."

Lydia looked at him sharply. "Bunker wasn't one of those men, was he?"

"I'm not sure. I can't very well ask him, I suppose."

"I'll see to the child."

Child, hell, Saint thought as he walked back into his surgery.

# Chapter 7

"It's jasmine," Lydia said as she poured a bit into Juliana's bathwater.

"Anything would be better than what I smell like now." *Gentlemen like this scent, my dear. But don't use too much. It's very potent.* When he'd turned away, she'd poured nearly the entire bottle on her shoulders and chest and the skirt of the gown. She'd thought he would strike her, but he hadn't. He'd pulled the gown to her waist and bathed away the heavy musk.

The girl's words were true enough, Lydia thought. She wondered if Jules had been raped, but didn't ask, of course. She helped her out of Saint's nightshirt and into the porcelain tub.

"You need more flesh," Lydia said.

Jules remembered all the food Wilkes had tried to tempt her with. "Yes," she said. It didn't occur to her to try to cover herself. *He's changed me,* she thought. She wasn't at all embarrassed that Lydia was helping her, seeing her with no covering but her hair.

"You'll need some clothes," Lydia said as she helped Jules lather her long tangled hair.

"Yes, Michael said he'd get me some."

"Michael?" Lydia asked, a brow raised.

Jules smiled a bit at that. So he was still close-mouthed about his given name—Ulysses Michael. "That's his real name, at least part of it." When he'd told her his name one afternoon so long ago, she'd announced that she preferred "Ulysses" and burst into laughter. "Michael," she thought now. Such a kind name, a full name with depth and complexity. "Does everyone call him Saint?" she asked Lydia.

Lydia smiled. "Yes, and I'll just bet I can blackmail him now. You see, everyone wants to know what his real name is and he won't tell. Nor will he tell anyone how he got the nickname Saint."

"I know," Jules said. I'm acting normally, she thought. I'm sitting in a bathtub in Michael's house in San Francisco, and I'm acting like nothing at all happened to me.

"Well, if you decide to tell me, I'll doubtless become a rich woman by selling that tidbit," Lydia said. "Here, dear, let me rinse your hair."

When Juliana was tucked back into bed, she said to Lydia, "Michael told you about me?"

Lydia heard the shame in the girl's voice, and patted her hand. "Yes, he did. I hope you don't mind, for I'll never tell a soul. Saint will take care of you, my dear, you mustn't worry. He is a very responsible, thoughtful man."

"I know he is," said Jules, and closed her eyes. She wasn't worried. My family believes me dead, she thought. And Kanola's children have no mother now, her husband no wife. All Wilkes has is a broken jaw. She felt hatred, pure and raw. She was so locked into her private misery that she didn't hear Lydia leave the bedroom.

She fell asleep and dreamed. Wilkes was laughing, watching her as she drank some wine. Then she began to feel heavy, and dull, and very strange. She saw him lean over her and kiss her breast.

"No—"

She heard her own scream, and jerked upright.

"Jules?"

"No," she screamed again, seeing a man coming toward her. She rolled to the far side of the bed.

Saint stopped cold. He'd been outside the bedroom when he heard her cry out. He drew a deep breath and said quietly, "You had a nightmare, Jules. You're with me—Michael. Do you understand?"

She stared at the wall, mute. She whispered, "He made me drink some wine and he touched me and kissed me and fondled me." She gulped, hating him, hating herself, hating her shame.

Saint saw her fingers lightly touch her breasts. He should have killed Wilkes. For a long moment he couldn't speak. He pictured her naked, terrified, drugged, and Wilkes touching her. He fought down his own rage. She didn't need his fury, she needed to be reassured.

"Jules, it's all right. Come, look at me."

Slowly she turned to face him. She saw the compassion in his hazel eyes, and hated herself even more. He was being kind to her because he pitied her. She probably disgusted him. Thank God she hadn't told him any more.

"I'm all right now."

Saint forced a smile. "You certainly look fine," he said. "I like the damp hair. It makes you look like the little mermaid I remember so well. Do you remember all those times I helped you dry your hair so your father wouldn't get into a snit?"

That drew her out the way he'd hoped it would.

"I remember. I escaped most of the time, but once I didn't. It wasn't my hair, it was the sunburn. He didn't forbid me to swim until I was sixteen. I ignored him, of course. Then it was my brother, Thomas, who helped me sneak out."

Saint also remembered all the times he'd had to drag her out of the ocean and the bright sun so she wouldn't look like a broiled lobster. "How is your brother, anyway? I always liked Thomas."

"He is fine," she said. *And he's probably the only one of my family who's sorry I'm dead.* "He's a man now, Michael."

"Time has a way of adding years," Saint said.

To his immense relief, she suddenly giggled, a sweet, fresh sound that warmed him to his bones.

"I'm remembering what you always wore when you went swimming," she said.

So did he. He should have had more sense. Being half-naked in front of a child was one thing, but as he'd learned, it was quite another in front of an impressionable young girl. It had finally struck him when he'd seen her staring with very different eyes at him one afternoon as he'd walked out of the surf.

"You looked like Adonis," she said now. "Do you still have those frayed, cut-off sailor's pants?"

"You're embarrassing me, Jules," he said. It had seemed so natural to wear only those meager pants when he was swimming with her.

"Why? You're so beautiful."

He flushed. The last thing he wanted her to remember was a half-naked man. "Enough," he said, trying to sound cool and unconcerned. "After lunch, little one, I'm off to buy you some clothes. Unfortunately, I can't take you with me."

"Because of Wilkes," she said.

"Yes. Until I find out what he's up to, I can't risk him finding out where you are, or, for that matter, who took you away from him."

"He doesn't know it was you?"

Saint grinned. "You should have seen my disguise. I probably looked like a huge black bear, and the most villainous creature imaginable."

Over lunch they spoke more of their shared past. He knew she had to talk about what had happened to her, but he didn't want to rush her. Not yet, anyway. And, dammit, he had to figure out what he was going to do with her. But he knew what he had to do. He had to take her home. Oddly, he didn't want to face that prospect just yet. He realized he wanted to enjoy her company for a while longer. That, and see that she healed on the inside.

He ended up sending Lydia out to do some shopping for her because Delaney Saxton called. Evidently, the Saxton's four-month-old daughter was on her deathbed.

Saint was relieved to tell Chauncey Saxton that her daughter was just colicky.

"New mothers," Saint said, grinning at Chauncey, "and new fathers. I'll bet when Alexandra starts teething, I'll be spending most of my time here reassuring you that she's not try to bite through your finger because she's a cannibal."

"I can't wait until you have your own child, Saint,"

Chauncey said. "Then we'll just see how calm you are."

Unbidden, Saint saw a baby with bright red hair and green eyes. He blinked.

"What's wrong, Saint?" Del Saxton asked. "You sick too?"

"I'm an old fool," Saint said. "Now, if you two nervous parents will excuse me, I'll be off."

"Before you go, have a brandy with me in the library," Del said.

"That sounds like I'm not invited," Chauncey said.

"No, love, not this time. I need to calm my weak man's nerves. Come on, Saint."

Over delicious French brandy Del said, "I heard the strangest thing just this morning."

"Oh?"

"Yes. It appears that someone rescued a very pretty girl last night from the Crooked House."

"Good for that someone," Saint said.

"I agree. It's just that someone is probably in a very precarious position now."

"I can't imagine why," Saint said.

"I met Jameson Wilkes two years ago," Del continued. "He is not a nice man, which is an understatement. Evidently, according to my source, he's on a rampage. One can but hope that the someone who rescued the girl can trust all the men who helped him. If one of them spills the beans, there'd be trouble, real trouble."

"It sounds like one of them already spilled the beans," Saint said, looking at his friend.

"No," Del said. "I discovered what happened from Maggie. It turns out that one of the members of that little club at the Crooked House showed up at her brothel late last night. He told one of her girls, Lisette, what had happened, and she told Maggie."

"And Maggie told you. So now Lisette, Maggie, and you know."

"That's right. You may be certain that Lisette and Maggie won't say a word."

"That's a relief, certainly."

"I'm here if you need help, Saint."

Saint met Del's eyes. "Thank you," he said. "I've got to go now." He turned at the doorway. "How did Lisette and Maggie know the someone was me, if I may ask?"

"Size."

"Ah."

"Well, not just size. Maggie guessed because she knows how you feel about enforced prostitution."

"Let's hope no one else guesses."


There was no real choice, Saint knew. He had to get her back to Maui as soon as possible, for her own safety.

He said as much to her that evening over dinner. She was wearing a simple gray gown that Lydia had bought for her, and her glorious hair was pulled back from her face and tied with a black ribbon. She looked fresh and beautiful.

She didn't look like a fourteen-year-old girl.

"I don't want to go back there," Jules said after a long moment of silence. Lydia had already returned to her boarding-house and they were alone. "I want to stay here, with you."

That took him aback. "Jules," he said, "your parents must be frantic about you—"

"My parents believe me dead, drowned."

"Then their grief will cease shortly. It's your home. It's your life, it's—"

"I don't like my parents. Certainly you remember my father. He is just more so now. My mother is still fading like a wilted plumeria. My sister, Sarah, is such a prig, and she's become more and more insufferable and snobbish."

"And Thomas?"

"My brother is the only one I care about. You know that. He will escape soon enough—after all, he's a man and he's free. He can't stand our father either."

"Jules, you're young. No, don't interrupt me. Hear me out. You were brought here under terrible circumstances. Wilkes is looking for you. It's not safe for you. Besides, there's John Bleecher at home, and he no longer has pimples. You'll marry, Jules, and have babies, and eventually you'll forget all this."

"I thought you said I was young," she said, staring him down.

He had, dammit. He shook his head.

"I don't want to marry John Bleecher. I told you that." She shuddered, unable to help herself. "I don't want to marry anyone." But that wasn't true. She wanted to marry Michael. She'd wanted to marry him since she was twelve years old—well, maybe thirteen. He didn't love her, of course. He still thought of her as a silly little girl. He'd saved her, but now he wanted to be rid of her and continue with his life. He wasn't classically handsome like the princes in fairy tales. His face was strong, rugged, filled with caring, determination, and kindness. But his eyes were beautiful, and his mouth. She was being a fool, she knew it, but he was everything a man should be. And he'd saved her and she wanted him, only him.

"I don't want to go back," she said again.

But Saint was still hearing her say she didn't want to marry anyone, and he'd seen her unconscious shudder.

"Jules," he said, leaning forward to take her hand in his. "You will marry. You mustn't allow your experience to make you hesitant about marriage. A man who loves you, who cares about you, will make you forget. He'll understand, he'll help you."

"You know nothing about my experience."

He let go of her hand and sat back in his chair, his arms folded across his chest. "Why don't you tell me, so that I will understand."

*He'll hate me, despise me if I tell him.*

It was as if he'd read her mind, and, indeed, he guessed very closely, for he saw the loss of innocence in her eyes.

"Tell me, Jules. I have always admired you, cared for you. Nothing could ever change that. You're a fool if you think it could."

She wanted to cry, to scream. She did neither, merely stared at him.

Saint couldn't help himself. He was out of his chair in an instant. He pulled her upright and cradled her in his arms. He stroked his fingers through her thick hair, savoring the feel of it, savoring the fresh, sweet scent of her. "Nothing matters," he said, pulling her closer. "Please, don't continue to think what you're thinking. You did nothing wrong. You must believe that, Jules."

Suddenly, as if she were staring through a soft veil,

she saw him holding her like this, stroking her, speaking to her softly. She felt his strong hands moving over her. Then the veil thickened, receded, and she saw nothing more. She leaned her cheek against his shoulder.

*I love you, Michael. I've always loved you.*

The words rang clear in her mind. She'd said those words to him. But when? She raised her face and whispered, "I don't understand?"

"What? What is it you don't understand?"

"I just saw you holding me as you're doing now, but not really. And you were touching me and speaking softly to me."

He stiffened, and she felt it. She went cold all over. For an instant she saw herself quite clearly, jerking about, crying out, feeling things that were alien and wild and— And he was there.

"No, Jules," he said, shaking her a bit. He hated that bewildered look in her eyes. "It's not what you're thinking."

She raised her eyes to his face, arching her back against his arms to see him better. "Was it only a dream?"

She saw the truth in his eyes, and he knew it. "Let me explain," he said. "Come into the sitting room."

He took her hand, and led her into the small parlor. "Sit down."

She sat.

He walked to the fireplace and leaned his shoulder against the mantel. "Wilkes drugged you. You remember that."

"Yes, I remember."

"When I brought you here, you were very much under the influence of the opium. And when you recognized me, you thought we were in Maui again. The past became the present, Jules, and you were confused."

*I love you, Michael. I've always loved you.*

She'd embarrassed him horribly. She was embarrassing him now.

She rose to her feet. "I don't want to know any more."

She ran to the doorway.

"Jules, stop."

He caught her at the bottom of the stairs. He pulled her around and shook her. "Don't do this, dammit. You were not yourself, not really. You didn't know what you were doing."

Her eyes went wide, and he knew that she was remembering now, remembering in vivid detail.

"You touched me. Between my—" She remembered the touch of his fingers on her flesh, the wildness of it, the urgency, the frenzy, but she couldn't capture the actual feelings. They flitted away from her consciousness, leaving her more confused.

"Yes, dammit, I touched you and I gave you a woman's pleasure. I had to."

She became very still, trying to find something that made sense, that made her herself again. She said, "I don't know what a woman's pleasure is. I can't remember exactly."

"Oh God." He pulled her against him roughly. "I'm sorry, Jules. I didn't mean to say it like that."

"Did you take my virginity?"

"Did I what?" His mind was reeling.

"Jameson Wilkes said he was glad I was a virgin because the man who bought me would know it and be pleased. That was why he could charge so much money for me. But how would a man know? Did you know?"

"I didn't take your virginity. I'm not an animal, for God's sake. I wanted only to help you, to make you calm again. How could you ever believe that I would hurt you?"

"No, I know you wouldn't hurt me. It's just that I don't understand how a man could take something from me. I know that men can hurt women—is that what he meant about taking my virginity?"

"Yes," Saint said, and gritted his teeth. "Well, no, not really." He released her, running his long fingers distractedly through his hair. "It's complicated, Jules. It's something—well, it's something that your husband will explain to you."

"Then I will never know, will I?"

"Yes," he said firmly. "Yes, you will."

She was silent, her eyes cast down. He hugged her gently to him as a father would a child. "Would you like to sleep now?"

"Yes, I suppose so."

He took her to the small guestroom. "If you hear any knocking during the night, just ignore it. It's probably someone who needs a doctor. All right?"

"Yes, Michael."

# Chapter 8

"We're leaving on the *Carolina* Friday."

Jules dropped the collection of Lord Byron's poetry to the floor and started to rise from her chair.

Saint raised his hand to still her. "No, stay there, Jules, and let me finish. I will escort you, of course. It will take us about two weeks to reach Lahaina."

"I know exactly how long it takes," she said, her voice bitter. She clutched the arms of the chair until her knuckles showed white.

"Yes, I guess you do. Then you will be reunited with your family."

*And you will leave and I'll never see you again.*

She watched him come into the small parlor, making it seem even smaller with his presence, and for an instant, saw him wearing his ragged, cut-off pants. His legs were tanned, and long and thick with muscle. She saw him diving after her, dunking her, laughing with her. She felt a spurt of warmth deep in her belly. She felt his eyes on her and kept her face down. Maybe she should look at him straight, she thought. Maybe he would see into her mind and keep her with him. But no. He was giving her his very patient look; he was prepared to calmly demolish her every protest. But she wasn't a child any longer. But how to make him realize that?

She could only try. "I would like to stay in San Francisco, Michael. I could find a job. You wouldn't have to be responsible for me."

Saint raised a brow at that. "Just who would be responsible for you, then?"

"I am not a child, even though it pleases you to think so—still. I am a grown woman and I will—"

"No," he said, looking at her fisted hands, "you're not a child. But you are returning to Lahaina, Jules, and that's an end to it. Your family—it's where you belong."

"Michael, I could help you, really I could. Please, won't you just listen to me—"

Again he interrupted her, unable to bear her pleading. "Jules, please try to understand. I am doing what is best for you."

"I could be your mistress."

"My *what*?"

"Your mistress," Jules repeated. "Jameson Wilkes explained to me that a mistress belongs to only one man and he takes care of her. So I could continue to live here, and you could take care of me and I could do whatever it is a mistress is supposed to do."

Saint simply stared at her. He supposed he should be glad that Wilkes hadn't rid her of all ignorance and innocence during the two weeks he'd had her. "Jules, he did tell you what a mistress was supposed to do, didn't he?"

"No, not really. I told him that a mistress sounded like a whore to me and I wouldn't do it." Jules ducked her head, realizing that she'd just done herself in. "Not with just anybody. Just you."

"I see," Saint said. Handle this with kid gloves, he thought, and with some humor, if he could dredge up any. "Jules, I can't afford a mistress. I'm only a poor physician, remember? And if I could, you would have to parade about in awful gowns like the one Wilkes made you wear, and douse yourself in that smelly perfume. Surely you wouldn't want that?"

"I couldn't just be me?"

"Indeed not. A mistress is a bird of very different plumage—a simple, elegant cormorant is not allowed. There are different rules about mistresses."

"I don't believe you. Just what are these rules?"

"First of all, a mistress is not a lady. She isn't allowed to be around ladies. She's an outcast, if you will, and she has no rights, no security. She's taken care of only as long as the gentleman she lives with wishes it. It isn't pleasant, Jules."

"It would be pleasant with you, Michael," she said.

Saint walked to her, drew her out of her chair, and stroked his hands down her arms. "I don't want a mistress, Jules. And you are not mistress material. You're beautiful, vibrant, and you're meant to have a husband and a home of your own and children. The rest is nonsense and not at all for you."

"Do you already have a mistress?"

He thought of Jane—not a mistress, not Jane—but Jules saw the expression in his eyes and wanted to strike this unknown woman. "No," he said. "I don't have a mistress."

Jules stared up at him, not really believing him,

but knowing that Michael had never lied to her. What would he do if she kissed him? She raised her hand and lightly touched her fingertips to his cheek. "I'm glad you don't wear a beard," she said.

He got hard instantly. It wasn't her touch, or her words, it was the look in her eyes. She'd had the same look when he'd stroked his hand between her thighs and felt her and caressed her. It was a vivid image in his mind: her lashes sweeping down as she moaned, arching wildly.

He released her, disgusted with himself. He tried for a smile. "I'm glad you don't wear a beard either."

Her smile was as forced as his. "You said that I would get married and have babies."

"Yes, I said that."

"So I'm not too young for that."

"No, you're not."

"Then I'm an adult."

"Yes, an adult."

"Then, Michael, you have no right to tell me what to do. I'm a woman grown and I will make my own decisions. I want to stay in San Francisco. And if you don't want me, I'll just have to—"

"Wilkes would have you within twenty-four hours."

"I'll buy a gun and shoot him."

He wanted to throttle her. "You've become quite a talker in the past five years, haven't you?"

"I've always been a talker, and you know it. And don't think you got away with throwing in a cormorant to distract me. I wasn't distracted and you don't know anything about cormorants."

"Jules, the subject is closed. You will do as I say."

"But—"

He placed his fingertips over her lips. "No. Trust me, please."

He was implacable and she knew she'd lost.

*Lahaina*

Lahaina didn't have a natural harbor, only an open roadstead. Ships could always approach or leave it with any wind that blew. No pilot was needed. The *Carolina* approached through the channel between Maui and Molokai, then let the trade winds carry it close to Lanai and in toward Lahaina. Saint and Jules stood on deck watching the harbormaster climb aboard to give Captain Rafer a copy of port regulations. Chase boats and tenders waited to take the few passengers and sailors into the town and to sell goods to those who remained aboard.

"I'd forgotten how beautiful it is here," Saint said, looking at the lush green hills that rose behind the town of Lahaina. Jules said nothing, but now he didn't expect her to. "And there's the taro patch. Is it true, Jules, that Kamehameha worked there to show his subjects the dignity of labor?"

"Not that I ever heard," she said, her voice clipped, "but I suppose it's a nice story. Makes him sound noble and all that, which, I suppose, he was."

He fell silent. He'd tried every ploy he could think of to make her less resentful of coming home, but nothing worked. His laughing, bright girl had withdrawn into herself.

He felt the now familiar surge of impatience with her. It was as if she'd built a very firm, impenetrable wall between them. During their voyage, she'd been firmly polite, and a stranger.

And she'd said not a word about the two weeks she'd spent with Wilkes, even when he'd asked her three evenings before, following the only storm during the two-week voyage. He hadn't seen her for nearly twenty-four hours, his services as a doctor in demand from the moment the storm hit. "I'm tired as hell," he'd said, joining her at the railing.

"You look it," she said, not turning.

"Thanks for your concern."

Jules turned to face him, and shrugged. "I hope all those green-faced, vomiting passengers paid you well. Will you be able to buy yourself a prostitute when we reach Lahaina?"

He stared at her, and automatically shook his head.

"But it's just one night, doctor. Nothing expensive or demanding, like having a mistress."

"Do you always turn sarcastic when you don't get your way?"

She saw the weariness in his eyes, but bit down on the tug of concern. "Yes," she said, "I do, particularly if the *man* making the decision is a blind ass."

He smiled, just a bit, and forced himself to look away from her, out at the endless expanse of ocean. "I think the last woman to truly enjoy insulting me was my mother. Of course, she did it with humor."

"I'll just bet she was laughing after she birthed you. That's why she called you Ulysses—revenge."

"Can't say I blame her," Saint said. "I weighed eleven pounds. Poor woman used to tell me that the real Ulysses—from what she'd read—searched and searched for nigh onto twenty years before he came home, and that's how she felt after nine months hauling me around inside her."

"As I said, revenge."

"Ah, but she tempered it with 'Michael'—that's innocuous enough, surely."

It wasn't innocuous, it was the most beautiful name she'd ever heard. She said, "Lydia told me that she could make a fortune in blackmail if only she could find out what your real name was and where you got the nickname Saint."

"My friends never give up. It's like a contest now. They come up with all sorts of ploys to make me cough up the facts, and I sidestep." He turned around and leaned back against the railing. "God, I'm tired. And a doctor is supposed to be able to cure anything and everything. As if I could do anything about seasickness."

"I would have helped you if you'd just asked me," Jules said.

"Thank you, but it took all my resolution not to throw up, given the stench in the cabins. No reason for you to turn green, and you would have, I guarantee it."

"I never get sick," Jules said with all the confidence of a young person who thought of illness as weakness.

"I hope you never do," Saint said. There would probably not be a better opportunity, he thought, silent for few moments. "Jules, your friend Kanola— did Wilkes's sailors rape her?"

She heard Kanola screaming, saw that awful man with that thing sticking out from his belly, and tried to shut off the awful memory. "I don't know. Wilkes dragged me to his cabin, said he would protect me."

She wanted clarification of exactly what rape was, but was too embarrassed to ask.

Thank God, he thought, she hadn't seen it. He had absolutely no doubt that Kanola had been raped, repeatedly.

"Then what happened?"

His voice was matter-of-fact, she had to keep calm and in control, but it was difficult. "She managed to escape the men and jumped overboard. She couldn't have made it to shore. We were too far away."

"I'm sorry," he said, wishing there were something a bit more he could say. "I know that Wilkes drugged you once before you arrived in San Francisco, and that he touched you and kissed you."

"No."

"You told me that, Jules. I don't want what happened to eat at you, Jules. I don't want you to bury it deep. It truly helps to tell a friend. Tell me what he did to you. Then you can forget it."

She jerked away from him and snarled at him, her voice vicious, "What do you care what he did to me? You want to hear all the details, Friend?"

"What did he do, Jules?" he asked again, not allowing her to anger him. He heard the remembered fear in her voice and knew that her spate of words was bravado—no, more like protection, self-protection.

"I think," she said finally, "that I should begin to call you Saint. That's how you're acting, of course. A saint—so full of human caring and kindness, so anxious to make the poor little creature forget her nightmare. You can go to hell, Saint."

Saint was not a violent man. In fact, once, when he was only fourteen years old, he'd gotten into a fight with another boy and broken his jaw with one blow. He'd been appalled. Now, he thought, looking at her set face from beneath lowered lashes, he wouldn't mind at all breaking his rule. A good thrashing would, at the very least, make him feel a hell of lot better. He'd said nothing more, for there was nothing to say.

Jules said now, pointing toward a small knot of native women on the dock, all of them dressed garishly, "There are the prostitutes. But I don't see my father or any of his friends—many times he goes to the dock when a whaler comes in and rants and screams about Satan, and evil, and disease."

"I don't know much about the Satan or evil part," Saint said calmly, ignoring the bitter irony in her voice, "but I sure as hell know about the disease." He saw that the two sailors who were at the oars of the tender were already waving and shouting toward the women.

There were about a half-dozen other ships, most of them whalers. The long, narrow dock was bustling with local people hawking wares, and here and there in the distance Saint could see a black frock coat. Either a businessman or a preacher, he thought, or one of those useless diplomats from Oahu.

"Come," he said, and helped her out of the tender. Her hand was cold. "I'll be with you, Jules."

She allowed him to assist her, then pulled her hand away. They walked into Wharf Street. Saint glanced briefly toward the fort, built in the early 1830s and now used mostly as a prison. It was looking a bit the worse for wear. Dwight Baldwin's home looked as neat as a pin, set back from Front Street, its paint fresh, its garden neat and green. He and Baldwin, a Protestant medical missionary, had been good friends during Saint's stay in Lahaina. He started to ask Jules about him, when she suddenly pulled off her bonnet and shook her head. Her bright flame hair drew several glances, then a loud gasp.

"Juliana, my God, it is you."

Saint turned to see a young man staring at Jules as if looking at a ghost. It was John Bleecher, the planter's son. He wasn't pimple-faced now, Saint noticed. Indeed, he was a handsome young man, well-formed, open-faced, and at present, pale as death.

Jules was very still. She moved closer to Saint, saying only, "Hello, John. How have you been?"

John roused himself. "Saint? Dr. Morris? Yes, it *is* you. Juliana, what happened? Everyone has believed you dead. Kanola's body—well, it washed up on shore, and since you had been seen with her, we all thought—"

"Yes, I know," Jules said, interrupting him in a curt voice. "She's dead, but I'm not. I survived."

"I don't understand," John said, wishing he could fling himself upon the pale, beautiful girl he'd wanted for two years now. But there was something terribly wrong. What was she doing with Saint Morris? He'd been gone for a long time now, five years.

"John," Saint said pleasantly, "why don't you help us with the luggage? I want to take Jules to her home."

"Jules—? Oh, yes, certainly."

Saint watched the young man pick up Jules's one small valise. No, he thought, she couldn't marry him. He wouldn't suit her; he wouldn't understand her. He would stifle her spirit without realizing what he was doing. He would also paw her endlessly and scare her witless.

It was none of his business. He would stay the two days the *Carolina* would be in port, then return to California. He would never see her again. Something deep inside him rebelled.

Etienne DuPres's house was on Luakini Street, just one block behind the Baldwin house. It was set back from the busy street, its white clapboards gleaming in the sun. Saint heard Jules draw in her breath when she saw her brother, Thomas, clad only in trousers and an open white shirt, turn onto the street and wave to John Bleecher. Saint saw the shock on his face, but Thomas, unlike John, showed no hesitation. He gave a loud whoop and ran full tilt to his sister and swung her up into his arms.

"Thomas." Jules buried her face in her brother's neck.

Saint saw the front door to the DuPres house open and Aurelia DuPres slowly walk onto the narrow veranda. Saint saw her clutch at her flat bosom, then faint dead away. He'd forgotten how damned vaporish the woman was. Doubtless all the wretched clothes and tight corset she wore didn't help matters.

By the time he reached her side, there were people everywhere, and pandemonium.

Saint had also forgotten how much he disliked Etienne DuPres. There was no joy in the man, only grim, unremitting purpose. He was tall and very thin, his black broadcloth made him look gaunt. His eyes were not sparkling and alive like his daughter's, but a pale cold gray. His hair was thinner now, the black streaked with white.

They were all seated in the small parlor, Jules's

mother fluttering her hands, Sarah, Jules's older sister, silent and stiff, watching her sister, her lips a tight seam. Thomas was carrying on in his exuberant fashion, seated cross-legged on the floor beside Jules's chair. Even though he was dark-haired and tall like his father, he had Jules's openness and joy.

Etienne DuPres stood tall and silent next to a fireplace that was never used. He'd hugged his daughter briefly, then set her away. For a moment Saint thought he looked to be in pain—a good sign, he thought, that he'd missed and grieved for his younger daughter. Etienne DuPres said now to Saint, "How did you get my daughter?"

Saint smiled toward Jules and said, "You are the luckiest family alive. Your daughter is safe and well."

Before he could explain further, Reverend DuPres said, his voice even colder, "We understood that Juliana had drowned. She was forbidden to swim, but that is another matter. I would like to know what happened to her, and how you got her."

"I was taken by a man who wanted to sell me," Jules said. "In San Francisco. Michael saved me."

There was a moan from Mrs. DuPres, and Saint prayed the damned woman wouldn't faint again. Sarah said in a shrill voice, "Taken? Whatever do you mean? Why would anyone do that?"

Jules said, "His name is Jameson Wilkes. I believe you've met him, Father. He decided I was well-enough-looking, and took me to San Francisco. He wanted to sell me to a man so I would be a mistress."

Thomas DuPres roared, "Damnation, Jules. That miserable bastard. God, I'll kill him."

"You will be silent, Thomas," Reverend DuPres

said. "So," he continued, looking down at his daughter, "you were in the company of this evil man for two weeks, and he debauched you."

Jules paled. "If you mean by 'debauched' that he hurt me, no, he didn't. He wanted to save me because he would get more money for me if I were a virgin."

"How dare you speak like that in front of your mother and sister. Merciful Lord, to be cursed with such—"

"That's quite enough." Saint rose, his very size intimidating, his quiet voice instantly reducing Reverend DuPres to silence. "Your daughter is safe and well. She was not debauched. And even if she had been, I don't see that it would matter. What matters, sir, is that your daughter is with you again."

Etienne DuPres said nothing. He'd done his best by the girl. But she was willful, just as her scarlet-haired grandmother had been. She shouldn't have come back. He felt rage flow through him, rage and shame. He looked at her again, then walked from the room.

Jules sat before the small dressing table, slowly brushing her hair. She didn't look up when Sarah came into their bedroom.

"I am glad you are alive, Juliana," Sarah said.

Then why do I want to shiver at your tone? Jules wondered. "Thank you," she said, not breaking count with her hairbrush.

"You've been gone well over a month. Everyone was very upset. Father preached a marvelous sermon for you. He touched but once on your disobedience and your perfidy in swimming in the ocean."

"Now he can unpreach it," Jules said.

Sarah, as was her habit, stepped behind the narrow screen to undress. "John is going to marry me."

Jules raised her head at that, looking toward the screen in the mirror. His affections were short-lived, she thought. But she wasn't angry at him; she was immensely relieved. "I am glad for you," she said. "John is very nice."

Sarah fingered the buttons on her long nightgown. "I saw how he was looking at you this afternoon. But he won't go back to you. Not now. Not after what you've done."

"But I didn't do anything," Jules said.

"So you say," Sarah said. "As for Saint, well, you're better off with him. You should have stayed with him."

Jules turned on the stool and eyed her sister silently for a long moment. She would be pretty if only she would smile—not just her mouth, but her eyes. Her hair, unlike Jules's, was a soft brown and didn't fly about her head in wild curls. "Sarah," she asked, "do you love me?"

"Yes, I suppose so," Sarah said, "but I want John."

"But you said you're marrying him. You have him, Sarah. He has nothing to do with me."

Suddenly Sarah seemed to collapse. She covered her face with her hands, and sobbed.

Jules, appalled, quickly went to her. "What's wrong, Sarah?"

The sobs continued, and Jules stood helplessly, watching her sister's body shake.

"John means nothing to me, please believe that," Jules said. "He loves you. Why else would he marry you?"

"You fool," Sarah whispered, raising her tear-stained face. "He went crazy when Kanola's body was discovered and we were told that you'd been with her. Crazy, do you hear? But I wanted him, Juliana. I've always wanted him. He grieved. And I—well, I comforted him."

"Well, of course you did. I'm certain he comforted you too.

"You stupid fool," Sarah screamed at her. "I let him have me. That's why he's marrying me now. He has to. Dear God, I could be pregnant right now, and here you are, back again. I hate you."

Jules stepped back, her face white. Very slowly she stripped off her white nightgown and began to dress. It didn't occur to her to step behind the screen, and her sister's shocked gasp only made her smile, a small, bitter smile.

"What are you doing now?"

"Nothing," Jules said.

"He did debauch you, just like Father said. Taking off your clothes without a thought! It's disgusting."

Jules turned a puzzled look to her sister. "Didn't you take off your clothes with John?"

Sarah shuddered. "No, of course not. It was dark. I just let him—well, I know that *you* understand what he did." She shuddered again, and Jules suddenly felt very sorry for John Bleecher.

She finished dressing in silence.

"Where are you going?"

"Out," Jules said, and quietly slipped from the room. The house was dark. Everyone was in bed. Jules carefully propped open the back kitchen door and walked quickly toward the beach along the back streets. She could hear sounds of revelry—men's laughter and women's giggles—and now it had a new meaning to her. She saw not a soul. When she reached the deserted beach, she stripped off the hot, restricting gown and walked slowly down the beach toward the ocean, clad only in her short chemise. There was a half-moon, and as usual, the sky was clear, the stars dazzlingly bright. Gentle waves crested with barely a sound and slithered onto the wet sand. She didn't wade into the water, but skirted the waves and sat on an outcropping rock, hugging her arms about her knees.

She'd been gone for such a short time, really, but everything had changed. And everyone. No, that wasn't true. She saw her sister's face, the streaming tears. Priggish Sarah had made love to a man. She'd obviously disliked it.

Jules saw her own life as series of days spent in silent despair and nights spent thinking of what she couldn't have, and swallowed down tears.

It was as if she'd conjured him up. She sat very still, watching Michael, magnificently naked, stride through the surf toward the beach. He was running his hands through his thick hair, then shaking himself like a mongrel dog.

As he came closer, Jules let her eyes fall down his body. She had never before seen a naked man—only Michael when he'd worn those meager pants. Now he wore nothing. The hair was thick on his chest, narrowing as it snaked down over his flat belly. She knew that men stuck themselves into women. For a moment she stared at him objectively, wondering how it would work, and how it would feel to touch him there. How it would feel to have him pressed against her, naked.

He turned a moment, looking back over the water. Her fingers tingled as her eyes traveled down his back to his long legs. Old Lanakila carved figures in smooth, glowing wood. Michael looked as sculptured and perfect as the most beautiful of Lanakila's statues. Suddenly he twisted about and his eyes met hers, and held.

He made no move to cover himself, merely stood there, the water lapping over his feet, looking at her.

# Chapter 9

She was staring at him, staring intensely at his sex, now swelled and jutting out. Before he'd seen her, he had been thinking that Maui was indeed a Garden of Eden, so lush and warm and vibrantly beautiful. Jules fit into his image as naturally as the moonlit waves lapping over his feet.

Very slowly he walked toward her. Her bright hair was in wild disarray, down her back and over her shoulders. She was wearing only a simple white cotton chemise that came to her knees.

He said nothing, merely stopped in front of her. She sat very straight on the edge of the rock, her hands folded primly in her lap, her eyes wide on his face. He dropped to his knees in the sand, feeling the coarse grains against his legs. He stretched out his hands and placed them on her thighs. Slowly he pulled her legs apart. He slid his hands upward beneath her chemise, his fingers wet and warm on her thighs. He clutched her buttocks, lifting her, and brought her down against him.

She cried out softly, and Saint shook himself free.

He was reeling with the vividness of the fantasy that had held him. He knew that what he'd imagined could easily happen—right now. He felt himself swelling.

He called out, his voice distant, "What are you doing here, Jules?"

"I didn't know anyone else would be here," she said, her voice too high, breathless.

"You didn't answer my question."

"I had to get away from the house, from Sarah."

Had priggish Sarah been tormenting her? "I see" was all he said. He walked briskly up the beach, aware of her looking at him. He found his clothes and dressed himself. He pulled on his boots, then straightened. The bulge in his trousers had diminished, thank heaven.

When he turned, she was standing very quietly, watching him. Moonlight flowed over her face.

"I'm staying with the Baldwins," he said. "I'm going back now. I will probably see you in the morning."

God, he sounded like a cold, uncaring bastard. He stopped in his tracks. "Jules," he said, his voice gentle now, "don't let Sarah hurt you. She doesn't understand."

"Sarah is Sarah," Jules said. She raised her chin. "I shall be quite all right, thank you."

He merely nodded, turned on his heel, and left the beach.

A shudder went through him.

I should paint a picture, Jules thought, and call it *Family at the Breakfast Table with Prodigal Daughter*. She nearly laughed aloud at the thought of Koli bringing in a fatted calf so everyone could rejoice over a feast at her return. Her father was sitting stiff and unyielding in his high-backed chair. Her mother was pulling apart a soft piece of bread, her thin fingers nervous and anxious. Sarah said not a word, merely toyed with the fresh papaya. Thomas, sensing the tension, kept his head down and wolfed his breakfast, as was his wont.

*I don't belong here. I don't belong anywhere.*

"Today is Saturday," Etienne DuPres announced. "Will you be going to the plantation, Thomas?"

"Yes, Father. John and I have some business to discuss."

Jules saw Sarah's head come up at Thomas's words, saw the desperate yearning in her eyes as she asked, "Will John come back with you for lunch?"

Thomas flashed a quick glance toward Juliana. "I imagine nothing could keep him away."

"John is going to marry our Sarah," Aurelia DuPres said in her thin, high voice. "Of course he will come."

Etienne gazed a moment at younger daughter. She looks like a wanton, he thought, just like her damned grandmother, even with her hair plastered against her head and tied securely.

"Juliana," he said abruptly, shoving his chair back and rising, "you will come with me to my study. I wish to speak to you."

Juliana escaped the house long before noon. She didn't want to see John Bleecher. She didn't want to see anyone. She kept to the back streets, but she saw many people she knew. The missionary contingent merely nodded to her and kept going. The natives were open, friendly, and glad to see that she was still alive. She knew she should visit Kanola's husband and children, but she couldn't bring herself to do so yet. The pain was too fresh. She walked south along Waine'e Street today, past the Episcopal cemetery. She didn't turn toward the ocean until she reached Shaw Street. It was narrow, and muddy after a brief morning rain. She lifted her skirts, kept her head down, and continued walking. Her mind kept returning to the conversation with her father that morning. Not really a conversation, he had stood on high, like God, and made a pronouncement.

When she reached the beach, she pulled off her shoes and stockings without hesitation, set them on a rock, and walked toward the water. Men were out on their canoes fishing, and two young children were playing in the waves. Naked-masted whalers were farther out in deep water. She walked farther down the beach, pausing every once in a while to examine an interesting shell that had been washed up. She didn't pay any attention today to the birds, nor did she even spare more than a passing thought to the fish.

The hem of her skirt was soon soaked, but for the first time in her life she simply didn't care. What else could her father do in any case?

She turned away from the water and walked barefoot to Maluuluolele. She stared at the small island in the center of the pond. It was a tiny island, Moku-ula. How many years had it been a home of Maui chiefs? She couldn't remember. Even King Kamehameha III had received visitors here in the recent past, showing them the large burial chambers holding the ornate coffins of those long-dead chiefs.

"Juliana."

She froze in her tracks at the sound of John Bleecher's voice.

She turned slowly to face him. "Hello, John. I thought you would still be at my father's house."

"No, I left. I had to see you, talk to you."

I will not hurt Sarah, nor will I hurt John, Jules swore to herself. "I will be leaving Maui soon, John."

"I know," he said. God, she was beautiful. His fingers itched to touch her, to feel her beautiful wild hair.

"I really want to be by myself, John, if you don't mind."

He said nothing, merely walked toward her, stopping but inches from her. She looked up at him and was taken aback at the unfamiliar look in his blue eyes. She cocked her head to one side, silent.

"We're alone," he said more to himself than to her.

"I suppose so."

Suddenly, without warning, he grabbed her, hauling her against him and pressing his mouth against hers. Jules was too startled for a moment to struggle. "John," she cried out, and felt his tongue thrust into her open mouth.

She began hitting him then, twisting to free herself. She hadn't realized before that he was so strong.

"Stop it, Juliana," he said at her in a voice she'd never heard. "Damn you, you know I've always wanted you, not Sarah. And now I know the truth. You've given it to how many men now?"

"Given what, for God's sake? Let me go, John. How dare you do this?"

But he didn't let her go. He seemed wild. She felt pain in her ribs, but didn't cry out. "Don't act the innocent with me, Juliana. I know now, all of it. Sarah told me what you've done. It won't make any difference to have one more man, will it? God knows, you've been flat on your back for Saint."

For a moment Jules lost her fright in sheer shock. What had Sarah told him? "You think I'm a whore?"

He answered her with a groan and buried his face against her throat. When his hands grabbed her breasts, and she cried out, seeing Jameson Wilkes over her, his fingers stroking her, squeezing, hurting. She went crazy in that moment, clawing, kicking at him, her breath coming in loud jerks. John hurled her to the ground and slammed his body down on top of her.

He was hard and punishing against her belly—she could feel him through the layers of clothing. Dear God, he was going to hurt her, and she knew now that this was what rape was.

Saint washed his hands and wiped them on the white towel Dwight Baldwin handed him.

"Thanks for coming in with me, Saint," Dwight said. "We've only the twelve patients right now, but just you wait a couple of months."

"My pleasure. You still treat more syphilis than anything else?"

"Lord yes, it never ends. The poor fellow you just examined, what do you think?"

"You've got to take the leg off today or he'll be dead tomorrow."

Dwight Baldwin sighed. "That's what I thought too. Dammit, it was a stupid, needless accident. It happened on the taro plantation, and Elisha Bleecher didn't bother to bring him in until yesterday evening.''

"Exhort him with hellfire and brimstone tomorrow from the pulpit," Saint said.

"Won't do a bit of good, I'm afraid, but you may be certain that I shall. Come, let me walk you out."

"Have you got ether around?"

"No, but I do have chloroform. Thank God we no longer have to put our patients through such agony. Didn't you tell me that you were an actual witness to the first use of ether in 1846? At Massachusetts General Hospital, wasn't it?"

"Yes," Saint said, "I was. It started out a circus, with all the other doctors and medical students laughing derisively, and ended in complete and utter silence. I'll never forget Dr. Warren's face when he made his first incision. The patient didn't move, didn't utter a sound. When it was all over, he turned to the audience and said in the most bewildered voice I've ever heard, 'Gentlemen, this is no humbug.' "

"I remember hearing that one doctor walked up to the patient and began slapping him, still unable to believe that he wasn't faking."

That hadn't happened, but it made a good story, so Saint only nodded to Dwight. "Now, if only we can get our colleagues to use ether on women in labor." Saint knew Dwight Baldwin as a man of infinite compassion and caring for his fellowman, but like many men, religious or otherwise, he believed firmly that it was the scheme of things for a woman to undergo childbirth with nothing to ease her agony.

Today Dwight didn't take the bait. He was silent

for many moments, then said calmly, "I heard about Juliana DuPres."

"Yes," Saint said. "I told you about her adventure and mine last evening."

"That's not what I meant," Dwight said, sighing.

"I know. I bet everyone has heard things," Saint said. "It will pass. She'll be all right."

Dwight gave him an incredulous look, but Saint had turned to speak to an old man who used to bring him fresh fish at least three times a week. He'd set the old man's broken leg and taken the fish as payment. Old Kama had simply never stopped bringing him fish.

Saint and Dwight Baldwin parted some minutes later. Saint made his way to the DuPres house, only to be told by Mrs. DuPres that Juliana had left. Saint thanked her, frowned, and set out to find her. He tracked her to the south of town.

When he heard her screaming wildly, frantically, his guts twisted. "Jules—"

He ran toward the sound, and broke through the bushes that blocked his view. He saw Jules on her back, fighting, screaming, with John Bleecher on top of her, grinding himself against her as he ripped at her clothes.

His mind went blank with rage. With a loud roar he threw himself upon the younger man.

"You goddamned little bastard." He grabbed John bodily off Jules. He smashed his fist into John's gaping mouth, and the force of his blow sent the slighter man staggering back.

"You filthy pig," Saint shouted. "I'm going to break your bloody neck."

Jules managed to pull herself upright. She saw Michael strike John, heard John's yowl of pain. He would kill him! She saw her brother running toward them, and shouted at the top of her lungs, "Thomas, help. For God's sake, hurry."

It was like trying to stop a train, Thomas thought frantically as he threw himself on Saint's back. "You'll kill him, Saint."

Saint came out of the black rage. He saw John Bleecher's bloody nose, heard his moans of pain.

"What the hell is going on?"

Saint very slowly straightened, closed his eyes a moment. He said in an emotionless voice, "That little bastard was trying to rape your sister." He smiled grimly. "I think he needs cooling off."

Saint picked John up, one large hand grabbing his collar, the other the seat of his breeches. He carried him to the ocean, waded in, and tossed him out into the waves, facedown.

He was still smiling when he came back to where Jules and Thomas were standing. It was a ghastly, grim smile.

The smile disappeared at the sight of Jules's white face. She was standing rigid, staring at him but not really seeing him. "She'll be all right," he said more to himself than to Thomas. "Jules," he said as he reached out for her, only to see her shudder and stumble backward.

Jules sank slowly to her knees. She raised wide, bewildered eyes to Saint. "He said I gave it to every other man and I should give it to him. He said Sarah told him what I'd done."

"That stupid, jealous bitch."

"Enough, Thomas," Saint said, turning briefly toward the young man.

Suddenly it was too much. Jules saw herself sprawled naked on Wilkes's bunk, saw him touching her, leering at her. She felt John grinding his body against hers. She clutched her arms about herself and rocked back and forth on her heels. "No, no, no," she said, her voice singsong.

"Oh God, Saint," Thomas said, terrified. "Do something."

"Take John away from here, Thomas," Saint said quietly. "Leave me alone with her. Don't let anyone else come along, all right?"

John was staggering toward them, and Thomas quickly turned to run to him. Saint saw Thomas grab John's arm none too gently and drag him off. Thomas said something, but Saint couldn't make out his words.

He waited a few more minutes, then dropped to his knees in front of Jules. He clasped her chin in his hand and lifted her face. Her eyes were unseeing, her lips still moving, her only words "No, no—" He slapped her hard, and caught her so she wouldn't fall. He saw her blink, shudder, then cry out. Gently he drew her against him, rocking her in the circle of his arms. "It's all right now, Jules. Everything is all right. No man will ever hurt you again. I promise."

He included himself in that promise.

He drew a sigh of relief when she slumped against him and began to cry. He was becoming stiff in the kneeling position, and slowly sat down, pulling Jules down beside him. He kept her face pressed against his chest, his arm supporting her.

"He's sending me to Canada," she whispered in a deadened voice, "to Toronto, to live with his older sister Marie, who's a spinster and does good works. He said he wouldn't abide my shame here, wouldn't abide all the shame I've brought on *his* family."

Saint closed his eyes a moment. God, what was he to do now? He said, "I will speak to your father, Jules. He will not send you to Canada."

Jules wanted to tell him that there was absolutely nothing he could do, but she didn't say it. He'd already saved her; he'd already done much too much for her.

"John said that I'd given it to you."

What a way to talk about sex, Saint thought, so angered at John Bleecher that if the young man had appeared, he would have started beating him again, with great relish. He clamped down on his anger and said quietly, "John Bleecher is a spoiled, thoughtless little rich bastard. I don't know what your sister said to him, but I fully intend to speak my mind to her."

He felt Jules's head shaking against his chest. "No, please, Saint," she said. "Sarah loves him and she let John have her. He's got to marry her. She's just afraid that he won't, now that I'm still alive."

"She deserves to be horsewhipped."

To Saint's relief, he heard Jules laugh. It wasn't much of a laugh, but it was a start. She was resilient, his Jules. "I agree," she said, "And you may be certain that I'll blister her ears."

"Good. And you may be certain that I'll speak to your father. Canada, for God's sake."

Saint faced Reverend Etienne DuPres across the man's large mahogany desk. What a paltry, mean-spirited specimen he was, Saint thought. No humor, no love, just the kind of fanaticism that kills the spirit, doesn't save it. He said without preamble, "I've come about Jules."

"Her name is Juliana," DuPres said, distaste plain on his face.

"Fine. In any case, I've come to speak to you about your younger daughter. She told me that you intend to send her to Canada."

"Yes, that's right. I will not abide her presence here any longer than I must. She is a blight on her family. My sister will take her in hand."

"May I ask why you consider her a blight?" Saint asked calmly, too calmly.

"Come, Dr. Morris," DuPres said, his hands shaking. "I have no doubt that you, along with many others, have enjoyed my daughter's body. I will abide no harlot in my house."

"Didn't you listen to her? Didn't you hear what she had to say? None of it was her fault, and, I might add, she is still a virgin. She is the furthest thing from a harlot. She is pure and innocent."

"Dr. Morris, I understand that many men, once they've taken a woman, don't wish to be bothered with her anymore, you included, evidently. I am her father, more's the pity, and I shall do what I believe best. Now, sir, you will excuse me."

Saint wanted to hit him, but he remembered John Bleecher's bloody face and moans of pain. He remembered how he'd sworn never to hit another who had not his strength. He stared a moment at Jules's father, wishing he could fathom the way the man's mind worked, but he couldn't, of course. He also realized that there was nothing more he could say. He knew now what he had to do. He knew he had absolutely no choice in the matter. He said nothing more, merely turned and strode out of the man's study and his house.

Etienne DuPres stood quietly for a long time, staring at nothing in particular, his mind working furiously. He had absolutely no doubt, just as he'd said, that Saint Morris had debauched his daughter. And Juliana, with her grandmother's wild blood—well, he knew her for what she was, had known since she was a little girl what she would turn out to be. And now, he thought, nodding at himself in approval, he knew what he would do. He sat down at his desk and began to write.

# Chapter 10

Saint quietly slipped into the back of the Waine'e Church. It was cool inside, for the building was of stone. It could seat nearly three thousand Hawaiians, most of them packed together on the floor. There were calabash spittoons for the tobacco-chewing chiefs and ships' masters on the far side of the huge room. This Sunday morning, however, there were only about three hundred souls waiting to hear the Lord's words. Saint thought cynically that the souls gathered were so few because Dwight Baldwin, who normally preached at the Waine'e, was across the island ministering to a dying woman, leaving Etienne DuPres to exhort the flock.

He spotted Jules with her family at the front of the church, her face, beneath her plain bonnet, pale and set. He sat back, crossed his arms over his chest, and prepared himself to be bored.

But he wasn't. He was enraged.

After two hymns were sung, Reverend DuPres walked to his pulpit, read from the Scriptures, and spoke briefly and generally of the sins of the flesh. Noting new in that, of course. It was one of Reverend

DuPres's favorite sermons. Then he paused a moment, and Saint could have sworn that he smiled.

"It is difficult," Reverend DuPres said, his voice filling the large room, "for a man of God to be cursed with an offspring who has no moral responsibility, despite all the pious teachings she's received, despite the model of a virtuous mother and father." He paused a moment, aware of the gasps of surprise, aware that he had everyone's attention. Saint tensed. No, he thought, DuPres won't, he wouldn't, not to his own daughter.

"As most of you know, particularly those of you who know my family well, we believed my younger daughter dead. Just as that virtuous woman Kanola is indeed dead, and with our Savior in heaven. The difference between these two women is obvious. The one chose death rather than submit to the wanton evil of the flesh. The other chose to debauch herself, to wallow in sin."

Saint heard a snicker from one of the sailors. He looked at Jules and saw that she was rigid as a statue. Her mother's head was bowed, but Sarah, curse her, was smiling. Thomas's face was red. Saint was barely aware that he had risen and was walking the long distance toward the pulpit. Rage pounded through him like storm-tossed waves to the shore.

"My daughter Juliana DuPres," Reverend DuPres said, "has debauched herself. Indeed, she has a true sinner's disregard for what is good and Christian, and dared to come back to Lahaina—in the company of one of the men who taught her—"

"You goddamned bastard, shut up."

"I will not shut up," Etienne DuPres shouted back

at Saint, slamming his fist on the wooden pulpit. "No, I will speak the truth, Dr. Morris. My daughter has proven herself to be a harlot, a slut. And you, sir, have added to her sins. Even yesterday, she tried to seduce, yes, seduce, my virtuous daughter's fiancé, John Bleecher. A fine upstanding young man who was appalled and who would have none of her, of course."

"Father, that's a lie," Thomas DuPres roared, jumping to his feet. "He tried to rape her."

"She is to be reviled, cast out—"

Reverend DuPres got no further. Saint rushed to the pulpit, grabbed him by the lapels of his black frock coat, lifted him a good foot off the floor, and shook him as he would a rat. "You miserable lying worm." Saint drew back his arm and slammed his fist into DuPres's jaw.

Etienne DuPres collapsed unconscious to the floor.

The place was pandemonium.

Saint turned and very calmly walked to where Jules was sitting, both the white community and native Hawaiians scurrying out of his way. "Jules," he said, "come with me now."

She raised empty eyes to his face.

"Come." He took her hand.

"Juliana, no, you can't," her mother said, but Jules ignored her. She placed her hand into Michael's and he led her from the church.

His heart pounded against his ribs. He closed his eyes against the bright sun, unaware that he was squeezing Jules's hand too hard.

When he opened his eyes, he didn't look down at her, merely kept walking toward the beach. The sound of the breaking waves usually soothed him, but not this time. He led Jules to a palm tree and said quite calmly, "Sit down, and stay out of the sun. It's quite strong today. I don't want you to get sunburned."

"I have my bonnet on," she said, but she moved to stand beneath the palm fronds.

"All within the space of twenty-four hours I've wanted to kill two men," he said. "I, a physician, a saver of life."

She raised her head and saw the pain in his eyes.

"It is my fault," she said. "You mustn't blame yourself. You are—too good and kind. Perhaps he was right—my father, that is. I did choose to live instead of end my life as Kanola did. I suppose I would have allowed myself to be debauched to survive. No, Michael, don't blame yourself. I am truly sorry."

Saint shook himself. He was a damned fool, carrying on about himself when it was Jules who was suffering. "God forgive me, I'm sorry." He pulled her against him, comforting the both of them. She was utterly passive.

"Jules," he said after some moments, his breath warm against her temple, "I was there only because I wanted to speak to you after the service, away from your family. I arranged with Reverend Baldwin yesterday to marry us. When he returns from tending his patient, he will."

Jules wanted to yell and laugh at the same time. She knew what her father had said to Saint the day before; her mother had told her. She knew why he wanted to marry her. He was honorable; he felt responsible for her; he felt pity for her.

"I should have killed myself," she said. "Then no one would hate me and revile me now."

His arms tightened around her and she cried out, unable to help herself.

Saint didn't apologize. He said, "Don't you ever say such a stupid thing again! Listen to me, Jules. Even if you had been raped by a dozen men, it wouldn't have been your fault, and I wouldn't feel any less respect for you. For God's sake, if a woman dies in childbirth, is she to blame?"

"But it's true, Michael. All of them, except for Thomas, wish I were truly dead."

"You are not to die. I won't allow you to die until you're well over eighty. You will forget your damned father, your weak, silly mother, and that mean-spirited sister of yours."

She pulled away from him and he let her go. She said over her shoulder, "It isn't fair that you feel constrained to make me your wife. I will go to Canada."

"No, you will go nowhere, save back to San Francisco with me." He paused a moment, then asked, "Did you guess that your father would treat you as he has? Is that the reason you wanted to stay in San Francisco?"

"I don't know. I can't see that it's particularly important now. I do know that my father was closeted with John Bleecher last evening. Michael, how could John lie like that?"

"Forget the little bastard. Jules, will you marry me? Will you do me the honor of becoming my wife? Will you come home with me to San Francisco?"

She said, "Wouldn't you prefer me as your mistress? Isn't a wife more expensive?"

"No, I wouldn't, and frankly, I don't remember how expensive a wife is."

Jules blinked at that. "You've already had a wife, Michael?"

"Yes, in Boston. Her name was Kathleen and she was an Irish girl. Only seventeen, but I was a wordly twenty-year-old. She left me to return to Dublin to fetch her mother. She died there of cholera, as did her mother." Saint paused, aware that he felt nothing but a faint regret now. Indeed, he could no longer see Kathleen's face in his mind's eye.

"I'm sorry," Jules said. She felt guilty suddenly because she was glad Kathleen was dead and out of Michael's life.

"It was many years ago, and there's no reason for you to be sorry. She wasn't part of your life." Saint's voice was natural now, and he was in firm control again. "Now, Jules, your answer, please."

It wasn't really a question, she knew, but she didn't say that aloud. She wanted to ask him if he loved her, but she didn't ask that either. He didn't. She also knew, in that moment, that she had enough love for both of them. Maybe the Lord did move in mysterious ways.

"Yes," she said. "Yes, Michael, I would be honored to marry you."

He felt as if a great weight had been lifted from his shoulders. His friends had teased him many times about taking a wife. They would doubtless be delighted. And she wasn't a stranger to him. He had watched his own wife grow up—at least he'd known Jules in her most formative years. And liked her and enjoyed her company.

"Come here," he said, "and let me kiss you."

As soon as the words were out of his mouth, he felt another, equally heavy weight descend. He couldn't and wouldn't force her to be a wife in more than name, not after what she had been through.

To his surprise, Jules walked back to him, stood quietly in front of him, and raised her face. He quickly placed a chaste kiss on her pursed lips. They had been friends, and they would continue to be friends. Nothing would change that. He would never hurt her.

Jules opened her eyes. "Thank you, Michael," she said.

"Certainly," he said. What did she think, he wondered—that he would ravish her here on the beach, like John Bleecher?

He caught her hand in his and they walked from the beach together.

Dwight Baldwin wished he'd been present at the church that morning. Certainly he'd been appalled to hear that Saint had assaulted a man of God, but he was willing to make allowances when he heard what Etienne DuPres had said. He smiled at Saint now as he stood beside his new bride. He looked immensely relieved, and he was smiling, thank the Lord. Poor Juliana looked numb. Perhaps everything would work out well between these two very good people. He would send many prayers heavenward to that end.

"You may kiss her now, Saint," Dwight said.

Saint dipped his head and touched his mouth to hers.

Mrs. Baldwin, a placid, plump woman, hugged Jules, and to Dwight's surprise, Jules said with some of her old enthusiasm, "I'd forgotten how beautiful your garden is, ma'am. The kukui, bananas, guava, kou—"

"Don't forget the grape arbors," Saint added. "Surely, Mrs. Baldwin, you remember what a naturalist Jules is. Have you any new plants to show her?"

"Figs," said Mrs. Baldwin. "If you like, Juliana, we can serve you some at the wedding dinner."

Jules turned wide eyes on her hostess. "Wedding dinner? But there is no one to come."

Dwight said, "Of course we're having a celebration dinner, my dear. You and Saint have many friends here. True friends, you know, remain just that."

"I do not wish," Jules said to Reverend Baldwin, "for you to be in disagreement with my father. It could not be comfortable for you. You have already done so much for me—for us."

He wanted to tell her that he thought her father was the most unnatural creature imaginable, but he didn't. There was no reason to upset her further. "I will be just fine, Juliana. You are not to worry about anyone save your new husband, and I think the poor man is becoming faint from hunger."

"I agree," Saint said. "You are to talk about me, my empty stomach, and not about the Baldwins' garden."

Jules took him at his word, and to his consternation, began to tell the Baldwins about his fine and selfless work in San Francisco.

"I think that soon you will be as noble as your nickname, Saint," Dwight said with a crooked smile sometime later in the crowded Baldwin parlor. "You've got yourself a fine woman."

"Yes," Saint said, looking over to where Jules stood speaking to several local Hawaiian families. "I never thought this would happen, even two days ago." He shook his head. "Life is bloody strange."

Dwight laughed. "I'm just glad you weren't already married. Then we would have been in the stew."

Saint said before thinking, "No, marriage wasn't for me. I—"

Dwight patted his arm. "You'll think differently—quite soon, I would imagine. My, my, look who is here."

Thomas DuPres, dressed in his Sunday black suit, stood uncomfortably in the doorway, his hands nervously picking at the rim of his hat.

Saint, without another word, strode to his new brother-in-law and extended his hand. "Thank you for coming, Thomas."

Behind him he heard Jules's voice. "Thomas." He stepped aside and watched brother and sister embrace, Thomas awkwardly patting Jules's back.

Saint said, "After everyone has left, Thomas, why don't you stay awhile? We can talk. As for you, my dear," he said to his new wife, "would you care for a glass of punch? I'm sure Thomas is also very thirsty."

Before the evening was over, Saint was approached by two ships' captains. Captain Richards of the *Occidental* said, "Wilkes has been a thorn in my side for years, Saint. David Gascony and I were talking. When we get to San Francisco, we've decided to look the bastard up and—"

"And what?" Saint asked, touched and amused by their concern. "There's nothing any of us can do, unfortunately. If you and John made a fuss in San

Francisco, my wife's reputation would be seriously damaged, and she would be hurt even more than she has been here."

"Damn," said David Gascony. "I hate to think the bastard will simply get away with it."

"At least," Mark Richards said, stroking his full whiskers, "you didn't let her bastard of a father get away with his rotten words, blast him."

Dwight Baldwin said, humor lacing his voice, "I agree completely, Mark. Would you believe it? Etienne called me to his house to take care of his jaw. I tell you honestly, I was sorely tempted to finish the job. I covered the entire side of his face with iodine, Saint, and told him in all seriousness not to talk for at least three days."

The men laughed. Jules looked up at the sound of Michael's laughter, and blinked. She thought it was the first time he had truly laughed since she'd seen him again. It was a wonderful sound and she thought: He's my husband. My husband.

"I'll tell you something else, Saint," Dwight said a little while later. "Etienne knew I was going to marry the two of you. He just looked at me, didn't say a single word, and I swear to you, I think he was delighted. In fact, it occurred to me that he may have perhaps denounced his daughter to force your hand."

"Then he is indeed a despicable creature," Saint said. "I tell you, Dwight, if heaven is populated with a congregation like him, I don't think I want to get past Saint Peter."

"One saint telling another saint to remove himself? Impossible."

Dwight arranged with his friends the Markhams

to lend a small house to the newlyweds. It was located near Makila Point, only a fifteen-minute carriage ride south of Lahaina. Saint didn't want to be alone with Jules, but there was nothing he could do save accept the Markhams' offer with good grace. He waited until Jules went upstairs with Mrs. Baldwin to pack her few things before speaking to Thomas. Dwight, a gentleman of great understanding, left them alone in the parlor.

"I hate him," Thomas said without preamble. "I hadn't realized how much until I saw how he treated Juliana. And John Bleecher—dammit, Saint, the fellow's paltry, a coward. He and Sarah deserve each other."

"I agree with everything you've said, Thomas," Saint said, lowering his body into a comfortable chair. "The question is, what are you going to do?"

Thomas DuPres drew a deep breath and said, "I want to go to San Francisco with you and Juliana."

Saint saw the pleading and defiance in the young man's eyes, and slowly nodded. "Yes, I think that would be a good idea. Unfortunately, Jules and I won't be leaving until next Wednesday, aboard the *Oregon*. Where will you stay until then? I assume you know that your sister and I are expected to be alone."

"I've already asked my friend Hopu. Hell, Saint, I'd sleep on the beach if I had to."

"Have you thought about what you want to do when we reach California?" Saint held his breath, fearing he'd hear Thomas spout off about finding gold and becoming rich overnight. He was blessedly surprised when the younger man said, "That's easy. I want to be a doctor, like you."

Saint said on a slow smile, "Excellent, Thomas."

He rose and clasped his hand. "Will you say good-bye to your parents?"

"I don't know," Thomas said truthfully. "Perhaps by Wednesday I'll be able to, but not now."

"I know what you mean. Now, let's drink a bit of Dwight's excellent brandy."

"Father has always hated Juliana," Thomas said, swishing the amber liquid in his glass some moments later. "She's so different, you know."

"I've often wondered about that," Saint said.

"I overheard him talking to my mother about Juliana some years ago—complaining, of course. I think it's all because—and you won't believe this—my mother's mother was a French actress, and Juliana is the very image of her. Evidently my grandmother called my father a petty bourgeois, told my mother she was a stupid twit to marry such a pious prig. My father, of course, could just barely overcome his scruples to marry my mother. And he quickly removed her from all sinful influences."

"I begin to understand," Saint said. "Hair as red as sin and eyes just as wicked, is that it?"

"Yes, I suppose that's it. But it's paltry, Saint, to dislike a person—your own child, for heaven's sake—all because she resembles someone else."

It was more than "paltry," Saint thought later; it was an illness that no physician could cure.

It was a beautiful, calm evening, the eaves breaking gently onto the shore, their white crests gleaming nearly silver under the half-moon and brilliant stars.

"We're married," Jules said, staring out over the water from her perch on some volcanic rocks.

"Yes," Saint agreed, wishing she weren't sitting so

close to him. "Yes, we are. Is it all right with you, Mrs. Morris?"

"Yes," she said, turning to face him. "I promise I won't be very expensive, Michael. I like that—Mrs. Juliana Morris."

There was humor in her voice and it pleased him inordinately. He took her hand in his without meaning to. Her flesh was warm and soft. "That's a relief," he said, smiling at her, "because I don't have that much money. It isn't unusual for my patients to pay me with favors."

"I'm fortunate then," she said with great insight, "else you might have had more trouble rescuing me, isn't that so?"

"Yes, that's so," he said, releasing her hand. A strand of thick hair blew across her face, and without thinking, he reached up to smooth it back. She grew very still, her eyes unwavering on his face.

He rose abruptly, keeping his back to her. He looked down at himself and cursed. "It's late, Jules," he said. "Go to bed."

Jules stared at his rigid back. "I think I'd rather go swimming," she said.

He quivered at that, remembering that night on the beach, her eyes on his naked body. He closed his eyes a moment, but he saw her in his fantasy, saw his hands widening her legs, saw his hands stroking up her thighs to lift her hips, to bring her down on him.

"Go to bed," he repeated.

"But don't you want to—?"

He whirled around. "Damn you, Jules, get into the house. I am your husband, and you'll obey me. Now."

# Chapter 11

Jules woke up abruptly, disoriented. She stared about the small bedroom and for a brief instant thought that Wilkes was there, and she was again his prisoner.

When she read Michael's brief note, propped up on the kitchen table, telling her he had gone into Lahaina to fetch some food, she felt at first relief, then anger.

Why hadn't he awakened her? She felt as if she were in some kind of quarantine. Was he afraid that she would be stoned for a harlot if she were to show her face again?

She stripped off her modest cotton nightgown, wrapped her swimming sarong around her, and left the house.

"Jules, I'm back."

There was no answer. Saint saw her rumpled nightgown on the floor and shook his head. He knew where she was. He closed his eyes a moment. Please, he prayed, she wouldn't, couldn't, swim nude as he had done that night.

He strolled onto the beach, shaded his eyes against the bright morning sun, and searched for her bright head. He felt his heart pound when he finally spotted her. Dear heavens, she was out so far. Did she want to kill herself? He turned cold at the thought.

He was standing on the beach when Jules, having caught a big wave, was carried nearly to his feet on her stomach. She was laughing. He watched her stand and wring out her hair. The sarong molded her young body, leaving very little to the imagination—at least to his imagination.

"You swam out a good half mile," he said, his voice rough, hands on hips.

Jules smiled at him. "Good morning. Yes, I did. I had to, you know. The reef sharks like the deeper water on the far side of that coral reef." He followed her pointing finger.

"I see," he said. "Come along, I've got our breakfast. Can you cook, Jules?"

"I can try," she said, giving him a sunny, guileless smile. She'd determined a good hour ago that she wouldn't make him feel guilty for leaving her alone. She wouldn't nag him or make him sorry he'd married her. She wouldn't say a word about spending the night by herself. She would be the perfect wife.

"That sounds ominous. Perhaps together we can keep ourselves from starvation."

She wanted to tell him how very handsome he was in his loose white shirt and black trousers. But he looked preoccupied, so she merely nodded and trotted after him into the small house.

He said, not looking at her, "Why don't you change first?"

"Actually, I'd like to get the salt water off me. There's a fresh spring just a few hundred yards away."

"Go ahead, then. I'll see what I can do about feeding us."

When Jules returned some thirty minutes later, Saint realized that he had grown concerned not ten minutes after she'd left. "Next time," he said, "I'll go with you."

"All right," she said. "This looks delicious."

They feasted on eggs, fresh papaya, and bread. "You, Michael," Jules said, sitting back in her chair and patting her stomach, "are an incredible man. You can do everything."

"Your hair is dry," he said, disregarding her praise as he eyed the riotous curls.

She touched her fingers to her hair and sighed. "I'll have to tie the mess down with a ribbon."

"No, leave it the way it is. I like it."

She looked so pleased with the meager compliment that Saint added, "Your hair is beautiful. I've always thought so."

She actually flushed with pleasure, and he rose abruptly from the table, turning away. He closed his eyes. Lord, he didn't want the responsibility for this fairy creature. She could be too easily hurt. "What would you like to do today?" he asked. Three days and two more nights, he thought. He'd slept outdoors the previous night. Thank heaven they weren't in Massachusetts, in the winter.

"I wish we had time to go to the volcano and see the sunrise. It's very spectacular."

"We don't, unfortunately. Any other ideas?"

She was silent for a long while, staring down at her folded hands. "Kanola and I were swimming off Makila Point when Wilkes kidnapped us. I thought

I would be frightened to swim here again, but I wasn't. Is that unnatural?''

She was such a curious little thing, he thought, staring at her. ''No,'' he said finally. ''It means that you've got lots of common sense.''

''That or no sensibilities,'' she said. ''When Mrs. Baldwin took me upstairs last evening, I told her about it—Makila Point, that is. I thought she was going to faint.''

''You didn't tell her any of the rest of it?'' he asked carefully.

''No, of course not.'' She lowered her eyes. ''She asked me if there was anything I wanted to know about my wedding night.''

Saint swallowed convulsively. ''And?''

''I already know everything, Michael. I just asked her if men stuck that thing into—'' She broke off, her face as red as if she'd been in the sun too long.

He smiled, unable to help himself. ''I understand. What did Mrs. Baldwin say?''

''She said yes, that was true, and that it wasn't too bad, not really, but that she was certain that you would be very careful. I told her that it sounded very strange to me.''

''Did she say anything else?''

Jules nodded. ''Yes, she said that it wasn't strange really and that you were a doctor.''

''Those two things go hand in hand? I'd never considered that before.''

She saw the amusement in his eyes, and grinned. ''Now that you mention it, it doesn't make much sense, does it?''

''Not an ounce,'' he agreed. ''Now, Jules, since you

haven't any ideas to speak of, I think I'll go swimming."

Saint decided that Jules's idea of the male thing that was stuck into women had originated with him. At least Wilkes hadn't paraded about in front of her naked. He suddenly remembered her few words about the sailors. She'd seen a sailor's penis—the sailor who had raped Kanola, probably. He also wondered a few minutes later as he was stroking through the water if Jules would mind lovemaking with him. She certainly seemed interested. He hadn't seen a patch of fear in her eyes when they'd spoken of her conversation with Mrs. Baldwin. Despite the chill of the water, he was hard. "Damned randy bastard."

That evening, they strolled to the beach to watch the sunset. "I'll miss this," Jules said as the sun dipped finally over the horizon, casting the sky in vivid red for a few moments. "I feel a bit like Eve being tossed out of the Garden of Eden."

Saint, who was wearing only a shirt and his cut-off pants, dropped down on the sand and leaned back on his elbows. "Do you cast me as Adam?" he asked.

"I don't think so," Jules said, turning to stare down at him. "I didn't corrupt you."

"I don't think you could corrupt anyone, even if you tried your damnedest."

"I looked at you, very closely, Michael."

He knew immediately what she was talking about. He said, "Yes, I know. Am I the only man you've ever seen with no clothes, Jules?"

She shook her head and said, "You're beautiful."

"That's a novel thing to say about a man, particularly a huge hairy beast like me. But I thank you."

Jules looked away from him, out over the water. "You changed, even while I was watching you."

Deep waters, he thought, shifting his weight a bit. "A man," he said, "is very simple in terms of function. When he wants a woman, he becomes larger."

"Yes," she said, "you did." She suddenly turned her eyes to his face. "Did you want me?"

"I think I just hoisted myself on that evil petard," he said, striving for some humor. "What I should have said is that sometimes a man's body reacts even when he doesn't want it to. Sometimes a man can find himself very embarrassed, and for no reason at all."

In the darkening evening light, he couldn't make out the expression on her face, but he knew she'd stiffened.

"Jules," he said, "do you want me to make love to you?"

"You mean kiss me and touch me and stick—"

"Yes, all of that."

"I don't know." She sighed, hugging her arms around her knees. "I guess I speak so openly to you because I know you won't do anything to hurt me. Like John Bleecher."

"No, I would never hurt you."

"When I woke up this morning, I thought for just a moment that Jameson Wilkes had me again. And sometimes when I close my eyes, I can see John, and I feel that awful fear. Of all of it, I guess it's the feeling of absolute helplessness, that because I'm a woman and not as strong, a man can do whatever he pleases to me. I hate that. It's not right."

"No, it isn't. But not many men are like that, Jules. Most men admire and respect women, just as I do. Shall I tell you what I would like?"

"Yes, I suppose so."

"I would like for you to trust me enough to tell me what happened to you during your time with Wilkes."

He saw the distaste, the fear. He barely heard her whispered "No, oh, please no." He swore to himself in that moment that he wouldn't touch her until he could be certain she wouldn't be disgusted by him, and afraid. He rose to his feet and dusted the sand off his clothes. "I think I'll go for a walk. Jules, if ever you do want to talk about it, I'll be around to listen."

"All right," she said, her voice small, thin. She watched him walk down the beach. She almost called him back. But she didn't. Slowly she lowered her face and sobbed against her hands. If she told him, she knew he would hate her. He wouldn't denounce her as her father had done, oh no. He would remain polite to her, and very kind. But she would disgust him, and she didn't think she could bear to see the distaste for her in his eyes.

The next morning, Saint watched Jules speak to Kanola's husband, a tall, sleek man who worked at the Government Market selling fresh meat. His name was Kuhio, and it was soon obvious to Saint that he blamed Jules for his wife's death. They were speaking Hawaiian, but Saint could make out a few of Kuhio's words: *hoomanakii, ino, hookumakaia*. And Jules saying over and over the word *minamina, minamina*. Something about her regret, her sorrow.

But Kuhio kept repeating that she was vain, wicked, sinful, a mistress of betrayal.

Finally Saint stepped between them, bowed to Kuhio, and took his wife's hand. "Come," he said.

"He told me that he wouldn't let me near his children after what I'd done."

"He's grieving, that's all. It is convenient for him to have you to blame."

She raised wide, strained eyes to his face. "He told me that I was more wicked than my father had said on Sunday."

"Stop it, Jules. Oh, damn."

"Well, if it isn't my innocent little sister," Sarah said, closing her parasol with an abrupt snap. "Were you speaking to Kuhio? You needn't worry, Juliana, Father has given him money to recompense him for you killing his wife."

His hands clenched, but he couldn't very well hit Jules's sister, though in his mind, she deserved it.

Jules simply stared at her sister, her eyes bewildered, pleading.

Saint said now, "How well you're looking, Sarah. I do hope that you and John Bleecher marry before your belly swells."

Sarah gasped, then gave her sister a look of utter hatred. "You had to malign me too, didn't you? You evil, wicked girl."

"Of course," Saint continued, smiling, "after you marry John, I imagine you'll have to keep a keen eye on him. I do hope he doesn't give you syphilis, Sarah."

"You filthy creature, you deserve each other."

"And I think, my dear, that you and John Bleecher will make the perfect couple. He can make love to you in the dark, then go find himself a helpless girl to force. Do send your sister a letter announcing the birth of your first child."

"John will kill you for that."

For the first time, Saint felt his rage get the better of him. "I would like to get my hands on that worthless little bastard. Again. Is he hiding his black-and-blue face?"

"Please, please, stop," Jules whispered, grabbing her husband's hand. "Sarah, you can't mean all those things you said—"

"Shut up, Jules. No apologizing to this jealous bitch. Good day, Miss DuPres."

Saint pulled her away with him, ignoring the startled, curious glances cast their way. Let them all gossip, he thought, it wouldn't matter. Tomorrow they'd be gone.

They'd walked into Lahaina, and now they began their walk back to Makila Point. Jules didn't say a word.

Neither did Saint. What could he say?

Saint jerked awake, jumped to his feet, and ran into the small house. Jules was screaming, sobbing as if her heart were breaking.

"Jules," he nearly shouted at her as he sat down beside her on the narrow bed. She was writhing, her body twisted in the single sheet that covered her. She cried out again, "No, oh God, no."

He grabbed her shoulders and shook her. "Jules, wake up. Come on, sweetheart, wake up."

Jules felt his hands on her, heard her man's voice, and struggled wildly. "No, don't touch me."

He didn't want to slap her as he'd done before,

but he didn't see much choice. He drew back his hand, then paused. He saw her eyes slowly open in the dim light, saw her blink. "Michael?"

"Yes, Jules. It's all right now. You're safe, with me." Had he repeated the same words to her before?

She drew a shuddering breath, but she couldn't stop the sobs. She couldn't seem to break away from the awful dream.

"Jules, tell me. Tell me what you were dreaming." He felt only a moment of guilt, using her vulnerability against her. But it was for the best, dammit. "Tell me."

She gulped down the tears, and buried her face against his bare chest. "He tied me down on his bed, my arms and legs apart. He took all my clothes. He touched me and told me how lovely I was. He told me that he would keep me naked so I would get used to being looked at. He told me that the man who bought me would want me like this. Oh, God."

"It's all right," Saint repeated, stroking her hair. "It's all right now."

It seemed as though the dam had burst, he thought, listening to her harsh breaths, seeing through her eyes what had happened to her.

"He threatened me. He told me if I didn't behave for him, he would bring in some of his men and let them play with me. He made me walk about in front of him naked. Then that night he drugged me, and put his hands on my breasts, and kissed them, and I felt so strange, and so frightened. He kept touching me—he never let me wear any clothes until that awful red gown. He told me he wanted to take me, but I was worth too much money to him as a virgin." She reared back in his arms, her eyes wild. "I laughed at him and told him he was an ugly old man."

"Good for you," Saint said. "Well done, Jules."

"I did it only once," she said, more calmly now. "I was too frightened of him to put up much of a fight after that." She buried her face against his chest again. "He even made me relieve myself in front of him, and bathe. I felt like a cheap, worthless nothing. He wouldn't stop fondling me. God, I hated his hands, and how he looked at me when he was touching me."

He held her tightly against him, rocking her slightly. At least it was all out now. He knew the moment she got a hold on herself and came completely awake. He felt her stiffen.

"Jules," he said, shaking her, "no, don't think what you're thinking."

She sniffed, then very slowly pulled away from him. He let her go and she sank back down on the pillow. She closed her eyes, thinking that even in the dark she could make out the disgust and distaste on his face. All because of a stupid nightmare. She turned her face away.

"Jules," he said quietly, lightly touching his fingertips to her hair. "Do you feel better now?"

Feel better? She wanted to die.

He repeated his question.

"Yes," she said. "Please, Michael, I want to go back to sleep."

The bed creaked as he rose. There was absolute silence for several moments, except for their breathing. He was staring at her—she knew it, she could feel the condemnation flowing from him.

Saint sighed, turned, and left the bedroom.

The next morning when he called her for breakfast, she sidled out of the bedroom as if she'd been hiding. She wouldn't meet his eyes.

"We're leaving this afternoon on the *Oregon*," he said, toying with his bread.

She said nothing.

"Is there anything you would like me to fetch for you from your parents' house?"

She raised her head, but still didn't meet his eyes. "My surfboard is hidden behind the house."

"Unfortunately, the water is too cold for surfboarding in San Francisco. I remember you were quite good at it."

"Yes, I am. I will miss that wild feeling." Her voice broke on a sob. "Kanola taught me when we were very young."

This is no Garden of Eden, he thought. This is more like hell we're escaping. He said sharply, "Enough, Jules. Your life has changed—neither you nor I can deny that. But everything will work out. I promise to be a good husband to you. I promise you'll never starve."

"If we're ever on the edge," she said, "you can always sell me to the highest bidder."

He stood abruptly, his chair falling to the floor, and placed his splayed hands on the tabletop. "If you ever speak like that again, I will thrash you." His anger was immense, but when he saw her flinch, it dissolved immediately. "And if you ever cower away from me, I'll thrash you. Damn you, Jules, I am not Jameson Wilkes, nor am I John Bleecher." She didn't reply, but then again, he didn't expect her to. He straightened, a bit chagrined by his display, and said more calmly, "Your brother will meet us at the dock."

But Thomas wouldn't meet them at the dock. Later that morning, Dwight Baldwin rode his swaybacked mare to the small house on Makila Point. "Saint," he said. "Juliana."

Saint shook his hand, saw the troubled look in his gray eyes, and said quietly, "What's wrong, Dwight?"

Reverend Baldwin sent a worried look toward Jules.

"What's wrong, sir?"

"I'm sorry," Dwight said. "Thomas was beaten up last night. No, no, he'll be all right, but he's in no shape to travel for a while."

"His injuries?" Saint asked, his voice tight, controlled.

"No internal injuries, as best I can judge," Dwight said. "But he's got a couple of broken ribs, and a broken leg. He'll need to stay in bed for several weeks."

"Who did it?" Jules asked.

"John Bleecher and some of his friends. The bunch of them left the island early this morning, bound for Oahu. I suppose they'll stay away until it's forgotten. John's father, when I spoke to him, claimed that his son was conducting some business for him on Oahu. He said his son had nothing to do with any of this and Thomas is a liar." Actually, Elisha Bleecher had been far more colorful in his speech.

"Is Thomas at home, sir?" Jules asked.

"Yes. Reverend DuPres is in something of a quandary," he added. Saint knew exactly what he meant, but Jules, who was concentrating on her brother, didn't seem to hear his words.

She said, "I must see him, Michael, before we leave."

"Yes," he agreed. Jesus, the last thing he wanted was to face her damned father again, but there was no hope for it.

He heard Jules whisper, "It's my fault, all of it."

# Chapter 12

Unfortunately, Saint saw, there were no signs of iodine on Reverend Etienne DuPres's jaw.

"Get out and take my harlot of a daughter with you." He tried to slam the front door.

Saint, without much effort, pushed him back.

"It's your fault," Jules's father yelled as he fell back, shaking his fist at Jules. "Your poor brother, beaten because he tried to protect you!"

"Ah, so now you will admit that John Bleecher attacked your daughter and not the other way around?"

"I admit nothing."

"Father," Jules said, "I would like to see Thomas."

Saint saw the man's face flood with rage, and quickly said, "We will both see Thomas. After all, he was to accompany us back to San Francisco today. Come, Jules."

"No." Saint shoved him aside as if he were naught to be bothered with. "You little slut—you should have been destroyed the moment you emerged from your mother's womb."

Saint turned at the foot of the stairs and said, "If you do not keep your mouth shut, sir, I will break your jaw. This time, I will ensure it is broken. Do you understand?" He took one step toward the man.

"This is my house."

"Fine," Saint said. "Remember that this is also your daughter and that I, sir, am your son-in-law. I assure you, that fact is the only blot I know of in my family history." He shook his head. "You really are quite a paltry man."

He felt Jules's hand on his sleeve, and turned to walk up the stairs with her. "Easy, sweetheart," he said. "You knew it wouldn't be pleasant. Ignore him. He is not well."

"I have come to realize that he is rather narrow," Jules said. She looked up at him a moment. "Even if your children were awful, you wouldn't treat them like he treats me, would you?"

"If they looked like you, I'd give them huge hugs."

Thomas managed a grin when his sister and Saint came into his bedroom.

"Good Lord," Saint said on a whistle, "you look colorful enough to become a country's flag." He walked to the bed, lifted Thomas's hand, and took his pulse.

"I'll live, Saint," Thomas said. He winced slightly when Saint gently placed his hand on his belly and pressed here and there.

"Yes," Saint said, "you most certainly will—we need more good doctors. I'm taking Jules away today, Thomas. You of all people understand that she must leave. I am leaving money with Reverend Baldwin. When you are well enough, you will book passage and come to San Francisco. All right?"

Thomas closed his eyes a moment and choked down his tears. "Yes, Saint," he said. "God, everything has been such a muddle, and now this."

"I know. Now, tell your sister that you're going to live." Saint rose and stood aside.

"Stop looking at me as if I were on my last legs, Jules," Thomas said to his white-faced sister. "Don't be a fool. Come on now. I'm fine, just fine. Don't you believe your husband? I'll be with you in a month, you'll see." The spate of words exhausted him, and he laid his head back heavily on the pillow.

"Thomas, I'm so sorry," she said.

"Women," Thomas said, biting down on the awful pain in his ribs. "Watering pots and silly twits, all of you. Cut line, Jules. You heard Saint—I'll be fine." He was beginning to feel like a parrot. But birds didn't want to kill, he thought, and to kill John Bleecher would give him the greatest pleasure at the moment.

Jules leaned down and kissed her brother's pale cheek. She stroked her fingertips over his bruised jaw. "I love you, Thomas. We will both build a fine life, you'll see."

"Lord, I know that," he said. Anything to keep away those damnable tears.

Jules kissed her brother again, and stepped back.

"You take care, Thomas," Saint said, shaking his hand.

"Yes, Saint, I shall." He lowered his voice. "Please take good care of my sister. She is so—hurt."

"I will, Thomas, I will."

They were not to escape Reverend DuPres's house with no more confrontations. Sarah, her eyes puffy from crying, her face pale as wax, was standing in the hall below, waiting for them. When she saw her sister, she screamed, "You miserable bitch. God, I hope you die, you don't deserve to live."

Saint squeezed Jules's hand. He wanted to feel some sympathy for Sarah, but couldn't seem to find any within him. He said, "You are a bore, Miss Du-Pres. Let's just hope you aren't a pregnant bore."

"Shut up, damn you."

"Such language from a missionary's daughter," Saint said. "So, John Bleecher has left you high and dry, so to speak. After he tried to kill your brother. And before that, he tried to rape your sister. You have excellent taste in men, it would appear."

"I hate you," Sarah screamed, hands fisted at her sides.

"Were I you, Miss Sarah, I should be careful what my dear father overheard me say. I wouldn't put it past him to toss you out on your ear for your slut behavior. After all, how much is a father expected to take? Two sluts for daughters? Come, Jules. We have a date with the *Oregon*."

Jules followed him silently from her father's house. She paused a moment in the road and stared back. "So much unhappiness," she said in a low voice. "Poor Thomas."

"Yes and yes," Saint agreed. "You are well out of it, sweetheart. And Thomas will be out of it soon."

It was evening, and Saint knew he couldn't tarry any longer on deck. He was alone now, the other few passengers having retired sometime before. As he stared out over the endless expanse of ocean, he remembered the first time he'd ever seen the sea. He'd been with his Uncle Rafe fishing on the Chesapeake Bay. Then they'd ridden to the Atlantic and the thirteen-year-old Saint had wanted only to sit on a rock and stare at the savage beauty of the crashing waves. He pulled away from the railing and sighed. He'd seen the small cabin, the single narrow bed, and gulped. Well, he would simply have to deal with it. After all, he was a man, not a randy boy.

He walked along the companionway and quietly opened the door to their cabin. He pulled up short. Jules stood in the middle of the small space, her hands clutched around her stomach, bent over.

"Jules, what's the matter?" He was at her side in an instant, his gut wrenching in sudden fear. To his surprise, she straightened immediately and flushed a vivid red. He cocked a brow at her. "I'm waiting," he said. "What's wrong? Do you hurt? Are you feeling seasick?"

"No," she whispered, looking utterly miserable. "I'm not seasick. You know I'm never seasick."

"Then what's the matter?" At her continued silence he said, "If you don't talk to me now, I'm going to poke and prod around."

"My stomach hurts," she said in the thinnest voice he'd ever heard.

"Your stomach? Was it something you ate at dinner?"

She shook her head, mute.

"Jules—" he said, his voice threatening.

"My stomach is cramping," she said.

"Ah," he said, relief flooding through him. "You've begun your monthly flow." He saw that she was ready to sink through the floor in embarrassment. "It's all right, sweetheart. I'll give you some laudanum in water. It will make you sleep, and when you wake up you'll feel just fine. All right?"

Now, he thought as he pored several drops of laudanum into a glass of water, he wouldn't have to worry. He had five days of enforced nobility. He silently handed her the glass of water. She drank all of it, and just as silently handed back the glass.

"Now," Saint said, "why don't you get into your nightgown? You'll be very sleepy soon."

There was no screen, and he left her alone for a good five minutes. When he walked back into the cabin, she was sitting on the side of the bed, covered neck to tie in a white lawn nightgown.

"Do you feel any better?"

She shook her head, not looking at him.

"Do you have bad cramps every month?"

She shook her head, still not looking at him.

"Does your back hurt?"

"No," she said, looking now at her toes.

There was a single chair in the small cabin. Saint sat down and patted his thighs. "Come here, Jules."

She looked at him, horrified. He only smiled at her.

Slowly, Jules padded over to him. He held out his arms, and she sank down onto his legs. He gently pulled her against him and held her.

He felt her tense with cramp.

"It will be gone soon," he said, lightly kissing her hair.

"It's nothing to you," she said in a muffled voice.

"Nothing? What it is is natural. However, I do not believe in pain when it can be alleviated. Now, you just relax, and I'll tell you about Louis the fourteenth."

"He was a French king," Jules said.

"Yes, in the seventeenth century. He was called the Sun King. In any case, when he was born, he came into the world with two teeth. The queen, his mother, was appalled, and very wisely refused to put him to her breast. You can imagine the wariness of the two wet nurses. I remember reading that they were well compensated for their stoicism."

Her head fell against his chest. He continued, his voice growing softer, "There's another story about poor Louis. It seems that he had a rather embarrassing problem that involved his backside. He had what's called a fistula. The surgeons operated successfully, and the courtiers, to show their sympathy for their king, proceeded to have similar operations."

Her breathing was even and soft. She was asleep.

"For a while very few gentlemen in the court were able to sit down." He eased her back into the circle of his arm. Her thick dark lashes were fanned against her pale cheeks. He hadn't really noticed before that her brows and lashes were a dark brown, not a washed-out red as one would expect. And not one single freckle, even on the bridge of her nose. A nice straight nose, he thought. And a lovely mouth, a passionate mouth. He continued to study her, perhaps really seeing her for the first time. "You've grown into quite a beauty," he said softly, lightly touching his fingertips to her throat. "And now you're my wife and my problem." No, he amended to himself, his responsibility.

He carried his sleeping wife to the bed and gently laid her on her back. He looked thoughtful for a moment, then shrugged. He stripped off his clothes and slipped in beside her. The damned bed was so narrow he could feel the warmth from her body.

When he awoke the next morning, he realized that he was precariously close to falling off the bed. Jules, he saw, turning to face her, was sprawled on her stomach, her arms and legs spread, as if she were floating in the water. He was normally a light sleeper, but he'd never stirred, even when she'd begun her takeover. He smiled, then rose and bathed.

Dressed, he returned to the bed and sat down beside her. "Jules," he said, gently shaking her shoulder.

A very heavy sleeper, he thought, and shook her again.

"Hmmm?" Jules pulled up to her elbows and slewed her head around. "Michael? What's the matter? Where—"

"We're aboard the *Oregon* and it's morning, and how do you feel?"

Jules ducked her head and said, "I'm just fine, thank you."

"Good. Why don't you get dressed and join me in the dining room?"

When Jules entered the long, narrow dining room on the main deck of the *Oregon*, she saw a knot of men, her husband in the middle of it. As she neared, she heard laughter, then Michael's voice saying, "To this day, it's called 'burking.' "

"Good God," one heavily whiskered gentlemen laughed, "and to think I'd believed medical science had advanced to the point of curing people, not killing them."

Saint laughed, then spied his wife. He excused himself. "Hi, sweetheart."

"You're quite a storyteller," she said, remembering his outrageous tale about Louis XIV. "What's all this about 'burking'?"

"In Scotland, not very long ago, a man used to supply the medical school with dead bodies for dissection. Unfortunately, he got into the deplorable habit of strangling people to get corpses. And that was called 'burking.' "

"His name was Burk, I presume?"

"Yep, and he was hanged, finally. After some sixteen-odd folk ceased to exist due to his greed. The medical school paid handsomely for bodies."

"You have quite a talent."

"It comes in handy, like last night," he added, smiling down at her. "Patients, in my experience, need to be distracted. You're sure you feel fine this morning?"

"Please—yes."

"We're married, sweetheart," he said, and tucked her hand through his arm. "And I'm a doctor. Two valid reasons why you should never be embarrassed with me."

"If you say so," she said, not believing him for an instant.

"I do say so. Now, onward to food. I have a lot of body to maintain."

The day was warm, the weather calm and clear. Jules became acquainted with the remainder of the passengers, met Captain Drake, and listened to her husband charm everyone who came into his orbit.

She wasn't asleep when Saint slipped into the bed beside her. She reached out to touch his arm, and realized he was quite naked. She gulped.

"Michael? Would you tell me a story?"

He laughed and turned onto his side to face her. It was probably a fine idea, he thought. He himself needed to be distracted this time. "Well, let me see. Did you ever hear the story—? No, I think I'll tell you about some of my friends in San Francisco. You've probably heard me mention their names— Delaney and Chauncey Saxton."

She nodded.

"Well, Del is a very rich man. He wasn't, not at first. He was one of the argonauts—that means he came to California in 1849 with the first group of men to search for gold. He found it. Unlike most others, he used the gold he'd discovered wisely. He owns a bank, is a partner in many other businesses in the city, and owns three or four ships that go to and from the Far East. He'll make you laugh within three minutes of meeting him. He's very witty, you see, and gives his witty wife, Chauncey, quite a time of it. She's English, beautiful, and now a mother. She's also very rich in her own right. You'll like her, I'm sure of it."

"Won't she think I'm not a very nice person, after what happened?"

"Jules, if you don't stop that foolishness, I'm going to beat you."

He reached out his hand to touch her shoulder, but instead connected with her breast. He sucked in his breath and drew back his hand as if burned.

"I'm sorry."

"No, no," Saint said. He grinned into the darkness. "You see, Jules, I'm not in the habit of sleeping with my wife. Are you sleepy now?"

"Yes," she said, lying without hesitation.

She lay awake a long time, listening to her husband's deep, even breathing.

Saint, the light sleeper, awoke the next morning aware that something was very strange. Jules was lying on top of him, her head resting against his throat. His sex was hard against her belly.

He realized he was lying in the middle of the bed, and in her sleep, she'd just tried to find some space. "Damn," he said. Very slowly he eased her off him.

"Michael?" she said in a sleepy, slurred voice.

"Yes, sweetheart. Go back to sleep."

To his relief and regret, she did, curled up on her side, her hand fisted beneath her cheek.

When he rose from the bed, he cursed himself, even as he turned again to look at her. Her nightgown was bunched about her thighs—long, slender legs, so white and so soft-looking. He pulled a sheet over her.

# Chapter 13

Saint learned in the next several days that his young wife was quite a storyteller in her own right. He came into the dining room one afternoon after treating a fellow passenger for an abscess on his leg, and saw Jules siting at a table, her hands gesticulating while she talked. He moved closer, saying nothing, his eyes on her face. When he'd known her as a young girl, he'd thought her fascinatingly aware of everything around her, but in the endlessly curious manner of children. Not so, he had come to realize. She'd managed to nurture her curiosity, her complete excitement with life itself. Even the events of the previous month and a half had only dimmed her spirit for a while.

"The whole thing about the *kapus*, you see, was to curtail the native women's freedom. They couldn't eat with the men, couldn't eat certain foods—bananas, coconuts, pork, even baked dog."

"Good heavens," said Miss Mary Arkworth, "what was there to eat then?" Miss Arkworth, who had lived on Oahu for a number of years and who knew the answer very well, could have added that all the *kapus* were supposedly religious in nature, but she didn't. She was enjoying the very bright Mrs. Morris's enthusiasm too much to dampen it.

"Sounds fine to me," said Nathan Benson. "Let them eat cake if they're not allowed baked dog."

"Well, Mr. Benson," Jules said, "it's all well and good to joke about it, but there was a story about a little five-year-old girl who ate a banana. Instead of killing her, which was the punishment for breaking a *kapu*, they ripped out her right eye."

Amid the gasps of outrage, Saint asked, "Weren't all the eating *kapus* gotten rid of by a woman?"

She smiled at him, as if he were a very bright pupil, and nodded. Her audience quieted, leaning forward to listen. "You see," she said in a confidential voice, "after King Kamehameha the first died, his queen, Kaahumanu, announced to her young son that she would be his *kuhina-nui*, or vice-king."

"Smart lady," said Mr. Benson.

"Indeed," said Jules. "And she was a very brave woman. To break the eating *kapu*, she ate a banana in front of the king, Liholiho. He, dear boy, ignored it. Then she had the temerity to eat a meal in his presence."

A natural storyteller, Saint thought, smiling at her.

"What happened?" Miss Arkworth demanded.

"Nothing, not a single thing. Kaahumanu broke him down. Finally, at a banquet, the king went to the women's table and began piling pieces of food into his mouth. The vice-king—a woman—won."

"What became of her?" asked Mrs. Benson.

"She died of old age," said Jules.

"Odd," said Saint. "I thought she died from overeating."

Jules shot him an impish grin. "Well, like most Hawaiian women, she was immensely fat. That, you know, is what is considered beautiful on the islands."

"Now, Jules," Saint said when they were alone a few minutes later, "Victorian prejudices have started taking hold. Many of the Hawaiian women are forcing their healthy bodies into those awful whalebone corsets. You didn't tell all the truth."

She nodded and said sadly, "Civilization is not always such a wonderful thing. And," she added, grinning up at him, "I didn't want to ruin the impact of my story."

Saint cupped her face between his large hands. "You, Mrs. Morris, are a natural."

"A natural what?" Jules asked, her eyes coming to rest on his mouth. She felt a bit breathless and somewhat strange, as if his fingers and his palms were warming her from the inside out.

Saint felt her lean toward him and immediately dropped his hands, saying lightly as he did so, "A natural teller of tall and not-so-tall tales. Now, would you care to stroll on deck?"

"I suppose even naturals must have exercise," she said.

His dreams became vividly erotic, jerking him awake to stare into the darkness, covered with sweat and harder than the bedpost. He rose several mornings before dawn, unable to lie quietly next to Jules, listening to her even breathing, the soft sighs that made him wonder what her dreams were made of. Certainly not of sex, he told himself. Perhaps of fear and dread of men, but not of sex, not of him.

They were but four days out of San Francisco

when he could bear it no longer. He stayed in the small parlor where the gentlemen smoked and gambled until very late, unable to face lying down in that damned narrow bed beside his young wife. He drank too much, lost one hundred dollars at vingt-et-un, and made his way to the cabin well past midnight.

Jules was on her side, facing away from him, the sheet pulled to her chin. He eased out of his clothes, and slipped in beside her. She didn't stir.

He slept fitfully, until finally he was lost in that vague, blurred state that seemed so real, so very vivid. Jane Branigan was beside him, touching him, laughing and teasing him, and he was in such great need of her he thought he would die. Then they were lying together and he was stroking her body, calling, "Jane, my God, Jane." He felt her soft breasts, felt her nipples tauten from the teasing of his fingers. God, he wanted her, and now.

"Jane," he whispered, nuzzling against her throat. She wasn't naked, as she should have been. She was wearing something, and the starchy material scratched his mouth. He felt nothing but urgency, and rose over her, pulling the nightgown up above her breasts. The touch of her warm flesh made him crazy. His hands and mouth covered her breasts, her smooth, soft belly. He lay atop her, moaning aloud. His sex, pressed against her closed thighs.

"Jane," he said, moving restlessly over her. "I can't wait, Jane."

He pulled her legs apart and pushed forward. But she wasn't ready for him, wouldn't let him enter her. He was frantic now, not understanding.

"Jane," he said again, "what's wrong?"

Jules came abruptly awake. She heard Michael's

voice repeating a name. Not her name. Jane. She was suddenly aware that a man, a huge man, was covering her, pressing her down into the mattress, and she cried out, her mind blurred with sleep. Then something deep within her cried out, refusing to accept the terror of a dream. No, she was with Michael. It was he covering her, pressing against her.

He was moaning, telling her between gasping breaths to relax, to give in to him. But something was terribly wrong. *Telling Jane to relax.* Suddenly his hands was probing against her, that male part of him pushing forward against her.

Saint felt wild with need, frustrated and angry that he couldn't enter her body. He felt Jane trying to push him away; then he heard a sharp cry of pain.

"Michael—no—please."

He came awake. "Jane," he said, then drew in his breath sharply. In the dim light of dawn, he saw Jules sprawled beneath him, and he was trying to force himself inside her.

"Oh God, no." He pulled himself up and rested on his haunches, his head in his hands. He'd very nearly forced his wife without realizing what he was doing.

Jules lay very still. He was on his knees between her widespread legs. "Michael?"

"I'm sorry," he said, hating himself more at that moment than at any other in his entire life. "I'm sorry, Jules. I didn't hurt you, did I? Are you all right?"

She frowned at him, uncertain, becoming more bewildered by the moment. "I don't understand."

He rose from the bed, shrugging into his dressing gown. Of course she didn't understand. Lord, it was difficult enough for him to comprehend.

"Who is Jane?"

He turned slowly to face her, and was relieved to see that she'd pulled down her nightgown and was leaning against the pillows.

He walked to the bed and sat down beside her. "I know you don't understand, Jules." He paused a moment, uncertain what to say. Finally, "I was dreaming, a result of all the damned whiskey, I suppose. I didn't realize what I was doing. Jules, I didn't hurt you, did I?"

"Just a bit. I was surprised. Who is Jane?"

He slashed his hand through the air. "It's not important. Look, sweetheart, I can't continue sleeping with you. I can't trust myself not to—well, take advantage of you. You were frightened, weren't you?

Of course she'd been frightened. What could one expect? But he hadn't been trying to make love to her; it had been another woman he was dreaming about. She closed her eyes against the awful hurt. She turned her head away from him. She had to know, even though it hurt so much. "Who is Jane? Who is this woman you were dreaming about?"

How could he tell her that in a dream he could act out what he wanted, that his immense desire for her, to be justified even in the recesses of his mind, had to transfer itself to another woman, a woman he wouldn't hurt, a woman he knew wanted him?

His head was ached, and he needed to clear his mind. He began to dress. He could feel Jules watching him, but he said nothing. All his concentration was on escaping, both from her and her question and from himself and his reprehensible behavior.

He sat down in the single chair and pulled on his boots. "I'm going out for a while, on deck." He was

out the door and gone before she could gather two
words together.

She didn't cry. She didn't do anything, save lie
there looking up at the darkened ceiling of the cabin.
He hadn't return by the time she fell asleep, the sun
rising brightly in the morning sky.

Jules saw him immediately when she came into the
dining room late that morning. He'd returned to
bathe and change while she'd still slept, she realized
from the wreckage in the cabin. He was avoiding her.

Who was Jane?

She drank a cup of coffee and nibbled on a slice
of bread and butter. He made no move to separate
himself from his cohorts and come to her.

Saint was aware of her the moment she walked
into the dining room. She looked a bit pale, a bit
tired. He himself felt like the proverbial piece of cow
dung, but he'd refused to take anything to ease his
hangover. God, he deserved every shard of pain that
sliced through his damned head. This can't continue,
he thought sometime later, so weary of pretending
to listen to his fellow passengers that he couldn't
bear it. He rose finally and escaped. He made his
way to their cabin. She wasn't there.

With a lagging step he went on deck, finding her
seated beneath the mainsail on a pile of coiled rope.

"Jules," he said.

She looked up at him but only nodded.

He ran his fingers through his windblown hair.
"Look," he said abruptly, "I've come to—"

"To apologize?" she said when he faltered. "You
have already apologized. It isn't necessary for you to
do so again."

"Perhaps 'explain' is the more apt word."

"Is Jane your mistress?"

He said sharply, "I told you I don't have a mistress."

"I don't know any other word for it. You make love to her, don't you? You care for her."

"Yes and yes, but it's not the same thing."

"Does she live in San Francisco?"

She was speaking so calmly, with far less enthusiasm than she used discussing the dolphins they'd seen yesterday.

"Yes," he said, "she does. She is a very nice person, Jules."

"Why didn't you marry her?"

"Because I don't love her, dammit."

"I see," she said. "A pity you didn't rescue her. Then perhaps you would have—married her, that is."

"I did rescue her, but not in the same way."

She arched an eyebrow, saying nothing.

He sat beside her on the coil of rope. The mailsail flapped overhead and the wind whipped through his hair. The smell of salt permeated everything. He wanted to tell Jules to get into the shade, for her fair complexion was turning a distinct red, but he didn't. "Her name is Jane Branigan, and she's a widow with two boys. Her husband died in one of the gold camps and I simply helped her to get started on her own. She owns a seamstress shop and is doing well now."

"Does she know about me?"

"She knows that I was taking you back to Maui."

Jules closed her eyes, fighting against the burdensome pain. He'd more than likely made love to Jane Branigan while she, Jules, was staying in his house.

"She will be upset?"

"I don't know. We are good friends, Jules."

She raised her chin. "Perhaps I shall have some good friends who are men."

"Perhaps you will," he said.

"Perhaps I shall even dream about them and call out their names and not yours."

"Jules," he said, "I am truly sorry for what happened. It is difficult for a man to be very close to a woman and not respond to her. It is also very common for a man to dream about sexual things so vividly that they almost become real. Women do it too."

"I don't."

"Perhaps someday you will understand what I mean. I any case, it won't happen again, I swear it to you."

Jules wished at that moment that he hadn't awakened, that she hadn't cried out. It would have been over with, and she felt now that she could deal with any fear better than this. She said, "When we are home, you will continue to see this Jane?"

He hadn't thought about it. It was the kind of thing that shouldn't happen. A man married, his wife a virgin, and he so damned randy— She was so beautiful, his Jules, so bright and vivid, and so very vulnerable. He would simply have to become a monk. He had no choice in the matter. A saint who was also a monk. He supposed it fit.

"No," he said. "I will see her, of course, as a friend, but I won't have sexual relations with her again. Marriage, for me, means fidelity."

"Fidelity seems to have no bearing on anything," Jules said, and quickly rose, beating down her skirts as the ocean breeze swirled around her.

"Just what is that supposed to mean?"

She ignored him, merely shrugged. "I must fetch my bonnet."

"Yes," he said, his voice showing his weariness. "Yes, you should. You're becoming quite red."

# Chapter 14

"Now, Molly, you're an old hand at this. Breathe slowly, light shallow breaths. That's it." Saint gently wiped Molly Tyson's sweating brow with a cool damp cloth.

"I was so scared you wouldn't be here," Molly said as a contraction eased. "I heard you'd gone off to those Hawaiian Islands."

"Yes, I did, but my timing is always exquisite, and so, it appears, is yours. That's it, Molly—no, don't tense up. Here, squeeze my hand. That's it."

"Damn, it hurts. How could I have forgotten how bad it hurts?"

"I know. Scream if you want to. I know I would." She wrung his hand, her back arched up, her body rigid, in a contraction. "All right, Molly, the pains are coming closer now. Let me see how far along this little fellow is."

He rose and walked to the basin of hot water that Molly's eldest daughter, Elizabeth, had provided. He washed his hands, then returned to the bed. He wished there were another woman to be with her, but there wasn't, and he wasn't about to let twelve-year-old Elizabeth in here. As for Ranger Tyson—the man was useless as a fish flopping on the beach when Molly had a baby. As Saint eased his hand into her, he was grateful that Molly wasn't embarrassed or a prude. Lord knew, he'd had to deliver babies when the women were suffering as much from embarrassment at his presence as from their labor pains. "Things are coming along just fine," he said after a moment. "Not much longer, Molly." He returned to the chair beside her bed and took her hand again.

"In a little while I'll give you some chloroform. No, don't tense up. Incidentally, did I tell you that Queen Victoria had chloroform used when she birthed her seventh child last year? If the Queen of England allows it, it's sure to spread."

"I don't know, Saint, Ranger isn't so certain, and Father O'Banyon says that the Bible preaches that women should have pain with childbirth and—"

"To hell with Ranger and Father O'Banyon," Saint said, interrupting her. "Neither of those blessed gentlemen has to do any of the hurting. I've heard that ridiculous argument about women and sorrow until I'm ready to kill. Now, you just think about this new little tyke. You're lucky you aren't an Indian wife, Molly. Did I tell you about the Indian tribe—I can't remember the name—but if a woman in labor wasn't birthing quickly enough, they tied her to a stake out in a field. Yes, indeed, it's true." He grinned at her incredulous look, knowing she was now distracted. "Then, Molly, a brave would ride full tilt toward her, veering away only at the last instant."

"Oh God, that's awful."

"Yes, but you can imagine that such a fright would do something. Evidently it worked, or I can't imagine that they'd continue scaring the woman out of her wits. That's it, Molly, pant."

He administered the chloroform about ten minutes later. The birth of Molly's third child, a boy, came quickly after that. The chloroform didn't stop all pain, but it certainly lessened the utter agony a woman felt in the last minutes of labor.

"You just get your breath, Molly," Saint said, grinning down at her, "and I'll take your beautiful baby out to Elizabeth."

"Tell Ranger, if he isn't too drunk, Saint. He wanted another boy."

Over an hour later, Saint mounted his horse, Spartan, and rode north back to the city. Ranger Tyson was partner in Hobson's Stables in San Francisco. Instead of money in payment for his services, Saint had bargained himself free stabling and feed for Spartan for six months.

Saint breathed in the crisp, fog-filled air. It was near to dawn, streaks of crimson had started to slash across the horizon. Why, he wondered, rubbing his jaw wearily, did women always tend to start their labor at night? He'd left Jules asleep, at least he hoped she'd been asleep.

They'd arrived in San Francisco three days before on a foggy, chill afternoon. Jules, used to the balmy weather of the islands, was shivering violently by the time they'd gotten to his house. Lydia Mullens, bless her, had wrapped Jules up and poured hot chocolate down her. He remembered clearly his feeling when he'd stepped into his surgery. It was as if he'd been living out of time. Everything was again as it had been, as it should be, except that he had a shivering wife upstairs. She hadn't been cold before, but then, she'd spent all her time in the house.

"Damn," he said aloud with no particular heat, rubbing his hand over Spartan's satiny black neck.

Spartan nickered.

Saint grinned, staring between his horse's ears. "Well, old boy," he said to his horse, "life isn't the way we left it, is it? The question is, what the hell is going to happen now?" Spartan didn't nicker again.

Saint was tired to his bones, but it was a comforting physical weariness that he appreciated. At least he wouldn't have to endure those damned draining erotic dreams for a while. As for Jane Branigan, she'd behaved with great understanding when he'd visited her the day before. It was almost as if she'd expected it, he realized, thinking back to her words.

"She isn't all that much a child then, I gather," she'd said, pouring him a cup of coffee in her small kitchen.

"She's nineteen," Saint had said. "Not a child, no." Had he given her the idea that Jules was still in puberty?

"And I don't suppose, you being as you are, that we'll be seeing much of you anymore."

"Of course you'll be seeing me. I'm fond of the boys, Jane. It's just that—"

"I know, Saint," she'd said quietly, "I know. Honor, fidelity, and all that."

"I suppose so," he said. He remembered that dream he'd had aboard ship, and clenched his fists at his sides.

His thoughts veered again to his young wife. Jules had withdrawn from him after that last damned fracas aboard the *Oregon*, and he supposed he couldn't blame her. Lord, how should she have reacted when he'd very nearly forced her and called out another woman's name? Later, when he'd found Lydia unpacking Jules's clothes in his bedroom, he hadn't known what to say. He didn't want to sleep in the spare room—the damned bed was too short for him.

And he couldn't sleep with her. It was simply too much.

To his surprise and silent relief, Jules had taken the matter out of his hands. He'd been called away to treat a broken hand—the result of a fistfight, of course—and when he returned that evening, he saw that she'd moved all her things down the hall to the spare bedroom.

He didn't know what to say to her. It was odd, he thought, frowning slightly. He'd never in his life been so damned obsessed with sex. Sex was just something that went along naturally with everything. But no longer.

There was Jules, smiling, chattering gaily, primarily with Lydia, until his—no, *their*— housekeeper had left for the night. Then she'd become quiet and withdrawn again.

He'd settled quickly back into his routine. As for Jules, he wasn't certain exactly what it was she did when he wasn't there.

"Spartan, what about Jameson Wilkes?" he said aloud to his horse. Spartan nickered, but at their entry into the city, and not in response to Saint's profound question. Already, men were up and about. He returned greetings and continued toward Hobson's Stables on Market Street.

"The bastard," he continued to his horse after a

moment, "is bound to discover that Jules is married to me. What the hell will he do?" *He won't believe she's a virgin anymore. She won't have any more value to him.* "True enough," he said in response to his silent observation.

He left Spartan at the stable in the capable hands of John Smith, an unlikely name for an unlikely gnomelike individual, and walked the short ten minutes to Clay Street and his house.

He suddenly thought of Jules pregnant with his child, of Jules giving birth, and he felt a knot of fear. He hadn't exaggerated his birth size to her. He'd been enormous, but his mother, bless her humorous soul, had been a large-boned woman, capable of carrying him and birthing him without too much danger to herself. Jules wasn't large-boned, and he realized he didn't know how wide her pelvis was. He closed his eyes a moment, tripped over a discarded piece of pipe in the street, and cursed. He let himself in quietly, and eased into his bed.

"You have some visitors, Jules," Lydia Mullens said to her young mistress the following afternoon.

Jules bounded to her feet, her book dropping to the floor beside her chair in their small parlor. "Visitors?"

"A bright voice said behind Lydia, "Please forgive us for just barging in like this, but we couldn't wait for an invitation from Saint. Married. Agatha and I had to meet the new Mrs. Morris."

A very lovely young woman with high-piled chestnut hair came gracefully into the parlor and stuck out her hand. "How do you do? I'm Chauncey Saxton, and this is Agatha Newton. Oh, how beautiful you are—not that any of us doubted it for a moment. Saint has the most stunning taste."

Jules took the gloved hand. "My name is Juliana, but Michael calls me Jules."

"Michael?" said Agatha Newton, arching an eyebrow. "Lordy, so the dear man does have a real name. I'm Agatha, my dear."

"Hello," Jules said, a bit dazed. Agatha Newton was an older woman, massive-bosomed, with a booming, very kind voice.

"I'll bring in some tea, ladies," Lydia said. "You just sit down, lovie, and entertain the ladies."

"Mrs. Mullens," Chauncey Saxton said, "must think she's died and gone to heaven. A lady, finally, in Saint's house."

"Please," Jules said, waving her hand, "please do sit down. Michael told me about the Saxtons and the Newtons, of course. He said you were all dear friends."

"Yes indeed." Chauncey said. "Jewels, huh? You mean like diamonds and emeralds?"

"No, actually, J-u-l-e-s," she said, spelling out her nickname. "Michael didn't want to distort my real name too much."

"Just wait until I tell Horace—my husband, you know—Saint's real name. Lord, the dear boy is in for a thorough razing."

Jules smiled, relaxing for the first time. "Actually, 'Michael' is only one of his real names," she said.

"Both ladies leaned forward in their chairs, questions on their faces.

Jules laughed. "No, I must have loyalty to my husband."

"Where is Saint, or Michael, by the way?" Chauncey asked.

"There was a problem of some kind. He said something about having to go see Maggie."

"Ah," said Chauncey. Her husband, Delaney, had told her about the new Mrs. Morris's experience. Now wasn't the time to bring up Maggie's profession, or the probable profession and sex of his patient.

Lydia Mullens came into the parlor at that moment, carrying a tarnished silver tray. 'I didn't have time to polish the thing," she said apologetically to Jules. "In fact, Saint's never used the tray before."

"Things are very different now," said Agatha with great complacency.

"Now, Jules," Chauncey said after sipping the delicious jasmine tea, "Agatha and I are here to invite you to a small dinner party at our house. Saint has already accepted, but we wanted to meet you and invite you in person. It's time you met some of San Francisco's fair populace."

Jules felt a bolt of excitement. "That would be wonderful. Oh dear, I must buy a new gown, and I must ask Michael if—" She broke off suddenly. "Michael said it was all right?"

Chauncey paused a moment, suppressing a frown. What had this poor girl been through? What indeed was her relationship to Saint? She said finally, in a very firm voice, "Of course Saint agreed. He's very proud of you and wants you to get out and about. Why don't you accompany me tomorrow, say, to Monsieur David's? He's an excellent modiste—but that's a woman, isn't it? Well, whatever he is, he's quite good and has a marvelous selection of lovely gowns, many of them from Paris."

"I should appreciate that," Jules said. But she was worried about money. Clothes were expensive. Perhaps Michael didn't wish to spend money on things like that.

Agatha and Chauncey stepped into Chauncey's open carriage some thirty minutes later after a thoroughly satisfactory visit. Chauncey said to their driver, Lucas, "Let's go to the Newtons' home now, please."

"She's very—" Agatha broke off, shaking her gray head.

"Vulnerable? Frightened? Wary?" Chauncey said.

"Yes, I suppose all of those things."

"I shouldn't care if she were a wretched individual," Chauncey said. "We must take care of her, for Saint's sake."

"Don't you mean Saint Michael?"

Jules felt excited, yet very tense. Michael didn't return home until late in the afternoon, and by that time she was nearly incoherent with anxiety.

"Hi, Jules," he said, striding into the parlor. "How was your day?" He shrugged out of his light coat and tossed it to a chair back. "What's wrong? Do you feel ill?" He'd looked at her only a moment, but he was so aware of her that he sensed almost instantly that something was different. He watched her glide her tongue over her bottom lip.

It affected him as strongly as if she'd thrown herself naked upon him. This has simply got to stop, he told himself. I will not be a slave to my damned body.

"Michael, do we have any money?"

He blinked at that. "Enough. Why?"

"Mrs. Saxton and Mrs. Newton were here and they invited us to a party and Chauncey said she'd take me to Monsieur David's for a new gown and I didn't know if you would mind or if you would want—"

He held up his hand.

"He sounds very expensive," she said, ignoring him in an effort to get it all out at once, "and Father, well, he never—"

Saint felt that damned elusive pain at the pathetic trailing off of her voice. She looked up at him, hopeful as a child, but certain that a treat was to be denied. But she wasn't a child, dammit.

He said, very gently, "Jules, of course you must have a new gown, several in fact. Do go with Chauncey. And don't worry about money, all right?"

"But—"

"No butts. Don't worry."

"But Lydia told me how, many times, you have to barter for things, and how people owe you favors, and I don't want to be a burden to you, at least more than I already am."

That made him angry. Damn Lydia anyway for her big mouth. "Enough, Jules. You are not a burden, and don't you ever speak like that again, do you understand me?"

She wilted at his anger. "I'm sorry. It's just that I *am* a burden. I don't do anything, nothing at all, and I'm—"

He couldn't bear it. He strode swiftly to her and gathered her against him. She was rigid for a moment, then leaned against him. He breathed in the sweet scent of her hair, felt her small bones beneath his fingers. He closed his eyes and held her. "I want you to be happy, Jules," he said finally, his warm breath against her temple. "There is enough money, I promise. I could have ten burdens like you and it wouldn't matter. In fact, I'd like it very much."

He could still feel her uncertainty, her resistance, and said, "I think you would look lovely in pink."

"Pink?" She squeaked, looked up into his grinning face. "With my hair?"

"That's better." Without thinking, he quickly kissed her pursed lips. She flushed. Get her mind off you attacking her again, you ass. "How about an emerald necklace, then? To match your sparkling eyes?"

She smiled at that, naturally this time. "You truly don't mind, Michael?"

"Idiot," he said, squeezing her. "Now, would you like to ride out to the ocean with me? There are a number of birds I would like to have you identify for me. Talk about ignorant—all I can recognize is a gull and sometimes a cormorant. They've got long, skinny necks, don't they?"

She gave him a brilliant smile and he thought: She's my wife, she belongs to me, and I want her to be happy. He remembered so vividly that single night when he'd brought her pleasure. Damn, he wished he could stop thinking about it, forget it. He released her, knowing that if he continued to hold her, she would feel how hard he was. He wouldn't frighten her. Never again.

He bundled her out of the house before he could be trapped by another patient. He rented a mare for her from Ranger Tyson, the proud new father of another Tyson, and made their way to the ocean, very slowly, for Jules wasn't all that used to riding.

"When you go with Chauncey tomorrow, be sure to buy yourself a riding habit, all right?"

Jules pulled her cloak more closely about her. "I've never had a riding habit," she said.

"In royal blue," Saint said. "Now, sweetheart, what is that damned bird over there on that sand dune?"

"That, I believe," said Jules, "is a snowy plover. And that one," she said, excitement and fun in her voice as she pointed to another bird, "just might be a wandering tattler."

He grinned over at her. "I know quite a few wandering tattlers, and they all speak English. You wouldn't be making that up, now, would you?"

"No, sir. I love the name, don't you? I've really never seen one in the flesh-and-feathers before, but it does look like a bird in one of my books."

"Books?" he asked. "I don't recall seeing any."

She was silent for a long moment, saying finally, "I have two of them. They're in Lahaina in my father's house. I had hidden them under my bed and forgot about them in all the excitement."

"Tomorrow," he said, "or the day after, we will replace them for you. Also any more books you want. My library is rather meager." He saw that she would argue with him, and added quickly, "If you see a small plant, maybe it's a yerba buena, which is, just in case you don't know something I do, the original name of San Francisco."

Jules nodded, knowing his intent, and said, "I will look. And perhaps we'll see a Bonaparte gull."

# Chapter 15

"Now, Dan Brewer is my husband Del's partner at the bank," Chauncey was saying to Jules. "We're trying to find him a wife, but the pickings here in San Francisco are still quite slim. Another gentleman you'll meet is Tony Dawson, part-owner of the *Alta California*, another one of those bachelors. You recall that young lady I introduced you to before lunch? The one who treated me like I had the plague, and looked right through you?"

At Jules's nod, Chauncey continued, "Well, my dear, that is our own lovely Penelope Stevenson. A more snobbish, gossiping, ill-humored female you'll never meet. Her mother looks like a ship under full sail and her father, Bunker—well, he's jovial enough, I guess. Ah, there's Lucas with the carriage. I must get home to feed Alexandra now. Would you like to come with me?"

But Jules had just spotted a small bookstore, and remembering Michael's promise, said, "No, I think I'll browse a bit more." She pointed to the bookstore across Kearny Street.

"That's Mr. Jointer's shop. You'll like him. Very well, Jules, I'll see you Thursday evening. It was such fun, and you'll look exquisite in all your new clothes."

Jules thanked her once again, her hand not too steady as she thought about the awful amount of money she'd spent at Monsieur David's.

"Give my love to Saint."

Jules watched Lucas, a pirate of a fellow if Jules had ever seen one, help Chauncey Saxton into the open carriage. He was, Chauncey had told her, married to her longtime maid, friend, and housekeeper, Mary. "And therein lies a story," she'd said, shaken her head, and laughed.

Jules waited on the sidewalk, waving her hand until the carriage was swallowed up in the incredible traffic along Kearny Street.

She gathered up her skirt and began to weave her way among drays, beer wagons, lumber wagons, and myriad types of men, who all stared at her to the point of embarrassment. She remembered Chauncey's words. "There are so many lonely men. We have more and more women and families moving here all the time, but still so many men have no one. For the most part, you needn't worry, they're quite respectful." And they seemed to be, she saw.

She'd just see what Mr. Jointer has in stock, Jules told herself. She wouldn't buy anything, not today. She had reached the shop when she chanced to look up. Her body went rigid. Jameson Wilkes was walking toward her, looking every inch the successful businessman in a dark gray suit. Jules grabbed for the doorknob, but it didn't turn. She looked blankly at the small sign in the window: CLOSED UNTIL 2:00. Oh God, what was she to do?

He saw her. She saw him stare a moment at her, not at first recognizing the girl dressed in the dark blue muslin gown, her wild hair held firmly in place beneath a small bonnet. She knew the moment he realized who she was. *He can't do anything to you. There are dozens of people about. He can't do a thing!*

Jules squared her shoulders and looked at him insolently, contemptuously.

"Well, well," Jameson Wilkes said, giving her an appraising look as he drew to a halt only a foot away from her. "As I live and breathe. If it isn't the new Mrs. Morris." He swept off his hat and gave her a mocking bow. "I must say, my dear, I think I prefer you in your natural state, sprawled on your quite lovely back on my bed. But then again, ladies' clothes tend to drive men's imaginations wild."

She felt a searing pain in her stomach and recognized it as fear. He couldn't do anything to her. "Well," she said, "if it isn't that dishonorable, filthy pig of a man. Mr. Wilkes, your clothes bespeak a civilized man. How strange and how disturbing that appearances are so deceiving."

He sucked in his breath, wanted nothing more than to fling her over his shoulder, perhaps beat her senseless, and remove her to his house. He wouldn't force opium down her, oh no. He wanted her to know everything, feel everything he would do to her. Instead, he said with a short, humorless laugh, "How very brave you are, my dear Juliana. And so very insulting."

"It is quite easy to be so with you, sir. Although *sir* denotes a gentleman, doesn't it? How silly of me to make such a mistake."

"You think you've won, don't you? You think

yourself safe from me, don't you? You and that damned husband of yours."

"Well, of course. I am married to an honest man, and—"

"And he saved you that night. Ah yes, I found that out, but not until you'd returned from Maui with him, married. He and his Sydney Ducks, the worthless scum—"

"Certainly like should recognize like! But in this case, Mr. Wilkes, their actions were noble and honorable. I should prefer any number of them to you."

Jameson Wilkes got a hold on himself, but it was difficult. The smart-mouthed little bitch. God, he wanted to touch her. "And how do you like marriage, my dear? As I recall so well, you didn't know at all what it was men did to women. Do you like your husband plowing your little belly with that huge rod of his? Ah yes, I know he's a large man— heard it from many of our more colorful ladies in this city. They're pining for his return to their beds."

Her face went white. She knew he was lying, knew Michael wouldn't touch another woman. "You are a pig and a bastard," she said, her voice almost pleasant. "If ever you speak to me again, my husband will kill you. Or I will."

"Such language from a missionary's daughter," he said, his eyes glittering down at her.

"One must be appropriate at all times," Jules said. "Unfortunately, I do not know appropriate language to fit your character. Perhaps the Sydney Ducks do."

With that parting shot, she turned on her heel and marched away from him, her head held high. She didn't pause even when she heard him laughing behind her.

"We will see, Juliana," he yelled after her. His muscles were knotted with tension. He forced himself to take slow, deep breaths. The thought of Saint Morris taking her, sating himself, made him want to spit, which he did. He suddenly remembered how very pale she'd become suddenly when he'd spoken so mockingly about her husband plowing her belly. Why? Or had she turned pale at the thought of Saint Morris fucking whores? He strode thoughtfully across the street. Could it be, his thinking continued, that the bloody doctor was soft, had listened to his young wife's pleas, and hadn't yet taken her? He was, after all, a doctor, a man reputed to be kind and gentle, despite his great size. It was something to think about, indeed it was. After all, he had married her out of obligation, nothing more. Wilkes's lips thinned. It was impossible to believe she was still a virgin, even though he wanted to, very much. No matter. He would still have her. He rubbed his hand over his stomach at the familiar burning pain.

He had all the time in the world, and he knew he must go very slowly and carefully now. Saint Morris was a highly respected man, with powerful friends. But Wilkes would find a way. He was smiling when he entered the El Dorado saloon some ten minutes later.

James Cora was leaning against the long mahogany bar, a thick cigar in his mouth. "Looks like you just won yourself a pot of money," he said.

"Not yet," Wilkes said, "but one never knows. How about a whiskey?"

"If I tell Michael," Jules said to her mirror, "he will go after Wilkes. But Michael is honorable, and

Wilkes isn't. He would hurt Saint, I know it. He would hire men and they would hurt him, maybe even kill him."

She turned slowly from the mirror, not knowing what to do.

"And it would be all my fault."

"Did you say something, Jules?"

Jules whirled around at the sound of Lydia's voice. "Oh no, I was just thinking out loud."

Lydia frowned at her young mistress. She didn't look well. She said, "Saint's downstairs taking care of a Chinese who got his arm cut open. If you want to talk to him, he'll be done in ten minutes, I'd say."

"Yes, thank you, Lydia."

Saint was gently suturing Ling Chou's thin forearm. "Did you know that old Bonaparte wanted to march on China after he'd gotten Russia?"

Ling Chou, who was gritting his teeth, not making a sound, because a man shouldn't complain, blinked at Saint. "No hear that," he said.

Saint hadn't either, but he said, "Yes, sir. Way back in 1811"—*was* it 1811? he didn't remember—"when he was making his plans, he said to his military advisers, 'After Moscow, it's on to Peking, to make myself emperor of the world.' " Saint set the last stitch. "Of course with men like you there, Ling Chou, the little man wouldn't have stood a chance. Sometimes I think it's a pity that he didn't go to China first— would have saved a lot of trouble for England and France. I'll just bet there wouldn't have been a Waterloo. You men would have taken care of him just fine.

"You think so, Saint?"

Saint deftly tied off the last stitch. "Sure do," he said, "and I'm all done here. Good job, if I say so myself. Now, I'm going to clean this off real good and bandage it. You come back in three days and I'll change it. Don't get it dirty or wet, you hear me?"

"I hear," said Ling Chou. When Saint finished the bandage, Ling Chou paid him, counting out the five dollars in meticulous fashion, bowed, and walked slowly to the door. "Bonaparte, huh," he said, turning. "Who is Bonaparte, Saint? And who is this Waterloo?"

Saint grinned. Hoisted on his own petard. "Just a fool general, Ling Chou, long dead, and a place that won't ever forget him."

"I see," said Ling Chou with great dignity.

"I've got to come up with some stories about real Chinese people," Saint said to himself as he straightened up his surgery. "That one was off the mark entirely."

He nearly knocked Lydia down as he walked out of his surgery. He caught her arm to steady her. "What's this? Sorry, Lydia, but where's the fire?"

"I just wanted to talk to you before you see Jules."

A thick brow went up. "What's wrong?"

"I don't know, but she's upset about something, and she wouldn't say anything to me. She looked pale as a clean sheet."

Saint was silent for many moments. Finally he said, "I'll take care of it, Lydia."

But there was another patient at the door, this time one of Jane's boys, Joe, and he had a black eye as impressive as any Saint had ever seen.

"Won't you come back with me, Saint? Mom won't get mad if you're there."

"Coward," Saint said, grinning at the boy. "You've

got a while to come up with a heart-wrenching tale to tell her. She'll still probably tan your butt, Joe."

Joe looked glum. "You never come by for dinner anymore. Mom doesn't say much, but I know she misses you. All of us miss you, Saint."

At the door, Jules paused a moment at the boy's words. Oh, damn, she thought, wanting to escape, but knowing she couldn't, not now..

"Hello," she said just before Michael and the boy saw her. "I'm Jules." She thrust out her hand to the boy, and he took hers automatically. "My, what a beautiful assortment of colors. Reminds me of the moorish idol—that's a fish, you know—yellow and black and some white thrown in for good measure. I do hope you gave a good account of yourself."

Saint saw Joe staring at Jules as if he couldn't believe his eyes. He cleared his throat. "Joe, this is Jules, my wife. I'll tell you what. Both Jules and I will come over to see your family sometime soon. All right?"

"You're awful pretty," Joe said. "I didn't know Saint got hisself married."

"Hisself is very married," Saint said, grinning at his wife. "Of course she's pretty, Joe. Now, you run along home and face your medicine. Sorry, but there's no way I can hide that eye."

"Not even a black patch?"

"Now, that's a fine idea," Saint said, appearing much struck. He thought of Jane's face when her son walked in looking like a miniature pirate. "Hold on a minute, Joe. I think I just might have one lying about."

"I've never seen hair that color before," Joe said as Saint disappeared into his surgery. "It's awful red."

"Yes indeed," Jules said. "I'd much rather have hair your color."

"Nah, I'm a boy. Girls don't want to look like boys."

Don't think it for a minute, she thought, staring at the thick thatch of dark blond hair. Did his mother have the same color hair? Was she as pretty as her son was handsome? Probably. Hadn't Chauncey Saxton said that Saint had exquisite taste in women?

"Here you are, Joe." Saint carefully fitted the black patch over Joe's eye. "What a swashbuckler you are. Do you like it, Jules?"

"Very impressive," she said. "You look a bit like Lucas, the man who works for the Saxtons. Your mother will be so taken aback, she just might forget to chew a strip off you."

"I doubt it," Joe said, staring at himself in the window. "Thanks, Saint. A pleasure, ma'am," he added awkwardly to Jules.

Saint chuckled after the boy had left. "Cute lad," he said, eyeing his wife from the corner of his eye.

"Yes, he is, very."

Saint clasped Jules's hands, and brought her close to him. "Now, what's wrong, Jules?"

"Wrong? Whatever do you mean, Michael?"

"You went out with Chauncey Saxton, and now you've got a long face. Didn't you find any gowns you liked?"

"Certainly, but they needed altering and will be delivered tomorrow."

"Did someone say something to you?" She was so guileless, he thought, her eyes gave everything away. He could see her trying to think of a quick lie, and shook her. "What happened?"

"I met Penelope Stevenson."

"Oh no, not that godawful twit. Did she say something unkind to you?"

Penelope hadn't, but Jules nodded.

"What?"

"She said I was a—an adventuress."

"Jules," Saint said very patiently, "I am still the master storyteller in this house. Don't try to outmaster the master. If you don't tell me the truth, I'll—well, I don't know what I'll do. Maybe beat you, or lock you up and not feed you for three days."

*I'd rather starve and be beaten than have Wilkes hurt you*, she thought in silent misery.

"I'm waiting."

She shook her head, stubborn as a mule. He looked at her, his frustration mounting. There came a knock at the front door. Another damned patient. He released her. "Don't you dare try to make up another story before I get back to you, Jules."

"Michael," she said after him, "would you like me to assist you? I've got a very steady stomach, you know."

"No, certainly not," he called back when he saw who his patient was. One-armed Johnny. The last thing he wanted was for Jules to meet one of the most dishonest little bastards in the city.

"Saint, I've got a friend who got coshed on the head. "He's bad, Saint, real bad."

"All right. I'll be right along. Jules, don't wait dinner for me. This might take a while."

"Good-bye," she said. "Take care."

With One-armed Johnny to protect him, he didn't have a thing to worry about, he thought, giving his wife a reassuring wave.

Her shoulders drooped when the front door closed behind Michael and that disreputable-looking man. She walked slowly into the parlor and stared about her. At least back home she could have spent hours wandering the beach and swimming. Identifying birds, feeding the fish, just enjoying the sun on her face—playing with Kanola's children. But Kanola was dead. So much had happened in such a short time. Too much, and yet not enough. Not only did she now have a husband, she was also a prisoner.

She decided to write to Thomas.

"Well, if it isn't Saint Michael and his lovely bride! Come on in, both of you."

Saint shook his head. "You've done me in," he said to Jules. "All right, Del, have your sport, but my wife is sworn to silence."

"You mean silence about your other name?" Jules asked, and he squeezed her until she squeaked.

Del Saxton grinned as he led Saint and Jules into the parlor. "Here's our guest of honor, Chauncey," he said. "Lord, you picked a beauty, Saint," he added.

"Don't show your true colors just yet," Chauncey said, buffeting her husband lightly on the shoulder. "Remember you're a very married man with a child to boot. Lovely, Jules, really lovely. The gown is perfect for you."

"I agree," Saint said. "The green nearly matches your eyes, sweetheart." He'd had the strong urge, when she'd come downstairs to join him, to rip that lovely gown off her. Her shoulders were bared, milky white above the lace. "Lovely" wasn't the word he would have chosen for her. Her waist looked minuscule and he guessed that Lydia had pulled her stays very tight. He disapproved of that, but Jules had looked at him with such eagerness, such hopefulness, that he said nothing about the damned corset. "Beautiful," he'd said.

"Truly? You're not just saying that?"

"No, I'm not just saying that."

She'd fluttered about for a moment, then said, "It cost so much money. And all the underthings, and the gloves—"

"Don't be an ass, Jules. I thought I told you to leave the money to me."

Even now, in the middle of the Saxtons' parlor, knowing he should have himself well under control, he wanted to lean down and kiss her white throat, and her shoulders, and the soft swell of her breasts. Lord, he wanted—

"You're looking lost to this world, Saint," Chauncey said. "Come, have a glass of sherry."

He pulled himself together and forced himself to look at his wife without lust in his eyes. "Would you like some sherry, Jules?"

"I've never tasted it before," Jules said, looking shyly up at her husband.

"Just a little, Chauncey. I don't want a drunken bride."

The Newtons arrived a few moments later. Horace eyed Jules with an experienced connoisseur's eye and nodded. "Well done, my boy. Aggie here told me what a pretty filly she was, but she didn't go far enough."

"Better, I suppose, than a nag."

Agatha hugged her briefly. "You'll have to get used to all the gentlemen looking at you like you're a new dessert, my dear. Just wait until Tony and Dan arrive."

Tony Dawson, a journalist to his fingertips, hadn't, unfortunately, heard about Jules's background, and asked her over the first course of terrapin soup how she'd managed to tie herself to a big oaf like Saint.

She sent him an agonized look, her tongue frozen in her mouth.

"Jules comes from one of the Hawaiian Islands, Tony," he said. "I knew her when she was a skinny little girl. I must admit, age has brought some astounding changes."

"Hawaiian Islands," Tony repeated, his interest aroused. "However did you get together again?"

Chauncey said brightly, "Haven't we some champagne, Del? Agatha, won't you try one of Lin's delicious rolls? Dan, some more peas?"

She couldn't sit here like a puppet and let everyone protect her. She said, "I came to San Francisco and we met again, Mr. Dawson."

"Call me Tony. Everybody does, you know."

"My father is a minister in Lahaina, Maui," she continued, seeing that he was as confused as ever, but too polite to probe. "Michael was a doctor there."

"Michael?" Tony said, clearly startled, and thankfully snagged that new tidbit.

Saint sighed. "That's right, Tony. But please, I feel more comfortable with 'Saint.'"

"It fits so well," Del said.

Dan Brewer, Del's partner, who had been told of Jules's experiences, said quite gently, "You're a fortunate lady, Mrs. Morris. We hope you will be happy here. The weather, I'm certain, isn't quite the paradise that Maui is, but nonetheless, I think you'll find it pleasant most of the time."

Saint would speak to Tony later. In fact, he thought, he'd been a fool not to realize that something like this was likely to happen. He caught Tony's eye and gave him a simple nod.

Saint found himself looking again and again at his wife's lovely throat and shoulders. He said suddenly to Jules, "You need a necklace—emeralds, I think. Del," he continued, "tell me where I can find some jewelry for my wife."

"Oh no," Jules said. "I don't want—that is, I don't need—"

"Certainly," said Del Saxton. "Emeralds, with perhaps some sapphires, would look lovely on you, Jules, particularly with that gown."

"I agree," Chauncey said. "Diamonds are too harsh, I think. Yes, emeralds and sapphires. Vibrant and warm."

"It's settled, then," Saint said, reaching under the table to squeeze his wife's hand. "I'll come see you in the morning, Del."

Agatha said to the table at large, "It's nearly September. Do you think Brent and Byrony will be home soon?"

"The Hammonds," Saint said to Jules. "Brent owns the Wild Star and he and his wife went to Mississippi to take care of the plantation he inherited."

"Brent is arrogant, lovely to look at, and dangerous," Agatha said. "I have a feeling, though, that Byrony has him well in hand by this time.

The talk continued for a while about the Hammonds, and Jules chewed on her baked chicken. She was very aware of her husband, the way he used his hands when he spoke, his long, blunt fingers, the deep, full laugh. She remembered Wilkes talking of Michael and all the women he'd slept with. It wasn't true, she knew it wasn't.

She should tell him about meeting Wilkes. No, she couldn't. She felt miserable.

After dinner, Chauncey brought Alexandra downstairs to be admired. Jules held the baby, such a beautiful child, and her eyes met Michael's.

"I love babies," she said.

Saint's guts twisted. He watched her as she spoke soft, meaningless words to the baby, watched her eyes light up with pleasure when Alex grabbed her finger and held it tightly. And he laughed when Jules blinked and said, "I think I'm wet, Chauncey."

"Oh dear, indeed you are. Come with me and we'll make sure your gown isn't ruined. Del, do take Alex up to Mary for repairs."

When Jules followed Chauncey from the room, Saint joined Tony Dawson. "I should have told you, but I forgot. It isn't for publication, of course."

When he finished, Tony Dawson whistled softly. "Jesus, Saint, I'm sorry. I didn't mean to embarrass her."

"You didn't know. Forget it, Tony."

"That poor girl. Thank God you were here, Saint, and put a stop to it."

Del joined them shortly thereafter, laughing a bit. "The joys of fatherhood," he said. "Ah, I see you've told Tony. There is something else, Saint. Wilkes is entrenching himself quite thoroughly here. One sees him everywhere. Are you worried that he will try to make things difficult for you and Jules?"

Saint said without thinking, "If he knew she was still a vir—" He broke off, appalled. "I think I'll have some of your whiskey, Del. Excuse me."

Tony started to say something to Del, but Del shook his head and said, "Shit."

# Chapter 16

Brent Hammond, Jules thought, was more than lovely, he was probably the most beautiful man she had ever seen. He was tall, lean, and his incredible dark blue eyes glistened with pleasure and pride as he listened to his wife, Byrony, telling the Saxtons and Michael about Wakeville.

"So you see," Byrony concluded, "not only are we shortly to be real parents, but we've also got an adopted family of about four hundred former slaves. And that's why it's taken us so long to come home."

"Wakeville, huh?" Del Saxton said. "It has quite a ring to it. Now, my dear Mr. Hammond, I have a feeling that we need to talk of finance, don't we?"

Brent Hammond grinned. "Well, maybe just a bit, Del. Many of our people are quite skilled, but I'm afraid I'll need a loan to buy seed and machinery and lumber. Buying all the land, and tents to keep everyone out of the rain, about wiped me out. The land is so rich—Lord, I think you could grind any kind of seed in the world into the earth with the heel of your boot, and you'd end up in three months with—"

"The largest tomatoes," Byrony continued, "the

largest cabbages, heavens, every kind of food. We'll be self-sufficient in no time at all—''

"And of course we'll need to build houses and stores and a church," Brent said.

"That's quite an act you two have," Saint said, grinning back and forth between Brent and Byrony Hammond.

Jules found herself simply staring at the couple. They'd actually transported former slaves to California and were planning their own town. "I wish I had some money to donate," she said to Byrony. "But I do have a lot of time and I could do something to help."

Byrony patted her hand. "I appreciate that, Jules, and you may be certain that I'll be knocking on your door." Suddenly Byrony blinked, then broke into surprised, bright laughter. "Brent, he moved."

Brent Hammond gave his wife a long, lazy look. "He always kicks up a dust when we're in company. What do you think, Saint? A spot of brandy to quiet him down?"

"Nope, let the little devil move about. You feeling all right, Byrony?"

She said. "Oh yes, not even one moment of nausea. But I'll tell you, Saint, Brent is driving me crazy. You would think that this is the first child ever to be conceived."

"By me, at least," Brent said. "I'm still not convinced that the rest of you could manage it half as well."

Jules's eyes flew to her husband's face. He was smiling at Byrony Hammond.

"Brent," Chauncey said to Jules, "believes the rest

of the male population adheres to the medieval paint-
ings showing conception through the ear."

"Really, love," Del said over the laughter, "a most
unladylike observation. Even Saint is blushing, and
Jules's face is as bright as her hair."

Unabashed, Saint said, "I was just trying to picture
in my mind how that would work."

"You're terrible," Jules said.

"I have to be somewhat outrageous to keep up
with Chauncey, sweetheart." He continued to Brent,
"Are you going to keep the Wild Star?"

"We haven't decided yet. I think Maggie's interested in buying me out, but it's such a steady stream
of income. I don't want us to starve in Wakeville."

"Byrony," Saint said, "before I forget, do come see
me tomorrow. I want to make certain everything is
all right."

It was the first time Jules realized that her husband, who was a man, was also a doctor, and that
he would actually see and touch other women. It was
disconcerting. She heard him continue to Brent, "It
occurred to me that besides medical help, your folk
are going to need clothing. Tell you what, Brent, I'll
contract with Jane to make clothes."

"I'll get Horace to pay half," Del said.

"Don't forget Bunker Stevenson, Sam Brannon,
and I'll bet we can even enlist James Cora to help."

"A ball," Chauncey said. "A subscription ball,
that's what we need."

"With costumes, love?" Del asked. "Like the first
time we met?"

"Yes, indeed, and we could invite all the upper
crust, charge them a fortune, and Wakeville would
shortly be on the map."

"We can even ensure that Lloyd Marks is there," Chauncey said. "He draws the maps," she added to Jules.

"I think," Del said, "that the Stevensons would be delighted to hold the ball at their home."

"Yes indeed," said Saint. "You can hint to Bunker that we'll all do our damnedest to find Penelope a husband out of the flock of men who will be there."

"If," Byrony said, "we could just convince Tony Dawson to be a bit mean, he'd make a perfect husband for Penelope."

Planning the Wakeville ball went on for several more hours. Lydia served all the food in the house and cleaned out Saint's liquor supply. When the last of the guests had left, Jules sighed and walked back into the parlor.

"What a scene of devastation," Saint said, following her.

Jules was silent a moment, then turned to her husband. "What will you do to Byrony?"

"Do? What do you mean?" He cocked his head to one side.

"I mean, she's pregnant."

"Ah," he said. He walked to his now thoroughly embarrassed wife and took her hands in his large ones. "Yes, she is pregnant. Yes, I will examine her, thoroughly. She is a patient. I want her to go through childbirth with as little difficulty as possible, and I want her child to be as healthy as possible. That's all there is to it."

"You don't—that is, you won't touch—"

He broke off her pitiful string of words. "Come sit down, Jules." She did as he bid her, and he moved to stand by the fireplace. "You may be certain that I am not a slave to lust, my dear. As I said, Byrony, outside my office, is a good friend. Once inside my office, she is a patient."

"But she's so beautiful."

"True. And it bothers you that I will be touching her intimately?"

"Yes."

"Well, that's straight talking. In medical school, a long time ago—"

"Not more than nine years."

"Well, then, nine years ago, when I was a young man rather than a doctor, I got terribly embarrassed, more than my female patients, I'd wager, when I had to examine them. Embarrassed, not lustful. I remember once that my hands were actually shaking, and my face was red as a beet. But, you see, Jules, that young girl I was examining was very ill. She hurt. She trusted me to make her feel better. The fact that I was a young man made no difference. Pain tends to dissolve embarrassment, you know."

Jules lowered her head. "You must think I'm an awful fool."

"Not at all—well, just a bit, sweetheart. As my wife, I realize it must be difficult for you to understand that a female patient has no more sexuality to me than a male patient. But it's true."

"But I'm not your wife," she said, and bit down hard on her lower lip.

"Of course you are," he said sharply, disregarding the true meaning of her words. "Now, do you believe me? Trust me?"

"Yes, of course. I'm sorry, Michael." She fingered the beautiful emerald necklace about her throat that he'd give her two weeks before. He was so generous to her, so kind, and here she was questioning him like a shrew. She wanted to apologize again, but instead she heard herself asking, "Have you gone to see Jane Branigan?"

"Yes," he said simply. "I would have taken you with me, but I wasn't certain that it would be wise."

Jules swallowed. "Did you kiss her?"

"No."

"Did you want to?"

Yes, he thought, he had wanted to. He hurt from need. And he didn't know what to do about it, because he'd promised Jules he'd be faithful. He lied easily: "No."

"And if Jane got sick, you wouldn't feel anything if you had to touch her?"

"Of course I'd feel things. I am fond of her, Jules. I would be frightened that she would be too ill for me to help her."

"And if I were ill?"

He smiled at that. "I'd be scared silly. So don't get sick, all right?"

Jules felt as though she'd dug a hole a good ten feet deep and leapt into it. She fought to get out. "Thomas should be here soon," she said.

"Yes, he should," Saint said, relieved at her change of topic. "I've been thinking about him, and probably the best thing for him would be to go back East, perhaps to New York, to medical school."

"But he's so young."

"Not at all. He's twenty-two, isn't he?"

She nodded.

He looked at her closely. She was beautiful, he was used to that, but she also looked a bit pale and too thin. He frowned. Surely she couldn't be lonely.

Chauncey and Agatha both spent a good deal of time with her—she was always visiting Chauncey to play with Alexandra. Now that Byrony and Brent were back, he was certain she would become friends with Byrony.

He hadn't touched her. He couldn't bear it. When he went to bed at night, he was careful to keep his door closed. It was another tangible barrier that kept her safe from him. Even when he woke up during the night, his breathing harsh, his sex aching, he'd see that closed door.

"Jules," he said suddenly, "are you happy?"

She didn't look up at him. *No, I feel like I'm living a half-life. I'm frightened that Wilkes will take me every time I leave the house. I'm afraid that Wilkes will send men after you.*

"Of course," she said, now raising her head. He flinched at the haunted look in her eyes, but he didn't know what to do. Dammit, he thought, so frustrated that he wanted to yell. How much longer could they continue living like this? He knew she had to have time, time to forget, to heal, but God, it hurt. He heard himself say in a tight, very controlled voice, "I want you to be happy."

"Yes," she said, "I know that you do."

The day before the subscription ball, Thomas Du-Pres arrived in San Francisco. He looked fit, handsome, and darkly tanned, and Jules didn't want to let him out of her sight. He limped only slightly. Saint, pleased to see his wife laughing, chattering like a magpie, her face flushed with pleasure, sat back drinking a brandy, watching the two of them. Unlike Jules, Thomas had brownish-red hair and his eyes were brown. But, he saw, they both had the same stubborn chin.

"I must say, Thomas," he said during a brief lull in the conversation, "you're looking much better than I thought you would. No more pain?"

"Narry a bit, Saint. Reverend Baldwin gave me a clean bill of health three weeks ago, said my leg was mending just fine, then told me to fatten up before I came here. He said you'd blame him, Saint, if I showed up on your doorstep looking like a scarecrow. Jules," he continued to his sister, "we've both been disowned by our father, but I didn't think you'd mind particularly."

"No, not really," Jules said. "Thomas, is Sarah happy now? Is she all right?"

"If you mean by that is she pregnant," he said in a hard voice, "the answer is no, she isn't. She is the most godawful female, and now with John Bleecher gone, she's become a total shrew."

Saint saw that Jules was upset, and said quickly, "Perhaps things will be better for her soon."

Thomas threw his brother-in-law an incredulous look, but said nothing.

It was nearly midnight when Jules yawned loudly. "Time for you to go to bed, sweetheart," Saint said, rising with her. "Thomas and I will be up shortly. You can take him about tomorrow." He gave her a chaste kiss on her cheek. Thomas squeezed her tightly, and held her a moment.

"I'm so glad you're here, Thomas," she said. "Oh, you'll be in the spare bedroom, second door on your right upstairs." With those words, she left the two men alone, one smiling, the other staring after her, the meaning of her words like a death knell in his mind. He'd been an idiot not to realize that Jules would have to move back into his bedroom. He closed his eyes a moment, picturing her in a pristine, virginal nightgown, curled up beside him.

"Saint, you want another brandy?"

He shook his head. Thomas kept him up another hour, discussing medicine. If Thomas noticed that his brother-in-law was distracted, he was polite enough to ignore it.

Please let her be asleep, Saint thought when he very quietly opened the bedroom door. She was, and sprawled in the middle of the bed on her stomach.

He sighed, undressed quickly, and slipped in beside her. Too late he realized he should have worn one of the nightshirts Jane had made for him. She didn't awaken, but before he fell asleep, she was curled up next to him, her arm thrown over his chest.

Saint, a light sleeper, awoke immediately at the sound of knocking on the front door. It was barely dawn. He rose instantly, and dressed more quickly than he ever had in his life. He took one last look at his sleeping wife, now curled up on her side, before he slipped out of the bedroom.

There were three scruffy-looking individuals, two of them supporting the third, whose face was pale and drawn with pain. "Limpin' Willie told us to bring you old Sam here, Doc. He got hisself knifed in the back."

Saint wondered if the knife wound, which turned out not to be too bad, was the result of a victim fight back. Sam pressed fifty dollars in his hand an hour later, and staggered out again, supported by his friends.

\* \* \*

Jules was so excited she could scarcely sit still in the swaying carriage. Thomas, his costume that of a pirate, complete with a black eye patch, looked dashing. Saint wore a black broadcloth suit and a long black velvet cloak and a black velvet mask.

"Your stays too tight, little sister?" Thomas asked her. "You're jumping about like one of those Mexican beans I read about."

"Oh no, I just can't wait to get there. Michael, we've never waltzed together before. And Chauncey told me that the orchestra is all the way from Sacramento. Do you really like my costume? Agatha said I look the perfect shepherdess, and if she had any sheep, she'd give—"

"Lord, do you run on, Jules."

Saint took her hand into his. He wanted to tell her that she looked so exquisite in the draped white gown that he wanted to touch and kiss every inch of her, dressed and undressed. "You are perfect," he said in a light voice. "I also like your hair piled up like that—very effective. Ignore your brother. Brothers aren't supposed to appreciate their sisters."

"Everyone will know who you are, Jules," Thomas said, eyeing her hair, "even with your mask on."

And everyone did, of course. But Jules didn't care. Even if she'd been completely disguised, Saint's size would have given her away.

They waltzed, chatted with friends, admired costumes, mentally counted the money the ball was bringing in, and drank champagne. Saint had watched Bunker Stevenson very closely when they'd arrived. If he had been one of the men at the Crooked House that night, he didn't show it. Even when Saint looked him straight in the face, his eyes hard and flat as he introduced Jules, Bunker showed no sign of recognition or embarrassment. He hadn't been at the Crooked House, Saint thought. As for the others, doubtless many were here and they would recognize Jules. But they would say nothing. They wouldn't dare. He grinned at Penelope, gowned in a dampened Regency-style dress, her very nice nose in the air, as was her wont.

But Penelope was excited, even though she had no trouble disguising the fact.

Until she met Thomas.

"Well," said Penelope, eyeing Thomas without much interest, "I understand that you are Mrs. Morris's brother. Good evening, Mrs. Morris."

Jules nodded.

"Yes," Thomas said pleasantly to Penelope, "quite a curse, wouldn't you agree? But then again, she's such a beautiful curse and she makes me laugh."

Penelope, who had been ready to dismiss the young man, retrenched, deciding to give him just a bit of her attention. "I have decided I will waltz with you, Mr. DuPres," she said, offering him a dazzling smile.

"Your decision is gratifying, Miss Stevenson, but I haven't asked you, ma'am. I do believe I'm thirsty. Jules, would you like a glass of champagne?"

It required all Jules's efforts to keep from bursting out laughing. Penelope, red-faced, stared at Thomas, hands clenched at her sides.

"That was marvelous, Thomas," Jules said as they moved away. "Chauncey Saxton told me Penelope was such a snobbish twit, and so full of herself."

"True, but she's very pretty," said Thomas. He

tossed down his champagne. "She just needs a man to teach her manners. Now, Jules, I want to do some dancing."

"With Penelope?"

"Not yet. Let the girl suffer for a while. By the time I ask her, she'll be appropriately chastised, and eager."

Jules, who had never seen this side of her brother, blinked up at him. "Pretty sure of yourself, aren't you?"

Penelope didn't appear to be suffering at all, Jules thought. As usual, there were many more gentlemen than ladies, so her hand was claimed for each dance. Still, her eyes sought out Thomas, and glittered.

Thomas ignored her.

"Finally," Brent Hammond said to Jules a while later. "A waltz, ma'am?"

"I'd like that," Jules said.

He was a graceful dancer, and Jules quickly found herself following his lead with ease. "Michael said your wife is in fine health, sir."

"Yes," he said, his eyes searching out Byrony in the throng, "but I told her not to tire herself. It appears, however, that she's doing just that."

"It's so exciting. I can't blame her. I've never been to a ball before."

Brent looked down at the lovely girl in his arms, really seeing her for the first time. "You're a natural dancer," he said, smiling at her. "Saint's a lucky man."

"That, sir, is what I keep telling him."

"I don't suppose I can convince you to tell me Saint's other names? 'Michael' is inoffensive enough. Come, tell me."

Jules laughed, shook her head, and inadvertently stepped on his toes.

"How about where and how he got the nickname Saint?"

"Your wife is waving at you, sir," she said as the music came to a halt.

Brent watched her glide into another dance with Dan Brewer. He made his way through the crowd toward his wife. To his surprise, he saw Penelope Stevenson standing with Jules's brother, Thomas. She looked absolutely furious, and Thomas, interestingly enough, was looking ready to yawn with apparent boredom.

Jules released her husband, but only for five minutes, she told him, to speak to several men. The orchestra wasn't playing, and she looked about for Chauncey or Agatha. They must have gone upstairs to the ladies' receiving room. She walked to the French windows along the side of the ballroom. It was a beautiful, clear fall evening. She slipped out onto the balcony and leaned her elbows on the railing. It was nice to be alone for a bit. But only for five minutes. She wanted to dance with Michael again. She wished desperately that she'd managed to stay awake the previous night, but she hadn't. She didn't even know if he had come to bed, for when she'd awakened in the morning, he'd been gone. She sighed, and for once didn't admire the beautiful azaleas on the balcony. Something had to be done, but she simply didn't know—

"Ah," a soft voice came from behind her, "the little lamb left alone to the wolf."

Jules whirled about to faced a man wearing a light gray cloak and a gray mask.

"Who are you, sir?"

"I've been watching you all evening, my dear. You seem very sure of yourself, surrounded by all those people. I had almost despaired of finding you alone. It would appear that you've made quite a few friends."

"What," Jules said, suspicious now, "are you talking about?"

"I must also tell you that you look more beautiful than I had imagined. Is it possible, my dear, that you occasionally miss me, think of me?"

"Your jest, sir, is wearing a bit thin. Have you perhaps visited the punch bowl too many times?"

"Really, Juliana, don't you recognize me?"

She did, very suddenly, and felt herself go cold. He didn't have to remove his mask. "Get away from me."

He lunged for her, grabbed her arm, and pulled her against him, away from the open windows. "No," she yelled. His hand slapped down over her mouth.

She struggled wildly, bit his hand.

He sucked in his breath, and for an instant his hand eased and she jerked her head back and screamed.

"You damned little bitch." In the next moment she felt searing pain as his fist crashed into her jaw. Flashes of stark white exploded before her eyes, and then there was nothing.

# Chapter 17

Thomas DuPres, quite satisfied with his latest skirmish with Penelope Stevenson, strolled through the chattering groups of people toward the long bank of French windows. He'd seen Jules going in that direction a few minutes before, and wanted to talk to her. Lord, it was an opulent house, and like Jules, he'd cataloged and duly appreciated all the flowers arranged in huge pots throughout the ballroom. He saw Penelope waving imperiously to him, grinned to himself, and quickly eased out onto the balcony. It was no wonder the girl was spoiled rotten; he just might be also had he been raised as she had been, doubtless given anything she wanted. For the moment, he would let her suffer.

He looked about for Jules but didn't at first see her. He called her name softly—just in case, he told himself, there were any lovers out here.

He suddenly heard a man curse viciously. He whipped about and searched the shadows at the far end of the balcony. He saw his sister struggling with a man wearing a long cloak and mask. The man struck Jules and she crumpled where she stood.

He yelled as he sprinted forward, "You bastard, what the hell are you doing?"

Jameson Wilkes saw the young man running full tilt toward him. He gave Jules one final look, so furious he wanted to howl. He started to draw out his derringer, but decided it was too risky. He'd heard her strike her head when she'd fallen, and for an instant he felt tearing fear that she was terribly hurt or even dead. "Dammit, no." He wasn't certain if it was a cry to her or a cry to some unhearing god. He wrapped his cloak tightly about him and vaulted gracefully over the balcony railing.

"Jules." Thomas was only vaguely aware that the man had disappeared. He knelt beside his sister, saw that she was unconscious, and quickly lifted her into his arms. He drew to an abrupt halt just outside the French doors. No reason to cause a riot, he thought. He eased her down and slipped inside. He found Saint speaking to Del Saxton.

"Come quickly," he said. "It's Jules. She's been hurt."

Saint felt fear ripple through him. He said nothing, merely hurried after Thomas. When he saw her, pale and small, lying unconscious against one of the long windows, he forced himself to be calm. *I'd be scared silly*, he remembered telling her when she'd asked him what he'd feel if she were ill. And he was.

He felt for her pulse. Strong and steady. He heard Thomas saying to Del, "I think he struck her jaw. When he saw me, he jumped over the railing."

Saint lightly ran his fingers over her jaw, relieved, for it wasn't broken. But why was she still unconscious? He turned on his heel to look up at Thomas. "Did she fall?"

"I think so."

So she'd hit her head on the stones. He lifted her

just a bit and quickly found a growing lump behind here left ear. "Damn," he said.

"Wilkes?" Del Saxton said.

"I don't know," Thomas said. "Of course, I've never seen Wilkes before, and this man was wearing a mask—a gray mask and a cloak. Is she all right, Saint?"

Saint closed his eyes a moment, getting hold of himself. "I'm getting her home right now," he said. "Thomas, stay here, and you too, Del. No reason to upset the guests."

"I'll have Lucas bring around our carriage," Del said. "It will be quickest."

She was still unconscious when Saint lifted her into the carriage some five minutes later. "She'll be all right," he said to Thomas and Del. God, he hoped he was right.

"Are you certain—?" Thomas said.

"Stay here. I'm the doctor, remember?"

Lucas whipped up the horses. Saint pulled Jules onto his lap and pressed her head against his chest. The short ride was the longest in his memory.

"Thanks, Luc," he said over his shoulder. "Don't worry."

Saint carried her upstairs and eased her down onto the bed. Our bed now, he thought. He undressed her as gently as he could. "Damned women's corsets," he muttered, pulling the stays loose. He left her in her shift and methodically examined her.

Enough was enough, he decided a few minutes later. He slapped her face, saying as he did so, "Come on, sweetheart, wake up now. I'm scared silly, and you don't want your husband a dithering idiot. Wake up, Jules."

Jules heard a man's voice, but it made her head hurt, a dull, pounding pain. "No," she said, trying to pull away. "No."

"Come on, love."

The light was dim, and he was shadowy, just as the light had been on the balcony at the Stevensons' ball, and she thought he was Jameson Wilkes. "No—"

*Oh God*, Saint thought, *not again*. From her fear, he was quite certain that it had been Wilkes.

"It's me, Michael. Michael," he repeated, not touching her. He waited patiently for her to quiet and regain her wits.

"Michael?" Jules managed to focus on him. "Wilkes, he tried to—"

"I know. But he didn't. Thomas saved you, sweetheart. You're home with me now. And safe."

Of course, he'd said that before. And he'd lied.

"My head," she whispered. "It hurts really bad."

"When you fell, you hit your head. You've probably got a concussion, but you'll be all right. How does your jaw feel?"

"I don't know, all I can feel is my head." She shivered and Saint pulled a blanket to her chin.

"I can't give you any laudanum, at least not yet." He held up three fingers. "How many, Jules?"

"Three."

"And now?"

"Six."

"Good."

"The ball. I wanted to waltz with you again."

"We will again, soon, I promise. God, you scared me silly." He took her limp hand in his and brought it to his mouth. He kissed her fingers.

"He's crazy," Jules said, watching her husband holding and kissing her hand through a haze of pain.

"You're certain it was Wilkes?"

"Oh yes. He mocked me, just like the other—" She broke off, appalled.

Saint was silent for many moments, studying her pale face. "What other time?"

She wanted to lie, but knew he wouldn't brook a lie. "A while ago, that first day I was with Chauncey."

"Would you mind telling me why you didn't inform me of this?"

He sounded so controlled, so very calm, that she said honestly, "I was afraid that he would hurt you."

He went rigid.

Jules didn't notice. She was trying desperately to control the pain. "I knew he couldn't hurt me—there were so many men about on the street. But I thought if I told you, you would go after him. You're so honorable, but he's a snake. I couldn't bear it if he hurt you."

"Jules, look at me."

"Yes," she said.

"Do I look like a man who could be hurt?"

"He would hire people. He would—"

"I think you'd best be quiet now. God in heaven, I don't believe this."

Saint rose, ripped off his black cloak, and hurled it to the floor. He was so furious he couldn't think straight. He forced himself to take slow, deep breaths. "Jules," he said, very calmly now, "I am your husband. You are my responsibility. If you don't trust me to take care of you, you reduce me to nothing. Do you understand me?"

"No," she said, then cried out.

"Oh damn," he said, angry with himself now for upsetting her. Some doctor he was. He sat down beside her and gently probed the lump behind her ear.

"I don't want to cry," she said, but her head felt like a melon being battered against the ground. Tears seeped from the corners of her tightly closed eyes. Saint wanted to find Wilkes and kill him. But he couldn't leave her. He cursed again, pulled off his boots, and eased into bed beside her. "Come here against me," he said. "In a little while I can give you something for the pain. But not yet, sweetheart. I'm sorry, but I can't take the chance." The chance she'd never wake up.

He could feel the waves of pain each time she tensed. Very quietly, his voice soothing and low, he started to speak. "Did I ever tell you about the Siamese twins I saw born in Boston? They were male, and attached from their waists to their knees." No, no, he thought frantically. That story had a ghastly ending. "They lived happily ever after. But there was this man, way back in the fifth century. Actually, he was the Emperor Justinian, and his wife was the Empress Theodora. Interestingly enough, the empress had been a prostitute before she married Justinian and won a crown. In any case, the both of them wanted to eradicate prostitution. Her way didn't work, of course, but it was quite an interesting approach." Saint paused a moment, and Jules said in a sleepy voice, "Yes? Go on, Michael. What did she do"

He smiled. "Well, what she did was to build a beautiful palace-prison, and she had five hundred prostitutes taken there. They were treated very well. In fact, they could have whatever they wanted, with the exception of one thing: no men allowed. It is said that most of the women committed suicide in their despair, and the remainder soon died of boredom and vexation."

He heard her giggle. She said in a blurred voice, "Vexation? I love you, Michael, but I think you made that up."

He swallowed, unable to think of anything to say. She didn't know, didn't realize, what she'd said. "I didn't make it up," he said.

She didn't answer. She was asleep.

"It was vexation. I know the feeling well," he said, and kissed her on the cheek.

He woke her during the night, forced her to tell him who she was, who he was, and how many fingers he was holding up. At last, early the next morning, he gave her some laudanum in a glass of water, and watched her fall into a deep, healing sleep.

Thomas was waiting for him downstairs, still dressed as a pirate, pacing furiously. He was so angry he couldn't speak, and Saint, after reassuring him for the tenth time, sent him to bed.

Lydia was furious and appalled, and Saint winced at the sound of her crashing the pots and pans about in the kitchen, each of them probably a substitute for Wilkes's head.

Then Del Saxton arrived, his face grave and worried. He said without preamble, "How is she?"

"She will be fine. I gave her some laudanum just a while ago and she's sleeping soundly now."

"I've put a search out for Wilkes. Apparently the man's not a complete fool. It appears he's left the city. I also ran into Limpin' Willie early this morning. He's ready to spit nails and will get the Sydney Ducks out scouring for him."

"Thank you. I had intended to—well, it's done. Thomas is still asleep." He stopped and drank some strong black coffee, offering some to Del.

After several moments, Saint said more to himself than to Del Saxton, "Wilkes approached her before, but she didn't tell me." He gave a bitter laugh. "She was afraid he would hurt me. *Me.* The little fool was worried about protecting me."

Del studied his friend for many moments. "You can thank me for keeping Brent away, at least for a while. He's of course rather upset with you because you didn't tell him about Wilkes."

"What the hell was there to tell, for God's sake?"

"Calm down. Don't you want your friends to be concerned? No, don't answer that. I've been thinking," Del continued after a moment.

"And you're going to dose me with your damned advice whether I want it or not."

"Yes, I suppose I am. Listen, Saint, I assume that Jules is still a virgin. If you'll remember, you let that fact slip."

Saint winced.

"It seems to me," Del said, "that there are two ways to protect her. The first is to find Wilkes and kill him. That would be difficult, because he's gone to ground. The second—and certainly more pleasurable—way would be to consummate your damned marriage and get her pregnant."

"Pregnancy doesn't necessarily follow sex, Del," Saint said.

"You've got to try, Saint. No matter this weird obsession Wilkes has for her, I can't envision him wanting to kidnap a pregnant woman."

"No," Saint said very softly, utterly serious now.

"You can't continue playing the benign father to your wife. Chauncey tells me that Jules is crazy in love with you. What the hell is going on, Saint?"

Saint rose and walked to the fireplace. He looked down into the empty grate. Crazy in love with him? What utter nonsense. A young girl's infatuation mixed with a strong dose of gratitude—fleeting, ephemeral as the San Francisco fog. He said without turning, "Jules has been hurt very badly. Whatever feelings she thinks she has for me, if I tried to make love to her, she would be terrified. I had hoped she would forget, and perhaps—" He shrugged. "Last night, when she regained consciousness, she thought I was Wilkes. If you had seen her face, you wouldn't suggest such a thing. I will not hurt her. I will not force myself on her."

Jules looked blankly at the partially open parlor door. She felt dizzy. Slowly she tied her dressing gown more closely about her. It was odd, but she didn't remember thinking Michael was Jameson Wilkes. Had she truly looked terrified? The men's words wove in and out of her mind, fighting with the laudanum. She heard Michael's low, intense voice. "No, no more, Del. I know you mean well, but—"

"You're my friend, dammit. You of all men leading a celibate life. How much longer do you think you can stay sane living like this? And face it, Saint, you can't keep Jules a prisoner, and you simply can't be with her all the time."

"I'll think of something," Saint said.

She heard Del Saxton rise from his chair and move toward the door. She pulled herself upright, and wobbled back up the stairs. Her head began to pound again and she curled up under the covers, closing her eyes tightly.

When she woke, Thomas was sitting beside her.

"Michael?" she whispered.

"Sorry, love, he's with a patient. How do you feel?"

"I had this strange dream," she said, then closed her mouth. It hadn't been a dream. Her mouth felt full of dry wool. "Can I have some water, Thomas?"

"Certainly, love. A moment, there isn't any up here. I'll be right back."

Of course there wasn't any water there. That's why she'd dragged herself downstairs earlier. And heard them talking, Michael and Del Saxton.

After she'd drunk her fill, Thomas said, "You look like one of those skinny little lizardfish, all pale and limp."

"I've always believed lizardfish were perfect."

"Well, you're not. Saint filled in all the things I didn't know about Wilkes. There have been a good dozen people in and out of here all morning. I think half the male population of San Francisco is looking for that bloody bastard."

She looked at him. "Do you think he's really gone for good?"

"I don't know," Thomas said. He stroked her hair back from her forehead. "How he could want you— a tangled little raggamuffin—well, it's beyond me."

*He wouldn't want me if I were pregnant.*

She said, "Tell me about the ball. Did you have a good time?"

"After what happened to you, very little. Del and I kept it under wraps, so not many people know."

"I thought you said people were trooping in and out all morning."

"I mean friends, not acquaintances."

"Michael has a lot of friends," Jules said.

"And so do you, love."

"Thomas?"

"Yes?"

"Have you ever made love to a girl?"

"Good grief, Jules. Ah, Saint, you're just in time to save me from embarrassing questions."

"What embarrassing questions?" he asked, smiling from Thomas to his wife.

"I asked him if he'd ever made love before," Jules said, "to a girl."

"Shall I leave, Thomas, so you can say what you will to this inquisitive wife of mine?"

"No," Thomas said. "Actually, Saint, I think that knock on her head must have addled her wits."

"I think that happened a long time ago," Saint said, and sat down on the bed beside her. "How is my impertinent patient?" Why, he wondered, had she asked such a question of her brother? He decided that he really didn't want to know.

Jules managed a shy smile. "I'm all right," she said. "Truly, even though I do look like a ragga-muffin."

"That sounds suspiciously like a brotherly de-scription."

"Sure was," Thomas said. "Now, Jules, you behave

yourself and do as Saint tells you. I'll leave you to her, Saint. I'm off to see Bunker Stevenson. Of all things, the old buzzard wants to talk to me about my future."

"Bunker? What future? He's not a doctor."

"Lord only knows," Thomas said, grinning. "If I'm not here for dinner, don't miss me, all right?" He left the room, whistling, his walk cocky.

"That young man," Saint said, "is going places."

"I think this must have something to do with Penelope. Thomas was marvelously nasty to her last night."

"Intrigued the little twit, huh?"

"Thomas did say that she needed a man to teach her manners. It seems he's decided he's just the man to do it."

Saint laughed. "What a pair you two are. Now, Jules, let's see how that lump is doing."

She expected an explosion of pain, but there was only a dull throbbing at his touch. He was very close to her, his eyes intent—his doctor's look, she thought. She felt his warm breath on her cheek. "I'm sorry," she said.

"So you should be," he said, still intent on his examination. "But we won't speak of it again for a while. Not until you're back in top form."

"I'm going to be twenty next month," she said.

"Are you, now? I'd forgotten."

"I'm not fourteen anymore, Michael."

His hand stilled for a moment. He said slowly, "No, you're not. You want to know something else, sweetheart? You've got a very colorful jaw."

She didn't want to talk abut her wretched head or jaw, she wanted to talk about being celibate, but she was so drowsy. "When I'm in top form," she said, her voice slurred, "then I'll do—"

Saint pulled back and looked down at his sleeping wife. "What will you do?" he asked. He gently smoothed the curls from her face. Twenty years old. His mind leapt forward without pause. So many women had children by the time they were twenty. He frowned to himself even as his hand slid beneath the cover and rested lightly on her belly. He stretched his fingers, measuring the distance between her pelvic bones. He whipped his hand back, but he couldn't stop the thought. She wasn't as small as he'd believed she'd be. He left the bedroom, not looking back.

"It makes me so bloody angry I want to yell."

Jules smiled at Chauncey. She was sitting up in bed, feeling quite marvelous, really, despite Michael's insistence that she remain off her feet for another day. "Michael says Wilkes has disappeared," she said.

"It's true, if all of Saint's criminal friends say so," Chauncey said. "Thank God Thomas was there."

"Indeed," Jules said. She added, tired of speaking of Wilkes, "I understand your dear friend Penelope is undergoing a transformation."

Chauncey was distracted, as Jules had hoped she would be. "Lord, how I would love being a fly on the wall in the same room with your brother and dear Penelope. As to any transformation, I should live so long. What do you think?"

"Oddly enough, Thomas likes her. He says beneath all those layers of shrewishness beats only half a shrewish heart."

"I wish him luck. Oh, incidentally, the most ironic thing has happened. I suppose it's divine justice and all that. Did Saint tell you about the Butlers up and leaving San Francisco just yesterday?"

"Who are the Butlers?" Jules asked.

"Oh dear, I should have known Saint wouldn't say a thing about it."

"The cat's escaped, Chauncey, you might as well tell me."

"It's a rather long story."

Jules groaned. "Not another storyteller."

"All right, it's a very short story. You see, Ira Butler married Byrony DeWitt, who is now Byrony Hammond. He married her because, in truth, his half-sister, Irene, was pregnant with his child."

Jules could only stare at her.

"My sentiments exactly," Chauncey said. "In any case, Byrony agreed to pretend that she was pregnant and that Irene's child was hers. She didn't know then that the child was the result of an incestuous union. She found that out later. Del had the marriage annulled, and Byrony married Brent. It always bothered me that the Butlers got away with their deception, for Byrony was hurt very badly. Just a couple of days ago, if what I've heard is right, a new maid walked in on them, in bed. Their house of cards collapsed. I understand they've left to return to Baltimore."

"That is amazing. Poor Byrony, I had no idea—"

"Not many people do. Just our little group, I suppose you'd say. Now, my dear, I think I'll leave you alone. Saint told me not to tire you."

"Oh, Chauncey. How much money did the ball make for the Hammonds and Wakeville?"

"Nearly fifteen thousand dollars," Chauncey said. "Both Brent and Byrony are ecstatic, needless to say. Now, you rest, and I'll see you tomorrow."

Jules wondered before she fell asleep why people's lives were never so simple as one would imagine. Her first thought upon waking several hours later was: Tonight I'm going to seduce my husband. I'll prove to him that his nobility is no longer necessary. The next time I see Jameson Wilkes, if there is a next time, I'll stick my pregnant stomach out at him.

# *Chapter 18*

"Jesus, I'm tired."

Jules looked at her husband and smiled. *You won't be soon.* She said, "I'm sorry. A difficult patient?"

"Make that plural. How do you feel, sweetheart?"

"Just fine, top form and all that, and you aren't going to sleep downstairs tonight, are you?"

Saint swallowed, automatically drawing back from her. "I don't want to disturb your sleep," he said.

"But what if I wake up during the night, ill? Do you want me to crash a chair against the floor?"

Saint sighed. "I suppose I could sleep in the guest-room with Thomas."

"In that case, I could simply shout, I suppose," Jules said calmly, watching him closely. "Of course, that might hurt my head dreadfully."

Saint floundered about for reasons, any reason in fact, to stay away from her. Finding none for the moment, he said, eyeing the tub, "You had a bath."

"Yes, and Lydia washed my hair for me."

"I see," he said, beginning to inch toward the door.

Jules played her ace. "Please don't leave me alone, Michael. It's nightmares—and I'm frightened."

She thought she heard him curse very softly, and kept firm control over the smile that threatened to break free. "Very well," he said, and his voice sounded like a condemned man's.

He turned off all the lights and undressed in the dark. Jules didn't mind. She rather hoped he wouldn't wear one of those ridiculous nightshirts. But he did.

"Good night, Jules," he said as he slipped in beside her, hugging the far side of the bed.

"Good night," she said, and prepared to wait. Not too long, just enough time for him to relax.

"Michael?"

"Yes?"

He sounded too alert. Well, there was no help for it. "What do you think of celibacy?"

She heard him suck in his breath. "Go to sleep, Jules," he said, his voice harsh.

"Do you think it's more difficult for a man to be celibate than a woman?"

She was going to drive him crazy. He inched closer to the far side of the bed. She was so bloody innocent.

"I don't like being celibate."

"All right, Jules," he said, turning toward her, "what the devil is going on?"

"Aren't we married?"

"I repeat, what the devil is going on?"

She sought the word Del Saxton has used. "I think we should consummate our marriage."

"No."

"Why not?"

"Jules, please, no. I am not such a monster, and you are hurt, and I won't add to it, do you hear me?"

He continued, his voice jerky, about how he didn't want her to be afraid of him. She said nothing, merely waited until he had gotten it all out of his system.

When at last he fell silent, she smiled into the darkness and squirmed over to him. She took his face between her hands and kissed him. She missed at first because it was so dark, but then she felt his mouth beneath hers. "No," he said, trying to shove her away.

She clung like a leech. She wanted to tell him that she loved him, but knew that he didn't want to hear that. It would make him feel guilty because he didn't love her. She said in the most seductive voice she could manage, "I want you, Michael. You are my husband. I am a woman, not a child. Please."

Saint felt her words crash through him. "Jules," he began, "I will not hurt you."

"Why would you hurt me?"

He'd turned to face her, his strong hands clasping her shoulders. "Any man would hurt you—if not physically, then—"

"You think my weak woman's mind would snap or something?"

She managed to slip one hand free, and with unerring instinct let her fingers rove down his belly. He gasped, now trying to escape her. "Stop it."

Her fingers found him, hard through the nightshirt. "No," she said, "I won't stop. You are my husband, and you owe me certain things. You keep telling me that I'm your responsibility. Well, be responsible."

"Get your hand off me, Jules, or I won't be responsible for—"

She laughed.

"You damned little—" He had no time to search out the right word. She pressed herself against him, her hand between them, holding him real firm.

"I am not afraid, Michael. Not of you, in any case. Please, be my husband."

"Oh damn," he said, still not moving. Suddenly she released him and moved away. He was aware of relief and dreadful disappointment.

He reached out his hand, not really meaning to, thinking that perhaps she was upset and needed reassurance. His hand met bare flesh. Her shoulder. She'd pulled off her nightgown. Very slowly he rose from the bed. He lit one lamp, turning to face her.

A sheet was pulled just barely over her breasts. She looked very beautiful, her eyes luminous, her hair tousled about her face, her shoulders white—he didn't think he could breathe.

She was smiling at him.

"You look silly in that nightshirt," she said.

"Yes," he said finally, "I suppose I do." He pulled it off, standing very quietly at the end of the bed, naked. He was aware that she was studying him, and his sex, the focus of her attention, thrust outward.

"Have you seen enough yet?"

He watched her lick her lower lip. "Oh no," she said, holding out her hand to him. "Please, Michael, don't be afraid of me."

"I am afraid *for* you, Jules. Look at me, for God's sake."

"I have, and you're beautiful. You were perhaps more romantically beautiful that night on the beach when you came out of the water—"

"I am not beautiful. I am a big, hairy man, and

you know very well that if I touched you, you would hate me."

"And be terrified of you?"

"Yes, damn you."

"Aren't you getting cold standing there with absolutely no clothes on?"

She was goading him, and doing it very well. She let the cover slip, on purpose of course, and obligingly he looked at her breasts.

"Jules," he said, reaching for his dressing gown, "you don't know what you're asking. I would touch you and caress you, and I would come inside your body. It would bring back all the pain and fear you felt with Wilkes."

She felt a surge of warmth at the very graphic image his words created in her. Wilkes and her experiences with him were a million miles away. As were those with John Bleecher.

"Please, Michael." She wanted to touch him, wanted to feel his body covering her. She wanted him to kiss her and tell her how much he wanted her, how much he loved— Her thoughts broke off at that. He didn't love her, at least not yet he didn't. She would make him love her.

"Please," she said again. "Come to bed, Michael."

"You're my wife," he said very quietly to himself. He chucked aside the dressing gown and climbed into bed beside her.

He lay quietly, still uncertain. Then she was pressed against him, her breasts against his chest. He swallowed, and without further thought, he brought her to him. "Oh God," he whispered, put her onto her back. He lowered his head and lightly touched his mouth to hers. Lust shot through him; he trembled with the force of it. He had to go slowly, very slowly. If he frightened her, if he hurt her, he would never forgive himself. He called on every bit of experience he had. He remembered his wedding night with Kathleen, her pain when he entered her that first time. It was a pity that women couldn't be like men in that regard. No maidenheads, no pain. He drew a deep breath. Very slowly. He merely kissed her, giving her time to decide, to pull away from him, or to react to him. He felt her hand stroking down his back.

"Jules," he said into her mouth. "Let me love you, it's better that way."

"Why? I want to touch you."

"Because I won't be able to control myself," he said. He took her hands and drew them above her head. The cover came only to her waist. "You are so white—" He said his thought aloud: "You are a man's dream."

"And you are my dream," she said, looking at him while he studied her. She felt his warm breath on her breast. Would he touch her there, as Wilkes had done? Make her feel ashamed and somehow dirty?

But when his mouth closed over her, she felt a moment of utter terror. She didn't move, didn't make a sound. He was very gentle, his tongue playful. He raised his head and looked at her in the dim light. "I don't know where to kiss you first," he said. "I want all of you at once."

He came back over her and clasped her to him. He kissed her ears, the tip of her nose, smoothed her eyebrows with a fingertip, told her over and over how beautiful she was. "Now, you must learn how to kiss properly."

She smiled at that, and waited, willing her mind to ease, to allow her pleasure with him.

"Part your lips," he said, and she did. She felt his mouth, firm and warm, felt his tongue glide slowly over her lower lip. "Breathe through your nose, Jules," he said, and tested the waters. "Excellent," he said, smiling down at her.

"Now, I want to feel your tongue. Yes, that's it." He thought he would explode. She was so giving, so trusting.

He released her wrists and she brought her arms about his back. When his tongue went into her mouth, then quickly withdrew, she was surprised. He laughed, and said into her mouth, "I will come into you like that, Jules. But I doubt I'll leave you so quickly. I'll probably want to stay inside you—" He broke off—he had to. Odd how his own words, his own images, were making him crazy.

"When?"

He closed his eyes a moment, willing himself to control. But he couldn't help himself. He eased on top of her, balancing himself on his elbows above her. "When you are ready for me," he said, and kissed her again, slowly, thoroughly.

Jules felt him against her closed thighs. She wanted to feel him, and tried to open her legs.

"No," he said. "Not yet, sweetheart." Saint wanted to caress and kiss every inch of her, but he held back. The thought of her freezing in embarrassment made him stop cold. But if he didn't bring her pleasure, he would hurt her, he knew it. Slowly he eased off her. "No," he said softly when she tried to press herself against him, "no, just lie still." His fingertips stroked over her bruised jaw, downward, feeling her shoulders, her breasts.

He lowered his mouth and suckled her breast. He felt her stiffen just as she'd done the first time he'd touched her, but he continued, praying that she would ease. She did, a bit. He let his hand move slowly over her ribs. Keep talking to her, he told himself. It would distract her. "I've got to fatten you up," he said, pressing the palm of his hand over her ribs. "Did I ever tell you about that young boy that I—"

"Michael," she said, cutting him off, "can I touch you? Can I feel your ribs?"

"Yes."

Jules swept her hands over his chest, downward, reveling in the feel of him. So different from her, so incredibly powerful. She pressed her fingers against his flat belly, but before she could go lower, he let his own palm rest on her woman's mound. She froze, rigid as a stone.

"Don't be afraid, sweetheart."

"I'm not, not really. It's just that I didn't think that you would touch—"

His fingers found her. Familiar territory, he thought, caressing her more deeply, that first night he'd given her release clear again in his mind. He loved how she felt. He closed his eyes, wishing that his mouth could replace his fingers. But it was too soon for that intimacy.

"What's wrong?" Jules asked in a high, thin voice. She didn't know what to do. She felt exposed, vulnerable, and his fingers made her feel pleasantly strange, yet embarrassed.

"Nothing. You're perfect."

"Are you certain? You're not just saying that?"

"No," he said, raising his head to kiss her again. "I'm not just saying that." He wanted desperately to draw her upward and kiss her, taste her, and bury himself in her. But he knew he couldn't. Not yet. He let his fingers find a rhythm that seemed to please her, for she gasped suddenly, and dug her fingers into his shoulders.

"Michael, please, I don't know—I can't—"

"Yes, love," he said. "Just lie still." He continued to caress her as he raised himself over her. Slowly he parted her legs. He sat back on his heels a moment, watching her at the touch of his fingertips. He studied her legs, sleekly muscled, unlike those of many young women of her age.

"Jules," he said, his control gone. "Please, hold still."

His fingers left her, but she was tense with anticipation as she watched him guide himself toward her. She felt his fingers parting her. She didn't know what to do. He would come inside her. Yes, she wanted that. She felt that male part of him pressing against her, felt the incredible heat of him. She could hear his breathing, knew that he needed her, needed her now, this moment. She tried to relax, to open herself to him. He entered her, his fingers still parting her to ease his way, and she felt herself stretching. Painfully. She felt his hands on her thighs, holding them apart, and he came deeper into her.

"Jules, love."

She opened her eyes and stared at him. She was in awful pain.

"You've a maidenhead, and—" He groaned in his throat, and went in.

Jules yelled, she couldn't help it. He was deep and it hurt badly. She stuffed her fist into her mouth, not wanting him to know.

"No, Jules, hold still." She was trying to rid herself of the dreadful pain. She felt his fingers find her again, and stroke her, but the very nice sensations didn't return. He groaned suddenly, arched his back, and shoved forward until she took all of him.

He balanced himself on his elbows when he had enough strength to do so, and looked down at her. Her face was pale, her eyes closed, her eyelashes wet spikes on her cheeks. He cursed. He'd given her very little pleasure. Slowly he drew out of her, feeling her shudder at the pain.

"God, I'm sorry," he said, pulling her against him. He stroked her back, eased his hand up beneath her thick hair to knead the muscles of her neck. "Jules, are you all right?"

She thought about it. She felt very sore, as if she'd been battered inside, which, she supposed, she had. But he'd tried to be careful with her. It hadn't been all that bad. "I'm fine," she said. "Truly Michael."

But he felt her tears against his shoulder. He'd forced her, given in to his lust. He was no better than Wilkes. "Never, never again," he said to himself, unaware that he'd whispered the words aloud.

Jules felt as though he'd slapped her. No, please, no, she wanted to yell, but she said nothing. Her head was beginning to hurt, just like the rest of her. She wanted to talk to him, but her mind was numb with pain. She buried her face against his shoulder.

Saint felt her shudder, and hated himself. He lay awake long after he heard her even breathing and felt her body relax against him. He eased away from her, rose, and doused the lamp. He slipped into bed again and drew her back into his arms. He could still feel himself tearing through her maidenhead, feel her struggling against him. But he hadn't stopped. No, he'd continued hurting her, letting his lust rule him. She was so precious to him, he realized. So fresh and vital. He couldn't bear the thought of her awakening and flinching away from him, fear and wariness in her eyes. It brought him nearly physical pain. Why, he wondered, on the vague edge of sleep, had she wanted him? Seduced him?

When he heard the pounding on the front door, drawing him quickly from a fitful sleep, he knew relief that he wouldn't have to face her in the morning and see her fear of him. He was out of bed and downstairs within moments.

It was a fisherman from Sausalito, whose wife was vomiting blood. Saint left the house. She would be fine, he thought, walking beside the fisherman, his black medical bag tightly held in his right hand. And he was the last person on earth she would want to see when she awoke.

Jules woke early the following morning, and reached for her husband. His pillow was cold. He was gone. A patient, she thought. He'd had to leave to take care of a sick person. She rose gingerly from the bed, aware of soreness between her thighs. Then she saw the blood, and gasped aloud. There was also blood on the sheets.

She knew it wasn't from her monthly flow. She forced herself to be calm, and bathed away the blood. It seemed to have stopped, and she felt an overwhelming relief. She dressed and went downstairs.

"Good morning, Jules," Lydia said, eyeing her young mistress closely. "No head problems this morning?"

Jules shook her head, and forced a smile. "No, I'm fine, really. Is Thomas up yet?"

"Up and gone. That young man has more energy than a hungry mosquito."

Jules wasn't very hungry herself, but she managed a cup of coffee and a slice of bread. "Did you see Michael?" she asked finally.

"No, he must have been called away."

"Did he leave a note or anything?"

Lydia shook her head. She saw the pained look in Jules's eyes and wondered about it. A short time later, she had no more reason to wonder. She saw the bloodstains on the sheet. That damned fool man had better get home soon, she thought, pulling the sheets off the bed.

Jules paced the parlor. She realized she was terrified at the thought of leaving the house by herself. She could see Jameson Wilkes waiting for her.

Where was Michael?

Saint was very gently drawing a sheet over the fisherman's wife. She had died, and there was nothing he could do. She'd been ill more than a week, her husband had admitted to him on the boat ride across the bay, and now she was dead, never regaining consciousness in the last two hours.

And she had been young, not much over thirty, Saint guessed. He left the small house, the husband sitting at the kitchen table, a bottle of whiskey in front of him.

Saint wandered along the one dirt street of Sausalito. Life seemed particularly burdensome. There was one saloon, the Little Willow, and even though it was early afternoon, he walked into the dim, rather smelly room and ordered his own bottle of whiskey.

He knew rationally that the woman's death more than likely couldn't have been prevented, even if he'd seen her sooner. Damn, doctors didn't know a thing. He took a long pull on the whiskey. He hated death. He hated pain and illness, but even more than hate, something embedded deeply within him forced him to do what he could. And now he'd given his wife pain, gratuitous pain. He'd known better, but he'd allowed her, in all her ignorance, to seduce him.

And he'd left her alone to face her thoughts.

He drank deeply, telling himself yet again that he was the last person she would want to see after the debacle of last night.

Jules wandered up to their bedroom late that afternoon. She paused in front of the long mirror and stared at herself. She remembered his words: *Never, never again.* Was she so unattractive, then? Slowly, after she'd locked the bedroom door, she undressed. Naked, she approached the mirror again and studied herself. She had never seen another woman naked, so she had no comparison. She didn't think she was ill-looking. She wasn't fat or bowlegged, or flat-chested. He had touched her, everywhere. She lightly touched her breasts. There wasn't the same feeling of warmth she felt when he touched her. She stared at her belly, at the cluster of red curls. He'd even caressed her there. She didn't flush with embarrassment, she simply continued staring at herself. She'd probably made him feel guilty, acting like such a watering pot. He hadn't hurt her all that much.

*Never, never again.* But she had hurt him—that, or he hadn't enjoyed her, taking her only because she'd demanded it of him. How could he have enjoyed it when she'd fought him, and cried like a silly fool?

Tears stung her eyes. Everything had gone awry. She'd hoped that he would change toward her, but not this way. Slowly she sank to her knees in front of the mirror and buried her face in her hands.

Saint pulled himself together when he heard a man talk about all the bloody fog rolling in. "Unusual this time of year," the man said to his companion. "No way out now."

That brought Saint to instant sobriety. "Fog?" he asked the man.

"Yep. You're from the city, ain't you?"

'Yes, and I must get back."

"Ain't nobody going out in that damned soup. Sorry, mister, but you're spending the night here."

Saint paid his shot and went outside. The man was right. He couldn't see a foot in front of him. San Francisco could be a thousand miles away, and in any direction. He thought of Jules and cursed. He should have left her a note, dammit. She would worry, and there was nothing he could do about it.

There were no inns in Sausalito, so he walked back into the saloon.

# Chapter 19

Saint didn't get back to San Francisco until late the following afternoon. He felt dirty, tired to the soles of his boots, guilty, and he didn't want to go home. As he strode long Clay Street, his eyes on mud puddles that could bring the unwary low, he imagined the look on Jules's face when she saw him. Disgust, revulsion—God only knew. For a moment he allowed himself to remember the intense pleasure he'd experienced, but of course, the pleasure had been all his. He kicked a stone viciously out of his way. Life, he decided, had become bloody hell.

He drew a deep breath and opened the front door of his house. "Jules," he called.

Jules, who had talked herself into fatalistic calm, heard his voice and forced herself to walk slowly from the parlor into the entrance hall.

"Hello," Michael," she said, not meeting his eyes. His presence made her feel vulnerable, exposed. "Are you hungry? Lydia made a delicious beef stew, and there's freshly baked bread. Thomas isn't here. I believe he is again with Penelope Stevenson, teaching her manners, no doubt."

Saint wanted desperately to take her in his arms, to stroke her bright head, to comfort her, but he was afraid to. He needed comforting himself. He smiled painfully, knowing she was putting on an act for him, trying to behave naturally, hiding her true feelings about him.

"I need a bath first," he said. "I'm sorry, Jules, about a lot of things. I should have left you a message, but I expected to be home soon. I was called over to Sausalito, across the bay, and couldn't come back any sooner because of the fog. Please forgive me—a doctor's lot and all that."

She raised her eyes to his face. For a brief instant his expression was unreadable; then she knew she saw pity in his eyes. She rocked back on her heels, hating him, hating herself. He'd found her lacking, found her still to be a child, not a woman, and now he was stuck with her. She wanted to yell, but she didn't. She said nothing, merely looked away from him. "Yes," she said, "yes, there was fog." She hadn't known the fog was all that heavy, but of course she hadn't been out of the house. She'd been too afraid to leave. No, not really afraid. She hadn't wanted to leave because he might return at any moment.

"What happened to your patient?"

"She died. I could do nothing for her."

"I'm sorry," she said.

He slashed his hand through the air. "There was nothing to be done for her, as I said. Now, I think I'll go up. I won't be long, Jules."

He wasn't long and the dinner was indeed well prepared. Saint said nothing more about his trip to Sausalito. He didn't want to burden her with particulars. In fact, he said very little, not knowing what to talk about to her. He was drinking a cup of coffee, screwing up his courage, and finally said, "Jules, I want to apologize, to tell you how sorry I am for what happened, for what I did and—" He broke off suddenly, seeing her clutching a knife.

There was a loud knock on the front door.

It wasn't a patient. It was Brent Hammond.

"You stupid bastard," Brent said as he walked into the house.

"Good to see you too, Brent," Saint said. "Come in, won't you? Would you like a drink?"

"Nope. I want to talk to you."

Brent saw Jules from the corner of his eye, and quickly turned to smile at her. "Good evening," he said. She looked pale, and no wonder.

Jules nodded, and looked a question at her husband.

Brent answered for him. "I need to speak to your husband for a little while, Jules, if you don't mind. Byrony sends her love."

"Not at all," Jules said, and went upstairs. She'd never felt so alone in her entire life. She hated the house, the bedroom, hated the wretched mirror that showed her looking miserable.

In the parlor, Brent said, "Now, my friend, I've had a talk with Del."

Saint walked to the sofa and sat down, his arms behind his head. "Go ahead, I doubt I can stop you unless I plant my fist in your face. Since Del has said his piece, do feel free to dose me as well."

Brent smiled. "No advice. I've come with an offer for you."

"Look, Brent, why don't you just go back to your beautiful wife and leave me alone."

"If I recall correctly," Brent said, "you were very involved in my affairs not too long ago."

"That was different," Saint said. "You were acting the fool, wearing blinders, and poor Byrony—" *Oh God, that sounds like me.*

"Like hell," Brent said pleasantly, cutting off his thoughts. "Now, just listen." He sat forward in his chair, his hands clasped between his knees. "You are my wife's doctor. You will deliver our child when the time comes. In return, I wish to begin payments to you on sort of an installment plan. Your wife needs protection. I will provide that protection. His name is Thackery, and he's very smart, strong, and loyal. He's a black man, a former slave from Wakehurst, and a fine marksman. He will live here until Wilkes is taken care of. He will be with your wife when you can't be. He will be her bodyguard and protect her with his life. Now, what do you say?"

Saint wanted to tell Brent to take his Thackery and throw him in the bay, but he didn't. Brent was right. And he was a good friend. Saint sighed. "All right."

Brent cocked a dark brow. "Marriage seems to have mellowed you a bit. Made you more reasonable, more amenable. Thackery is waiting outside. Would you like to invite Jules down to meet him?"

"Probably," Saint said, rising. He wondered how Jules was going to react to having a bodyguard. "Let me fetch her." He turned in the parlor doorway. "Brent, thanks."

"My pleasure, old son," Brent said.

Jules gave Thackery a fat smile. She had to take him off guard, a difficult task at the very least. In their first week together, he went everywhere with her, never interfering in what she wished to do, merely staying stolidly with her, his presence forbidding to strangers and a relief to friends. Jules liked him. But now she had to distract him. Ah yes, the dress shop owned by Monsieur David. The perfect place.

"I would like to look at some gowns, Thackery," she said, waving toward the shop.

"Certainly, Mrs. Saint. I'll be right here when you come out."

*Mrs. Saint.* She'd tried to make him call her Jules, but he merely smiled at her and continued with "Mrs. Saint." Jules nodded and walked, shoulders back, into the store. She pretended to be interested in the new shipment of gowns from France. Every few minutes she peered out the window. Damn, Thackery hadn't moved an inch.

She spoke briefly to the dapper Monsieur David, then slipped out the back of the store. The gun shop, run by Marcus Haverson, was just a block down Kearny Street. She'd stolen some money from Michael's strongbox just that morning. No, she amended to herself, it was her money too. After all, wasn't she Mrs. Saint?

Ten minutes later, she was the proud owner of a derringer. In another ten minutes she had rejoined Thackery.

Thackery arched a black brow. His young mistress looked mighty pleased with herself. There wasn't one package in her arms. He wondered what she was up to. This jaunt of hers into a dress shop, looking all sorts of innocent and guileless, was unusual, and he was suspicious. She was a handful, but he didn't mind that. She was never boring. But she was unhappy. He was quite certain of that, even though she never said anything particularly unhappy. She was bright, chatty, interested in everything they saw. They'd visited the Russ Gardens, the old Dolores Mission, even the racetrack. But still—

He supposed it natural for her to be wary of that bastard Wilkes. But he would see to that man if he ever dared to show his face. No, it wasn't all Wilkes, he didn't think. He wished he could figure it out. Her husband was a very nice man who, as far as Thackery could tell, treated his young wife like one of those pieces of Dresden china Mrs. Hammond loved so much.

"I didn't like anything," Jules said, which was true. She twisted her hands a bit, aware Thackery was suspicious. To her relief, he didn't say anything. It didn't occur to her until later that she didn't know a single thing about guns. She eyed the long-barreled gun tucked into Thackery's belt, realizing she had to trust somebody. It was late afternoon, but she said to Thackery, "I would like to ride to the ocean. We're very close to the stables. All right?"

Thackery merely nodded. He would have preferred a visit to the Saxtons. He and Lucas were becoming friends, and he was fascinated by Lucas's tales of the gold fields.

When they reached the ocean, he listened with half an ear to Mrs. Saint carrying on about some long-legged birds that were skittering across the sand dunes. A bird was a bird, for God's sake.

When Jules saw that they were quite alone, she paused a moment, drew a deep breath. "I bought a derringer, Thackery. I want you to teach me how to use it."

"So," Thackery said on a deep breath, "that's what you were up to."

"Will you teach me how to use it?"

Thackery scratched his head. "No, ma'am," he said. "That's *my* job. Ain't nobody going to get to you while I'm here."

"If you don't teach me, I will sneak away and practice by myself. You know I can do it, Thackery."

"You need to have your bottom thwacked, Mrs. Saint," Thackery said, his eyes calm on her face.

Jules said nothing, trying to stare him down. But Thackery was made of stern stuff. "I'll tell Dr. Saint," he said.

"He won't care."

Thackery looked thoughtful. "Why not?"

She looked to him as though she wanted to cry and spit all at the same time. She said finally, "I am his cross to bear. You must know that he saved me, Thackery, then had to marry me because my father kicked me out. He didn't want to, but he's honorable. He really doesn't care what I do or don't do, just so long as I don't bother him."

Thackery heard the pain in her voice, and his reaction to it shocked him. He knew loyalty, indeed he did. Both the good Lord and Thackery knew how much he owed Mr. Hammond. But he'd sworn he'd never trust another white. Until Mrs. Saint. Poor little mite. When he'd been a slave, it had never occurred to him that a white man or white woman could know a moment of unhappiness. Whiteness seemed to him then to be the key to all that was pleasant on this damned earth. Well, maybe white folk in California had more problems than those in Mississippi. He looked at Mrs. Saint, saw the pleading, the defiance in those eyes of hers, and knew he had to say something, do something.

"I could just take that little thing away from you, Mrs. Saint."

"You try it, Thackery," she said flatly, her eyes narrowed, "and I'll—well, I'll make you very sorry."

"You just would, wouldn't you? No, don't answer that. I ain't going to help you, and that's that."

He wouldn't budge, and after another few minutes of fierce arguing, Jules gave up. She refused to speak to him all the way back to San Francisco. His last words before he left her at home were, "I'm going to the Wild Star to see Mr. Hammond. You just keep that damned toy put away, you hear?"

"I hear," Jules said, and stomped into the house.

"What are you doing here?" Jules asked Thomas a few moments later. She was surprised to see him at home.

Thomas gave her a big smile. "I came home to ask Lydia to make something special for dinner. Penelope is coming."

"Does she have manners yet, Thomas?"

"If she throws her peas at you, I'll put her bottom in the air," he said, grinning. "Oh, yes, the Hammonds are in the city, and Saint invited them also. Seven o'clock. All right?"

Jules nodded. "Where is Michael?"

Thomas scratched his head. "I think he said something about seeing a Mrs. Branigan."

Jules sucked in her breath. His mistress. No, she amended, not his mistress. His lover, his former lover. "Why?" she asked, and immediately regretted asking.

"How would I know, sis? He's a doctor, isn't he?"

But Saint wasn't being a doctor, not on this visit. He sat in Jane's parlor, a cup of tea balanced on his knee. The boys were outside playing at last, and Jane was fidgeting about, straightening the pillows on a chair.

"Well?" Saint asked.

"It's your wife, Saint," Jane said, watching him closely. She saw him close his eyes briefly, saw the pain.

"What about her?"

"Joe saw her today. She bought a gun at Haverson's. I thought you should know."

Saint stared at her, disbelieving. "He's wrong," he said flatly. "There's no earthly reason for her to buy a gun. Thackery is with her all the time."

"Joe assured me it was true," Jane said. "That boy likes to fight, but he doesn't lie. You know that, Saint."

"Hell and damnation. Sorry, Jane." He set down the teacup and rose to his feet. "I don't bloody believe this." He began pacing in ferocious silence.

"You should also know," Jane said, "that she visited Maggie the other afternoon. I heard it from a man who came to pick up his shirts. He didn't understand why Saint Morris's wife was visiting a whorehouse."

"Shit," said Saint. "Sorry, Jane."

"There appears to be a serpent in paradise."

Yes, he thought, the serpent was his damned sex.

"Saint," Jane said, moving to him and laying her hand on his shoulder, "I'm sorry, but I thought you should know." She regretted her sarcasm, and wanted to make amends. "Please, Saint, if you want to talk about it, you know I'm a good listener."

"There's nothing whatsoever to talk about," he said. "I suppose I knew things weren't going all that well, but there's nothing like keeping one's eyes closed, is there? No, don't answer that, Jane. I've got to be going. I have the dubious pleasure of having Penelope Stevenson to dinner this evening."

"Good luck, Saint," she called after him, but he didn't hear her.

Saint entered their bedroom close to an hour later. Jules was splashing in the tub. He paused in the doorway, wondering whether or not to retreat. She saw him and fell instantly silent.

"Hello, Jules."

Jules sank down a few inches in the water. Why should she be embarrassed? He knows—everything. "I shall be finished in just a moment," she said.

Saint made the mistake of allowing his eyes to leave her face. He swallowed, and backed up. "I'll be downstairs, Jules. I need a bath also. Just call me when you're finished."

He disliked her so much he couldn't bear to be in the same room with her? She was sorely tempted to climb out of the tub and hurl the water at him. But she didn't. She said only, "How sorry I am that you had to work so very hard this afternoon. What was wrong with Mrs. Branigan, anyway?"

He forced his eyes back to her face. He thought of the damned gun, of her visit to Maggie. Here she was attacking him like a shrew for his visit to Jane. For God's sake, he'd told her he wouldn't sleep with Jane anymore. He said, "Why, nothing at all was wrong with Jane. Nothing at all. Not everyone I visit is ill, you know."

She wanted to yell at him, but she lowered her head. She heard his harsh breathing, heard the bed-

room door slam, then listened to his retreating footsteps down the corridor.

"He's a miserable man," she said. "I guess that
makes us about even, since I'm a miserable woman."

Penelope had never before been in Saint Morris's
house. It was dreadfully small and not at all well-
appointed. Well, she was here and she supposed she
must make the bet of it. After all, Saint was Thomas's
brother-in-law. She greeted Saint with cool politeness
and tried her rarely used charm on Thomas's sister.
What wild red hair, she thought.

"How nice to see you again," Jules said, wondering for perhaps the dozenth time what Thomas saw
in this dreadful girl. Her voice could chill the wine.

"Yes," Penelope said. "Dr. Morris," she added,
gracefully inclining her long neck. "My parents send
their regards."

"How about a glass of sherry, Pen?" Thomas
asked.

Jules watched Penelope turn a beguiling smile on
her brother. Pen? Penelope's voice softened a much
as her eyes. "Oh yes, Thomas, that would be very
nice."

Saint was markedly silent until the Hammonds arrived, full of good cheer and laughter. Byrony's stomach was well-rounded now, and her skin had a
glowing, almost translucent look. "As I live and
breathe," Byrony said in a very sweet voice. "Penelope, how very delightful. How I wish the Saxtons
were here also."

Penelope didn't know what to do. She felt Thomas's squeeze, and she forced a big smile. "Hello," she
said. "It is very good to see you both again. Mother

is so pleased with the amount of money we raised
for your slaves, Mr. Hammond."

"There are no slaves in California," Byrony said
sweetly.

"Yes, Pen," Thomas added, "you must begin to
listen and perhaps read the newspaper. It would give
you all sorts of useful information."

Brent Hammond was watching this interplay with
some interest. He said to Saint, "Your brother-in-law
has more guts that I. Does she always roll over and
play dead when he tromps on her?"

"He does handle her," Saint said, "and very well,
it appears. I doubt you'll hear too many sly innuen-
dos out of her tonight."

"How is Thackery?" Brent asked.

"Fine," said Saint. Brent followed his friend's gaze
to Jules. She looked lovely in a dark green silk gown
that was fashioned low on her white shoulders. Her
flame-colored hair was intricately arranged in thick
coronet braids atop her head. Curling tendrils trailed
down on either side of her face.

"I spoke to him briefly before we came in," Brent
said. "He informs me that you wife is a handful.
But when I questioned him further, he became as
closemouthed as a clam. I fear he's shifted his loyalty
to your wife."

Saint didn't want to talk about it. He didn't even
want to think about it, at least not this evening.
"Does Byrony have any more nausea in the mornings?" he asked.

Brent arched a questioning brow, but allowed the
shift in topic. "No, she informs me she's healthy as
I am, but fatter. You don't expect any problems,
Saint?"

Saint did, but he didn't say anything. No sense in making Brent worry. If the child grew large, Byrony would have difficulties, for her pelvis was narrower than Jules's. "No problems," he said aloud. "Just make certain I'm around a couple of days before she's due to deliver."

"We'll be settled in Wakeville for the winter. You don't mind trekking down? You'll stay with us as our guest. Jules also, of course."

"That would be fine. And don't worry, Brent."

"If you insist. Incidentally, Maggie was telling me that Jules— "

Saint raised his hand. "No, I don't want to hear it. I've already been informed. I intend to speak to Maggie tomorrow. Now, let's join the ladies and masterful, romantic Thomas."

To her profound surprise, Penelope found that she was enjoying herself. Certainly the fact that Thomas squeezed her hand in a meaningful way occasionally under the table made her smile, but she hadn't imagined that she would actually enjoy having dinner with a gambler and a girl from Maui and a doctor. And a pregnant lady.

". . . and then Limpin' Willie told me that he returned the hundred dollars to the man's pocket and sent him on his way," Saint said. "He told me the fellow had one of my bandages on his arm. Thought I'd be upset if he did him in after I'd fixed him up."

He paused a moment to let the laughter die down.

"I think you should run for mayor, Saint," Byrony said. "You would gain more votes than any man in the history of San Francisco."

"Saint," Thomas said, sitting forward in his chair,

"tell us the story about Napoleon and his one experience with a cathartic."

"In front of the ladies, Thomas? And I believe you've already told it. Needless to say, he refused any further treatment of that sort."

"What's a cathartic?" Penelope asked.

"The opposite of an emetic," Thomas said, hooting with laughter.

"Thomas."

"Yes, Pen?" Thomas asked, his face as innocent and guileless as his sister's was when she wanted to fool Thackery. Which evidently she had. She hadn't spoken one word directly to him all evening. He wanted to be alone with her. He wanted to yell at her and shake her. He wanted— Oh no, you damned randy bastard. Not that, not again.

He sat back and pretended to listen to Brent describe their progress at Wakeville. Lydia's roast beef sat like leather in his stomach, as had her attempt at Yorkshire pudding. He sipped at his wine, looked at his wife's face.

What was he going to do with her? He'd hurt her badly, but that didn't excuse her recent behavior. He supposed he would have to speak with Thackery, have the man keep a closer eye on her.

"Michael?"

He was jerked out of his fog. "What?" he said, turning to Jules.

"The ladies will be in the parlor," she said, rising. He quickly stepped to her side and politely held her chair. She didn't look at him.

"We won't be long," Saint said.

Another two hours passed before they were alone. Thomas left to drive Penelope home, and Brent, his voice light and amusing, claimed his fat wife needed her rest, which gained him Byrony's elbow in his ribs.

Saint said without preamble, "I want to talk to you, Jules."

"I'm tired," she said, moving toward the parlor door. "I'm going to bed. You know, Michael, it's that rather large piece of furniture up in the bedroom. Good night."

"Jules."

He jumped to his feet and came after her. "You come back here."

Jules paused at the top of the stairs, curled her lip at him. "Oh no. It seems that the parlor has become your bedroom. I have no intention of speaking to you there."

"Damn you," he said, and stalked up the stairs after her.

# Chapter 20

Let him come in, Jules thought, stomping into the bedroom. She stopped in the middle of the room, turned, and faced the open doorway.

Perhaps she should begin taking off her clothes—that would stop him in his tracks.

Her fingers went to the long row of the buttons.

"Don't you dare," Saint said, coming into the room. He paused a moment, then slammed the door closed behind him. "Leave those buttons alone."

"Why?" she asked, unfastening yet another. "Would you find it so very repulsive? I thought doctors were quite used to seeing naked women."

"I want to talk to you, not see you with nothing on but your hair." What game was she playing?

Jules sat down on the swivel chair in front of the dresser, folded her hands in her lap, and began to twiddle her thumbs. "Yes?" she asked.

We used to be such good friends, he thought, staring down at her, his frustration mounting. She used to trust me, to love me. No, not that. She loved him as a child would an older brother. He said, "Why did you buy a gun today?"

She started to deny it, but knew it would do no

good. "So," she said, "I cannot even trust Thackery. When did he tell you?"

"He didn't."

"Then how do you know?"

"It doesn't matter. Now, where is it?"

She didn't move. He grabbed her reticule from the dresser and riffled through it. She said noting, merely stared at him.

There was no gun in the reticule.

"Where, Jules?"

Now was the time for a lie. Otherwise, he would tear the room apart looking for it. "I decided that Thackery was right. I don't need a gun. He will protect me."

Saint stopped, turned slowly, and looked at her. "Are you telling me the truth?"

"Why shouldn't I? I told you, I realized it was silly for me to have it. Besides, I don't know the first thing about derringers."

"I see. Just what did you do with it, Jules?"

"I threw it in the ocean this afternoon." She lowered her eyes. That wasn't a good lie at all. All he had to do was ask Thackery.

"If I discover that you aren't telling me the truth, I will thrash you."

She said nothing.

"What I should do is buy Thackery a leash. A short one."

She still said nothing, and kept her eyes on her thumbs.

"Another matter," Saint said after a moment. "I understand you paid a visit to Maggie the other day. No, let's not repeat how I found out. Suffice it to say that I did, quite by accident. Would you care to tell me why you went to a brothel?"

"I wanted to meet her. Chauncey Saxton told me how very nice she was."

"She runs a brothel," Saint said. "It doesn't matter how nice Maggie is. If you wish to make a friend of her, you will invite her here, you understand?"

"She won't come here."

"Then that's an end to it."

"No."

"What?"

"I said," Jules said calmly, "that I shall do as I wish. And *that's* an end to it."

"Jules, listen to me." He stopped, knowing that nothing he said would make any difference. She thoroughly disliked him, so why should she care what the hell he thought about anything? He suddenly remembered Victoria, her body viciously beaten by a mean drunk. God, he hated prostitution. Even willing women could be brutalized, just as Victoria had been. "Several months ago, Maggie called me to the brothel. One of the girls, Victoria is her name, had been badly hurt." He paused a moment, realizing that he didn't have her complete attention. "Actually, the man had not only beaten her, he had used her unnaturally, and torn her." Should he be more graphic? He couldn't bring himself to be. "I had to stitch her up, Jules. She was ill for several weeks."

"Why are you telling me this? It is terrible, of course, but it has nothing to do with me."

He frowned. "I don't know. I don't want you hurt, Jules."

"Then why did you go visit Jane Branigan?"

"She wanted to speak to me, that's all. Nothing more."

"About what?"

"It's not important."

"Are you going to sleep here tonight?"

"No, I'm sleeping downstairs. I'm expecting a patient. He's coming up to see me from San Jose." That was a bloody lie, but what else could he tell her? No, I won't sleep here or I'll strip off your nightgown and force you. Again.

"Good night then, Michael."

He nodded, and turned to leave.

"You needn't be quiet when you leave to see Jane Branigan," she called after him. "I'm a very heavy sleeper."

A muscle moved in his jaw. "Good night, Jules," he said, and left the bedroom.

Jules heard the front door open and close some fifteen minutes later. She turned off the lamp beside the bed, flipped onto her stomach, and cursed into the pillow.

It was only a week until Christmas, and the days had shortened. It was only a bit after four in the afternoon, and Jules had to move to the window to read the letter. It was from her sister, Sarah. It was a petty letter, in which Sarah described in great detail her wedding to Tory Dickerson, a visiting planter from Oahu. "Good for you, Sarah," Jules said aloud to the silent parlor. "Now maybe you'll be just a little bit happy." She folded the letter, then took it up to Thomas's room, propping it up on his pillow.

She was alone, Lydia having left an hour earlier to buy Christmas presents.

She wandered about the house, looking into Michael's surgery. There were several glass-fronted cabinets, two chairs, a desk, and a long table, where, she supposed, he examined people. She studied the bottles in the cabinets, but without much interest, for she recognized only a few of the labels. He'd been gone most of the day, called by David Broderick's servant to come to his house. Broderick, it seemed, had broken his leg.

She grabbed her cloak, placed her derringer, now loaded, into her reticule, and stepped out into the growing darkness. She didn't see Thackery. Perhaps he was off visiting Lucas. She had told him at noon that she wasn't going out today. Well, so much for him. She would take care of herself.

She would go visit Maggie. Certainly it was too early for Maggie to be entertaining men. Her eyes narrowed as she walked toward Kearny Street. Where are you, Mr. Jameson Wilkes? I'm not a virgin, not anymore, but I certainly would like to see you.

She became aware of the number of men staring at her. There were catcalls and whistles and some lewd comments, but she ignored them, stared straight ahead. She saw some women, gaily dressed, and knew they were prostitutes. She was nearly at Portsmouth Square when she heard an astonished voice from behind her.

"Good God, Jules, is that you?"

She turned slowly, recognizing Brent Hammond's voice.

"Hello, Brent," she said. "How are you this fine day? No fog, but Michael tells me there's not much during the winter. It's getting dark so much earlier now, isn't it? How is Byrony?"

"What the hell are you doing here?" Brent said, eyeing her. Where was Thackery?

"I'm visiting Maggie."

"Like hell you are."

"Your language is foul, sir, and it's really none of your business. It was nice seeing you. Now—"

"Stop, Jules. Does Saint know what you're up to?"

"Up to? I am a free person, Mr. Hammond. I am out walking and visiting, just as I suspect your former slaves can now do. Good day, sir."

Brent ground his teeth. Then he smiled, his charming smile. "Very well. Do allow me to escort you to Maggie's apartment. I'm certain she's very anxious to see you, particularly here."

Jules was nonplussed. Finally she nodded. Brent took her arm and led her through the alley to the back entrance to the Wild Star. When they reached the top of the stairs, he steered her to the left.

"A moment, Brent. Maggie is—"

"I imagine that Maggie is visiting Byrony," Brent said. "Come along."

Of course, Maggie wasn't in the Hammonds' apartment. Byrony was seated in front of a glowing fire, reading. She looked startled, then pleased, greeting Jules warmly and offering her a cup of tea.

After the amenities, Brent said to his wife, "I will come back in a little while, love. You and Jules can visit."

"How lovely. Give us at least an hour, Brent."

Jules was in a quandary. The major reason she'd wanted to visit Maggie was her husband's taboo. But how could she tell the glowing Byrony Hammond that she didn't want to stay? She gave Brent a slow nod.

"Just so," Brent said to her. "Later, ladies."

He tracked Saint down in front of his house, Saint having just returned from the Brodericks'.

"How nice to see you, Saint," Brent said. "My, do you happen to know where your wife is?"

Saint waved a hand toward the house. He paused, seeing no lights in the windows. "All right, Brent," he said in a resigned voice. "Where is she? What has she done this time?"

"Why, she's with my wife," Brent said. He added, "Of course, when I just happened to see her, she was on her way to see Maggie. Thanks to my perfidy, she is with Byrony, her guns spiked."

"Damn," said Saint.

"Yes. I guess my next question is, where is Thackery? Your wife was quite alone, trying her best to ignore all the very interested men."

"Jules very probably lied to him and told him she wasn't going out of the house. Thackery will have a fit when he finds out."

"And you, Saint?"

"I don't like fits."

"No, you don't, do you? But marriage seems to have brought you as many confusions and complications as it brought me. I don't know what's going on, Saint, and you're probably dying to tell me to go to hell—"

"Why?" Saint asked, sighing. "You did well by my wife, and I thank you. Lord knows, *I* can't seem to handle her."

Brent eyed his friend closely. "You might try thrashing her."

Saint laughed. "Yes," he said, "yes, I just might. Well, I'm off to fetch her. Thanks again, Brent."

Before he could leave, Thackery returned, a laughing Thomas with him.

"Hi, Saint," Thomas said. "What's going on? There aren't any lights in the house."

Thackery said very quietly, "Tell me where, Dr. Saint, and I'll go get her."

Perhaps it would be better, Saint thought, if Thackery brought her home. "She's at the Hammonds' apartment, above the Wild Star."

Thackery nodded, touched the brim of his hat, and went into the growing darkness. Saint turned to his brother-in-law. "Lydia should be back soon. You hungry, Thomas?"

"Yes," Thomas said. He laughed suddenly. "I won't be seeing Penelope this evening. She tried to give me orders about a certain something, and I informed her—well, I told her she could spend some time alone to think about her woman's modesty."

"Good God, Thomas," Saint said as they went into the house. "Whatever did the girl want you to do?"

Thomas looked thoughtful as the two men went into the parlor. Saint lit the lamps and took off his coat. He looked tired. Damn Jules anyway. Whatever was she up to?

"Drink, Thomas?"

"Sherry, please, Saint."

The two men relaxed a moment, drinking in silence. Saint said again, "What did Penelope want you to do?"

"She wanted me to make love to her."

"Penelope? Good God."

"Exactly," Thomas said. "I told her she should be ashamed of herself." He grinned in fond memory. "She is, of course, quite desirable."

Saint could think of nothing to say.

"She wants to marry me, you know, and since I'm as elusive as hell, I suppose she thought she would compromise me."

"And what did you say?"

"I told her no, and that this evening I was going to spend the night making love to a woman who expected nothing from me. For a while there, I thought she would expire with hysterics."

Saint shook his head. "Thomas, the gentlemen of San Francisco salute you."

Thomas sat forward in his chair, his glass between his knees. "Bunker wants me to come to work for him in the foundry. I'm not certain that's what I want."

"Doing what?"

Thomas shrugged. "Probably a glorified office boy to start with. Somehow, working for my father-in-law doesn't seem too smart a thing to do."

"No, I would agree."

"I want to be a doctor, Saint."

Saint leaned back, his arms behind his head. "I think," he said, "that you should determine if that is really what you want by working with me. I could teach you a goodly amount. If you decide in, say, six months that you wish to continue, I think you should go back East, to Boston or New York, for your formal training."

They continued discussing the pros and cons until Lydia arrived. Ten minutes later, they heard Jules's voice. Thomas watched Saint's face harden, his eyes go flat.

"Well," Thomas said, rising quickly. "I think I'll be going out now. I've got to spend some time with

Morton David, an interesting man. Of all things, he's an actor, Shakespeare and all that." Thomas paused a moment in the doorway and said quietly, "Good luck, Saint."

Saint heard him greet his sister with an affectionate "You look like hell, Jules. Go comb your hair."

Jules knew Michael was in the parlor, but she didn't want to see him. She went upstairs and stayed there until after Lydia had left. She came down only when he called.

She eased into her chair at the foot of the dining table. He handed her the several dishes, saying nothing.

"I trust you had an interesting day," Saint said, laying down his fork.

"No, not really," Jules said.

"Oh? You found Byrony boring?"

"No, she was quite charming. She wanted me to ask you if she could come by tomorrow."

"Certainly."

He wasn't angry. It made her wary. "Michael," she said, taking the offensive, "I am bored. I do nothing except sit around and brush my hair."

"Fine, I'll dismiss Lydia and you can take over her duties."

That shut her up, Saint thought, but only for a moment.

"So, if I can't be anything else, you'll allow me to be your housekeeper?"

"What else do you want to be?"

"Would you pay me what you pay Lydia?"

"Probably not—you haven't her experience or skill."

He sat back and watched her, knowing he'd spiked her guns.

"You think I'm afraid to work?"

"Jules, I don't think you're afraid of a damned thing, more's the pity."

Yes, she wanted to tell him, she was afraid of more things than she could count. Why wasn't he angry with her, yelling at her, for going to see Maggie?

"Aren't you angry with me?"

"Yes, of course."

But he didn't care enough to yell at her, she thought. She didn't know what to say. She watched him rise. He'd opened his shirt at the neck and she could see the hair on his chest. He was so handsome, she thought, her eyes going down his body. But he didn't love her, he didn't even like her, not anymore. She gave him nothing but trouble.

"I'm going out," Saint said. "Incidentally, Jules," he added, stopping a moment in the doorway, "Thackery will be here."

"Ah yes, my jailer. Give my regards to Mrs. Branigan."

He paused and said, his voice hard, "You will cease using Jane as a bone of contention between us. She is a fine woman. I admire her and respect her, but that is all."

She lowered her head, saying nothing.

# Chapter 21

January was a brooding month, Jules thought, and pulled her cloak more closely about her. The air was thick with swirling fog and a chilling drizzle that made her bones ache with cold. She thought of Maui, pictured herself running along the beach, the warm trade winds in her face. She wondered if she'd ever become accustomed to this bitter climate. She supposed with a shake of her head that she should count her blessings. After all, she could have ended up in Toronto.

She'd managed to lose Thackery. She'd gotten quite adept at it over the past couple of weeks. She was hunting again. It added excitement to the game to think she was also the hunted. Wilkes was there, waiting for her, just as she was searching for him. She knew it, she could practically feel him.

It was odd, but Wilkes had become the focal point of her life. It was odd and, she realized, pathetic. But she had nothing else.

Both Thomas and Lydia knew that Michael slept in the parlor. Lydia had said nothing, but Thomas had not been so reticent. Indeed, she thought, seeing his face in her mind's eye, he'd been appalled and angry.

"What the hell is going on, Jules?"

She'd merely looked at him, not at first under-standing his attack.

"Saint," he nearly shouted at her. "Your husband, little sister. I find to my chagrin that my brother-in-law, the owner of this damned house, is sleeping like some sort of extra guest downstairs. What is wrong with you?"

"Nothing," Jules said.

That had brought him up short. His features soft-ened just a bit. "Look, Jules, I realize that all is not well with you two, but you don't even allow him to sleep in his own bed?"

"He doesn't want to," Jules said.

"Oh, come on, Jules." Thomas said in disgust. "You're not exactly a troll. I don't understand any of this."

"It's very simple, Thomas," Jules said, her voice hard. "Michael didn't want to marry me in the first place. He had to, if you'll remember. In terms of sleeping with me, he's not interested." That wasn't precisely true, but all the rest of it was hardly Thom-as's business, after all.

Thomas looked shocked. "He's never slept with you?"

"Once. That, it appears, was more than enough. Now, Thomas, is there anything else?"

He saw tears sparkling in her eyes, and without another word gathered her in his arms. "This isn't right, love," he said quietly, stroking her hair. "I'm sorry, Jules. Damn, after all that happened to you, well—is there anything I can do?"

She shook her head against his shoulder. "Don't embarrass Michael, please, Thomas. He doesn't deserve it, it's not his fault. He's making the best of a bad bargain.''

But there was something Thomas could do, and he had done it two days later. He'd moved out. The short note he'd left his sister simply said that it was time to make his own way. And he'd thanked her for her hospitality.

Thomas had been gone a week now. Jules started momentarily at the shadow of a man in an alley to her right. Nothing. Jules had moved that same day back into the guest room.

And the siege of polite indifference had continued.

That voice, Jules thought, freezing. It was Wilkes, she was certain of it. She clutched her small derringer, fear trickling through her, fear and excitement. At last. Her eyes glittered in anticipation, her fingers tightened about the trigger.

But it wasn't Wilkes. It was a man, a very dirty man, dressed poorly, and he was drunk.

"Little girlie," he said fondly, staggering toward her. "My Anna had red hair, like a flame, she did."

"Get away from me," Jules said, backing up a step.

"Anna?" he said, his eyes bleary, his voice shaking.

"No, I'm not Anna," Jules said, and tried to pass him. He let her go, and she heard him make a whimpering noise behind her. Poor man, she thought. She turned slightly to look at him, worried that he might hurt himself. She jumped as two hard hands grasped her shoulders, jerking her around. This man was neither drunk nor dirty, and his eyes were alight with unexpected pleasure.

"Well, well, you're dressed awful nice, ain't you? Awful pretty, too. How much?"

"I am not a whore," Jules said, her heart pounding. "Go away."

"How much?" the man repeated. She saw in a detached manner that one of his front teeth was gold. "I'm rich and you're just too pretty to let go. Come now."

"Go away," she said again, and pushed her hands against him. He didn't even notice that one hand held a gun.

"It's almost dark," the man said, tightening his grip. "I don't mind the alley. Do you like it standing up? I won't pay you as much as I would if I could stick it in you in a nice bed. Come on now, little honey."

She tried to jerk away from him, but it was no use.

Suddenly his hand was flattened over her mouth and he was dragging her backward toward the filthy, dark alley.

"Stop fighting me. I'll pay you, and you'll like it."

He was strong. Oh God, what had she done? Her mouth was cotton dry. He was going to rape her.

She felt his mouth pressing wet kisses on her face, felt his hands tugging at her cloak to get to her breasts.

"Stop it."

She felt his hand wild on her breast, kneading, pressing her back against a brick wall.

"You just hold still," he said, and lifted his hand from her mouth. She yelled, a high thin sound that broke off abruptly when his hand yanked up her skirts.

His hand was pressing against her stomach, jerking at her underthings. She started hitting him, and the

derringer struck the side of his face. He drew back
in stunned fury.

"You little bitch," he said in utter astonishment.
"Why'd you do that? You ain't nothing but a—" He
stopped abruptly, seeing the derringer. He grabbed
her wrist and jerked it forward. But she wouldn't let
it go. There was a loud popping noise.

Jules watched as the man spun away from her,
clutching at his shoulder. Blood oozed from between
his fingers. He stared at her, his expression disbelieving. She dropped the derringer into her reticule
and sagged against the wall.

"Mrs. Saint, what the hell—"

Thackery, whose practice was to keep well behind
her, came bursting into the alley.

"My God, you shot him."

"He thought I was a whore," Jules said, her voice
too calm, Thackery thought, eyeing her white face.

"What did you expect? Walking about by yourself,
daring someone to come along—oh damn."

Thackery gathered the moaning man and hauled
him upright. "Mrs. Saint, fetch me a carriage, now."

Jules dashed into the street and yelled at a passing
beer wagon. It cost her all the money she had to
convince the man to drive them back home.

When Lydia opened the front door, she gasped.

"Get Dr. Saint," Thackery said, and carried the
man to Saint's surgery.

Saint was daubing iodine on a miner's leg. "Now,
there, Lewis, you'll be—" He broke off when the
door burst open.

"Later, Lewis," he said, and motioned for Thackery to put the man on the table. Saint said nothing,

all his attention on the bullet wound. It was high on the man's shoulder, and the bullet had gone clean through. The man moaned and struggled. "Hold him, Thackery," he said, not looking up.

"Damned little whore shot me," the man said. He stared up at Saint, confusion and pain on his face. "Why would a whore shoot me? I told her I'd pay her. I ain't no liar."

"Maybe she didn't like brown eyes," Saint said, his hands busy. "Just hold still, you're not dying, for God's sake."

"She shot me," the man repeated, his eyes dazed now from shock.

Saint got the bleeding stopped. He bathed the wound, spread on a thick layer of basilicum powder, and tightly bandaged the shoulder. "You'll be good as new in a week."

The man merely looked at him, and Saint asked Thackery, "Do you know who he is?"

"With that beautiful gold tooth? Maybe the president," Thackery said.

Saint lightly slapped the man's face. "Name. What is your name?"

"Avery. I made me a good-sized strike. I was here celebrating, at the Oriental Hotel, and the little whore shot me."

"At least he won't have to spend the night in the parlor," Saint said. "Thackery, hail a hack for him and get him back to his hotel."

"Dr. Saint," Thackery began, knowing the time for reckoning had arrived.

"Well, what?"

"Before I get him out of here—"

Saint eyed Thackery.

"It's Mrs. Saint," Thackery said. "She shot him."

Saint said nothing. He didn't move. His face was unreadable.

"She didn't mean to, but he was trying to force her."

"Don't defend her, Thackery. It isn't necessary. Get him out of here, please."

Thackery lifted the man in his arms. Saint followed him silently, not looking at his wife, who was standing in the entrance hall, watching, not moving.

When the front door closed, Saint walked into the kitchen. Lydia was pounding at some bread. "I want you to go home," Saint said. "Now."

Lydia wiped the flour from her hands, her eyes studying Saint's face. She wasn't blind, nor was she deaf. "I don't know if I should," she said.

"Leave, Lydia," Saint repeated. "I won't kill her." He gave a short, harsh laugh. "I'm a physician, remember?"

Lydia sighed. At least, she thought, he would speak to his wife. That, she supposed, was better than the deadening silence that pervaded the house.

Jules watched Lydia slip out the front door. She felt numb, blessedly numb.

Saint looked at her a moment, then said, "Come here into the parlor. You need a brandy."

She followed him, standing quietly in the middle of the room until he pressed a glass in her hand.

"Drink. All of it."

She did, and fell into a paroxysm of coughing.

He didn't touch her. Her face was red when she caught her breath.

"Finish it."

She did, then gave him the empty glass. Very carefully Saint set it down.

He held out his hand.

Jules simply stared. She loved his hands. The fine sprinkling of hair, the long fingers, their blunt tips. She had loved it when he'd touched her, caressed her.

"Give me the gun," he said.

She opened her reticule and looked at the very small instrument that could very easily have killed that man. She couldn't bring herself to touch it. She shuddered, unknowingly, and gave the reticule at him.

Saint took the derringer, opened the chamber, and took out the second bullet. He then dropped the gun to the floor and stomped on it. Once, twice. It broke into three pieces.

"Now," he said, "I believe it's your turn, Juliana."

"Juliana?"

"I believe," he said, his voice as cold as Toronto winters must be, "that 'Juliana' is more appropriate than 'Jules' for a whore. 'Juliana' is also more appropriate than 'Jules' for a liar."

His words broke over her, filling her with his disgust, and she began to shake; she couldn't help it.

"You might consider trying tears," Saint said, making no move toward her. "Though this time, Juliana, I promise you they won't work."

"No, no, I won't cry," she said.

"Refreshing," he said. He walked away from her— he had to—to the fireplace. He leaned his shoulders gratefully against the mantelpiece. "Would you care to tell me what happened?" he asked, his voice very polite, very calm.

"Nothing, not really. He pulled me into an alley. I was frightened and we struggled. The gun went off by accident, Michael."

"Such a short, almost boring tale," he said. "Fortunate for your conscience that the man, Avery—not a bad fellow really, I imagine—won't die."

As if drawn by a puppet's string, her chin went up.

"Would you mind telling me why you were out alone?" He waved a hand toward the window. "It's dark, and was almost dark when you were out there. Obviously you thought you'd lost Thackery."

"Yes," she said, "that's what I thought."

"I believe I asked you a question, Juliana."

What could she tell him? When she really didn't understand her own motives? "Wilkes," she whispered, her eyes on her shoes.

"Wilkes? What the hell does he have to do with anything?" At her continued silence, he said, "Have you changed your mind about him? Do you want to find him, give yourself over to him?"

"No."

"No what? I would appreciate some specificity."

"I was out tracking him."

He could only stare at her. "Tracking him," he repeated. "If you managed to find him, you wanted to kill him?"

"Yes," she said. "I'm tired of being a prisoner. I'm tired of being a helpless victim."

"Tracking Wilkes—dear God, I don't believe this."

"Why not?" She saw that he was looking at her as if she had suddenly announced that she was going to jump into the bay. "At least," she said, now more angry than numb, "he wanted me."

"What did you say?"

"Nothing, I didn't mean that. It's just that . . ."

"That what?"

"I don't know what to do."

"Charming," he observed. "So blatant stupidity is the answer. Your woman's mind—well, I should have faced it sooner, shouldn't I?"

"What do you mean my 'woman's mind'?"

"I was wrong to say that. Rather, it's more the case that you're still an ignorant child. Selfish, reckless, silly, and so uncaring of anyone else that—"

"I am not uncaring. I did not mean to hurt that man. And I am not a child. Ask Wilkes. He didn't think so."

They were going about in circles. Accomplishing nothing, resolving nothing. But he simply felt too overwhelmed and too furious with her to continue. What he wanted was to thrash some sense into her.

Jules felt his eyes on her, brooding, questioning, grim now with determination.

"What are you going to do?" she asked, hating herself for her high, thin voice.

"I'm going to do something I should have done months ago," he said. "Since there is no reasoning with you, since I can't be certain you won't continue to lie to me with great regularity, I shall just have to do something much more basic."

He strode toward her.

"What?" she said, backing away from him.

"Since there's no one here, I don't have to haul you upstairs."

"Why do you want to 'haul' me?"

He didn't answer her, merely pulled her against him. For a brief moment Jules believed he would comfort her, tell her that everything was all right, that he understood.

In the next moment he'd sat down in his chair and pulled her over his legs.

"No," she yelled, twisting on his lap, trying to pull away from him.

His hands pulled up her gown, jerked away her underthings. She felt the cool air on her bare bottom.

"Very nice," Saint said, and slammed down his palm.

Jules yelled, and arched wildly. His hand came down again, harder this time. She felt pain, but her humiliation was greater, and she yelled all the bad names she could think of at him.

He laughed.

Saint lifted his hand to smack her bottom again, then drew up short. Her white buttocks were now slashed with red, and he could feel her pain. He laid his open palm on her, his fingers, of their own accord, kneading her. He felt a surge of lust, and raised his hand.

"If ever," he said, "you lie to me again, or do something so stupid, I'll use a whip on you. Do you understand me?"

"I hate you."

He brought his hand down again, not as hard this time, but dammit, he had to gain her compliance, and, for that matter, her attention.

"Do you understand?" He punctuated each word with a smack.

"Yes," she said.

"Excellent." He pushed her off his lap, and she landed in a welter of skirts on the floor at his feet, her underclothes about her ankles. He rose quickly, forcing himself not to look at her, for if he did, he knew he'd probably beg her forgiveness, hold her, and—

He didn't bother with a coat. He left, slamming the front door after him.

Jules touched her hand to her bottom. She struggling to get her underclothes back into a semblance of order, then straightened her gown. But didn't rise—she couldn't manage to do that just yet.

She leaned down, pillowed her head on her arms, and breathed in the dust from the carpet.

# Chapter 22

Saint sat by himself at a table at the Wild Star. His friends and acquaintances now kept to themselves, leaving him in solitary splendor, nursing his whiskey.

"Hisself is takin' things too serious," said Dancer Drake, the local boxer.

To Bear Paw Ryan, Saint had been just plain rude. "He musta lost somebody important," Bear Paw said by way of excuse for one of the most popular men in San Francisco.

Saint stared down at his whiskey, unaware that his behavior was leading to wild speculation. What am I going to do now? he was asking himself. It was a refrain that had no more acceptable answer now than when he'd first asked it months before. He kept seeing Jules's shocked white face. And her beautiful bottom, red-streaked from his smacks. He heard the sound of his hand striking her. He downed the remainder of his whiskey.

*I hate you.*

"Well," he said to his empty glass, "what the hell did you expect? You were beating her. Did you think she'd tell you how wonderful you were?"

He yelled for another whiskey.

Saint had never before raised his hand to a woman. His size and strength discouraged men from trying to prove their courage by baiting him. All it had taken was one small woman who had finally driven him over the edge. What had she done, anyway? *She lied to you, she went tracking Wilkes, and she shot a man.* That was a start, he thought, grunting at Nero when he slapped his whiskey shot onto the table.

Nero backed away from the table, saw Brent Hammond, and waved toward his boss.

"Mind if I join you, Saint?" Brent asked. "Excellent, don't mind if I do. Godawful weather we're having, isn't it? I imagine that Jules is having a problem with all the drizzle and fog, her being from Maui and all, huh?"

"Go away, Brent," Saint said, not looking up.

Brent sat down and leaned back in his chair. He studied his friend's face.

"Leave me alone, Brent," Saint said, his voice as rude as he could make it.

"I think I'll take my chances and keep you company for a bit longer. Thackery wanted me to find out what you'd done to your wife, actually. He's very worried about her." If the truth be known, Brent thought, Thackery was just as worried about Dr. Saint. "She pushed him too far this time," Thackery had said, shaking his head.

"I should have used a whip," Saint said suddenly. "And I will next time, damn her stupidity."

"Thackery feels guilty, feels he should have prevented what happened. He tells me that your little one, as he calls her—"

"Would you just shut up?" Saint sent Brent the

meanest look he could manage, but it wasn't as effective as he'd hoped. Brent laughed.

"Why don't you go upstairs, Saint? Any of Maggie's girls would be delighted to bring you some temporary relief."

Brent waited for the explosion, but it didn't come. He watched in astonishment as Saint appeared to consider his suggestion. "I probably should," Saint said at last. "It would at least protect her from me."

For a long moment Brent simply stared at his friend. He didn't know what to do or what to say. Finally he said very quietly, "Can I tell you a story, Saint?" He continued without pause, "When Byrony and I were first married, we didn't get along—my fault of course. She followed me to Celeste's house, thinking I was going to my mistress to sleep with her. Odd. In fact, I wanted to ask Celeste about preventing conception. Do you know that she faced me down? Yelled at me like a fishwife. I was so mad I was ready to strangle her."

"Your point?"

"Hmm, well, I guess it's that Byrony showed a lot of courage to do that. It wasn't quite the same thing, but just maybe Jules wants and needs your attention, and you've frozen her out. Neither Thackery nor I, I might add, can understand why you don't appear to give a good damn about you wife."

Saint scraped his chair back and rose. He wasn't aware that a goodly number of men were regarding him intently. "It's gotta be a woman," Bear Paw said. Limpin' Willie nodded sage agreement.

"You want to borrow a whip, Saint?" Brent asked with interest, not at all intimidated. "Really bring the little fool to her knees? Or you could send her back East with Thomas. And if Thomas isn't going back East, hell, send her there by herself. Get rid of the thorn in you side once and for all."

Brent's mockery slammed into him. It was time to end it, Saint realized, staring blankly through Brent. "Yes," he said, "it is time to get rid of the thorn."

Brent felt a moment of fear at what his words had wrought. He wondered if he should hit Saint over the head, if he should— No, he decided, violence was abhorrent to Saint. If he had indeed thrashed her, he wouldn't again. He watched Saint throw down several dollar bills and stride out of the Wild Star.

"You calm him down, Brent?" Nero asked.

"God only knows," Brent said. He rose and heaved a mighty sigh. "I think," he said, a grin on his face, "that I shall go upstairs and tell my wife how much I love her."

Saint had sobered up dramatically by the time he reached his house. It was completely dark. What did he expect? It was, after all, well after midnight. He banged about loudly, wanting her to wake up.

Jules was awake. After Saint lit the lamp in the spare bedroom, she was sitting up in bed, regarding him warily.

"How's your bottom?" he asked, sitting down beside her on the bed. Her hair was in wild disarray about her shoulders, her eyes large in the dim light.

She looked thoughtful a moment. "I am fine," she said finally. "Are you drunk?"

"I was, but not much now. I guess that's one benefit to being a large man."

"Did you come to hurt me again?"

"No," he said. "At least I hope I won't hurt you. I've come to end it all, Jules."

*Jules, not Juliana.*

"What do you mean, Michael?"

He grinned at her. "Well, first I want to have a look at your bottom. I was pretty heavy-handed with you."

She drew back a bit. "My bottom is fine, I told you."

"After I look at your bottom, I want to toss that nightgown of yours into the corner. Then I want to carry you to my—our—bedroom."

Jules couldn't believe his words. She began pleating the sheet between her fingers. "Why?"

"It's got to stop," Saint said. "I've been a bloody fool. I want you, Jules. I want you so badly I hurt most of the time." He paused a moment, looked at her searchingly. Her expression was unreadable, but of course he hadn't tried all that hard to read her expressions. "First, I want to see your bottom."

Jules felt a surge of pure joy. She knew that if she showed the slightest hesitancy, the slightest fear, he wouldn't touch her. He was her husband.

She smiled up at him. "All right," she said.

Saint hadn't expected that—she saw it from the shock on his face. He looked suddenly uncertain. Maybe it would be easier if he had drunk a bit more. Well, it was too late to give him more now.

Slowly Jules pulled open the three pink ribbons that fastened the front of her nightgown.

He watched her fingers.

"I would appreciate you looking at my bottom," she said. "I guess I do hurt. Maybe you broke something."

"No, there's nothing to break in your bottom," he said, his eyes on a white breast revealed by the parting material.

"Still—" She came up onto her knees and pulled her nightgown over her head. She balled it up and tossed it toward the corner. She placed her hands flat on her thighs, and didn't move.

Saint stared at her, not speaking.

Jules stuck out her breasts. She felt foolish, and at the same time, hopefully excited.

As if in a dream, Saint stretched out his hand and touched her breasts. He felt her quiver, and drew back his hand.

"You aren't frightening me, Michael," she said. She didn't want to fling herself at him, but neither did she wish to be covered with gooseflesh sitting there watching him watch her. "My bottom," she said, and stretched out on her stomach over his legs.

Saint looked down at the white expanse of back, to her very nice bottom, down her legs. "Your bottom—" he said, and laid the flat of his hand on her hip.

"Is my bottom all right?"

"Perfect," Saint said with great sincerity. "All of you is—well, white and soft and sweet."

That was the nicest compliment he'd ever given her. Jules turned over, and pulled herself onto his lap. "You said you were going to carry me into your—our—bedroom," she said.

"Yes, yes, that's what I said."

For an instant he simply couldn't believe this was happening. She was offering herself to him. After he'd been a nasty bastard to her, after— But what if he hurt her again? What if—?

"I'm getting cold, Michael," Jules said, kissing his jaw.

He rose, clutching her against him, and carried her to their bedroom. He wanted to see her, every inch of her.

He laid her on the bed and pulled a thick blanket over her. "Now you won't be cold," he said. He moved quickly, lighting a lamp, then stripped off his clothes. Still, he was worried, even as he slipped in beside her, beneath the blanket.

"Jules," he said, looking down into her face, not touching her yet, "the first time we made love, I did hurt you, badly. I'm very sorry for that. I know that you must have thought me an animal, a brute, as bad as Wilkes—" He broke off a moment, but Jules didn't interrupt him. Let him get it all out, she thought. "I didn't mean to hurt you—it was your maidenhead—the first time is tough for a woman and I couldn't stop myself. If you could trust me now, I think it could be better between us."

"I don't know," Jules said, managing a very serious frown. "It was truly awful that first time. You were a complete brute and used me so roughly. I didn't think you cared at all about me, and I thought I was going to die with the awful pain and—"

"Are you mocking me?"

She gave him a dazzling smile. "Me? Mock you?" She turned onto her side facing him, and her hand roved quickly over his chest to his belly.

"Jules."

"All you have to tell me is that I won't bleed this time. Is that true?"

He closed his eyes and remembered that wretched trip to Sausalito. He had imagined her waking up alone, but he hadn't thought about her bleeding. God, she must have been terrified. "There won't be any more blood."

"Good," Jules said with satisfaction, and gently clasped him in her hand. He was swelling at an excellent rate, and she loved it. "I want to kiss every inch of you."

"Seduced by—"

"Your wife, Michael. Now, would you please kiss me, and touch me, and love me?"

"I've been a bloody fool, haven't I?" he said, and kissed her deeply.

"Yes," she said, "yes, you have. I could never, ever be afraid of you."

He knew he had to go slowly, despite this wonderful display of enthusiasm. And he did, until Jules was driven to distraction.

He said against her parted lips, "Remember how I fondled you that first night, when you were drugged, and crazy?"

"Yes, I remember," she said, and felt hard against her thigh.

"I used my hand, my fingers, that night, Jules. Now I want to caress you with my mouth."

"Oh dear. I don't know, it seems so very—"

"Just trust me," he said. "It's the most natural thing in the world, I promise. It's something that a man loves to do."

When she felt his warm mouth against her, felt him lift her hips in his large hands, she felt only a brief instant of shock. She'd never imagined that he would— Her thoughts broke off and she felt tension building, felt her legs stiffening.

"Michael." She arched upward, offering herself to him fully.

"That's it, love," Saint said, dazed by her response. "God, the sweet taste of you, the softness—"

Her body began to convulse even as he spoke, and he felt her pleasure. He felt powerful, and tender, and so pleased that his own need was temporarily held in check. He caressed her until she quieted. He wanted her to experience every pleasurable feeling, he wanted— Again, he thought. Yes, again. He caressed her until she quivered, cried out. He thought his own world complete at that moment. So much passion in her, so very much passion.

"Now, don't be afraid," he said, and very gently he came down over her.

"Yes," Jules said, dazed, her body still awash with the marvelous sensations. "I'm not afraid. Not of you."

"I'll go slowly, Jules, very slowly." She watched his face as he guided himself into her. He closed his eyes a moment when he entered her, felt her stretching for him, and stopped.

"It's all right," Jules said, seeing his concern for her. "You are so beautiful, Michael. Please, please, come into me." He *was* like a god, a pagan god. She gasped in wonder as he came deeply into her, and she held him tightly. "Oh," she said. "You are part of me."

He cursed, arched his back, and threw his head back.

"Thank you, Michael," she said when he lay panting on top of her. Her hands stroked down his smooth back.

Saint felt shattered, then laughed at the thought. He knew he was too heavy for her, but when he made to move, she tightened her hold around his back.

"I love you, you know," she said. "I've loved you since I was twelve years old. Or was it thirteen?"

His entire body quivered at her words, and to his chagrin, he felt himself harden inside her. "No," he said, more to himself than to her, "I don't want to hurt you." He pulled out of her, rolled to his side, bringing her with him, and clasped her full length against him.

"You were twelve," he said, tangling his finger in her wild, soft hair.

"It seems forever. I'm sticky," she added, kissing his shoulder and weaving her fingers through the hair on his chest.

"Yes, I imagine so. Will you forgive me, Jules?"

"I will if you promise never to call me Juliana again."

"No, I shouldn't do that. I can just imagine some of our future arguments. 'Juliana' comes trippingly off the tongue when I'm angry with you."

"All right," she said. She sighed and moved closer. "That was nice, very nice. You can thrash me if you promise to end it like that."

"You didn't think at all about Wilkes, or about John—"

"No, not for a moment. My weak woman's mind has quite recovered. After all, Michael, I did take off my own nightgown and toss it into the corner, with no help from you."

"No more derringers?"

She hesitated, but just a moment. "No," she said,

shuddering a bit from reaction. "That was awful. I think I must have been somewhat deranged."

"No," he laughed, "just starved for your husband."

"You do have a lot to make up for," she said, slipping her hand between their bodies.

"Jules, you're probably sore. You are quite small, you know, and I felt you stretching to hold me, to take me into you."

"You don't know," she said, "you can't imagine what it feels like, Michael. I think it's much nicer to be a woman. You become part of me, you know. I possess you."

"Possess me?" he said, grinning as he kissed her temple. "I've never heard a woman say that before."

"You, inside of me, filling me. I like it very much."

He groaned, and she simply smiled up at him as he became a wild man. Until she became as wild as he. Her last thought before her body exploded into almost painful pleasure was that, at last, she was a woman, a wife, Michael's wife.

"Have I just been branded?" she asked after he'd calmed her and settled her against his body for sleep.

"Twice, branded twice. But," he added, his voice deep with satisfaction, "you've been pleasured three times."

"Such possessiveness," she said. She would make him love her, she thought, oh yes, she would.

"Michael?"

"Hmm?"

"Did you enjoy making love to me?"

He was silent for a moment, and she could practically see him grin. "It was all right, I suppose," he said. "You could have shown a bit more enthusiasm, of course. But all in all, I didn't fall asleep from boredom, did I?"

She slid her hand over his belly.

"Dangerous, Jules, very dangerous. Have pity, sweetheart, I'm an old man." But not that old; he wanted her again, powerfully.

"Do you know what I was thinking when you were over me, inside of me?"

He groaned. "I'm scared to know."

"How powerful you are, how beautiful, and your legs, so strong and—"

He slipped his hand between them to cup her breast. He said, "Would you like to know what I was thinking when I was covering you, inside of you?"

"You weren't thinking a single thing."

"Be quiet. I looked at you, so small, so delicate, so very female, and—"

She punched his ribs, and he laughed, a deep, satisfied laugh. "Don't try to outdo the master, Jules, else I'll continue with how I felt when you wrapped you beautiful legs around me, drawing me deeper—"

"Michael."

He eased her onto her back, kissed her breast, then said with all the triumph of a sated man who held a sated woman, "You're mine, Mrs. Saint, and don't you ever forget it."

"No," she said, so happy that she thought she would die from it. "No, Dr. Saint, I won't ever forget."

# Chapter 23

Lydia paused a moment in front of the closed bedroom door, started to turn the knob, then slowly drew back her hand. She walked to the smaller bedroom down the hall, saw that the door was open, and looked in. "Ah," she said. She took in the mussed bed and Jules's nightgown, a heap on the floor. "It's about time, Saint Morris. Yes indeed, about time."

She decided to take her leave thirty minutes later, a pleased smile on her face.

Upstairs, Saint, who usually woke quickly with his full faculties, slowly opened his eyes. My God, he thought, aware of the soft body curled against his. Sunlight poured through the windows, splashing across his face, and he smiled, a besotted smile he imagined, and tightened his arm about his wife's back.

Jules mumbled something in her sleep and obligingly nestled her cheeks against his throat. She's mine, he thought. He didn't wake her just yet, content to think about the pleasant turn the world had taken. He couldn't quite understand how she could still love him, but she'd said she did. Had loved him since she was twelve. A heady thought.

"You're a lucky bastard," he said to the bedroom. He'd prayed he could give her pleasure, but her naturalness had surprised him as much as it had excited him. He remembered so clearly the older woman who had taught him about women. Her name was Lottie. Older, ha? She'd been about the same age as he was now. She had seduced him, very gently, after he'd gotten word that Kathleen had died in Ireland. She had given him renewed life, then shown him how to satisfy a woman. He'd failed Kathleen, of course, but had been too ignorant to realize that she could and should enjoy sex as much as he. He'd learned since that most men considered it nearly a perversion if their wives enjoyed the marriage bed. More fools they.

Saint smiled, remembering Lottie's exact words. "You've quite an aptitude for this. Yes, I admire a man who enjoys his work."

He slipped his hand between them, again splaying his fingers to feel the width of Jules's pelvis. She would have his children, but not more than two or three. He would take no chance with her health, nor did he want her to bear a child every year until she was thirty. He wanted her to himself—himself and two daughters and a son. He was blissfully picturing a daughter, red-haired, vibrant, and loving, just like her mother, when he felt a smooth hand glide down his belly.

"Jules?"

"Good morning, husband," she said. "Goodness," she said as her fingers closed around him.

"What do you expect?" he asked, nibbling at her ear. "I've been thinking about you for the past five minutes."

"I think, Michael," she said, "that I have great power over you."

"At least part of me."

"Michael?"

"Yes, sweetheart?"

"Will you teach me things?"

"I'll teach you everything you want to know," he said with great conviction, and rolled her onto her back.

"Lydia."

Saint frowned. "Damn, I'd forgotten all about her."

"Oh dear, this is dreadfully embarrassing. Do you think she saw us?"

He laughed and kissed her deeply. "We're married, Jules. And no, I sincerely doubt that Lydia, once she'd been in the other bedroom, would dare open the door to this one."

Jules pressed her face against his throat. "I'll never be able to face her."

He breathed in the sweet scent of her hair and also the smell of sex. This bedroom, he thought, grinning, has never been so appealing before. "Tell you what, Jules," he said, his hand closing over her breast. "Ouch. Not quite so much enthusiasm, sweetheart."

She released him, and giggled. "Shall I kiss it and make it well?"

He gave her a wicked grin. "What a lucky man I am, married to a thoroughly lascivious woman."

"I think I like the sound of that," she said.

"I do too. Tell you what, Jules, let me give you some instruction first, all right?"

"What kind of instruction?"

"Just lie still and attend to what I'm doing."

When he lifted her hips in his hands and gazed

intently down at her, Jules found herself trying to squirm away. "It's daylight. You're looking at me."

"Yes," he said, his voice sounding hoarse in his own ears. "I'm not only looking, but I'm offering up thanksgiving to heaven. Now, you just be quiet, and don't interfere with a man's pleasure."

She decided she had no choice, and he thought he would yell with pleasure when he felt her ease and relax, offering herself to him.

"Now I can look at you," Jules said many minutes later. He was deep inside her, moving gently, rhythmically, and she watched every expression on his face.

"Oh no," he said after a while, and slipped his hand between their bodies and found her. It was he who watched her face at the moment of her climax, allowing himself his own release after she'd gained hers.

"The world is a very nice place," he said, squeezing her so tightly that she yelped.

When they ventured downstairs close to noon, Lydia was nowhere to be seen.

"Smart woman," Saint said, eyeing the food she'd left out on the table.

He'd wanted to spend the entire day in bed with Jules, but realized he'd been quite fortunate not to have already been rousted by a patient. It was Avery who showed up, the man Jules had shot.

Jules, who had scampered upstairs at the rapping on the front door, heard him say to Michael, "It hurts, Doc. Bad."

"Come in here, Avery," Saint said, "and let's have a look."

When he joined Jules sometime later, he saw that she was pale and looked very guilty. He took her in his arms and hugged her. "No, sweetheart, it's all right. The man is just fine. No infection. I gave him some laudanum."

"I feel so bad."

"I didn't charge him, not even for the laudanum, and you know how much I pay for that. How's that for salving you conscience?"

She nodded—reluctantly, he thought—then said unexpectedly, "Do all men consider a woman to be a whore if she's alone?"

"Of course not. Well, not always. It's San Francisco, sweetheart. So many of our females are prostitutes. Poor old Avery probably took one look at you and didn't give a damn about what you said to him. In the future—"

"I know, I know, Michael."

"What about Thackery?" he asked her sometime later.

Jules was thoughtfully silent for a long while. "I don't know," she said at last. "I do know that Wilkes is out there somewhere. I feel it, as odd as that sounds. I don't understand why he could still want me, but I know that he does. It really makes no sense, does it?"

It made no sense to Saint either, but he privately agreed with her. He said nothing, however, for it would only add to her fear. He said instead, "How about we find Thomas and invite him over for dinner this evening."

She brightened immediately. "Yes," she said, "I should like that, if—"

"If what?"

"If he leaves early."

"Greedy woman," he said.

*    *    *

Thomas was aware of the change the moment he saw his sister's face. "Well," he said, "how are you?"

"Wonderful." Jules hugged him close. "Lydia made your favorite dish—roast sweet potatoes and pork chops."

"Lead on," said Thomas.

They had no sooner got settled at the dining-room table than Saint said, "Why don't you move back here, Thomas?"

"But—"

"No, no, please," Jules said.

"I really don't think it would be wise, Jules," Thomas finally forced himself to say. "Just as for Saint, the sofa's a bit on the short side for me."

Jules flushed just a bit, then said, "You may have the spare bedroom. Michael has decided that he misses his old room, his old bed—"

"—and his young wife," said Saint. "I've finally tamed the little twit, Thomas."

"So I see," Thomas said, "so I see. It's about time. Did you beat her, Saint?"

"Not really," Saint said, frowning a bit at himself as he remembered her reddened bottom. "Well, not much, in any case. Just enough to get her attention."

"Ha." Jules said. "He's a brute, Thomas."

"I don't suppose I'm going to hear this story?"

"You mean the story of my pulling down her drawers and—"

"Michael."

"If you could bear all the laughter and the giggling, we would enjoy having you back."

"Michael."

"Very well, Jules, I'll do all the giggling. Thomas," Saint continued, "have you decided anything yet? Is the world to have another doctor?"

Thomas played with the mashed sweet potato on his plate for a bit. "I have decided that I can't go back East, Saint," he said at last. "I have no money and I can't drag Penelope with me."

"So," Jules said, "you've decided to marry her?"

Thomas nodded, grinning. "The problem is, of course, that she's never known a day's want in her life. And I refuse to take money from her father."

"You might have to," Saint said. He raised his hand to stem Thomas's protest. "No, listen to me. You've some years of study ahead of you, with no income. Either you negotiate a loan from Bunker, or you don't get married."

"But you did," Jules said.

"Only at the very end," Saint said, "and it wasn't easy for a while. Incidentally, Thomas, I was speaking to Dr. Samuel Pickett at the Seamen's Hospital about you. He needs good men, and at least he's an excellent doctor. You'd get good training there. Not as extensive as in New York or Boston, but adequate."

Thomas brightened. "He'd take me on, really?"

"Yes," Saint said. He didn't add that he himself would provide funds during Thomas's instruction period.

"You could live here, Thomas."

But Thomas was frowning. "What about Penelope?"

"You're having problems fighting her off?" Saint asked.

"Yes, I am." Thomas sighed. "And myself as well."

"You could marry and live at the Stevenson mansion," Jules said.

"Damn," Thomas said. "I don't know." He smiled suddenly. "Do you know what Bunker Stevenson offered me? He's willing to give me the foundry as a sort of wedding present. Penelope's dowry, I suppose."

"That sounds like a financially wise solution," said Saint.

"He wants me to run the place. I told him I wanted to be a doctor, and he stared at me like I was one of Jules's arc-eye ravenfish."

"If I were you, Thomas," Jules said, "I think I'd let Penelope convince her father that you'd be the greatest doctor in San Francisco, after Michael, of course. And it's an arc-eyed hawkfish, Thomas."

"I'm glad to see you happy, Jules," Thomas said to his sister later that evening when they were alone for a few minutes. "It's about time. Saint's a fine man, and for a woman, and my little sister, you're not so bad either."

"Yes," said Jules, "yes, he is." She heard Michael's booted step upstairs and smiled.

"You sure you want me to move back in?"

"Yes."

"All right then. Good night, love. I'll bring my meager belongings back tomorrow."

"I simply don't understand how we fit so well," Jules said, her eyes resting on her husband's sex. "You are so large."

"Fate," Saint said.

"And so different from me. Now, I want you to relax so I can begin my lessons."

Jules delighted in the results of her handiwork, and Saint thought he'd die from the pleasure of it. "No," he said, pulling her away, "no more."

She gave him a slightly dazed, very pleased smile. "I don't pull you away," she said.

"It's not quite the same thing," he said. "Now, it's my turn."

"Oh dear. Thomas—"

"I'll put my hand over your mouth," said Saint. "Just promise not to bite me inadvertently, all right?"

The first explosion rocked the house and the bed. Saint, instantly alert, leapt out of bed and rushed to the window. He could see nothing.

"What was that?" Jules asked, sitting up.

"God only knows. Whatever and wherever it was, I'll be needed. Thomas too."

He began to pull on his clothes.

"I'll come too," said Jules.

He started to tell her no, but saw that she would argue tooth and nail with him. And there wasn't time. "All right. Hurry."

When Saint opened the bedroom door, he saw Thomas in he hallway struggling into his shirt.

"I don't know," Saint answered the unasked question. "Jules, wear a cloak. It'll be chilly."

They found Thackery downstairs, dressed, and leading two horses. "It's the Stevensons' foundry, Dr. Saint," he said. "Gawd, you can see the flames from here." Thackery was right. To the south, the sky was streaked with bright crimson and orange.

Damn Bunker, Saint was thinking. Normally at this

time of night there shouldn't be anyone around. But Bunker liked to have night shifts at the foundry. He prayed there were no fatalities.

He lifted Jules in front of him, and Thomas mounted the other horse.

"I'll follow as soon as I can," Thackery said.

When they arrived at the foundry, or what remained of it, there were already a good thirty men there, passing buckets of water with incredible speed.

"Anyone hurt?" Saint asked Morley Crocker, the foreman.

"Thank God, Saint. Yeah, we've still two men unaccounted for, and a half-dozen wounded over there."

Jules ran to keep pace with her husband and Thomas. Flames leapt into the air, and cinders flew about them. Her cloak felt suddenly stifling in the intense heat. She heard men yelling, saw the devastation.

"Your foundry," she said blankly to Thomas.

"I think my decision has just been rendered much simpler," he said.

Saint was bandaging a burned arm when Dr. Samuel Pickett came. "No fatalities, thank God," Saint said. "The burns aren't all that serious, but we've got one man unconscious, shock probably. My wife is watching him and keeping him warm."

Jules stared down at the man's still face. His clothes were tattered with burn holes and there were black smudges on his face and hands. She took off her own cloak and covered him. She heard Saint telling Thomas what to do, and saw Dr. Pickett hovering over a man who was moaning pitifully. It started to rain, and Jules lifted her face to the cooling water.

The drops thickened and soon it was a deluge. Thank God. That should put out the bloody fire. Thackery appeared beside her.

"What happened? Do you know?" she asked.

Thackery shook his head. Suddenly he straightened and yelled, "Dr. Saint, no."

Jules whirled about to see Michael running toward the still-flaming ruins. She could barely make out the form of a man stumbling out, clutching his stomach.

Her heart stopped. She jumped to her feet and ran toward her husband.

Saint had almost reached the man when there was another loud explosion. Gashes of fire rent the sky, and debris hurled outward. Saint felt his body hurled into the air from the force of the explosion and thrown backward. Then he felt no more.

Jules knelt beside her husband, her hand pressed against his chest. His heartbeat was strong, steady. She swallowed, swearing at herself that she wouldn't succumb to the awful tears and sobs she felt building inside her. She eased down beside him and held his head in her lap. In the next moment Dr. Pickett was on his knees beside Saint.

"His heartbeat is steady," Jules said, blinking away the rain so she could see him clearly.

Dr. Pickett looked at her briefly. "You're Mrs. Morris?"

"Yes."

"You're doing just fine, ma'am. You just stay as you are and let me examine him. Nothing appears to be broken," he said after some minutes had passed.

"He's very pale," Jules said, watching the rain wash away the black streaks from his face.

"No wonder. He probably struck his head. You won't faint on me, will you, ma'am?"

"Of course not," Jules said, her voice suddenly stronger and more forceful.

"Stay with him, ma'am. I'll be back shortly."

Saint moaned.

"Hush," Jules said. "It's all right now."

He opened his eyes, felt a deep, searing pain, and closed them.

"Jules?"

"Yes. Do you hurt anywhere, Michael?" She leaned over him, protecting his face from the driving rain.

"Jules," he said very calmly, "cup the rain in your hands and wash out my eyes. Quickly."

She froze, but just for an instant. She lifted her hands, cupping them as he'd said, and soon they were filled with water. Very gently she splashed the rain into his open eyes. He winced, and she saw him bite his lower lip.

"Michael—"

"Again, Jules. Keep doing it."

She continued, becoming more adept each time. Finally he said, "That's fine. Now, there's a clean handkerchief in my pocket. Fold it and tie it around my head over my eyes."

"Saint, you're back to the world again, dear boy?"

"Samuel?"

"Yes, what's this, ma'am?" He wondered briefly if the young woman had finally cracked as he watched her tie the handkerchief around Saint's head. She smoothed it firmly over his eyes, then sat back on her heels.

"Thank you, Jules," Saint said. "You did fine, just fine."

Suddenly Samuel Pickett closed his own eyes, feeling sickness rise in his stomach.

"Michael," Jules said.

"Help me up," Saint said. "Now, Jules, I know you're looking at me as if I'm on the brink of dying. But I'm not, I'm all right. Come."

Both Jules and Dr. Pickett helped him to his feet. He swayed a moment, then stood firmly.

Slowly he raised his hands and pressed the handkerchief more firmly against his eyes. "I think, Sam, that my usefulness here is over."

"Is there much pain, my boy?"

"It's lessening a bit. Jules probably got most of the fragments, but—"

Jules stared at him, hugging his side. "You're soaking wet," she said, her mind refusing to accept what she knew to be true. "We'll go home, Michael, and you can have a hot bath and—"

Saint knew she was trying to keep a firm hold on herself, and he admired her vastly at that moment. "Jules," he interrupted her quietly, "get Thackery and Thomas."

"Not Thomas," Samuel said. "He accompanied some of the wounded men to the hospital after I assured him you were all right. The black man, is that Thackery?"

"Yes, it is. We're not going to lose anybody, are we, Samuel?"

"Perhaps the one man you did your damnedest to save. I'm not certain yet. Maybe old Bunker will escape with a clear conscience after all, but the foundry's gone. Now, Saint, let's get you home."

"Yes, Michael, we must go. You're going to catch a chill."

He turned at the sound of her voice and said, "Hush, sweetheart. Everything will be fine."

He paused a moment, squeezed his wife's hand, heard her gulp down a sob.

Dr. Samuel Pickett said, "I've got my buggy. Mrs. Morris, stay with him until I bring it around."

# Chapter 24

Jules was squeezing his hand so hard it hurt. If Saint had been able, he would have tried to reassure her. He said nothing. He was scared. The searing pain was lessening in his eyes, but he knew as well as Sam Pickett that even those pale flashes of white he'd seen briefly could fade forever, leaving him completely and forever blind. Dear God, a blind doctor would be good for absolutely nothing.

The buggy lurched into a muddy rut, and he groaned, unable to keep it inside. He felt Jules lightly stroke her fingertips over his forehead and move him a bit so that his head was firmly in her lap. He heard her say gently, "Everything will be fine, I promise."

He would have smiled, but it required all his concentration to control the damnable pain. She was sounding like him. Soothing and in control.

The buggy finally came to a halt, and Sam's voice said, "Mrs. Morris and I are going to help you down now, Saint. Just hang on a bit longer."

He said nothing, allowed them to assist him into the house. It seemed odd in the extreme to be stretched out on his own examining table.

"Now, my boy, I'm going to take off the bandages. It's likely that you've still got some fragments in your eyes, and I've got to get them out. Then—" Sam paused.

"Then," Saint said, "we'll bandage me back up and pray."

"Yes," said Sam.

Saint listened to Sam give Jules instructions, and forced himself to lie quietly. When Sam unwound the handkerchief about his eyes, he blinked and opened them.

"Anything, Saint?"

"Same as before. Pale white, like hoary ghosts from my boyhood, and that's it."

"That's as much as we can expect and you know it. You've got to hold very still now, as I'm certain you well know. Mrs. Morris, please hold his head very steady for me, and move that light closer."

Saint didn't move, didn't utter a sound when Sam, with a light touch he appreciated, removed more fragments from his eyes. "It looks to me like the cornea is cut, but of course that's to be expected. As for retina damage, impossible to tell. Now, Saint, I'm going to wash out your eyes again."

"You didn't tell me one damned story to keep my mind occupied," Saint said when his eyes were bandaged again.

"I should have, I'm sorry," Jules said, stricken.

"Don't be a fool, Jules," Saint said, turning toward the sound of her voice. "It was Sam's duty, not yours."

"Mrs. Morris," Sam Pickett said, "would you please fetch your husband some tea?"

Saint frowned at that, but bided his time, hearing Jules's skirt swish against a chair as she left the room.

Strange, he thought, he'd never noticed that sound before.

"How much pain, Saint?" Sam asked immediately.

"Enough. A bit of laudanum in the tea, Sam?"

"Yes. I didn't want to worry your wife. She's being a big help, Saint. Does she assist you with your patients?"

"No," Saint said slowly. "At least she hasn't in the past. We haven't been married all that long."

"I see. Do you agree that the bandage should stay in place for three days?"

"Sounds reasonable. Then we'll see, won't we?" Saint sighed. "At least I hope I'll see."

"If not then," Sam said, "we'll keep your eyes bandaged another four or five days."

They were talking about canes when Jules came into the surgery, balancing a tray on her arms.

"Just a bit, Saint," Sam said, pouring laudanum into the teacup.

Jules watched him silently. She knew Michael would never tell her if he were in pain. He was a man, and for some reason unknown and not understood by her, men thought it weak to admit to anything less than perfection. She desperately wanted to talk to Dr. Pickett about his eyes, and she suspected that they'd had a frank discussion while she, weak woman, had been in the kitchen.

She would ask Michael.

"Now, Mrs. Morris," Sam said to her with a kindly smile, "why don't you help me get this giant upstairs to his bed. He needs a lot of rest, and after working with you, ma'am, I think you can handle him quite well."

The moment he began walking, the pain seared his eyes. He knew they were red and puffy.

Sam helped Jules undress him. He was nearly asleep by the time he was on his back in bed. "Thanks, Sam," he said.

"See you in the morning, Saint," Sam said, nodded to Jules, and took his leave.

Even with his senses dulled, Saint heard Jules undressing. He wanted to tell her that he would be all right, but the words faded from his mind. He was asleep when she kissed him.

Jules sighed at the sound of knocking on the front door, and trotted down the stairs. The stream of visitors, all of them worried about her husband, had been steady, giving her little time to brood, which was probably just as well. Lydia was baking in the kitchen, for each guest must be offered food and drink.

Jules opened the door.

"Hello. I'm Jane Branigan. I heard about Saint. You are Mrs. Morris?"

She's lovely, Jules thought. Jane Branigan, tall, voluptuous, glossy black hair. "Yes," she said. "Please call me Jules. Come in, ma'am. Saint is awake. A lot of friends have been here."

Jane had managed to quash the jealousy in her worry about Saint. But now, faced by this vibrant girl, she felt herself grow cold. She told herself yet again that it was over, had been over for quite some time. She was now a friend, no more, no less.

"If I could see him for just a few minutes," she said.

"Certainly," Jules said, stepping back.

She wanted to dog Mrs. Branigan's heels, but held

herself back. No, the woman wanted to see her husband alone. So be it.

Saint felt a cool, soft hand on his forehead.

"Jules?"

"No, Saint, me, Jane Branigan. Your wife is downstairs. The boys send their love, of course, I just wanted to assure myself that you would be all right."

Because it was Jane, because he'd forced himself to provide optimism to all his friends during the day, because he was scared and angry and trusted her, he said, "I don't know, Jane. My poor wife just might find herself saddled with a damned cripple. God, I could become some sort of institution. People could say, 'Yes, there's poor old Saint, blind as a bat, you know, but tells great stories. Give him a few pennies and he'll talk as long as you want.' Shit."

Jane understood, but she refused to pity him, at least not now. She said, her voice laced with humor, "Don't forget that those people could also demand medical advice. I can just hear old Limpin' Willie saying, 'Saint, bless him. Told me to lance the boil on my leg, and I did, and my leg rotted off.'"

"Damn you, Jane."

Jane felt tears sting her eyes, and leaned over without thought and hugged him close. "You'll be all right, my dear, you'll see. I mean that literally."

Jules stood in the doorway, a surge of evil jealousy washing through her. Slowly she backed up, and returned downstairs to the kitchen.

Saint hugged Jane, a reluctant laugh emerging from his throat. "As I said, damn you, Jane. You don't let a fellow bitch at all, do you?"

"You complain all you like, but you know very well that pity is the last thing you need."

"Jane, be kind to Jules. I think she's very afraid, but of course she's a chattering, optimistic little bird around me."

Jane was silent for a long moment. In truth, though, it was a brief war. She said, "I suggest you give her a bit more credit, Saint. She is your wife. Now I must go. I will come back, tomorrow perhaps."

"Jane?"

"Yes?"

"Thanks."

Jane was relieved that he couldn't see the tears in her eyes. She met Jules in the downstairs entranceway. "Thank you, my dear," she said. "I'll leave you now. You must be exhausted."

"Yes," Jules said, unable to hate this woman, "it has been mad all day, and Michael needs to rest. I don't know what to do."

"You give the orders, that's what you do," said Jane. "Let him complain and snap, but you do know what's best for him. Good luck."

And she was gone, leaving Jules to stare thoughtfully at the closed front door. She's right, Jules thought, perfectly right.

"Lydia," she called.

Saint herd her light footfall on the stairs. "Jules," he said. "Wasn't that the front door? Who's here?"

"Who *was* here. It was Horace and Agatha Newton. They'll return tomorrow."

"Why?"

"I told him you needed rest. They understood and send their love."

"I'm the doctor," he said. "I think I'm well able to decide when I need rest and when I don't."

"I brought you some tea and fresh sponge cake

Lydia just baked," Jules said, her voice all calm, soothing.

He wanted to strike out. "Dammit, Jules. Don't you dare treat me like a mewling child."

"Here, love. Drink this."

He did, with ill grace. Jules sat on the side of the bed, studying his face. "I'll shave you, if you like," she said, gently stroking her fingers over the stubble on his cheeks.

He grunted.

She leaned down and kissed him. "I love you, Michael. After you're rested, I'll give you a bath. That you should like," she added, her voice as wicked as she could manage.

"You want to beautify me so you can have your way with me."

"Yes," she said. "And I can do whatever I wish to you, and you'll not gainsay me."

"Dear God, a blind man dying from overexertion. Wife takes revenge on blind husband. I think I'll give Tony Dawson some headlines for the *Alta* for when I expire."

Jules smiled down at him, noticing the slurring of his words as the laudanum took effect. He would sleep a good four hours, Sam had assured her. And he needed the rest. The best thing for him, she knew. His eyes would heal. She would make them heal.

Jules held his hand as Sam unwound the bandages. "Keep your eyes closed, Saint, until I tell you otherwise."

"Doctors," Saint said in disgust.

"Now, very slowly, open your eyes."

He did. He was praying, hard. Nothing but the

same shadowy pale white light. He wanted to curse
and cry. He swallowed, knowing Jules and Sam both
were holding their breath.

"Just the lights," he said. "I guess I need more
time to heal. Another week, Sam?"

Sam was disappointed, but not overly surprised.
He'd seen quite a bit of damage in the cornea. He
couldn't bring himself to look at Jules, as he now
called her. She was a strong girl, and he knew she
was silent because she refused to cry.

"Yes," he said calmly, "let's give it another seven
days. Is the light any clearer?"

"No, just pale and hazy."

"Hold very still. I want to take another look to
make sure all the fragments are out."

Jules was fighting the lump in her throat.

"Looks good to me," Sam said. "any pain?"

"No."

"Back on with the bandage." Sam looked at Jules.
He stretched out his hand and took hers, squeezing
it hard. "Why don't you put it on, Jules? You've a
light, sure touch."

It gave her mind direction, focus. She smiled at
Sam, looking up for his approval as she fastened the
bandage. He nodded.

"We've seen little of Thomas," Saint said, then
laughed roughly at his choice of verbs.

"I've got the boy working hard, as you can well
imagine. He'll be a fine doctor someday, Saint, a fine
doctor." He added a moment later, after sending an
assessing look toward Jules, "He's got grit, just like
your wife here. Seems to me, Saint, that not all your
patients need to come to me. Lord knows I'm old
and tired. Perhaps Jules here could examine some of

them, and you could tell her what to do. What do you think, Jules?"

"I think that's a fine idea."

"Good, I'll spread the word."

When Jules returned to the surgery, she stopped cold in the doorway. Saint had gotten off the examining table and was feeling his way toward her. He bumped his leg against a chair and cursed.

"To your right, about a foot away," she said in a calm, clear voice, "is your drug cabinet. If you walk straight, you'll come right to me."

He wanted to yell at her that every goddamned thing in the world was nothing but black, impenetrable black. He said instead, "Keep talking. Balance is still difficult."

"I shouldn't wonder," Jules said. "You're doing fine, Michael. As you come straight at me, stretch out your hands. But not too far apart, mind."

That did make him smile, a bit.

"Now, lower your arms, Michael."

He did, and encountered her breasts. He stood quietly a moment, concentrating on the shape of her. "You're beautiful," he said, and Jules moved quickly into his arms.

He felt her cheek nuzzling his shoulder, felt her arms tighten about his back.

"I'm glad you're my wife, Jules, but dammit, it's not fair to you and—"

She clasped her hands behind his back and squeezed as hard as she could. "If you finish that thought, you will make me very angry. Now, do you promise?"

"Promise what?" he asked, resting his chin on the top of her head.

"Are you truly glad I'm your wife?"

Her voice was muffled, and he wished more than anything that he could see her face at that moment. Her expressions were so open, at least to him. Now, he thought, he had to rely on the nuances in her speech. "Yes," he said.

"And we can work together with patients?"

Pleading, he thought. It was important to her, and, he realized, it wasn't such a bad idea for him. It would certainly keep his mind occupied.

"We'll try," he said.

But it wasn't Dr. Pickett who sent them their first patient, it was Limpin' Willie.

"Me name's Ryan," the huge, shaggy man said, standing in the doorway, his black felt hat in his hands.

"Do come in, Mr. Ryan," Jules said. "Come into the surgery. I'll fetch my husband."

"Limpin' Willie told me he'd rather come to you, no matter you can't see nothing."

Saint smiled. "Tell me what's wrong, Ryan."

"I got myself pounded on the back of the head a couple of hours ago."

Saint wasn't about to ask how the pounding had come about. Ryan sounded every bit as much of a villain as any other Sydney Duck. He asked instead, "Any dizziness?"

"Yep, a bit. When I walk."

"Any blurred vision?"

Ryan thought about this for a while, then nodded.

"Yes, Michael," Jules said for him.

"All right. Sit still now, Ryan. Mrs. Morris is going to hold up a finger. First follow it to the right, then to the left—"

Jules was scared to death that she wasn't following Michael's instructions exactly right. After each test, Jules told him the result.

Saint said finally, "Sounds to me like you got yourself a concussion, Ryan. Now, here's what you're to do. I don't want you to be alone for another twenty-four hours. When you sleep, have someone with you, have them wake you every four hours and ask you who you are and where you are. That's just to make sure that your brains aren't addled. Then—"

After the grateful Ryan had taken his leave, pressing money into Jules's hand, she returned to the surgery, a wide smile on her face. The smile dropped away when she realized Saint couldn't see it.

"This," she announced, "is the first money I've ever earned in my entire life. Fifty dollars, Michael."

He heard the excitement in her voice and said, "Come here so I can congratulate you."

He drew her down onto his lap. "Well done, sweetheart."

"We're a good team, aren't we?"

"Yes," he said slowly, "I think we are."

"Michael?"

"Yes?"

"I don't know if I can stitch somebody. I think I'd throw up all over them, and that wouldn't be very reassuring for the patient, would it?"

"We'll see," he said. "And now, wife, I think what I would like to do is spend the next hours upstairs studying your body with my hands."

"Oh," Jules said.

"Do you know," Saint said a few minutes later in their bedroom, "I can hear you take off each item. You're only in your chemise now, aren't you?"

He heard a whisper of a sound, and grinned. "Lord, now my imagination is becoming overworked. Comes here, Jules."

He was still completely dressed, but Jules didn't hesitate. She felt an odd kind of excitement as he lightly began to touch her.

"Your nipples," he said, his voice deep, "I can't feel their exact color. Pale pink?"

"Yes," she whispered.

"And soft as velvet. Now, let me see if they taste pink and velvet."

It had been too long, she thought, as his mouth caressed her. She felt the familiar stirrings deep within her, and arched upward to give herself more fully to him.

When, finally, she eased off him and rose, she thought he was asleep. But he wasn't. He said in a deep satisfied voice, "I feel like I really am a saint at this moment. Nearly dead and gone to heaven. Lord, woman, you've worn me to the bone."

"I will let you rest awhile now, Michael. Then we will see about this bone business."

There was no thought of seeing about bones or anything else. An hour later Thomas came dashing into the house, his face white and drawn.

Jules jumped out of her chair. "Thomas, what is wrong?"

"It's Bunker Stevenson," Thomas said. "The bloody damned man has had a stroke."

# *Chapter 25*

"I'll be right along," Saint said without thinking. He pushed back his chair, kicked his foot into one leg and sent the chair sprawling. To keep his balance, he grabbed at the table, knocking his plate to the floor. He stood perfectly still, his hands braced against the table.

"Shit," he said very softly.

Thomas jumped forward. "I didn't mean—that is— oh hell, Saint. I shouldn't have blurted it out like that. Dr. Pickett's with him, but it doesn't look good. Mrs. Stevenson, as you can imagine, is in hysterics."

"And Penelope?" Jules asked, her eyes on her husband's rigid body. She saw that his knuckles were white from clutching the edge of the table.

"She's all right. Hell, she can't collapse, not with her mother carrying on like a Bedlamite."

Jules didn't really hear her brother's words. She was too worried about Michael. What could she say? It seemed to her at that awful moment that anything to come out of her mouth would but hurt him more. Merciful heavens, he was hurting enough now.

"Thomas," she said very calmly, breaking the tense silence, "why don't you sit down a moment? I'll get you something to eat. You too, Michael. Would you care for some wine, perhaps?"

Saint wanted to lash out. Hell, if there were a full moon, which he couldn't see in any case, he'd howl like a crazed animal. He got a grip on himself, turning toward his wife. "Yes, thank you, Jules. A glass of wine would be just fine."

"Excellent. Why don't you sit here, Michael?"

He allowed her to take his arm and lead him to another chair at the table. His mouth was drawn in a thin line. When he heard her pick up his plate, he couldn't help himself, and shouted, "Damn you, leave it. I made the mess, and I'll bloody well clean it up."

Jules slowly straightened. She saw Thomas's startled look, and shook her head at him. No excuses, no pity. He wasn't a hurt child, to be soothed. He was a man and he was proud. And he was frustrated and angry. She supposed she would be also.

"No, I will clean it up," she said, a bit of humor into her voice. "Since for the time being you can't see a thing, I will be your eyes. Besides, Michael, the peas scattered all over the carpet. I don't want you to squish them with your big feet."

"Jules—"

"Thomas, tell Michael exactly what happened and what Dr. Pickett is doing for Bunker."

Jules listened with only half an ear to Thomas as she cleaned up the mess on the carpet. Then she poured each man a glass of wine. She said nothing, merely took Michael's hand and placed his fingers about the glass stem.

"Thank you."

"So," Thomas concluded a moment later, "Dr. Pickett thinks that the shock of the explosion at the foundry probably triggered the stroke. What do you think, Saint?"

"Perhaps," Saint said, well under control again. "That and the fact that Bunker is fat as a stuffed turkey, something I've spoken to him about many times, to no good effect. You say his entire left side is paralyzed?"

Thomas nodded, then said, "Yes."

"But his speech isn't terribly impaired?"

"Only a bit. That surprised Dr. Pickett."

Saint said, "I've been Bunker's doctor for over two years now. I tend to think that he'll make it mainly because he's so damned stubborn. But then again, helplessness and dependence tend to change one."

Talk about looking helpless, she thought, staring at her brother. Thomas looked drawn and worried and scared.

Thomas said, "The question is, what am I going to do now?"

"I think, Thomas," Jules said, "that it might be the best thing if you married Penelope now and moved into the Stevenson house. You aren't needed here, my dear, merely appreciated."

Thomas would have protested, but Saint said, "Jules is right, Thomas. Penelope and her mother are used to having a strong man about to take care of them. The two of you should probably marry immediately."

Thomas and Penelope were married one day before Saint's bandage was to be removed. It was a private ceremony at the Stevenson house, and Bunker was carried down by a servant and his driver to give his daughter away.

"I have never seen her so subdued," Chauncey Saxton said to Jules. "I'm beginning to agree with Del that this is probably all for the best."

"I certainly hope so," Jules said. "Thomas is my brother, after all." Penelope looked lovely, Jules thought, and then realized: *She's now my sister.*

It was a rather unsettling thought, given the fact that Jules's only sister, Sarah, hadn't played that role with much warmth or caring. Please, she prayed as the two solemnized their vows over the loud sniffling of Mrs. Stevenson, let it work out properly. Let Thomas be happy.

There was, of course, champagne, and heavier drinks for the men. Chauncey had helped with the buffet, and it was impressive. Jules was eating a lobster canapé when she heard Bunker say in his loud, carrying voice to Michael, his speech only slightly slurred, "Well, my boy, here we are, two war horses, shot down. But Dr. Pickett tells me you'll be eyeing that lovely wife of yours again in no time at all now."

Sally Stevenson, her mother's duty accomplished, was smiling now, accepting congratulations. But, Jules thought, she looked ill, her jowls noticeably sagging, as if the shock had aged her five years. She wondered if the shock was about her husband or her new son-in-law. Thomas had never said if his mother-in-law approved or disapproved of her daughter's marriage to him, a penniless young man. She must tell Mrs. Stevenson how very lucky she was.

Thomas didn't let his bride out of his sight, his

hand always either under her elbow or around her waist. Jules knew about desire and passion and she saw both in her brother's eyes when they rested on Penelope. As for Penelope, she looked somewhat dazed, her voice and movements mechanical.

Jules couldn't get near her husband. Friends surrounded him, unwilling to leave him alone. Some were studiously careful to avoid any reference to his blindness; others, like Bunker, spoke freely, then went on to other matters.

She moved closer, hearing Brent Hammond say to Michael, "You'll not believe how Wakeville is shaping up, Saint."

"Thackery gives me progress reports. And how is your pregnant wife, Brent?"

Brent grinned. "My own little fat spider," he said, winking toward his wife. "She says she feels fine and for me to stop driving her crazy, but—"

"I know, the first child and all that."

"Well, by the time the first perfect child makes his or her appearance, you should be back on your feet and back into your eyes."

Byrony joined the group. "He is driving me utterly mad, Saint. Would you please tell him that his part in this entire affair is well over?"

"Hell no," said Saint. He stretched out his hand toward Byrony, and clasped her fingers in his large hand. It took Jules a moment to realize that it was a thoroughly doctorly thing he was doing. She heard him say after a moment, "No swelling. Good, Byrony. How about your ankles?"

"Here I thought you were getting forward with my wife," Brent said. "Her ankles swell if she doesn't lie down every couple of hours."

"Just see, Brent, that she does lie down, then," Saint said, patting Byrony's hand. "Alone."

Brent moaned, and if it was possible for a woman to guffaw, Byrony did.

"It was well carried off," Jules said to her husband as Thackery drove them back home.

"Yes," Saint said.

"Do you think Thomas will continue wanting to be a doctor?"

"I don't know." Oddly enough, Saint was thinking about his rearranged closet. He'd always been neat and orderly with his belongings, but not sufficiently for a blind man. It had galled him to have Jules hand him each item of clothing in the morning. Usually she'd have to rebutton his shirt, for he always seemed to mismatch buttons and holes. He'd said nothing to her, but that morning she'd led him to the closet and had him run his hands over the array of shirts, then trousers, vests, and coats. All in magnificent order now, all arranged with darkest coats first, then the blues and grays. He'd managed to dress himself for the wedding, and he supposed he should feel good about it. But he didn't.

Jules eyed him with mounting frustration, but said nothing more. When she helped him into bed an hour later, she smiled into the darkness, slipped off her nightgown, and snuggled next to him.

He said nothing, nor did he move to touch her or kiss her.

Jules leaned down to kiss him on his closed mouth. "I love you, Michael," she said, kissed him again, and settled beside him to sleep.

She awoke suddenly at the sound of an anguished moan. It was still quite dark.

"No, dammit, no. Oh God, no."

Saint lurched sideways, tangling himself in the covers, crying out.

Oh God, she thought, and began shaking him. "Michael, wake up. It's a nightmare, love. Wake up."

She felt sweat on his forehead, felt the pounding of his heart beneath her hand. "Michael."

"What?" Saint came awake with a shudder. For a moment he held himself utterly still. Then very softly he said, "God, Jules, I'm so bloody scared."

She straightened the tangled covers, then pulled him close. "I know," she said against his temple. "I would be too. But, Michael, listen to me—" For a moment she could think of nothing to say, for this large, proud man was shuddering against her, and she couldn't bear it. "Listen to me," she repeated, stroking his thick hair, hugging him. "If you don't see tomorrow, then you will see next week. Your eyes will heal, I swear it to you."

And if they didn't? If he became completely blind? No, she couldn't, wouldn't accept that, at least not yet, and she couldn't allow him to give up.

"I dreamed that you needed me. You were hurt, I guess. I told you I would help you, and I smiled at you and began to tell you a stupid story. And then suddenly I couldn't see, and you were begging me to help you. I couldn't see."

He was clutching at her, his face buried against her breasts. He was shuddering as if he were freezing to death. "I was useless," he said.

"Michael," she said, "it was a dream, that's all,

just a dream. I would have been scared silly if I'd dreamed it was you who were in trouble. You know something else? I can prove that it was stupid."

He was listening to her now, and she smiled, kissing his ear. "You are incapable of telling a stupid story. You would have had me laughing and cursing you. If I had been doing any begging, it would have been to make you stop because I was giggling so hard." It wasn't good enough, she knew, not nearly. Jokes and humor were all right in their place, but not in the dead of night when monsters roamed freely through the mind.

"I will tell you something else. I know you married me because you are an honorable man. That, and you did care for me, or at least you cared for that child you'd known." She felt him tense. "No, it's all right. But the fact is that we are married. We are a partnership. We are to share in everything. And we will. You said something about helplessness and dependence changing one. Well, if it does happen, if you don't regain your sight, we will both of us change, and adapt and adjust. You would never be useless, and I think if you say that again, I'll hit you on your hard head."

Saint felt her words seep into mind like soothing balm. The fear, the ghastly pain of the dream, were fading, leaving his mind free and alert.

"Do you believe that I could ever love you any less if you were blind for the rest of your life? Have you no idea of what I feel for you? How much I admire and respect you?"

"Jules, I— Oh, dammit."

Suddenly it was too much. Jules burst into tears,

and she hated herself, but she couldn't stop. The dam had burst.

"Ah, sweetheart, no," he said, moving against the pillows so he could take her into his arms, protect her, soothe her. He realized that they'd just reversed roles, and he smiled a bit. "Jules, don't let me hurt you—my anger and bitterness, well, it's all within me, and I've heard it said that the loved one gets all the misery. Hush, don't cry so, you'll make yourself sick." He stroked her hair, kissed her, caressed her bare back. "I don't know how a bastard like me could ever attract a beautiful creature like you, much less have her care about me."

Her sobs lessened and soon she was hiccuping against his throat. "I'm sorry," she said after a few more minutes.

"About what?"

"You need me to be strong, and I just became what I despise—a weak, silly woman. I'm sorry, Michael, please forgive me."

"No."

It was as unexpected as it was angering. She reared up and stared down at him. She could see the outline of his bandage, the planes of his face, but she couldn't see the smile. "Just what the hell does that mean?"

He laughed, and she hit his chest with her fists.

"Some weak woman," he said, grabbed her arms, and tossed her onto her back. "Will I have to tie you down so I can have my way with you?"

"No, but only because I don't think you can manage it."

He moved on top of her, his knee pressing against

her closed thighs. "Open your legs, Jules," he said, his mouth against her throat.

The feel of him naked, covering her— "What will you do if I do?" she said, moving beneath him.

"I'll caress you with my mouth until you yell and then I'll come inside you, so deep that neither of us will know where the other begins or ends. And I'll fill you with my seed, and you'll feel it, and know that you are part of me."

When at last he loved her with his mouth, caressed her as he'd said he would, she couldn't bear it. The pleasure that convulsed her body was nearly painful in its intensity, a pleasure that held all their shared pain, and she cried out again and again. And when he thrust into her, a long, deep thrust, she clutched him, arching upward, yielding to him, opening to him, wanting him to become a part of her.

"My God, woman," he said many moments later when he could finally speak, "I never thought about doing that to that scruffy little girl in Lahaina, at least not consciously," he added, and laughed.

"No," she said, clutching her arms about his back, "don't leave me, Michael."

"I won't," he said, his fingertips stroking her face. Her teeth nipped his fingertips and he kissed her again. He felt the sweet, smiling curve of her lips as his tongue traced over her. Her eyes would be smiling too, he thought. At least, he wanted to tell her, at least I have seen you in the moments of your pleasure. He felt her legs tighten about his flanks, felt her smooth hands stroking down his back, and his body responded. He moaned as he filled her again.

"You are the most exquisite lover in the world," Jules said just before she fell asleep.

"Yes," he said, his voice deep with satisfaction. "I guess I am."

"No," Saint said very carefully, "it is still the same, Sam."

Jules wanted to moan like a wounded animal, but she didn't. She said nothing.

"Still the white?"

"Yes."

Sam laughed. "Excellent, Saint. You're healing." He clapped Saint on the back. "All you need now is rest, lots of it. No worrying, now, and no fighting with your wife."

"I don't understand," Jules said.

Saint reached out his hand and she quickly took it. "What Sam means, Jules, is that since what vision I have hasn't faded, it's hopeful, very hopeful." He drew her against his side and hugged her. "I do promise not to *fight* with her, Sam."

Dr. Pickett smiled, and in that smile was a prayer. He patted Saint's shoulder. "Well, you don't need me anymore. We'll try again in another week, Saint. Another thing, no more than two, three patients a day." He turned to Jules, his voice more serious now. "Rest, Jules. He must have rest. I count on you to handle him."

"I shall, Dr. Pickett," she said, "I shall."

After Jules had shown Samuel Pickett out, she returned to the surgery. "Here is your cane, Michael. Let's have some lunch and tell Lydia the good news."

She watched him like a hawk, of course, but bit down on her tongue when he bumped into a chair. To her great relief, he laughed. He listened to her right the chair, and said, "Tell me how romantic I look with this cane, Jules."

He did, she thought. It was ebony, with a carved lion's head. She'd said nothing about the cane before, uncertain as to his reaction. "Well, Michael," she said, slipping her arm through his, "if you looked any more romantic, I would insist that you rest now, without your lunch."

Jules insisted that both Lydia and Thackery join them in the dining room. At first Thackery looked at her as if she were speaking gibberish.

"For heaven's sake, Thackery," Lydia finally said, "would you please stop acting like a slave."

"But—" Thackery said.

"No, no more," Jules said. "Come to the dining room. Saint will tell you about Mr. Leidesdorff, the first black man in San Francisco."

That got him, Jules saw, and smiled at Lydia.

Saint, when applied to for the story, sat back in his chair and smiled in Thackery's general direction. "His name was William, and unfortunately, I didn't have the pleasure of meeting him. He died a young man, only thirty-eight, in 1848, and what with the inflation brought by the gold rush, his estate was worth over a million dollars. Just six months ago, as a matter of fact, our own John Folsom"—this said in a sarcastic voice—"hauled himself to Jamaica and bought interests from possible claimants to the estate, for, you see, William Leidesdorff left no kin. Lord only knows what will happen now."

Jules tapped her fork impatiently. "But the point is, Thackery, this is California, and everyone is free to do as he wishes here." It was on the tip of her tongue to have Michael relate Leidesdorff's tragic love affair, but she realized in time that it had been tragic simply because the man had been a mulatto, and therefore unacceptable to the white family.

"If you ate with your fingers," said Lydia, "that would be another matter entirely. And that's why Saint here doesn't invite all those Sydney Ducks to dine with him."

Saint chuckled, and Jules wanted to shout with the pleasure of the sound. She looked at Lydia, then at Thackery. We're becoming a family, she thought.

Two days later, in the early afternoon, Jules, with smiling firmness, helped her husband upstairs to rest. Lydia had gone to do some marketing, claiming she'd best get out now before the rains started again. As for Thackery, he'd left go to the Wild Star to see Brent Hammond.

When there was a knock on the front door, Jules sent a worried look upward, praying it wasn't a patient. She hated to turn anyone away, but Michael was more important.

It wasn't a patient, however. It was a young boy.

"Miz Morris?" he asked, his voice a lisp through the gap in his front teeth.

"Yes," Jules said.

"This is for you, ma'am," the boy said, thrust an envelope into her hand, and scurried away before Jules could say anything else.

She frowned at the envelope, for there was no name or direction written on it. There was one sheet of paper inside. She read:

*My dearest Juliana,*
*I trust you haven't forgotten me. I wished to send my condolences about your poor husband's*

*blindness. I am near to you, my dear, very near.
Do think about me, Juliana, and know that soon I
will have you again.*

It was signed with a bold "J. W.," nothing more.
Jules dropped the paper as if it were a snake to bite
her. She felt the familiar fear building, and wrapped
her arms about herself. She looked toward the windows, but the thick rain prevented seeing outside.
She thought vaguely that Lydia hadn't missed the
rain after all. Slowly she walked to the sofa and sank
to the floor beside it. She heard a small, broken
sound, and realized that it was from her own mouth.

# Chapter 26

Thomas sat behind Bunker's large, ornate mahogany desk, a medical book propped open in front of him. He realized that he'd read the same paragraph at least three times and hadn't taken in a single word.

He looked up with a snort of disgust and eyed the opulent library. Three walls were lined with bookshelves, filled with impressive tomes that nobody read. A thick, bright red Aubusson carpet covered the floor, a lovely carpet, he thought, if one could but see more of it. His mother-in-law had covered it with heavy, clumsy furniture that depressed him. He wondered for a moment how his wife would have decorated the library.

Penelope. His wife. She was upstairs with her mother. My beautiful bride of three days, he thought, and sighed. It had never occurred to him that Penelope wouldn't enjoy the marriage bed as much as he. His only experience with women had been with native girls in Maui. They had been loving, giving, and not at all reticent of telling him how to pleasure them. He'd learned a great deal, particularly from Kani, and when he'd finally gotten his new bride to bed, he was confident and anxious to begin his pleasure, and hers. She'd allowed him to kiss her and fondle her breasts, but when his hand moved downward, she'd acted as if he were insane—no, worse; as if he were a disgusting animal. He'd breached her maidenhead finally, his teeth gritted at her sobs of pain. And afterward, as he'd held her and stroked her and told her how much he loved her, she whimpered against his shoulder. Still, Thomas had been optimistic. The first time couldn't be very nice for the woman, but surely when he made love to her again, she would welcome him. She hadn't.

He realized, sighing more deeply, that he hadn't even seen her naked. Her modesty dictated that the room be utterly dark. How could she love him, he wondered, and not want to see him or enjoy him physically?

He forced his attention back to his medical book. Surprisingly enough, it had been his father-in-law who, only three days after his stroke, had presented Thomas with the needed medical books, saying that if Thomas wanted to be a damned sawbones, he might as well get started, since Bunker fancied he'd need him.

"Not exactly yet, boy," Bunker said. "Maybe later, when I really get ill."

"Mr. Thomas."

Thomas started at the sound of Ezra's deep voice coming from the library doorway. The man walked as softly as a prowling cat, he thought. "Yes," he said, but moved a bit in his chair, uncomfortable with a bloody butler.

"It's your sister, sir, Mrs. Morris."

Thomas rose quickly. "For God's sake, man, show her in." Was Saint blind permanently? No, that couldn't be it. He'd spoken to Dr. Pickett and knew that Saint was healing.

When he saw her pale face, every positive thought plummeted to his toes.

"What's wrong, Jules? It isn't Saint, is it?"

She shook her head. "No, he is resting at home," she said. "He must rest, you know, Thomas."

Thomas cocked his head at her. "Then you've come to see how your newly married brother is faring?"

"Not really," she said. "Here, Thomas, read this."

She thrust the paper into his hands. Frowning, Thomas unfolded the paper and read.

"That damnable bastard. Jules, when did you get this? Was it Wilkes himself?"

"No, a boy delivered it to me about an hour ago. I couldn't worry Michael with it. All he could do is rant and rave and worry, and I can't allow that. Thomas, why is Wilkes doing this? What am I going to do?"

Thomas was silent for a long moment. "Have you shown this to Thackery?"

"Not yet. I wanted to speak to you first, but Thackery suspects something is wrong. And no, I didn't come here alone, Thackery is outside."

"Wilkes is insane, he has to be to keep after you like this."

"Thomas, I'm afraid."

"Come, love, and sit down. Let me think about this. Would you like a cup of tea?"

She agreed, not really caring.

Ezra brought in a silver tray some while later, his disappointment evident when Thomas dismissed him.

"How is Bunker?" she asked as she stirred a bit of milk into her tea.

"Much better," Thomas said absently, then smiled. "In fact, he's a terror. He'll be back to his old self in no time, I think. Saint was right about his constitution. I begin to believe he'll outlive us all."

"And Penelope?"

"She is fine," he said abruptly.

Jules frowned a bit at this most unloverlike reply, but didn't dwell on it. She was too frightened.

"You were right not to sell Saint about this," Thomas said.

"Yes, I know, but I also realize that if he ever finds out, he'll be furious with me. He's so proud, you know, but—"

"Yes, but," Thomas said, interrupting her. "Thackery is your only protection. It is not enough, not with Saint helpless as a baby."

"Michael smashed my derringer," Jules said, wishing now that she'd bought a dozen of the deadly small guns. She saw the look of bewildered astonishment on her brother's face, and added quickly, "No, I refuse to explain. It doesn't matter now in any case." To her relief, Thomas let it pass. She watched him rise and begin to pace the library. He came to an abrupt halt, whirled to face her, a wide grin on his face.

"Here's what we're going to do. My new wife and I will move into your house until Wilkes is out of your life once and for all."

Jules's mouth dropped open. She waved a helpless hand at the opulent room. "Thomas, you can't take Penelope away from this. Our house is small, and

the spare bedroom would seem to her like a servant's room."

"She is my wife," Thomas said in a very stern
voice, "and she will do as I bid her."

"But your father-in-law—"

"Bunker is just fine and he's surrounded by ser-
vants. I am no longer needed here. Now, Jules, no
more arguments from you. My wife and I will arrive
this evening. All right?"

She gave him a dazed nod, and he walked her to
the front door. "Jules, you will tell Thackery."

"Yes, of course," she said. "Thomas, it just occurred to me that Michael will wonder why you and
Penelope are moving in with us. What should I tell
him?"

Thomas grew thoughtful. "Tell him that Pen needs
to get away from her parents for a while, more spe-
cifically, her mother. Tell him that if he doesn't mind,
we'll continue our honeymoon on Clay Street."

It had begun to rain harder, and Thomas fetched
her an umbrella. After he had handed her into the
carriage, he saw that Ezra was regarding him with a
great deal of interest.

"You'll take care of Bunker, won't you, Ezra?"

"Certainly, Mr. Thomas," Ezra said. "And you will
take care of your sister, sir."

Thomas nodded, not bothering to ask him what
and how much he knew, and headed up the stairs.
For all Thomas knew, Ezra might have eavesdropped
on their conversation. He paused a moment in front
of his and Penelope's bedroom, squared his shoulders, and walked in. He might as well face the un-
pleasantness now and get it over with.

\*   \*   \*

Saint cursed his blindness, for Jules's face always gave her away. He sighed. "That sounds pretty weak to me, Jules. Won't you tell me the truth?"

"You don't mind their coming here for a while, do you?"

"Stop dodging, sweetheart."

"Michael, please."

He heard the pleading in her voice, and said finally, "All right. If you and Thomas wish to keep your secrets, very well." He shook his head. "The thought of Penelope sleeping in our house is unnerving. I wonder if we'll survive it."

Penelope was wondering the same thing that evening. She'd said not two words to her new sister- and brother-in-law. She regarded Thomas from beneath her lashes in animated conversation with Saint. My husband, she thought, is a trifle bitter. And I am to obey him. And that's what he'd told her that afternoon when she'd simply stared at him.

"You won't, of course, haul your entire wardrobe there, Pen, there's not enough room."

"How much room is that?" she'd asked him.

Thomas had looked about the enormous bedroom, dripping with opulent furnishings, and smiled. "The bedroom is, as I recall, about a third this size. You'll like the bed, though," he'd added, giving her *that* look.

"I don't want to go," she said, digging in her heels. "I must stay here, Thomas. My parents need me."

"No they don't. I've already spoken to your father. He's as worried as I am. Our reason for going is valid. I assume that you don't want my sister to be kidnapped again."

"No, of course not, it's just—"

"Enough, Pen. Pack your things. We'll leave after dinner."

"But—"

"You are my wife and you will obey me. Now, do as I tell you. Another thing, Pen, you won't say anything about Wilkes's threat to Saint. He is not to know."

And that, Penelope thought now, had been that. She'd seen the small bedroom and shuddered. And the bed, it was so small. She sipped at her tea and tried to think of something to say to her sister-in-law. But it was Jules who spoke first.

"You are very lucky, Penelope," Jules said, smiling toward her brother. "Thomas is a fine man. I was his slave when we were children."

"Such an odd life you had," Penelope said.

"Yes, it was like a Garden of Eden. Despite our father's rigidity, we managed to run wild most of the time and enjoy ourselves immensely."

"I don't have my maid," Penelope said.

What do I say to that? Jules wondered. She mustered a smile and some warmth in her voice and said, "It is very kind of you to come, Penelope. I realize that this is not exactly what you're used to, but I don't think you'll be unhappy here, especially since Thomas is here also."

Penelope merely nodded, and Jules felt a wave of frustration. This, she thought, wasn't a very good idea.

The following morning, Thomas left to see Del Saxton, his explanation to Jules being, "Saint's Sydney Ducks need to be alerted, and I hope Mr. Saxton will know how to round them up." He'd kissed her cheek and left. Saint was with a patient, a man with a private problem, so her husband had told her, and thus her presence wasn't needed, or desired for that matter.

Jules wandered back upstairs, planning to see if Penelope had everything she needed. She paused outside the closed bedroom door, aware that Penelope was crying.

Oh dear, she thought. Had she and Thomas had a fight? What should she do?

She knocked, then entered. Penelope was still in bed, huddled under the covers.

"Penelope, what's the matter? Do you feel ill?"

Penelope froze, humiliation washing over her. "What do you want?" she asked, not looking at her sister-in-law.

"What's wrong, Penelope?" Jules asked, quashing anger at the cold words. "Come, we are sisters now."

"It's your damned brother," Penelope shouted, her cup filled to overflowing. "He's an animal, a brute, and—"

"*What?*"

"He forces me to do—things, and I hate it and it's awful and my mother told me it would be thus, but I didn't believe her."

The light dawned. Jules regarded Penelope's flushed face. "What did your mother tell you?" she asked.

"That men are animals, that they do unspeakable things to their wives, and we have to be brave and—bear it."

"And you believed her? By all that's rich, that is ridiculous. Don't you love my brother?"

Penelope stared at Jules. "Of course I love him. I shouldn't have married him otherwise."

"But you only wanted him to kiss your hand?"

Penelope drew back at the sarcasm. "I didn't know what it was all about. I don't like it, it's degrading."

"It? I assume we're talking about lovemaking."

Penelope shuddered at what she thought a most inappropriate term, invented doubtless by men.

Jules felt an odd mixture of pity and anger. Poor Thomas. And poor Penelope. "I think," Jules said, moving to sit on the side of the bed, "that you need to think of me as your mother for a while. Now, I want you to listen very carefully, Penelope, because I will not lie to you."

Penelope gave Jules her full attention.

"—and I told her that making love was more fun than anything else in the whole world," Jules told her husband that night in bed. "I explained things to her. I simply can't understand why mothers frighten the wits out of their daughters with such awful rubbish."

"Your mother didn't tell you frightening things about filthy men?" Saint asked, pulling her closer to him.

"No, she never told me anything at all. I think complete and utter ignorance is better."

Saint kissed her nose, then nibbled on her ear. "I hate to tell you, sweetheart, but unfortunately many men believe that their wives should endure their base needs. It's only whores who are supposed to enjoy lovemaking. Men are fools."

"You don't think Thomas is a fool, do you?"

"He is young," Saint said, "but no, I shouldn't think that he'd be inept. But I suppose you want me to speak to him? Just to make certain, you understand?"

"Explain things to my brother?"

Saint's hand cupped her breast. "In delightful detail," he said, and began to knead the soft flesh. "Did you tell Penelope how much you adored my touching you?" His hand slipped down between her thighs. "And kissing you?"

Jules sucked in her breath when his fingers found her. "Oh dear," she said, "do you think I should have been that specific?"

Saint felt filled with warmth and deep, deep feelings that so stunned him with their force and their unexpectedness that he couldn't speak for a moment. "Jules," he said finally, "I don't want to think about Penelope any more tonight. All right?"

"Yes," she said, "yes, all right."

Jules managed to find her brother alone the following morning. "What did Del say?" she asked without preamble.

"Not to worry," Thomas said, hugging her. "He said they'd start the search again for that miserable bastard. It shouldn't be long now, love."

She felt great relief, and to her chagrin, tears filled her eyes. "I am so lucky," she said, and threw her arms around her brother. "Thank you, Thomas."

"Perhaps," he said quietly, a bit of humor in his voice, "it is I who should thank you, my dear."

She gulped, not pretending to misunderstand him. "Penelope told you that we had a little talk?"

"Yes, though it took me a while to pry it out of her."

"You're not angry at me for meddling, are you?"

"No, little idiot." He gave her a wicked grin. "Actually, it pleases me mightily to know that Saint is such a caring husband. As for my wife, let us say that her attitude is changing. It's now up to me, I suppose, to be patient as a saint."

"My husband could give you advice about that," she said, grinning up at him.

Penelope came into the dining room at that moment, Saint beside her. "Good morning," she said, and when her eyes met her husband's, she blushed.

"Michael," Jules said as she ate her scrambled eggs, "would you like me to change the bandage this morning?"

"All right," he said. "Then, sweetheart, it's off for good in three days. It's time I saw my beautiful wife again, as well as my complaining patients."

Jules was silent a moment; she was praying.

"I'll provide the champagne," Penelope said, surprising everyone.

Saint chuckled. "Your father does have the best wine cellar in San Francisco. Think you can sneak some out of there, Penelope?"

Penelope felt herself smiling. Indeed, she realized, she felt comfortable and wanted. It was a heady feeling. "Yes," she said, joining in the laughter. "I shall lock Ezra in the cellar if he gives me any trouble."

"Or, love," Thomas said, leaning closer to her, "if you prefer, I could be convinced to have Ezra lock us in the cellar with the champagne. I can just see you now, Pen, your petticoats in wild disarray and a half-empty bottle in your hand."

To Thomas's delight, his wife giggled.

How could she have forgotten even for a moment? Jules thought that afternoon as she stood in the entranceway, another letter from Wilkes clutched in her hand. It read simply:

> *My dear Juliana,*
> *You force me yet again to withdraw. It is not over. Pray do not forget me.*

It was Penelope who found her, white-faced, rigid, and alone, huddled next to the sofa on the floor.

She took the crushed paper from her sister-in-law's nerveless hand, smoothed it out, and read it. She said nothing, merely helped Jules to her feet and drew her against her, hugging her.

Jules said, "God, I wish I had my derringer."

Penelope gently patted her back. "Why don't I purchase one for each of us?"

Jules could only stare at her.

"Yes," Penelope said again. "I believe I shall go out now."

And she did.

# Chapter 27

There was not a sound that morning in Saint's surgery. The small room was crowded. Thomas, Penelope, Jules, and Dr. Pickett all stood as still as stones, waiting. Thackery and Lydia were outside the open doorway in the entrance hall.

Jules could hear everyone else breathing. She was holding her own breath.

Dr. Pickett cleared his throat. "Saint?"

Saint said nothing for many moments. "Jules," he said finally, "is that a freckle I see on your nose?"

Jules stared at him, for the moment unable to accept his words. Then, at his slow smile, she flung herself into his arms, nearly knocking him backward. "Yes," she said against his shoulder, "it's a freckle. I don't know where it came from. I suppose I could use some lemon juice or something—"

"Or some cucumber lotion," Penelope said.

"Or just let me kiss that very cute freckle," Saint said. He drew her back, stared down into the dearest face he'd ever seen, and lightly kissed the tip of her nose. "Hello, wife," he said, stroking his fingertips over her face. "It's quite nice to see you again."

Thomas gave a loud shout and wrung Dr. Pickett's hand.

"It seems to me," Saint said after a moment, "that a doctor's surgery is the last place to expect such an excess of spirits."

But nobody paid him any mind. He accepted handshakes, back slaps, with a big smile and his deep laugh. Jules saw his eyes alight with pleasure, and she didn't believe she'd ever seen him so happy. She sent a prayer of thanks heavenward.

"Pen," Thomas said after a moment, "it's time to get on with the excess of spirits. And Saint's right—this surgery is too small for us."

"Actually," Penelope said a few minutes later when they were all in the dining room, "my father insisted I bring over six bottles of his best champagne."

"Drunk as loons by noon," Dr. Pickett said, raising his filled glass a few minutes later in the dining room. "To the return of the most saintly man in San Francisco.

"And the biggest tale-bearer," Lydia said.

"Could you rephrase that a bit, Lydia?" Saint said. He looked around the table at all his friends. It was a heady thing, this looking and seeing. "Lord," he said, his voice deep with his feelings, "it's good to see all of you again. Allow me to refill everyone's glass. If I spill any, it won't be because I'm not seeing straight."

Jules looked at Thackery and was surprised to see tears in the black mans' eyes. He met her gaze and said with a crooked smile, "I never drank champagne before."

"Your wife, Thomas," Saint said as he refilled Penelope's glass, "looks as content as a spring rose, and just as pretty. Is he a good husband to you, my dear?"

Penelope gulped, hiccuped, and laughed with Thomas's eyes on her. "He will improve," she said.

"Every day," Thomas said, "yes, indeed."

"Saint," Lydia said, "I've baked you your favorite apple tarts. If we're all not to be drunk under the table, I'd best serve them now."

Three hours later, Saint, a bit tottery himself, was giving out advice for hangovers.

But it was only the beginning. By evening it seemed to Jules that everyone in San Francisco knew that Saint had regained his sight. The stream of visitors was continuous. The women brought food, the men liquor.

At midnight Jules was so tipsy that Saint half-carried her upstairs to their bedroom. He called over his shoulder, "Good luck to you, Thomas." He grinned at the sound of Penelope's giggle.

"I don't believe I've ever seen you quite so sodden," he said to his wife as he undressed her. Jules looked up at him and grinned. He kissed her freckle again. "Do you think if we listen we'll hear some marvelous sounds coming from the other bedroom?"

"What if they listen, Michael?" she asked, her eyes nearly crossing in her effort to focus on his face.

"I fear," he said, voice stark with disappointment, "that all they would hear would be the sound of your unladylike snoring,"

She tried to punch him in the stomach, but missed. Her head spinning, she fell onto her back on the bed.

Saint grinned down at her, and quickly pulled off the rest of her clothes. For a moment he was on the sober edge. "God," he whispered, looking down at her. "I prayed I would see again. Do you know how beautiful you are, Jules?"

Jules was too giddy to care that she was sprawled on her back, her legs parted.

"That flame-colored hair, very delightful, sweetheart." She realized vaguely that he wasn't looking at her head.

"Michael," she said, and tried to cover herself, only to feel his strong hands pulling hers away.

"Oh no, you are mine, all mine."

She swallowed at the richness of his deep voice, then felt a wave of dizziness and giggled. "You have your clothes on," she said.

"Not for much longer."

To his chagrin, Jules was sound asleep when he turned back to her. He kissed her, drew her body against him. She'd lost weight. He looked a moment toward the lamp by the bed. I can see you, he silently told the light. I can see everything. I am the luckiest man on earth. He was loath to plunge the room into darkness. I will see the sun in the morning, he thought. And I will feel like the very devil and probably curse it.

The following afternoon, Saint *was* cursing, but not from a hangover. He was standing by the dresser in their bedroom, two pieces of paper in his hand. He closed his eyes a moment, utter fury washing through him.

He strode to the top of the stairs and bellowed at the top of his lungs, "Jules, come here. Now."

Jules, who was feeling a bit tentative, excused herself from her company and slowly, with great care, mounted the stairs. She heard Agatha Newton, Tony Dawson, and Chauncey Saxton laughing in the parlor, and wished they wouldn't be quite so loud.

"Yes, Michael?" she said, coming into the bedroom.

She stopped cold in her tracks, seeing him waving two sheets of paper at her.

"I was looking for a handkerchief," he said with great calm, "and I just chanced to come across these."

She looked at him helplessly.

"It is not that I haven't enjoyed having Thomas and Penelope staying with us," he continued, his voice becoming harder, "but this, Juliana. Damn you, how dare you?"

Juliana. She'd just regressed again. "Michael, you don't understand—" Her mouth felt dry as cotton.

"Yes? You can, I am certain, manage a marvelously competent explanation. You're rarely at a loss for glib words, are you? Well?"

"I didn't know why I didn't throw them away," she said, staring at those wretched sheets of paper.

"Juliana, damn you, answer me."

She raised her eyes to his face, and he cursed crudely.

"Do you have any idea how this makes me feel?" He waved the papers in front of her nose. "Less than a man—in fact, something far less than a tinker's damn. How dare you keep this from me?"

He grabbed her shoulders and shook her. The papers made a loud crumpling noise as they wrinkled between his hand and her shoulder.

"If I recall correctly, I said very nearly the same things to you before, didn't I? Did my feelings then mean nothing to you?"

She jerked away from him. "All right," she said, shaking her fist in his face. "I was protecting you, dammit. I love you and I couldn't allow you to be worried."

"I had every right to know that this vermin was threatening you again."

"No," she said, "no, you didn't. And stop cursing me. There was nothing you could have done in any case. If you don't remember, you were blind. Helpless."

He realized the justice of her reasoning, but was not ready to release the meaty bone of contention. "So, you, my little wife, made the decision that I was to be left ignorant. Is there anything else I should know? Did it not occur to you to tell me yesterday, when, if you will remember, I saw the light of day again?"

"I was too drunk and too happy," she said. "I forgot to tell you. Even if I had thought of it, I wouldn't have said anything. We were celebrating, remember?"

That halted him in his tracks, but for just a moment. "Then you should have told me this morning."

"You are acting ridiculously," she said. "I will have no more of your silly shouting and wounded male vanity. I would do the same thing again, do you hear? Now, we have company downstairs."

"I happen to be nine years older than you and twice your size," he said. "I refuse to be ordered about by a little twit now or ever. Do you understand me?"

"Damned arrogant man," Jules said, and shook her fist at him again. "If you wish to nurse your grievances, do so, Michael. I'm leaving."

He stared at her. " 'Damned arrogant man,' " he repeated, as if disbelieving of the words until they'd come from his own mouth. "That's what you think I am?"

"I do, if you continue to call me Juliana."

"Oh shit," he said, and thrashed his fingers through his hair. "Come here, you idiot."

She gave him a hopeful, tentative smile, and at the answer in his eyes, she threw herself into his arms. "I'm sorry," she whispered against his shoulder. "I did what I thought I had to do, what I thought was best."

"I know," he said, "I know."

He began kissing her, and her response was immediate and gratifying.

"Oh God," he said, reluctantly releasing her, "company downstairs, did you say?"

"You've a lot of friends, Michael," she said.

"Any chance of sending the whole bloody lot of them to the devil right now?"

"Probably not," she said, a wealth of disappointment in her voice.

He hugged her to his side. "Onward, love. Charm and all that."

He called me "love," she thought, dazed and so happy she wanted to yell. She paused. Perhaps it had just been another endearment, like "sweetheart."

At dinner that evening, Saint merely asked Thomas what he'd heard about Wilkes. Thomas drew a relieved breath, shot his sister a smile, and told his brother-in-law what they were doing.

As for Jules, she sent a conspiratorial smile toward Penelope. Both women now owned a derringer. When Jules had shown her how to fire it, she'd said, "Men aren't altogether reasonable. I am continually amazed that they actually believe that women are helpless creatures with even less sense. Here, Pen, you load it now."

Jules said nothing at all while Thomas and Saint discussed Wilkes. She watched her husband as he used his large hands to make a point, watched his beautiful hazel eyes change in intensity as he spoke. His white teeth gleamed with a wide smile. She imagined him naked, and felt warm deep in her belly. At that moment, Saint met her eyes. A brow arched upward, his eyes darkened.

Jules laughed, a nervous, silly sound that made Saint grin at her. "I don't think," he said to Thomas, "that I will ask your sister what she's thinking right now."

"Why not?' Penelope demanded. "Jules has very good ideas."

"Too true," Saint said. "Too true."

"I will tell you later, Michael, exactly what I'm thinking," Jules said.

"Or you could simply show me," Saint said.

"But Jules," Penelope said, "why don't you tell him now? This does concern you."

Thomas broke into merry laughter. He leaned over and clasped his wife's slender hand. "She can't, love, it would be too embarrassing."

"Oh, you are a wretched tease, Thomas DuPres."

Saint didn't believe that he would ever tire of watching his wife brush her hair. She was wearing the dark blue velvet dressing gown he'd given her at Christmas, and her thick beautiful hair rippled down her back. He was lying on the bed, his head pillowed on his arms. He said idly, "I explained things to Thomas, just as you asked."

Jules looked at him in the mirror, a grin on her face. "And what did my brother have to say?"

"Well, he looked very surprised, really. Astonished, I suppose you could say. As I recall, he said, 'Saint, are you certain that is how it's done? I thought the ear—' "

Jules threw her hairbrush at him.

He let it bounce off his chest, then tossed it back to her. "To be serious about it, I simply asked him how things were going with his bride. He looked greatly pleased. Of course, sweetheart, two gentlemen wouldn't discuss techniques or exact approaches, not like you ladies appear to do."

Jules rose from her chair and slipped off her dressing gown. She liked the feel of it and stood a moment, petting the velvet.

"Why don't you consider putting me around you? I imagine I'm much warmer than that dressing down."

She grew warm at the sight of him. "Have you never worn a nightshirt?" she asked, standing over him, looking down his body.

"No," he said, his voice growing thick as her eyes rested on his groin.

"You are so beautiful, Michael," she said, and slipped into bed beside him. "And much warmer than my dressing gown."

Saint did his best to slow her down, but it was impossible. She wanted him, and quickly. It was the first time they'd made love since he'd gotten his vision back, and he thought he would yell with pleasure as he watched her face at the moment of her climax.

Then he was deep inside her, thrusting frantically, beyond himself. He heard her moan softly when his seed burst from his body into her, and he knew that she was filled with him and that she was happy to be so. He pulled her onto her side, stroking his large hands down her back. "You are perfect," he said, kissing her temple. "And I love you, Jules. With all my heart."

She raised her face to look at him, and he said softly, "Don't cry, love."

She felt his fingertip wipe away the single tear that ran down her cheek. "I'm not. I was just thinking that perhaps I didn't hear exactly what you said."

He squeezed her, felt himself growing hard again. "Woman, you heard me right, and you know it. As you can feel, my body agrees with me. Will you rush me this time, Jules? Or will you let a simple man give you everything he can, and very slowly?"

Jules contracted her muscles and he moaned. "I don't know, Michael," she said. She came on top of him, and he helped her straddle him. He was very deep inside her. His hands covered her breasts, and she arched her back, her hair streaming over her shoulders and over his hands. When his fingers stroked downward to find her, she gasped. "I don't think I can, Michael."

He felt her hands close over his wrists, felt her thighs tighten about him. He thought he would never see anything so beautiful as the dazed sheen in her eyes. "Yes," he said, "come with me, now."

Her response was immediate.

Saint lay awake, the shadowy patterns cast in the far bedroom wall by the moonlight silvering through the window. Life, he thought, would be perfect if it weren't for that bastard Wilkes. During his several years at Massachusetts General Hospital, he'd dealt with the insane, people who were mindless yet utterly harmless, people who were mindless and violent, people who believed they were someone else, usually long dead, and people, he realized, who were obsessed with an object, an idea, or another person. His reason rebelled against the notion, but faced with Wilkes's actions, he could not deny it.

He'd assumed in the beginning that Wilkes wanted this lovely girl because she was a virgin and would bring him a great sum of money. But her marriage should have made him realize the futility of his wish. Unless all he wanted was revenge. But no, Saint's thinking continued, that didn't make sense either. He tightened his arms about his wife. There was no choice now, not really. He would have to kill Wilkes.

He would find Limpin' Willie in the morning. Perhaps Willie's criminal mind could aid him in finding Wilkes. Jules muttered something in her sleep and Saint smiled. He hoped she was dreaming of him and enjoying every bit of it.

He wondered now how long it would be before she became pregnant with his child. His body stirred at the powerful thought. He began to breathe deeply and slowly, a habit he had learned early in medical school, and one that put him to sleep within minutes.

The following morning, Jules and Saint helped Thomas and Penelope move back to the Stevenson mansion. Bunker, Saint thought, after he'd examined him briefly, would live to be ninety.

"Well, my boy," Bunker said, "it's good to have you back again. Not that I don't like Pickett, mind you, but—"

"Thank you," Saint said quickly, cutting him off. "Now, what you need are more rest and a daily dose of fresh air. Have your man Ezra drive you out every afternoon."

Mrs. Stevenson was a different matter, and Saint felt a stab of pity for Penelope when her mother fell on her, weeping.

"Leave go, Sally," Bunker told his wife sharply. "The girl's a married woman now and has lots of new responsibilities. And she looks happy as a tack." He turned back to Saint. "A good man, my son-in-law," he said, not bothering to lower his voice even though Thomas was within hearing distance. "He'll make a fine doctor, I don't doubt. Ah, yes, Saint, I'll help him right enough. Next time I have one of these damned fool attacks, he'll be here to get me over it."

"I will miss Penelope," Jules said to her husband as they got into the carriage. "She has changed so much. Even Chauncey said she was having to revise her opinions. Del just shook his head and said something about every woman being tractable if handled properly."

"And what did Chauncey say to that?"

"Something about she would take care of him later."

"I'm certain that she did," Saint said.

"I'll miss Thomas too," said Jules.

"At least I won't have to worry about clamping my hand over your mouth every night."

She poked him in the ribs. "Do you never think serious thoughts? Elevating thoughts?"

"Maybe they'll return in, say, five years."

"Or so," Jules said, tucking her hand through his arm. She gave him a sunny smile even as she felt a sudden surge of guilt over her new derringer. No, she would be very careful this time. She wondered what Penelope would do with hers, and had the inescapable feeling that her sister-in-law would keep it safe, and a secret from Thomas.

She was not at all surprised to see three patients waiting for Saint when they returned home. She was surprised, however, and delighted, when Saint asked her to assist him.

# Chapter 28

It was the middle of the afternoon. Patches of sun came through the bedroom windows, unnoticed by either Saint or Jules.

"That," Saint said many minutes later when his heart slowed a bit, "should probably be against the law." Her muscles tightened at his words, and he groaned, kissing her.

Jules wanted to moan and laugh at the sound of the knock downstairs on the front door. "I should be a banker, like Del Saxton," he said, slowly and very reluctantly pulled away from her. "Given the satisfied smile on Chauncey's face, I wager they spend many afternoons like this." He sighed. "I suppose I should count my lucky stars. That knock could have come ten minutes earlier."

He rose and quickly dressed. "You, love, are in no shape to be my assistant this time. Just lie there and think about me."

Before he left the bedroom, he leaned down and kissed her again, his hand gliding over her breasts. "You look well loved," he said on a strained laugh. He touched his fingers to the damp curls, then forced himself to straighten. "Don't move," he said. "Per-

haps I'll be lucky and the patient downstairs only
has a cold or a sprained thumb."

But the patient, a Chinese worker, had been beaten
and robbed. Saint was with him for hours.

"Will he be all right?" Jules asked him over dinner
that evening.

"It depends, dammit. There might very well be
internal damages, something we great doctors know
next to nothing about and could do nothing about in
any case. If he lives the night, he has a good chance.
And no, the men who did this to him weren't any
of Limpin' Willie's friends. Strangers, his friends
told me."

He was angry, and Jules noticed he'd eaten next
to nothing. To distract him, she began to talk about
the time he'd saved her from a jellyfish when she
was thirteen years old. Soon he was laughing, remembering how she'd yelped and how he'd had to
straddle her to keep her foot steady.

It was over a cup of Lydia's delicious coffee that
Saint sat back in his chair and said, "Byrony is due
to deliver in a week or so. I received a brief note
from Brent today. Would you like to visit the new
town of Wakeville?"

She nodded enthusiastically. "Oh yes, I should
love it. I was hoping we'd be going soon. I can't wait
to see what they've done."

Saint nodded, then shrugged with a show of elaborate indifference, saying, "We'll leave first thing in
the morning, then, before it's light."

Jules wasn't fooled for a minute. "You believe
Wilkes has someone watching the house?"

"I doubt it," Saint said, lowering his head so she

wouldn't see the worry in his eyes, "but I won't take
any chances." He saw that she would protest and
said quickly, "Jules, I don't like sneaking about like
thieves in the night, but dammit, I won't take any
risks with your safety. Now, I need to make arrange-
ments with Dr. Pickett to take over patients, and you,
my dear, need to write notes to Thomas and your
friends. Lydia will continue as if we were here." But
Saint was thinking to himself: Please show yourself,
you vermin bastard. I want to put my hands around
your damned neck. I want to destroy you as I would
a mad dog.

"Thackery will accompany us?" Jules asked, pulling him from his violent but very satisfying thoughts.

He nodded. "Now, why don't you pack for us and
I'll be off for a couple of hours."

It was drizzling before dawn the following morning, the fog thick and heavy. Ranger Tyson from
Hobson's Stables had provided a carriage and two
horses. "He still owes me" was all Saint said.

Jules felt the chill seep through her thick cloak and
moved closer to her husband in the dark carriage.
The seats smelled of old leather and tobacco smoke.
And, her nose twitching, the carriage smelled of sex.
It was a rather large carriage, after all.

She heard Saint speak in a low voice to Thackery,
and soon the carriage jolted forward.

They were nearly ten miles south of San Francisco
when the sun came up. The air was clear and there
wasn't a hint of rain.

"This is lovely," Jules said, staring out at the rolling green hills. "I can smell the ocean. I wish we
could see it."

"The land was too rugged to build a road closer," Saint said. "Perhaps someday."

"We'll stop for breakfast soon. Lydia packed us a hamper."

They stopped on a rise that gave a view of the ocean to the west and rolling hills to the east. The sun was warm and there was a crisp early-morning breeze. Jules stood for a moment near the edge of the rise, breathing in the clear air. Saint watched her a moment after spreading out one of Lydia's checkered cotton tablecloths. He loved the way the breeze caught tendrils of her hair, lifting them, and the shine of the sun through the flame strands.

"Beautiful," he said, lightly closing his hands over her shoulders.

"Yes," she said, leaning her head back against his shoulder.

She felt his hands ease beneath her cloak and cup her breasts. She shivered, pressed herself more tightly against him. "Shall I tell Thackery to go find the Northwest Passage or something?" Saint asked, kissing her ear.

Jules's stomach growled and Saint laughed. "I suppose that's my answer," he said, turned her around, and kissed her mouth.

They breakfasted on fresh, still-warm bread, butter, and jam, and coffee in one of Lydia's jars, wrapped in heavy cloths to keep it hot.

"This is decadent," Saint said, leading back a moment on his elbows. "How far to go now, Thackery?"

"Not more than another hour, Dr. Saint," Thackery said, and both Jules and Saint could hear the excitement in his voice. "The rains haven't been so bad so far, and the building never stops. Mrs. Byrony never stops either, and you should hear Mr. Brent yell at her."

The horses seemed to feel the excitement and quickened their pace. The first view of Wakeville came less than an hour later, and Jules sucked in her breath. "I don't know what I was expecting," she said, tugging at Saint's sleeve, "but this is incredible."

It looked to Saint as if Brent Hammond had managed to buy the most fertile acres in the area. And the activity was astounding. There was even a Village Street wide enough for two carriages side by side, with new buildings with sidewalks lining it. Nine out of ten faces in the new town were black.

"All this in six months," Saint said. Thackery turned the carriage off Village Street and pulled to a stop in front of a two-story white house with a wide veranda across the entire front. There were trees and flowers everywhere.

Brent Hammond came out of the front door at that moment, a very pregnant Byrony on his heels. An ancient black woman followed closely behind Byrony as if she expected her to keel over like a small ship.

"Ah," Brent said, grinning as he shook Saint's hand, "we've got the greenhorns from the big city."

"I'm afraid you can't get any closer," Byrony said, laughing as she tried to hug Jules. "This child is going to be born declaiming lines from a play. He certainly is dramatic enough in his movements."

Byrony said, "This is my keeper, Mammy Bath. Mammy, this is Mrs. Morris."

"Just look at that hair, little missis," Mammy said, reaching out gnarled fingers to touch Jules's hair.

"And all that pretty white skin. Now, you two little ladies come inside and rest."

Byrony said behind her hand to Jules, "And the big strong men will ensure the running of the world. Don't argue, Jules, it's no use."

Soon the little ladies and the strong men were seated at a huge dining table, plates of sausage, eggs, and toast piled in front of them.

"This isn't nirvana by a long shot," Brent was saying, "but we're working through the problems as they arise. We have few fights, fortunately, and no thievery except for a month ago when some drifters came into town. They saw all our black people and decided to help themselves." Brent shook his head, grinning.

. "He enjoyed himself immensely, Saint," Byrony said. "He was itching to bang some heads together and got his wish."

Saint watched Byrony with a professional eye. The child was large and it worried him. And Byrony, despite her smiles, looked tired. He heard her speak to Jules about their school.

"Little Tony, bless his heart, practically taught himself how to read and do figures. He's now in charge of deeds, births, deaths, and all the rest of the record-keeping."

"Yes," Brent said with a wry grin. "Little Tony— the fellow's nearly as big as you are, Saint."

It wasn't until that afternoon that Brent managed to get Saint alone. They were walking in the garden behind the house, Brent explaining what crops they were planting and how it was decided who did what. He broke off suddenly. "Well, what do you think, Saint?"

Saint didn't pretend to misunderstand. "She needs to be tied down," he said.

Brent curse softly. "Lord knows I yell at her enough, but she'll turn those big eyes on me and say, 'But there's so much to be done,' and I always fold. Some gambler I am."

"Tie her down," Saint repeated. "The child has dropped, Brent, which means that she'll go into labor in, say, three or four days. She needs to stay in bed now. I won't lie to you. The child is large, even larger than I'd expected it would be. She needs to have all her strength because her labor will probably be long."

Brent turned white.

Saint put his hand on Brent's shoulder. "I don't mean to scare you. Byrony will be all right, I swear it. But I don't like to tempt fate."

"I'll tie her down," Brent said. "Excuse me a moment, Saint, and I'll do it right now."

"Better yet," Saint said, "let me examine her now. I'll give her the orders. You're only her husband, Brent, I'm her doctor." Saint paused a moment, then said, "You haven't seen any strangers about, have you, Brent?"

"As in Wilkes, you mean, Saint?"

"Yes, as in Jameson Wilkes. I really don't know just how extensive his spy system is, but—"

"Yes, *but*," said Brent. "Try not to worry. I'll ask about."

Saint said nothing more, but Brent knew he was worried. Hell, all his friends were worried and would be until the vermin was destroyed.

They found Jules and Byrony in the parlor laughing and drinking tea. Byrony was busily sewing something. Brent said firmly, "Hello, Jules. Byrony, come along now, Saint's going to take care of you." He held out his hand to his wife.

Byrony grumbled a bit, but allowed her husband to help her out of the chair.

"Jules," Saint said, "would you please see to Brent here? Byrony, at last I've got you to myself. Let's go upstairs."

Brent looked as if he would follow, but instead sighed and flung himself down in the chair Byrony had just vacated. "Damn," he said. "Excuse me, Jules," he added.

"You're worried, Brent. I don't blame you, but Michael is the best doctor in the whole world."

He gave her a crooked smile. "He's also going to be the busiest doctor in the whole world. Everyone in town knows he's here by now. A goodly number have aches and pains. There'll be a line two deep tomorrow."

Upstairs, Saint helped Byrony sit down in a chair, then sat down on the edge of the bed. "Tell me how you feel."

"I've had pains already, Saint. Then they go away. I do try to rest, but—"

"Yes, I know. These pains, Byrony, tell me about them."

She told him of the sharp, low pains, finishing with, "I thank my lucky stars I didn't tell Brent. He would have gone crazy."

"Yes, it's just as well. Now, I'd like to feel this child of yours."

Byrony undressed while Saint waited outside in the hallway. She was swathed in a long white cotton nightgown when he came back into the room. He helped her lie on the bed, then very gently slipped his hands beneath the gown to feel her belly.

"No, Byrony," he said looking at her tightly closed eyes, "please, just relax." His knowledgeable hands lightly roved over her belly. "That's better." He decided to wait to examine her internally. Best to let her accustom herself to him first. He straightened her nightgown and took her hand. "Now, Mrs. Hammond, let's chat a bit."

Byrony was in bed by nine o'clock that evening. Saint looked at his wife and decided bed was the best place for her too. He felt a surge of pure lust and frowned. His hand, though, went around her waist, and she leaned into him, smiling up at him.

"You know something, Saint?" Brent asked.

Saint turned toward him.

"Never play poker, my friend. You'd lose." Brent chuckled, patted Jules's arm, and took himself off.

"What was that all about?" Jules asked.

"Brent saw the lustful look in my eyes, I think. He's right. I'd never win at poker."

"Would you care to play something else?"

"I suppose I have no choice?"

"None at all," she said, and dragged him upstairs.

# *Chapter 29*

The child screamed at the top of his lungs, so loud Jules wanted to clap her hands over her ears. Instead she held the wriggling little boy down while Saint vaccinated him.

"There," Saint said. "Stop your caterwaulin', Tobias. You'll live, I promise." He patted the boy's head and helped him up. "Now, you're going to live forever—"

"Yessir," the boy gulped.

The mother said, shaking her head fondly, "No guts at all. Yer little missis here is a real sweetie pie."

"Hi, sweetie pie," Saint said, kissing her the moment they were alone. "I'm about ready to drop, love. How about you?"

"A nice strong cup of tea would put me to rights, I think," She shook her head. "I think I'm temporarily deaf."

"Did I ever tell you that Napoleon had all his troops vaccinated if they had not already had smallpox?"

She blinked up at him and he grinned, adding, "I've done about eighty-five vaccinations today, and not a soul would have known who Napoleon even was. I had to tell that interesting fact to someone, just to keep my hand in.''

Jules clasped his hand in hers, silently studying the long, blunt-tipped fingers, the sprinkling of chestnut hair.

''Now, I wonder where you think my hand should be next?''

She kissed each finger. ''This is a start,'' she said. ''Now, you need to tell me how you managed to get enough supplies to vaccinate all the children.''

''A mistake, Jules, a simple mistake, at least that's what Sam Pickett told me. Some government fellow showed up at the hospital wanting to get rid of cases of what he believed were useless medical supplies. Needless to say, Sam nearly did a jig for joy, kept a straight face, and called me. And here we are and all the children are now protected, thank the Lord.''

''You're a perfect man, you know that?''

'That's what my mother told me,'' Saint said, ''but it was a number of years ago.''

He stopped a moment, and straightened her bonnet. ''The sun is strong, love. I do love that one freckle on your nose, but I don't know as I'd like to see more of the little fellows.''

She poked him in his ribs, laughing. ''You know that isn't a freckle on my nose—it's a liver spot.''

''I've aged you so quickly, hmm? I think I'd best do a thorough examination. If you have any more of these liver spots, I'll just have to do something about it.''

''What?'' Jules asked, taking a skipping step to keep pace with her husband.

He leaned down and whispered in her ear.

''Michael.''

* * *

Jameson Wilkes stared at her from his post in the narrow alley. He was dressed roughly, a felt hat pulled low over his forehead. The scratchy wool pants increased his anger at Saint Morris. He hated having to appear like one of the damned slaves in Brent Hammond's town.

He leaned forward and watched the breeze lift a waving curl off her forehead, watched her husband straighten her bonnet, and stiffened when the huge man who was her husband leaned down to whisper something to her.

*Don't touch her, you damned bastard.* He could barely keep the words from spurting from his mouth.

He'd lived with the dream of her, the fantasies of her that he'd woven over the months, and knew that he would have her, have her lying beneath him, helpless, yet wanting him as he did her. The reality of her shook him, as did her bright laugh. Reality, he thought, an odd word, something to avoid, to escape. He'd never heard her laugh before. He'd cursed himself again and again for ever taking her to the auction. He should have kept her with him, sailed from San Francisco and taken her to the far reaches of the earth. But for what reason? He shook his head, his thoughts tangled. His hand roved over his belly, rubbing frantically, and the pain made him think clearly.

Now she was married to that damned do-gooding bastard Saint Morris. If only he'd kept her with him, if only he'd managed to take her the night of the Stevensons' ball, if only—

He wanted her. And he was here, and he was going to take her, had to take her, and her husband, Dr. Morris. Oh yes, he had to see Saint Morris, had to— He winced at the increasing pain, but forced his mind away from it, forced his mind to plot, to come up with strategies. He had to have focus. No, he wouldn't dig into his opium supply until the pain made him want to howl.

His last grand gesture, he thought. His last gesture to affirm that he was alive, that he managed to win one last time. And he knew it was true. Juliana now represented both life and death to him. He smiled a bit, remembering how Hawkins had come to him, a huge grin splitting his ugly face. "Yessiree, they're off early, bound for the black town."

So easy, Wilkes thought. He wondered if Juliana now believed herself safe from him.

Saint Morris was here to deliver the Hammonds' child. Wilkes had only to remain out of sight and wait for his opportunity.

It would come, oh yes. He knew suddenly, at that precise moment, with the bright sun overhead, exactly when and how he would strike.


Jules was walking down the street beside Thackery and Little Tony, a black man who would intimidate the bravest of men. His size was formidable, his body hard with muscle, and he had the gentlest eyes Jules had ever seen.

She was listening to the two men talk. Although Thackery had never said anything to her, she realized now that he missed being here, missed being part of the town's growth. She silently cursed Wilkes.

"I must get back to work now, Miz Morris," Little Tony said, pausing a moment before a freshly painted wooden building. "This is where we keep all our records," he added, pride in his voice.

"Please call me Jules," she said, but knew that he wouldn't. Old habits were hard to break.

Little Tony nodded to her from his great height.

"Thank you for the tour," Jules said. "Now," she continued to Thackery, "why don't we go for a ride? I should love to see the land around the town and all the planting and all the new building."

Thackery agreed and they walked to the livery stable. "Little Tony was telling me how much trouble they're having with names."

Jules cocked a questioning brow.

"Slaves have only one name," he said tersely. "Outlandish names, given by white owners."

"What are you doing about it?"

"Mr. Hammond, he's made lists of names—real names—his missis too. All of us choose what name we want, then Little Tony writes out certificates."

"What name have you chosen?"

"Me? I was lucky. I just chose John. John Thackery."

Jules stopped and thrust out her hand. "A pleasure to meet you, John."

He gave her a big white-toothed grin and took her small hand in his large one. "As for Little Tony, he's now Mr. Anthony Washington."

"That's some name to live up to," Jules said.

They rented two horses and rode out. Jules was wearing her new blue velvet riding habit and a jaunty little hat. She felt happy and content. The morning was sunny and warm. The rolling hills surrounding the wide valley were green from the winter rains. They reined in occasionally so Thackery could show her how the plots of land had been divided up, pointing out the constant building of small houses.

"I think Mr. Hammond has every banker in San Francisco involved," he said. "The amount of lumber we need is incredible. Just look over there—"

There was a loud cracking sound. Jules whipped about to see Thackery grab his chest.

"Thackery—"

She tried desperately to keep him upright on his horse, but his weight was too great and he slid to the rocky ground. Jules was off her horse's back in an instant.

"Leave him be, Juliana."

Jules knew that voice—it had played in her dreams countless times. Now it was hard and cajoling at the same time. And filled with triumph and satisfaction.

"I must help him," she said, voice blank from shock, still disbelieving. She felt Wilkes's hand on her arm, felt him pull her about to face him.

"Look at me, Juliana."

She couldn't. She wouldn't.

His long fingers took her chin, forced her face upward. "You're insane," she said. "I am nothing, nothing at all to you. Why?"

Jameson Wilkes sought the depths of her eyes. He laughed. "If I could answer that, my dear, in a fashion you could understand, I shouldn't have lived in hell for so long a time. Come now, Juliana. We have a goodly distance to go."

"No," she said, her voice so calm it surprised her. "I must help Thackery."

"You touch him, my dear, and I'll put another bullet through his black hide." He saw the flaring of fear in her eyes, and knew he had found his lever. "However, if you come with me, I'll leave him as he is." He didn't want her fighting him, didn't want her struggling until she hurt herself. He saw the growing stain of red on the black man's chest and knew he would die in any case. But the man was tough, and Wilkes hoped he would make it back to tell Saint Morris. He was counting on it; that was why he hadn't put a bullet through the man's heart.

"You will die for this," Jules said as she walked to her horse. "My husband will kill you for this."

"Actually, my dear," Wilkes said, "your husband is at this moment helping Byrony Hammond. From what I could tell with all the excitement, she is now birthing her child."

Jules shut her eyes. When would she be missed? Would she be missed at all?

"Now, I believe I shall take your reins. Unfortunately, I cannot trust you to do as I bid you once we are away from your bodyguard." He grasped her horse's reins, pulling closer to her.

"Behave, Juliana, else I'll tie you up. Remember how I tied you up before? There is much we will do together."

Jules thought of her derringer, so safe and distant in the bottom of her valise. It was the oddest thing, but she wasn't particularly afraid, for the fear of the reality was much less than the fear of his shadow and his threats. The fear would come, though, she knew it. But before it numbed her mind, she knew she had to think clearly. She had only herself to rely upon. As Wilkes nudged their horses forward, she turned in the saddle to see Thackery. Pain seared through her. He was lying utterly motionless on his side.

"You are a filthy man," she said.

"Nothing a bath won't cure," Wilkes said. His eyes

darkened, and she flinched. "Ah, you're remembering those baths aboard my ship, aren't you? And how I watched you and admired you."

"No, I am remembering how I smashed your head. I wish only that I'd hit you harder."

"Such a pity," Wilkes said before turning his attention to the trail in front of them.

"What is?" Jules demanded.

"That you are married, my dear. I wanted to marry you, but now you'll just have to be my mistress. Please me, and I will keep you with me."

"I won't please you, I'll kill you."

He threw back his head and laughed. "You've lost your girl's terror, haven't you? Now that you know about fucking, I fancy you will please me in bed."

She shuddered and knew he saw it. She closed her eyes, but just for a moment. She had to keep alert, try to remember the way they were traveling.

Wilkes grew silent. He was thinking about his two men— Grabbler and Hawkins—scum, both of them. He didn't doubt for a moment that they'd want to share her. He considered not going to the caves where they were waiting.

When Jules suddenly dug her heels into her horse's belly, causing the mare to snort and read back, tearing the reins from his hands, he knew he would need them. He caught the flying reins before Jules could grab them, and brought the frantic mare back down.

He crowded his horse next to the mare. He saw Jules breathing hard, her eyes dilated. Without warning, he grabbed her about the waist and pulled her in front of him.

"How very stupid of you, my dear," he said.

Jules felt fear and rage flow through her. She began to struggle, striking at his face, her nails scoring his cheek.

He cursed, and dragged her off the horse. She fell onto her back, but the sharp stones digging into her body made no impression. She watched him pull off his belt.

She came up on her knees, and nearly fell back again, dizzy from the fall.

Wilkes grabbed her wrists, forcing them together, and bound them with the belt. He saw her flinch, and loosened the binding leather just a bit.

"There," he said. He clasped her beneath her arms and pulled her to her feet. For a moment he brought her against him. Jules went rigid.

"No, damn you, no."

"Well, not yet, at any rate," Wilkes said. He grabbed her chin to hold her still, and kissed her deep. Jules felt his tongue probing against her tightly pursed lips. She opened her mouth and felt him. She bit him, hard.

His yelp of pain brought her but a moment's pleasure. Her head reeled back at the hard slap on her cheek. She would have fallen had he not held her.

"If ever you do that again," he said, his face so close to hers that she could feel his breath fanning against her skin, "I will make you regret it. I might consider sharing you with Grabbler and Hawkins. I promise you, Juliana, you wouldn't like that. They are not gentle men."

She stood rigid, saying nothing. Wilkes studied her face for a long moment; then, satisfied that she understood him, he kissed her again. This time when his tongue probed between her lips, he felt her shudder. With distaste. That would change, he thought. Yes, she would change.

He hauled her in front of him on his horse again. He left her mare, knowing the animal would straggle back to the town eventually. He hoped it would. If her bodyguard didn't make it, the mare would. *I want that husband of yours to come after you. I want to kill that bastard, kill him slow.* He looked back to see the mare already trotting back toward the town, and smiled.

They rode for several more hours, southward, hugging the cliffs overlooking the ocean. He allowed his hand to move upward to cup her breast. He felt her suck in her breath, become rigid. He only smiled.

Jules closed her eyes against his hated hand. He was going to rape her. All the old terrors, the old nightmares, rose to choke her. She hated herself for showing him any reaction at all. Her only relief was that Michael was safe. With Byrony. But Thackery— Tears burned her eyes. Please, she prayed, let him be all right.

"Time to let Mammy Bath help you out of those clothes," Saint said, smiling at Byrony. "Call me when you're in bed."

Byrony's lips tightened as a contraction grabbed her belly. She saw Brent's white face, and tried to smile at him. It was she who said, "I'm just fine, love. You mustn't worry."

"Let's get this chile into the world, little missis," Mammy Bath said, and tugged at Byrony's arm.

Saint watched until Byrony disappeared from view at the top of the stairs. He turned to Brent. "If you like, you can stay with her for a while. Talk to her, distract her. First, though, let me examine her."

Brent nodded, his throat too tight from fear to let words out.

"That's right," Saint said on a grin, and clapped Brent's back. "You think celibate thoughts."

"Just wait until Jules is pregnant," Bent said.

Saint was silent a moment. "It's a sobering thought."

It would be a long labor, he thought a few minutes later, gently easing his fingers from Byrony's body. He forced a smile. "Just continue breathing easy, Byrony. That's it. Now, let me get your husband for you."

The pains were coming more quickly some three hours later, but still she was long from delivery. Brent was talking at his wife nonstop, nonsense, really, but it did distract her a bit.

Byrony yelled suddenly, her body arching upward.

Brent sent Saint an agonized look, and Saint said quickly, "Breathe slowly, that's it. Now, Byrony, did I tell you about what was done to the expectant fathers in a long-ago civilization? You listen to me now, and you too, Brent. You see, these folk were very advanced. For every hour the woman was in labor, her husband was hung upside down by his heels beside her bed. Even after the baby was born, the father had to look at his son or daughter upside down and nod in approval before he was released."

"Talk about celibate thoughts," Brent said.

"You made that up, Saint," Byrony said, her laugh cut off by another contraction.

"Nope, I swear. Now, the Siamese had an interesting method. After the birth of a woman's first child, she continued in her bed, exposing her abdomen and her back to the heat of a blazing fire not two feet distant from her. It was kept going night and day for an entire month, the husband in charge. The practice had at least one virtue—it allowed the woman all the rest she needed. What do you think of that?"

"I prefer Brent hanging by his heels," Byrony said.

"I'll hang myself by anything you want," Brent said as he wiped the sweat from her forehead. "Well, not anything."

Saint rose and stretched. He was racking his brain for more stories when he heard a shout from downstairs. "Stay put, Brent," he said. "I'll see what's going on."

He bounded down the stairs. Just inside the door lay Thackery at Mammy Bath's feet. His shirt was soaked with blood. Saint went cold.

He lifted the man in his arms and carried him to the dining table. "Mammy, get me hot water and my bag from upstairs quick."

He cut away Thackery's shirt and saw the bullet hole high in his chest.

"Dr. Saint."

"You just lie still, Thackery, just lie still."

"He got Mrs. Saint, he shot me and left me for dead, I guess. God, I let you down."

"It's all right—" Saint began, only to watch Thackery sink again into unconsciousness at the same time a piercing scream came from upstairs.

Brent appeared in the doorway a few moments later, his face white. "Saint, what the hell—"

"Wilkes has Jules. He shot Thackery."

"Damnation. Oh God, no."

Saint closed his eyes a moment, trying to think clearly, calmly. "Brent," he said at last, "listen to me.

Byrony's hurting, but the baby won't be here for a while yet. I want you to stay with her—hell, make up stories, anything. I'll patch up Thackery."

"Then what will we do?"

Saint knew he couldn't leave Byrony. Yet that bastard Wilkes had his wife. "I don't know," he said. "Go to your wife now."

Saint quickly dug out the bullet. He wanted Thackery conscious to tell him where Wilkes had captured her, but not before he's gotten the bullet out. He was a strong man, a healthy man. He would live. Mammy Bath stood at his elbow, handing him instruments, cloths as he asked for them. Within minutes Thackery's shoulder was bound firmly.

"Now the smelling salts, Mammy," Saint said. He waved them under Thackery's nose. "Thackery," he said, leaning over the man. "I know you hurt and I'll give you some laudanum in just a moment. Tell me where you were when Wilkes shot you."

"Better yet, let him tell me. You wouldn't know, Saint, even if he told you."

Saint moved aside and let Brent lean over Thackery.

For a moment the pain was so great that Thackery couldn't breathe.

"It's all right, John," Brent said. "Take your time."

"At the northeast edge of the valley near MacGiver's place. I saw him heading south with her, and west, toward the ocean. He knew, Dr. Saint, oh yes, he knew that Miz Hammond was going to have the baby. He timed it that way."

Saint patted Thackery's shoulder.

There was another piercing scream from upstairs, and both men froze.

# Chapter 30

Fear crawled through him.

"You've got to go," Byrony whispered. "You've got to bring her back safely. I have a saint to look after me. A real-live saint. Go, Brent."

Then she was lost to him and to reason, her eyes wild with pain.

A man shouldn't have to make such a choice, Saint thought, even as he gently rubbed Byrony's back to ease the contraction. He met Brent's eyes.

"Take care of my wife, Saint," Brent said. "I'll get Jules, I swear it. And I'll kill the bastard, you can count on that."

But *I* want to kill him, Saint thought, exhilarated by the rage that filled him.

He nodded then, unable to find words.

He watched Brent lean down and kiss his wife's pale lips.

Then he was gone. Saint listened to his pounding stride down the front stairs.

Saint walked to the window that faced the front of the house. He saw Brent tie a rifle to his saddle, saw the two guns in his belt. A half dozen men, all of them black, waited for him to mount.

The horses whinnied and reared. Then they were

gone, leaving only the thick welter of dust kicked up from the horses' hooves.

*It's just as well I didn't tell him,* Saint thought, walking back to the bed. He sat down beside Byrony and gently took her limp hand into his. "Listen to me, Byrony," he said, his voice low and insistent, pitched to cut through her pain. "The baby's turned wrong and I've got to straighten him. Byrony, do you understand me?"

He realized that she didn't. He called to Mammy Bath. "Come here and hold her. You heard what I told her?"

"Yes, Docta Saint, I heard."

It wasn't the first time Saint had wished his hands were smaller. There was no help for it, of course. He had to try to turn the baby. If he failed, he knew Byrony Hammond would die. *And what of Jules? What of his beautiful, sweet wife? What was Wilkes saying to her, doing to her?*

Saint shook himself and forced on the matter at hand.

"It is quite odd, I'll admit that," Jameson Wilkes said, and unconsciously tightened his arm around Jules's waist. But he'd wanted her too long, so long in fact that he could no longer remember when she wasn't in his thoughts. And in his opium dreams.

He sounded so reasonable, so *reasoning*, Jules thought, a stirring of hope going through her. "I can be nothing to you," she said, her voice as persuasive as she could make it. "You've only imagined that you want me. But I am a married woman. I am not a virgin any longer. Didn't you tell me that my virginity was my only value?"

"Yes," Wilkes said. "That's what I told you."

"Then why?"

He felt the agony in his belly growing stronger, and he was unable for the moment to answer her. The pain was the reality.

Her voice thin and high, Jules said, "You're old enough to be my father. Do you want a daughter? Are you so twisted that—?"

He tightened his arm about her waist, cutting off her breath. "Shut up," he said. He laughed humorlessly and said to himself, "Hell, what I need is your damned husband." His laughter fell away. No one could help him, cure him. He was tired now, and worried. And he felt so old, so damnably used up, finished. No. He shook his head and forced his mind into clear channels. He would handle Hawkins and Grabbler. The scum wanted the money he'd promised them more than a woman.

He watched the sun disappear in a ball of vivid red. He'd always been in awe of sunsets over the ocean. They were like a short burst of the most awesome Chinese fireworks. Never to see them again— He felt Juliana sag against him and breathed a sigh of relief.


"It's almost as if he wants us to track him," said Josh, a black man Brent had grown up with at his father's plantation, Wakehurst. He straightened, his eyes on Brent. "We saw Miz Saint's mare—"

"Which means he's carrying her on his horse, and that will slow him down," Brent said, shading his eyes toward the sun that was glowing fiercely over the ocean.

"That's not the point," Josh said.

"No, it isn't. I'm afraid I do know what the point is. Not only does he want Jules, he also wants Saint. Revenge, I suppose, since Saint saved her from him. Stole her, I guess, is Wilkes's reasoning."

But why did he wait until Byrony had gone into labor to take her? Did he believe Saint would leave her and come after his wife? No, he added mentally, Wilkes just wanted enough time. And, it seemed, he wanted Saint to be in a damnable position. The cruel bastard. "We've only got another hour of light," he said abruptly, and dug his heels into his stallion's sides.

But they hadn't found her when night hit. It was dark as pitch, only a sliver of moon, clouds obscuring the stars. They couldn't track any more until morning.

Brent didn't know what to do. He was faced with the most painful decision of his life.

"I'm sorry, Brent," Josh said, laying his huge black hand on his friend's arm. "Real sorry. But you can't go back, not now. Four hours there, four hours back. You'd be exhausted, and Miss Saint needs a functioning man, not a piece of dead meat."

Brent gave Josh a twisted smile. Then he closed his eyes, praying toward the cloud-strewn heavens, praying that his wife was all right, that Jules wasn't being savaged at this moment, praying that life would somehow become normal again.

"We need to build a fire," Brent said. "It'll be colder than a dead stone before long."

The cave was damp and chill despite the smoking fire in front of her. Jules drew her legs closer, kept her head down.

"She's a purty little thing," said Hawkins. "Lookee there, she knows I'm talkin' about her. She shook all over."

Hawkins chuckled and emptied his tin cup of the remains of his coffee.

"It's time for you to spell Grabbler," said Wilkes. "Take him something to eat while you're at it."

He felt better. The opium always dulled the pain, for a while at least. He'd not taken too much to dull his mind.

"You gonna fuck the little gal while we're gone?"

"Get out, Hawkins," Wilkes said.

"Looks awful cold, she does," Hawkins said. "A nice big man atween her legs would warm her up."

Jameson Wilkes looked Hawkins square in the face. God, he was a villainous-looking creature, his gaunt face covered with a thick black beard, hiding, Wilkes knew, a puckered, ugly scar that ran the full length of his cheek. "You want her or the money?" He forced himself to shrug. "It's up to you. You don't get both. And you know, don't you, my friend, that the money isn't with me."

Jules felt her blood run cold at Wilkes's emotionless voice. She kept her eyes on the cave floor. The dirt was soft and very black. She tried not to think of Byrony in agony, tried not to think of Michael and Brent.

"Hell," Hawkins said, the toe of his dirty boot kicking at the fire's embers, "a man can always get hisself some tail."

"Tell Grabbler the same thing," Wilkes said coldly. "With what you two will earn, you'll be able to buy all the whores you want."

There was no more talk until Hawkins had left the

cave. Wilkes said to Jules, "A pity, my dear, that I can't offer you a bath—or a bed, for that matter. I do apologize. I don't believe, however, that we will have to remain here much longer. Since it's dark, we'll be staying here the night. I suggest you get some sleep."

"Why are we remaining here at all?"

Wilkes studied her pale face in the soft glow of the fire. Her riding hat was long gone, and her beautiful hair was in riotous curls and tangles over her shoulders and down her back. There was a smudge of dirt on her cheek.

He was proud of her cold voice because he knew how afraid she was.

"I don't think you need to know that just yet," he said. No, he thought, if he told her, she'd become a wild thing.

"What are you going to do to me?"

"Not fuck you, my dear, as Hawkins so crudely phrased it. Not yet, in any case. Not until we're away from here and safe."

"Not ever," Jules said. "No, not ever."

"I know. Your huge husband would kill me, is that right?"

"No," Jules said. "*I* would kill you."

He swooped down and kissed her hard on the mouth, then moved before she could react. "Get some sleep, Juliana. If you need to relieve yourself, I suggest you ask me to be your companion."

Saint sat beside Byrony, his chin resting on his folded hands. The bedroom was in darkness save for the one lamp that cast dim shadows on Byrony's pale face. He'd finally given her some chloroform and she was asleep. He prayed she would regain some strength, because there were still hours before the child would birth itself.

At least he'd managed to turn the baby. He could still feel Byrony's pain, the dreadful stretching of her small body as he'd eased his hand into her. But the child was now head-down, as it should be.

He finally slept himself, fitfully, his thoughts of his wife. What had happened to her? It was twelve o'clock, midnight.

When Byrony awoke she lay for a moment in a painless, vague world that she quite liked. She saw Saint's face above her, gentle, kind, yes, so very kind. She ran her tongue over her lips.

"Some water, Byrony," he said, and helped her sip from the glass.

The pain was nearer now, bringing her to full awareness.

"Chauncey told me you'd tell me where you got your nickname, Saint," she said, trying for reason, for control over her pain-racked body.

"Yes," he said, "I'll tell you. You breathe deeply now, and when that contraction builds, I want you to push with all your strength."

"I don't think I have much more strength," Byrony said.

"Don't you talk like that," Saint said, his voice hard and cold. "You're young and strong. You're going to birth that baby soon. Do you hear me, Byrony?"

"I hear you," she said, her voice so hoarse and raw that she wondered he could even understand her. The contraction built, and she wanted to die, to do anything to escape the pain. But she heard his voice telling her to push, and she did, with all her might.

"Now," Saint said when the pain eased a bit, "let me tell you about my nickname. Look at my face, Byrony. Don't fight the pain. You know what you have to do and you will do it. Now, it was when I was a young man, at Harvard Medical School. Various folk would provide the students with corpses to dissect. Breathe sharp, shallow breaths, Byrony. Yes, that's it."

"I don't know if I want to hear any more of this story, Saint."

"It ends well, I promise."

He waited, hearing her scream, softer now because her throat was raw from her cries, saw her arch, and said, "Push, Byrony." He knew she was trying, but she was weakening.

*Jules, where are you?*

It was four o'clock in the morning. Nearing dawn. When most deaths and most births occurred. He shook himself.

Byrony struggled to hold to something real, not to be dragged into the endless pit. "Tell me, Saint."

"Yes, well, one day they wheeled in the body of a man who'd just expired at the hospital. The professor, Old Hook Nose, we young men called him, was waving his scalpel about, on the point of demonstrating to us stupid students how one was to proceed. But you see, Byrony, the man wasn't dead. I grabbed Old Hook Nose's wrist just as it was descending. There was a lot of shouting and cursing that I, a wretched student, would dare attack such a venerable man. But I'd seen the eyelids of the 'dead man' flicker. I thank the good Lord to this day that I'm a

large man. I had to fight off a good ten men, Old
Hook Nose included. Then, my dear, the supposed
dead man opened his eyes. It was he, Robert Gallagher, who named me Saint.''

"Saint, make it stop.''

He wondered briefly if she'd even understood him.
He held her, felt the awful wrenching pain, and knew
he must do something or she would be too weak to
birth the child. She would die, and the child with her.

"Byrony, listen to me.'' He clasped her face between his large hands, shaking her until her eyes
focused on his face. "I'm going to help you, do you
hear me? No, don't close your eyes. Look at me, Byrony. Here's what you'll do.''

He felt her tears wet on his hands and wanted
to weep himself. For her, for Jules. For poor Robert
Gallagher, who'd been run down by a carriage six
months after Saint had saved him from being cut
open by Old Hook Nose.

Dear God, what was happening? Sunlight poured
through the bedroom windows. He glanced a moment toward the clock.


"We got company, Mr. Wilkes,'' Hawkins said,
poking his head into the cave. "Six, seven men, riding slow, tracking.''

"Ah,'' Wilkes said, his eyes turning toward Jules.
He saw the wild hope in her eyes. "No, my dear, it
won't be your husband, at least it shouldn't be. He
wouldn't leave a woman in labor, now, would he?''

"I bet it's that gambler Hammond, the man who
started that damned town.''

"Yes, I suppose so. They're all so honorable,
aren't they?''

"They aren't scum like you," Jules said.

"Now, little girlie—" Hawkins began.

"Shut up, both of you," Wilkes said, and got to his feet. He cursed the damned pain, but managed to keep control. He wanted more opium, needed it desperately, but he couldn't allow himself to escape, not yet. He said to Jules, "You will stay put, my dear, or I will kill Mr. Hammond. Hawkins, you come with me."

Jules watched the two men leave. She scrambled to her feet, looking about frantically for a weapon, any kind of weapon. She clawed through the bedrolls. Nothing. She felt dirty, her bones ached from sleeping on the dirt cave floor, and she was more afraid than she had ever been in her life. Before, it had been just her. Now it was Brent.

She crept toward the cave opening and peered out. She could see Wilkes's back, Hawkins just behind him, and Grabbler off to her left in the notch of a pine tree. She saw the ocean beyond, calm, gray like a whitetip reef shark.

"This is it," Josh said, his voice low, nearly a whisper.

"Yes," Brent said, nodding. He looked up at the cliff above them and scanned the wall. He heard a horse nicker. He held up his hand for silence, then rode forward a bit.

He called out, "All right, Wilkes. We are here. What the hell do you want?"

"Hammond?"

"Yes, of course. You know that Jules's husband is with my wife. What do you want?"

*Jules*, Wilkes thought blankly. How odd. It

sounded ridiculous. He much preferred "Juliana."
Had her damned husband given her that nickname?
He wanted to kill him.

"You may be certain I don't want you," Wilkes
shouted. "I want you to take a message back to Saint
Morris. He'll come here alone, or he will never see
her again."

"Why didn't you just wait until he would track
his wife?"

"Very simple, Hammond," Wilkes called out. "She
wasn't out of his sight and wouldn't be until your
dear wife started her birthing pains. He would not
allow his innocent wife to be present, of that I was
certain."

Brent curse softly. Why had he imagined all sorts
of wily, bizarre plots on Wilkes's part? It was all so
simple really. And Wilkes was right, completely
right. It was the first time Saint had let Jules out of
his sight. Saint and Thackery had dogged her every
step.

"Now, as I figure it, Hammond, by the time you
get back to that town of yours, your baby will be
born, that or your precious wife will be dead. In any
case, Saint Morris will be free to come after his wife.
Give him my message."

Brent felt his jaw tighten until pain seared his face.
What the hell could he do?

Jules felt her blood run cold. Wilkes not only
wanted her, he also wanted to kill Michael. She
couldn't, wouldn't allow it. She didn't know what to
do. Suddenly she yelled at the top of her lungs,
"Brent, don't get Michael. He wants to kill him. Don't
let him leave Byrony."

"Jules, are you all right?" Brent yelled back. His

horse shied sideways, and it took a moment of his concentration to get him back under control.

"I'm all right," Jules shouted back. "Don't let Michael come here."

Wilkes was beside her, pulling her back into the cave. He flung her to the dirt floor. "You keep your mouth shut, Juliana, or I'll kill Hammond, and his men can deliver my message to your precious husband."

She stared at him, hatred filling her. At that moment she saw his face pale, saw him clutch at his belly. My God, she thought, he was ill.

"You stay put," Wilkes said again, his voice low, his teeth gritted, "or I'll plow your belly in front of your precious husband. You understand me?"

"I understand," Jules said. She was silent a moment, then said very quietly, "Do you want my husband for revenge or do you want a doctor?"

"Interesting question," Wilkes said, and laughed. "Don't move, Juliana." He walked from the cave, not looking back, for there was nothing she could do. Nothing.

Saint ripped off the sheet that covered Byrony. He couldn't allow it to go on any longer. He had to do it. "Mammy," he said, "take her hands and hold her steady. Byrony, you're not going to give up, you're going to push with all your strength."

"No, I can't," she whispered.

"Damn you, Byrony, do as I tell you."

He thought he saw a ghost of a smile on her white lips. He saw the contraction and splayed his hands over her belly. "Push," he shouted at her, and bore down with his hands. Almost, he thought, hope wel-

ling up in him. "Again, Byrony." This time he
slipped his hand inside her. He felt the baby's head,
gently found the tiny shoulders and pulled. He shut
his mind to Byrony's screams and eased the baby
from the birth canal. Damn him for a fool, he should
have given her more chloroform, but there hadn't
been time.

"My God," he said, cuddling the slippery little
body against his chest, fierce joy filling him, "it's a
boy you've got, Byrony. A beautiful boy."

Byrony was unconscious.

"Mammy, bathe our little fellow here. Ah, that's
it. A lusty cry. He's ready for the world. Then wrap
him in a warm blanket."

"I know," Mammy said, affronted, and Saint
smiled. The old woman was as exhausted as he was,
but still feisty as hell.

He worked over Byrony, more mechanically now,
because she would be all right. He'd taken the risk
and she'd survived. It was Jules who filled his
thoughts. Had Brent found her? What had happened? "Damn," he said. So many questions and no
answers. He realized his hands were shaking, fear
washing through him in great relentless waves.

Mammy Bath handed him the baby some minutes
later. The child was a carbon copy of Byrony, not
Brent. Honey-colored hair, fair-complexioned. Perhaps there was divine justice, he thought. Byrony had
done all the work, suffered more than a human being
should ever have to, so it was only fair that her child
look like her.

He smiled down at the wizened little face, his finger under the tiny chin.

"I'll bring a sugar tit for that little man," said

Mammy Bath. "His mama won't have no milk for a while yet."

"Good idea," Saint said, and began to pace the bedroom. He was still pacing when Brent Hammond burst through the door two hours later, his eyes going immediately to his wife.

Saint said quickly, "She's all right. You have a son and he looks like Byrony."

"She's all right?" His throat felt suddenly very scratchy, and tears burned his eyes. "She's not moving."

"You wouldn't be either. She's asleep. Your son is in the next room with Mammy Bath."

Brent dragged his fingers through his hair. "We've got trouble, Saint, dammit."

"Tell me while you look at your son," Saint said, and knew he had to remain calm.

# Chapter 31

The men rode steadily south, high on the cliffs above the ocean, Brent beside Saint at their head.

"Have you any ideas, Saint?" Brent asked.

Saint shook his head, his eyes straight between his horse's ears. "None other than getting my hands around that bastard's neck." Why, Saint continued to wonder, did Wilkes want him? If it were revenge in the man's mind, it was chilling. He had Jules, why him? Why the elaborate ruse?

Brent well understood and merely nodded. They had plenty of time to devise some sort of plan. He said finally, "I thank you for saving Byrony."

"She did all the work," Saint said. He arched an eyebrow at Brent. "She was pleased that the baby looks like her and not you, a swarthy pirate."

"Gambler, not pirate. Hell, I wouldn't have cared if the baby looked like you, Saint."

"The perfect child indeed. Incidentally, Brent, go see Maggie before you begin relations again with your wife. I suggest contraception. Another child in perhaps three years, then I'd be satisfied and call a halt."

Brent turned white and shook his head back and

forth. "I don't want her to go through that ever again. No way."

It was early afternoon when they reached the cliff.

"You can't just go up there, Saint," Brent said again. "He wants to kill you."

"He won't," Saint said. For a moment he wondered why he'd said it with such confidence. Hell, he had no reason to be confident. It was just that he had this feeling— So many things about Wilkes didn't make sense.

Brent sighed. "The two men he's got, we'll try to pick them off. Josh is the best shot I know, after Thackery."

"Thackery can give him lessons in another week or so. That man's as strong as an ox, thank God."

"I still don't like this," Brent said.

Saint shrugged. He was thinking of his confrontation with Jameson Wilkes.

Jules felt numb. She'd spent the entire morning feeling helpless. Hawkins had eyed her again, but she realized she wasn't afraid of him, nor was she afraid of Wilkes, not anymore.

She was afraid for Michael. He would come, she knew he would come. She didn't know what to do.

"Ah," Wilkes said, an odd relieved tone in his voice. "I do believe your precious husband has arrived."

Jules bounded to her feet and ran to the cave entrance, screaming, "Michael, no, go away."

Wilkes jerked her backward and flung her to the dirt. She scrambled to her feet.

"You stay put or I'll put a bullet through him before you can even see him."

Jules believed him. Oh, Michael, she thought, closing her eyes a moment, why did you come? Why do
you have to be so noble?

She prayed that Byrony was all right.

Then she heard his voice, strong and deep, coming
from below.

"Wilkes, can you hear me?"

"Good afternoon, Dr. Morris," Wilkes shouted
down. "I see you brought your friends. Leave them
down there and come up alone."

Without conscious thought, Jules ran at Wilkes,
grabbing at the gun in his belt. He whirled about,
caught her hand, and struck her with the flat of his
palm.

She staggered back, and he came toward her,
drawing his gun as he stalked her.

Saint felt the barrel of the gun in the small of his
back. He didn't pause, but continued walking until
he came into the cave entrance.

"Here he is, Mr. Wilkes," Hawkins said, and gave
Saint a shove.

Saint blinked rapidly to adjust his eyes to the dim
interior of the cave. Wilkes was holding Jules in front
of him, one arm across her breasts, the gun in his
other hand.

"Hello, Dr. Morris," Wilkes said. "I have wanted
to meet you. Very much. I believe it was you who
clipped my jaw."

"I was hoping," Saint said calmly, his eyes hard
on Wilkes's face, "that I'd broken your jaw that night
at the Crooked House. Did I?"

"No, no, you didn't. Of course, I have heard that
you aren't a violent man," he added.

"I'm not. But I realized months ago that I should

have killed you." He shrugged, looking over his wife's strained face. "Then again, I'm supposed to save lives. You have always posed me a difficult problem, philosophically, at least."

"Stay where you are, Dr. Morris." Wilkes pressed the gun against Jules's left breast.

Saint didn't move. He met Jules's wildly frightened eyes. "Are you all right, love?" he asked.

"Yes, yes, of course. You shouldn't have come, Michael."

"I'm your husband, little fool." He met Wilkes's eyes. "I *am* her husband, you know, in all ways. Now, what do you want, Wilkes?"

The gun jerked and Saint froze.

"You took her from me," Wilkes said in a low, hoarse voice, the pain in his belly nearly bending him double. God, he'd just had as much opium as he could take and still be coherent. "I wanted her and you stole her from me."

"That isn't how I seem to remember it," Saint said. "You were selling her. Hardly the same thing. All you lost was money."

"I would have gotten her back."

"Would you have? Really? After she'd been raped and abused? And what would you have done with her, Wilkes? Raped and abused her more?"

"Shut up, damn you. You know nothing about it."

"I know that you aren't thinking straight." *His eyes look odd. His flesh is gray. The flesh around his eyes and mouth is scored with pain.* "Let her go, Wilkes. If you kill me, she will kill you. Perhaps not today, but to-morrow or the next day."

"*She is mine.*"

"No, she is not."

Jules could bear it no longer. "Michael, I'll go with him, please, just leave. I don't want you hurt. Please leave."

He merely smiled at her, shaking his head. "He wouldn't let me leave even if he trusted your promise, sweetheart."

"No," Wilkes said, the pain so bad now that only through sheer will did he get the words out. "No, Doctor, you aren't leaving."

It was then Saint saw the spasm of pain on Wilkes's face. It was fearful, his mouth working like a death rictus. "Has she already tried to kill you?" he said.

"No, damn you. Oh, my God. My belly—"

Jules felt him ease his hold on her as his body bent forward with pain. She didn't think, merely acted. She sent her elbow into his stomach, and he screamed. Jules grabbed at the gun. In the next instant, Saint jerked away her hand, pulled the gun from Wilkes's unresisting fingers. He met Wilkes's glazed eyes. He felt a spasm of pity.

"You're dying, aren't you?" he said very softly, knowing that only Wilkes could hear him.

"I didn't need you to tell me, damn you." Wilkes was panting, his breathing an agony. He staggered backward.

"No," Saint said, "no, you didn't. How long have you lived on opium? How long have you had none to ease the pain?"

But Jameson Wilkes couldn't answer. His mind was clouded with agony, with strange broken images of the ravaged face of his wife, long dead.

Then Saint knew. He was on opium, to his limit.

"Michael."

Saint whirled about at Jules's shout, saw Hawkins looming in the mouth of the cave. He fired. There was another shot, and Jules saw a bullet slam into the wall of the cave. She watched, frozen, as Hawkins, a bewildered look on his face, stumbled forward, then fell on his face.

There was a loud shout from outside the cave. Then a rapid staccato, at least six more shots.

Suddenly Saint felt Wilkes's hands clutching at his wrist, bearing downward. Again he looked into Wilkes's eyes, and saw madness and more pain than a human being should have to suffer. Stomach cancer, he thought, a slow, agonizing death. He saw something else in his eyes, something he couldn't yet understand. Then he did. He realized, deep in his soul, that Wilkes could have shot him in the confusion. He saw another pistol lying in the dust very close to Wilkes and knew Wilkes could easily have grabbed it. He knew that Wilkes had made a decision. For a split second Saint wavered. He closed his eyes, knowing what was to happen, what the dying man wanted to happen. He let him bring the gun between them.

Jules was weeping softly. "No, please, no."

There was a muffled shot.

Jules screamed.

Neither man moved. Then Saint very gently eased Wilkes's limp body down to the cave floor.

Jules backed away, turning her head, unable to bear the fixed gaze in Jameson Wilkes's eyes.

Brent burst into the cave, drew up short, and slowly slipped his gun back into its holster. "He's dead?" He nodded toward Wilkes's body.

"Yes," Saint said. "Just as he wanted to be." *Thank*

*God, he didn't linger, even for a moment. Jules couldn't have borne that.*

"Josh shot the other man. I see you got this scum," he added, nodding toward Hawkins's body.

Saint nodded. He looked one last time at the man who had caused so such suffering, lived with such suffering, then walked slowly over to his wife. "Love," he said, taking her into his arms. "It's all over now."

Jules leaned against him, beyond tears now. She wrapped her arms around his back, burrowing her face into his shoulder, feeling his strong heartbeat against her. He rocked her, gently stroking his hand through her tangled hair. He looked over at Wilkes again, a strange sadness filling him. Had Jules somehow become twisted in his opium dreams into a fantasy to save him from himself? Or had he wanted her with him when he died, to complete some eerie ritual, some twisted dream? Saint doubted he would ever understand. He certainly wouldn't speak to Jules about it. She'd suffered too much already. And most of it had been for him.

"You're a godmother, Jules," Saint said. "Come, let's go admire Byrony's perfect child."

"I'm a godmother?" she repeated blankly, and he knew she was striving desperately for something real to hold on to.

"Yes, and I'll wager Brent will even let you suggest names for the little fellow."

"Yes, I will, Jules."

"I want to see my godson," she said.

"I'm proud as hell of you," Saint said, kissed her, and led her from the cave.

He became aware of Wilkes's blood on the front of his shirt.

There was so much hell on earth. But then, there were also other people who made life bearable, people who made meaning of things, who gave joy and love. And he had his wife, he had his Jules. He realized something then that would be with him throughout his life: He loved someone more than his own life. God, he was lucky. The fragility of life, the preciousness of life—

He pulled her tight to his side. And that's where she would be, always. Beside him, part of him.

Jules stared around the Hammonds' parlor, feeling disoriented for a moment, until Michael said, "You think we can make as cute a little boy as Byrony did?"

"What about me?" Brent said, grinning down at his wife. She was still dreadfully pale, but the sparkle was back in her eyes. Their child, Damon Michael, was sleeping in a crib beside her chair.

"What about you?" Saint said, his voice sardonic. "All you did was enjoy yourself, repeatedly."

"So true," Byrony said, giving her husband a radiant smile. "Jules, if ever you tire of that husband of yours, I will gladly take him. A very useful man. A caring man, and he told me the strange story about how saints are created."

Saint cocked a brow at her but said nothing. He was, quite frankly, surprised she remembered.

"I should offer the same for Brent," Jules said. "If it weren't for him, I should be on board a ship sailing for China."

No, Saint wanted to tell her, there would have been no ship. There would have been naught but an ending—and Wilkes had known it. Poor bloody bastard.

"I believe we should drink to how great we all are," Brent said. "Can Thackery have a glass of champagne, Saint?"

"Mr. John Thackery," Saint said, giving a heartfelt smile to the grinning black man, "has my thanks and good wishes for all eternity, not to mention free medical care."

"Excellent," Brent shouted. "Mammy—champagne for everyone."

"As for you, little one," Saint said to his wife, "I fully intend to cosset you and love you until I'm too old to move."

"In that case," said Jules, squeezing her husband's hand, her eyes twinkling, "I shall just have to give you my derringer."

"*Derringer?*"

"Yes, and you can stomp on it. Again."

"Jules, if ever I—"

"Perhaps Penelope will give hers to Thomas."

"What the hell are you talking about? Penelope? Don't tell me that the two of you—"

Saint broke off at Brent's laughter.

Byrony said, "Ah, the champagne."

"We'll give Saint the bottle," Brent said. "He looks like he needs it."

# *New York Times*
## bestselling author
# CATHERINE COULTER

| | |
|---|---|
| *The Countess* | 198506 |
| *The Deception* | 408586 |
| *The Rebel Bride* | 404327 |
| *Lord Harry* | 405919 |
| *The Duke* | 406176 |
| *The Heir* | 20682-7 |
| *The Offer* | 407946 |

To order call: 1-800-788-6262

SIGNET

## <u>Paperback Original</u>

# *New York Times*
## bestselling author

# CATHERINE
# COULTER

# BEYOND EDEN

From the bestselling author of *False Pretenses* comes an exhilarating and steamy novel. When her life is threatened by an unknown pursuer, wealthy Lindsay Foxe is forced to trust her safety to rugged private investigator S.C. Taylor, who alone has the power to free her from a past of betrayal and treachery....

0-451-20231-7

To order call: 1-800-788-6262

# Penguin Putnam Inc.
## Online

Your Internet gateway to a virtual environment with hundreds of entertaining and enlightening books from Penguin Putnam Inc.

*While you're there, get the latest buzz on the best authors and books around—*

Tom Clancy, Patricia Cornwell, W.E.B. Griffin, Nora Roberts, William Gibson, Robin Cook, Brian Jacques, Catherine Coulter, Stephen King, Ken Follett, Terry McMillan, and many more!

**Penguin Putnam Online is located at
http://www.penguinputnam.com**

# PENGUIN PUTNAM NEWS

Every month you'll get an inside look at our upcoming books and new features on our site. This is an ongoing effort to provide you with the most up-to-date information about our books and authors.

Subscribe to Penguin Putnam News at
http://www.penguinputnam.com/newsletters